ALSO BY JIM LYNCH

The Highest Tide

Border Songs

Border Songs

Jim Lynch

ALFRED A. KNOPF · NEW YORK
2009

THIS IS A BORZOI BOOK
PUBLISHED BY ALFRED A. KNOPF

Copyright © 2009 by Jim Lynch
All rights reserved. Published in the United States by Alfred A. Knopf,
a division of Random House, Inc., New York.
www.aaknopf.com

Knopf, Borzoi Books, and the colophon are
registered trademarks of Random House, Inc.

Library of Congress Cataloging-in-Publication Data
Lynch, Jim, [date]
Border songs / by Jim Lynch.—1st ed.
p.   cm.
"This is a Borzoi book."
ISBN 978-0-307-27117-4 (alk. paper)
1. Border patrol agents—Fiction. 2. Washington (State)—Fiction. I. Title.
PS3612.Y542B67 2009
813'.6—dc22   2008053514

This is a work of fiction. Names, characters, places, and incidents either are the
product of the author's imagination or are used fictitiously. Any resemblance to
actual persons, living or dead, events, or locales is entirely coincidental.
Manufactured in the United States of America
First Edition

For Denise and Grace

Part One

I

EVERYONE REMEMBERED the night Brandon Vanderkool flew across the Crawfords' snowfield and tackled the Prince and Princess of Nowhere. The story was so unusual and repeated so vividly so many times that it braided itself into memories along both sides of the border to the point that you forgot you hadn't actually witnessed it yourself.

The night began like the four before it, with Brandon trying not to feel like an impostor as he scanned the fields, hillsides and roads for people, cars, sacks, shadows or anything else that didn't *belong*, doubting once again he had whatever it took to become an agent.

He rolled past Tom Dunbar's dormant raspberry fields, where in a fit of patriotism Big Tom had built a twenty-foot replica of the Statue of Liberty, which was either aging swiftly or perhaps, as the old man claimed, had been vandalized by Canadians. Brandon reluctantly waved at the Erickson brothers—who laughed and mock-saluted once they recognized him in uniform—and rattled past Dirk Hoffman's dairy, where Dirk himself stood on a wooden stepladder completing his latest reader-board potshot at the environmentalists: MOUTHWASH IS A PESTICIDE TOO! Brandon tapped his horn politely, then swerved through semifrozen potholes across the center line to get a cleaner look at the fringed silhouette of a red-tailed hawk, *twenty-six*, the white rump of a northern flicker, *twenty-seven*, and, suspended above everything, the boomerang shape of a solo tree swallow, *twenty-eight*.

Brandon traversed the streets of his life now more than ever, getting paid, so it seemed, to do what he'd always loved doing, to look closely at everything over and over again. The repetition and familiarity suited him. He'd spent all of his twenty-three years in these farmlands and humble towns pinned between the mountains and the inland sea along the top of Washington State. Traveling beyond this grid had always disoriented him, especially when it involved frenzied cities twitching with neon and pigeons and bug-eyed midgets gawking up at him. A couple hours in the glassy canyons of Seattle or Vancouver could jam his circuits, jumble his words and leave him worrying his life would end before he had a chance to understand it.

Some people blamed his oddities on his dyslexia, which was so severe that one giddy pediatrician called it a *gift*: While he might never learn how to spell or read better than the average fourth grader, he'd always see things the rest of us couldn't. Others speculated that he was simply too large for this world. Though Brandon claimed to be six-six, because that was all the height most people could fathom, he was actually a quarter inch over six-eight—and not a spindly six-eight either, but 232 pounds of meat and bone stacked vertically beneath a lopsided smile and a defiant wedge of hair that gave him the appearance of an unfinished sculpture. His size had always triggered unreasonable expectations. Art teachers claimed that his unusual bird paintings were as extraordinary as his body. Basketball coaches babbled about his potential until he quit hoops for good after watching that huge Indian in *Cuckoo's Nest* drop the ball in the hole for a giddy Jack Nicholson. Tall women fawned over his potential too, until they heard his confusing raves and snorting laughs or took a closer look at his art.

Near dusk, Brandon wheeled up Northwood past the NO CASINO! yard signs toward the nonchalant border, a geographical handshake heralded here by nothing more than a drainage ditch that turned raucous with horny frogs in the spring and overflowed into both countries every fall. The ditch was one of the few landmarks along the nearly invisible boundary that cleared the Cascades and fell west through lush hills that blurred the line no matter how aggressively it was chainsawed and weed-whacked. From there, as thin as a rumor, the line cut through lakes and swamps and forests and fields. After turning into a ditch for a few miles, the line climbed one more hill before dropping again, slicing through Peace Arch Park and splashing into salt water. The park was all most travelers saw of the border, but locals drove into the valley to gawk at this ditch that divided the two countries and created a rural strip where Canadians and Americans drove on parallel two-lane roads, Boundary Road to the south and Zero Avenue to the north, just a grassy gutter away from each other, waving like friendly neighbors—until recently, that is.

Most passersby didn't notice anything different. The soggy, fertile valley still rolled out for miles in every direction until it bumped into a horseshoe of mountains—Alp-like peaks to the north, a jagged range to the east and Mount Baker's massive year-round snowball to the southeast—that gave the impression the only way out was west through the low-slung San Juan islands. There were still orderly rows of raspberry canes, fields bigger and greener than the Rose Bowl and dozens of pungent dairies with most of the cows hooked to computers that automated feeding and maximized the river of milk exiting daily in the metal bellies of tankers the size of oil trucks.

But a closer look hinted at the changes. Many barns and silos had nothing to do with cattle or farms anymore. U.S. border towns no longer served as burger pit stops for Canadian skiers dragging home from Baker. And nineteen-year-old Americans stopped rallying across the line for the novelty of legal drinking. Yet despite the slump in legitimate commerce, a curious construction boom was taking place on both sides. New cul-de-sacs rolled north like advancing armies, and young Canadians continued stacking trophy homes on abrupt hills with imperial views of America.

Brandon trolled Boundary Road past the home of Sophie Winslow, the masseuse who seemingly everyone visited but nobody knew. A black sedan cruised the Canadian side of the ditch, the driver avoiding eye contact and accelerating as Brandon closed in on his family's thirty-four-acre dairy with its three barns, one silo and two-story house that looked naked in the winter without blooming willows or a dinghy full of tulips pulling your eyes off its weathered planks. Overhead lights brightened the back barn, where his father, no doubt, was resanding teak already rubbed smooth as brass while obsessing over what he still couldn't afford, such as a mast, sails or a reliable diesel. A television winked through the kitchen window. Was *Jeopardy!* already on? The show exercised his mother's memory, as she put it, at least when she remembered to watch it. Brandon glanced back across the ditch at the row of houses along Zero Ave. Did Madeline Rousseau still live with her father? How long had it been since he'd even talked to her? You apparently couldn't bump into Canadians anymore. Spontaneity had up and left the valley.

He puttered past the Moffats' farm before pulling up for a closer look at icicles dangling from their roadside shed. He thumped his head unfolding from his rig, then snapped off a stout icicle, dipped its flat end into a slushy puddle and froze it like a spike to the hood of his idling rig while listening to the final mechanical exertions of the day— grumbling generators, misfiring V-8s, grinding snowplows. He stamped his thick-soled boots, trying to create room for his toes. The agency's largest boots were a half size too small and gave him the floating sensation of being detached from the earth. He heard the *rat-a-tat* of a downy woodpecker, *twenty-nine,* and the nervous *chip* of a dark-eyed junco, *thirty.* Brandon could identify birds a mile away by their size and flight and many of their voices by a single note. During the climax of spring, he often counted a dozen birds from his pillow without opening his eyes. Most birders keep life lists of the species they've seen, and the more intense keep annual counts. Brandon kept day lists in his head, whether he intended to or not.

He snapped off two smaller icicles, and then tried to moisten and freeze them to opposite sides of his original hood spike, but they wouldn't stick. He flattened their butt ends with his teeth, redipped them in the puddle and tried again. One held, then the other, creating for several seconds a glittering hood ornament before it toppled and shattered. He was eagerly starting over when he heard what sounded like crackling cellophane.

Deer often glided through at this hour. Or maybe the Moffats' turkeys had just busted loose. When Brandon looked up, he noticed it was snowing again, then counted seven child-sized shadows darting through the curtain of firs dividing the Moffats' farm from the Craw-fords'. Glancing toward the border, to see if others were hopping the ditch, he saw nothing but taillights. By the time he turned back to the trees, the shadows were gone. Grabbing his portable radio, he tried to summon the casual murmur he'd been practicing.

"I'll see if two-twenty-nine's in the area," the dispatcher replied in a similar disinterested mumble.

229 was Dionne. The thought of his trainer backing him up wasn't what flustered Brandon. It was the fact that two union guys had already warned him to always wait for backup, whereas Dionne insisted that all he ever needed was someone rolling in his direction. During his first solo patrol he'd heard her say on the radio, "I've got bodies," as if rounding up six Pakistanis were no more complicated than picking up a sixer at the Qwik Stop. She averaged almost twice as many arrests as any other agent and, as a result, was what the others respectfully, if begrudgingly, called a shit magnet.

Brandon loped toward the firs before remembering he'd left his motor idling and his Beretta on the passenger seat. Too late. He knew the trees opened into a leased pasture that led to Pangborn Road, where a van was probably waiting, and from there they were just minutes away from vanishing into the I-5 bloodstream. He ran harder once he made out the stampede of tiny footprints beneath branches the size of airplane wings, and two shadows finally bobbed into view. He shouted "Border Patrol!" for the first time in his life. To his ears, it sounded like a self-mocking falsetto. He might as well have yelled "Boo!" or "Ready or not!"

The shorter shadow glanced back, squealed and slipped to a knee before being hoisted by the other. What if they were just kids? Scaring children was another phobia of his. Babies loved him, but kids cowered no matter how small and friendly he tried to make himself.

Lumpy ground almost tripped him twice before he broke free of the trees into a mini-blizzard and a crunchy field. He knew the Crawfords' pasture was ditched for drainage, but he didn't know where and stumbled again, half-toppling before lurching back on track and spotting another five of them—or was it seven?—scattered ahead.

Even after the academy, a week as a trainee and four nights on solo patrols, he'd never pictured himself in actual pursuit. Everything had been in the abstract, like auditioning for some role he didn't want or expect to get. But what choices did he have? His father had forced him off the dairy and nobody else was hiring. So here he was, in painful boots, in a slippery pasture less than a mile from his home, *in pursuit*. Yet compared to faking patrols, this felt oddly relaxing, his body coiling into an efficient glide until Dionne's warning echoed inside him: *Assume everyone is carrying a nuclear device.*

The road was still sixty yards away and he didn't see any vehicles waiting, although he heard and then saw one howling toward them. The smaller shadow glanced back again and squealed. It was light enough to make out her anguished features. A woman? An Asian or a Mexican or . . . a woman. He had an urge to help her, but by the time he caught up with them he was too winded for words. He just lunged for their outer shoulders, simultaneously stubbing his left boot, cramping his right hamstring and catapulting himself horizontally into the sudden blaze of Dionne's flashlight.

That image soon made the rounds on both sides of the border, the first irrefutable evidence that Brandon Vanderkool's stint with the BP was more than a onetime sight gag like sending a dwarf to the plate to shrink the strike zone. Though Alexandra Cole didn't see it herself, she would later swear that Brandon flew twenty-six feet from takeoff to landing, which eventually went unquestioned alongside such facts as his flight occurred during a freak blizzard at dusk on March twenty-first, that he was unarmed at the time and wearing size-nineteen boots that were too small. As the story evolved it was ultimately seen as the beginning of a madness and temptation that blew through the valley, but that perspective came later. What made it an instant favorite was that for once a border bust had been made by someone everybody knew. And as it played out, the illegals Brandon tackled were not generic aliens, but rather a regal couple from some unknown nation.

From Brandon's vantage, he was simply airborne long enough to watch himself in flight, and he'd experienced enough similar out-of-body sensations to chalk them up to his *gift*. Regardless, he saw himself from above, his arms flung out like albatross wings until they collapsed around the runaways in a flying hug as he used their brittle bodies to break his landing. He heard a noise like a snapping wishbone before Dionne shouted his name. Her powerful light swung through snowflakes the size of chicken feathers, blinding him, his breathless apologies interrupted by the murderous screech of a barn owl. *Thirty-one.*

2

MADELINE ROUSSEAU was getting her feet stroked by an American smuggler named Monty when Brandon Vanderkool called.

The date with the bud runner had begun spontaneously enough with her being flattered by his appreciation of her Himalayan blue poppies. After he raved about her black tulips she'd hesitantly agreed to a drink after she helped close the nursery. *One drink*. He even warned her during her third margarita that he had a bit of a foot fetish.

"Yeah?" she'd asked. "How bad?"

"Well, I don't collect heels or anything, but I guess I'm somewhat of a voyeur."

"Then why're you interested in me?" She considered her feet her most exotic feature—half-moon arches and slender, shapely toes of ascending length. Still, she wanted to hear it.

A blush rose above his swashbuckling mustache. "Your personality, of course," he said, without glancing down at the sailing sandals she wore year-round. "But your arches are sublime."

She found it oddly endearing, how he peeped at women's shoes and held his breath when a waitress clomped by in spiked boots. Though he smelled like coconuts and sounded harmless, she knew she should have walked out once he admitted he'd been steered to her by Fisher, the same unreliable pothead she was waiting to hear from.

But by then her night had already swerved out of control. Rather than driving all the way to her White Rock apartment, she impulsively let Monty follow her to the moldy little guesthouse on her father's property across the ditch from the American border. Her regrets were in full bloom by the time he kneeled reverentially at the end of the futon and started massaging her feet with large, powerful hands. "I'm sorry," she said, "but this is too weird and I . . ." She was searching for the words that could free her feet when her cell broke into song and startled him into loosening his grip.

She was expecting a call about when she'd get paid, but not this soon. Had something already gone wrong? Fisher had assured her countless times how amazingly risk-free it all was. Yet in just three weeks she'd gone from reluctantly helping cultivate to waiting on money to indulging some smuggler who might be twice her age. Monty suddenly looked too old to run through raspberry fields with hockey bags full of what Fisher called product. She swung her feet free, plucked her phone from her vest and answered it.

"Madeline? This is Brandon, Brandon Vanderkool."

As if he needed a last name.

People talked about Brandon the way they discussed earthquakes, eclipses and other phenomena. His size, his "art" and the bizarre things he said and did had always generated chatter about Super Freak or Big Bird or whatever they were calling him at the time. After one January blizzard, he built a wall of what everyone gradually understood weren't snowmen but snow *penguins*. Another morning, he stood in his grassy driveway off Boundary Road and flapped his arms for twenty minutes with the rising sun at his back, puzzled drivers slowing down to see if he was all right. He didn't move his feet until the sun slid high enough to melt the frost everywhere around him except in his shadow, leaving behind a frost angel that clung to the grass several minutes after he strode off to the barn.

"Madeline?"

"Whaddaya need?" she asked. How'd he get her number? She pictured a tiny phone lost in his fingers, pinned against his massive ear, his body accordioned in a car or towering outside, his uneven grin torn between amusement and amazement, his free hand—the size of a first baseman's glove—air-sculpting whatever he was trying to say.

"We just caught some illegals hopping the border and running through the Crawfords' farm. Middle Easterners, maybe. Real small. Could be Iranians. No ID, strange accents. I don't know. Definitely not Mexicans or Koreans. Maybe Filipinos? Real small. Eyes like black olives."

She listened to his familiar halting rhythm, surprised he was this coherent. She'd initially dismissed her father's news flash about Brandon joining the patrol as yet another joke about Americans. "Guess who they've got guarding the country now?" But that was before she'd received Brandon's jumbled letter from the academy in which he rattled on about birds and constellations in the New Mexico sky.

She filled her lungs but her voice still squeaked. "So why're you calling me?" She glanced at Monty sulking on the futon and wondered why Brandon hadn't responded. Had the connection died? "Are you calling on behalf of the Border Patrol?" she asked slowly and watched Monty's bloodshots widen. How old was he, anyway? Forty? Forty-five? She pointed at the door.

A crackling delay continued on Brandon's end as if she'd stumped him or lost the call. Then he mumbled the words he wanted to say before repeating them at normal volume, fast and breathy. "Thought they were aminals at first. Chased them down in Crawfords' field. Got banged up pretty good. The woman is in St. Pete's. A woman. Didn't even know she was a woman until it was kinda too late. And the guy running with her came back because she was slipping. He saw me coming and still came back. You believe that? The woman was dressed like a genie. Or a princess. Told her how sorry I was, but she didn't know what I was saying. Hold on."

Brandon stranded her with static as the door clicked shut behind Monty. She stared at her blushing feet, her toes as pink as baby mice. Why was Brandon telling her all this?

"Madeline?"

"Yeah?"

"Called your father. Got no answer. So maybe he's out. But the lights are on. Called again. I think they crossed down the street from him. Why would anyone try to cross in the snow—I mean, leaving tracks and all?"

Madeline glanced out the steamed window toward her father's illuminated house. "Maybe," she heard herself say, "that's what they *thought* you'd think." She rubbed her foot with a towel, recalculating how much she'd drunk and ordering herself to focus.

"Know something?" Brandon said. "I think the most interesting people I'll meet these days will be criminals—or people about to become criminals."

The mini-fridge hummed a higher note. She had no idea what to say. Where was he headed? Did he know something?

"Ahhh," Brandon said. "Well, I hate to—"

Her cell beeped twice, then the battery died. Shit! What was he going to say? *What* did he hate? And why'd he really call?

She ran some water and frantically rinsed, soaped and toweled each foot. Should she ring Fisher on her dad's phone and tell him the BP called, or was it just Brandon being Brandon? This kept happening nowadays. She'd plan on *one* cocktail or *half* a joint, then fall into these time warps. How did Brandon get her cell number anyway? They hadn't been close since she was fourteen or fifteen, and they weren't *that* close then. How close did anybody get to him? She stepped outside and hurried toward her father's house along Zero Ave., disoriented by the blackness, skating across snow as slick as frosting.

She scanned the dark southern landscape for patrol lights or any signs that something had truly happened, but saw only house and barn lights. Was Mr. V still building that boat? She felt the wind shift across her face. "Can sailing be taught?" he'd asked her so earnestly years ago, as if her answer might provide the password to the afterlife. She'd wanted to tell him, *Yes, of course,* but there was something about him that wouldn't let her fudge it. "Either you're good at it or you're not."

That was back when the ditch was just a ditch, the Vanderkools just peculiar American neighbors and Brandon just an oversized kid who could watch barn swallows for hours and tell you which bird made which nest and which egg and which song. A year younger than she was, he towered above her like an adult once he turned eleven. And when he got nervous or excited his words came out wrong. Spluttering, Danny Crawford called it. Occasionally, in memorable gusts, he even spoke backwards. "Fair being not are you!" The first thought when people heard him derail? *Retarded.*

Her father was sprawled on the love seat next to a half liter of port and two roaches with Glenn Gould's piano clinking on repeat like the mutterings of a disturbed genius. The latest *Maclean's*—GREATEST INVENTIONS OF THE YEAR—covered his shallow chest, his bifocals balanced mid-nose, his neck bent at an angle that would only make him crabbier. Early pass-outs were common now that there wasn't any hockey to stay up for. From what Madeline could tell, the strike was realigning Canadian life. Couples were getting reacquainted, talking more, screwing more, divorcing more. A nation of men were rediscovering hobbies and remodeling kitchens or, in her father's case, smoking pot and piddling with inventions. Or, to be precise, *reinventions.*

He'd started the reinvention kick and the cannabis binge—she wasn't sure which came first—soon after being diagnosed and retiring a year early. And he'd taken to them both with a startling fervor. Professor Wayne Rousseau, the irreverent quote master, had been reduced to a daily toker who spent his waking hours reinventing gunpowder, the compass, the steam engine and who knew what else.

She played the three blinking messages without rousing him. "Mr. Rousseau? This is Brandon calling. Vanderkool. I mean I'm with the Border Patrol now and . . ." He rattled on disjointedly until he got cut off. Then a woman's soothing voice: "Wayne, it's Sophie. Call me if you want to hear about Brandon's big bust." Of course, that's who gave Brandon her number, the mysterious masseuse. The third call was Brandon repeating himself until he got muzzled mid-sentence. Madeline regretted being so curt with him. He needed someone to calm him down, and she hadn't even asked if he was all right. She glanced out the window, half-expecting to see him in the fields, yet saw only her own spooked reflection in the glass. She stared again at her father, his arms akimbo as if overacting his death. He'd always looked smaller and less imposing when he wasn't talking, but MS added a boyish vulnerability. And his death—maybe tomorrow, maybe in five years and seventeen days—nonetheless loomed. She nudged him awake, noticing the familiar odors of sour laundry, cheap wine and expensive pot. After he blinked and smacked his lips, she casually mentioned Brandon's calls and waited for his gears to catch.

He pushed his glasses higher on his nose and began clawing his thin beard. "This isn't their jurisdiction." Then a pause. "Does Nicole know?" Of course his first reaction would be outrage, his second to wonder what her older sister would make of it. "If the Border Patrol thinks it can run investigations on both sides of the border . . . ," he began, settling into lecture mode.

Should she slip away and call Fisher? She realized she didn't even know if Fisher was his first or last name. Meanwhile, the window was so large and the living room so bright that she felt like a target.

"When'd he call? Exactly when did that fucking giraffe call?" Her father looked around wildly, started to rise, then fell back with a wince, rubbing the right side of his neck with blackened fingers. "What'd he want? What'd he say? You didn't tell him anything, did you?"

"What could I possibly tell him?" Madeline said slowly, hoping she'd only have to say it once. She dimmed the lights and shut the blinds, trying to puff herself up to match his anger. But she'd always been amused that college students so earnestly studied the morality lines her father laid down, not realizing how often he lifted those lines and dropped them wherever he pleased. She poured him some seltzer on ice and gathered his pills. After watering the coleus, poinsettias and philodendron, all she truly wanted to do was tell somebody about her encounter with the foot man, someone who could sympathize and laugh and keep a secret that strange.

3

WAYNE ROUSSEAU rose long before dawn to reinvent the lightbulb.

Working in his basement by gas lanterns and candlelight—it
would've been a farce otherwise—he fussed for hours with spiral threads
of platinum, titanium, nickel and copper until he'd singed every finger
on his right hand. Nothing stayed illuminated for more than eleven seconds before flickering or exploding.

Over the prior week Wayne had tried Edison's first eighty-four filaments, sticking to the arduous chronology of cutting, securing, electrifying and unlatching each material and combination thereof inside a
replica vacuum tube he'd ordered from an oddball company in Montreal. Having completed less than a tenth of Edison's trials, he already
felt defeated and empty. Now he strapped tungsten inside the tube,
sealed it, hooked it up to the battery and lowered the switch. The bulb
lit briefly, flickered, then exploded. Wayne ripped off his goggles and
began sweeping the floor.

Edison and his lab boys tried twelve hundred materials—including
beard hair, playing cards and fishing line—before discovering a reliable
filament. Twelve hundred. The more Wayne inhabited Edison, the
more he wondered how a man cultivates a stubborn streak so pro-
nounced that it transforms a daily barrage of failures into stimulants.

Edison was thirty-two when he perfected the lightbulb. Thirty-
fucking-two. Half Wayne's age. Studying the dueling portraits of the
man—the visionary wizard who lit up the modern world and the

credit-hogging prick of incomparable dimensions—Wayne increasingly leaned toward the latter. No single man could have invented the music and motion-picture industries, the pull-cord doll and more than a thousand other breakthroughs. But how long would everything have taken without Edison? That was the question. Yank this prick out of history and the oddsmakers who studied that sort of thing swore the electrical revolution would have taken another generation and the recording industry probably longer. All this from an uneducated, nearly deaf dropout who wasn't sophisticated enough to realize that the things he imagined and demanded of himself and his underlings were not *possible*. And perhaps this was exactly the DNA, a quintessentially American prickishness, that all the giants possessed, whether Edison or Ford or Gates. They all turned less brilliant and more peculiar the closer you looked, didn't they? And maybe it wasn't just the Americans—most of the world's innovators were colossal bullies who shoved society forward. That was all Wayne was squeezing from his morning exercise. No enlightenment, no glory, no revelation. Just the metallic, back-of-the-tongue aftertaste of the impatient prick. He crossed tungsten off the list, fatigue blowing through him. Fucking Edison.

He hauled himself upstairs, a hot pain girdling his waist, into an alarmingly bright morning. He swallowed eleven pills, poached an egg, then flipped on the CBC in time to catch the back half of a report he knew would be retold on the half hour. The audacity! He knew exactly what to say if reporters called for comment. The paranoids were right! That's what he'd tell them. And maybe he'd mention the unusual messages he'd received from the Vanderkool boy the night before. Perhaps the Mounties would find that interesting. It's not a matter of when, he'd shout. They're already here!

But why wasn't his phone ringing? He bombarded the answering machines of friends at the college and *The Vancouver Sun*. He sent out thirteen e-mails and waited, hitting refresh every few seconds. No responses but a home-loan pitch and a credit-card con. He called Nicole, but his older daughter was *with clients*. It grew so quiet that the kitchen clock sounded boisterous. He ground espresso beans to hear himself doing something and swallowed two doubles. He played the repetitious news loud enough to make himself feel part of it, then slid across his slushy deck with half of yesterday's joint, pain sparking across his face as if the bones and ligaments holding it together were strung too tight.

He patted pockets for his lighter until he heard the garden hose and reveled in the sight of Brandon Vanderkool's father washing his enormous pickup once again, as if letting the big blue Ford stay dirty was as un-American as leaving the flag out overnight.

Norm looked bulkier than ever, almost a meter deep in the chest with a boulder head that reminded Wayne of those old Soviet leaders, all of which made the dairyman favor his left leg more than ever. Wayne descended his slick porch steps, one at a time, before shouting across the ditch.

NORM WASN'T CERTAIN what he'd heard other than his name, the word "Americans!" and some cussing alongside it. Knowing the likely mouth behind the noise, he ignored it, but the garbled yelling continued.

Unfortunately, Norm's driveway was within range of Wayne's deck. Though the professor lived on the other side of Boundary Road, the ditch and Zero Ave., he was still Norm's closest neighbor, if you could call him one. Used to be nothing but well-spaced farmhouses on both sides of the line until some Canadians sold border-front properties and a mini-suburb popped up with a view of Norm's dairy. *Ignore him*, he told himself, but instead he reluctantly shut off the water and rocked stiff-kneed to his side of the ditch like a man on stilts, squinting into the silvery glare and feeling at a sluggish disadvantage, having been up since three thirty on one cup of coffee. "What're you blaming us for today, Wayne?"

"You didn't hear?" The professor lit a stubby hand-rolled cigarette with a surfboard-shaped lighter. "Of course not. Why pay attention when you're always right? Well, your *drug czar* marched into Vancouver last night and told the owner of the Amsterdam Café that he runs a disgraceful business. That's the exact word he used: *disgraceful*. It's all over the CBC."

"What should he have called it?" Norm drawled as casually as he could, suspecting this discussion was foreplay for more agitating topics.

"Still don't get it, do ya?" Wayne cocked his head on a neck no bigger than Norm's wrist, shuffling to his left to keep the sun in Norm's eyes. "You act like *our* land is *your* land."

He studied Wayne's scratchy new beard. He'd had a Marxist goatee last week and was clean-shaven a month before that. Norm had hoped like hell the professor would move along once he'd retired, but here he was like some aging fugitive rotating through disguises. Nothing ever added up with Wayne Rousseau. Everybody heard about his wine parties—with fifty-dollar bottles on a teacher's salary—and then came his greenhouse. Growing tomatoes, Wayne? He'd always been more of a challenge than Norm had signed up for. The Cuban and Iranian flags he flew on Sundays just to piss people off were mild irritants compared to the nuke he dropped two years ago. "The deaths of innocent Americans are the direct consequence of their government's bloody foreign policy!" Instead of apologizing, the professor repeated it for every reporter who bothered to call, which led to Dirk Hoffman's reader board—ROUSSEAU IS A TERRORIST—and Wayne's retort, a flag that flapped for several gusty days before anyone identified it as representing Grenada.

"Imagine if a Canadian official, any official—our trade czar, our trash czar, our lost-pet czar, take your pick—barged across the border," Wayne shouted, as if his audience far exceeded one drowsy American farmer, "and called any one of your business owners anything less than magnificent."

"You said he called the business disgraceful, not the owners."

"The fuck's the difference, Norm?" Thinning smoke swirled above the ditch between them. "I know you think it's all pothead bullshit, but do you have any idea what I'd feel like most days without a half gram of this MC-9 Skunk Bud Number Three?"

Norm coughed. "That skunk doesn't seem to be helping you much today. And do you have to smoke it out *here*?" Norm felt his steam rising, but sensed Wayne hadn't started into whatever would truly rile him. "Does it have to be a performance?"

Wayne blew smoke through a yellow smile and leveled his swollen eyes on him. "How's Jeanette?"

Norm wished he'd already retreated instead of standing there breathing illegal secondhand smoke wafting across a ditch he hadn't crossed since Customs spotted an old DUI on his record and sent him back. He promptly vowed never to step foot in Canada again, though he'd grown up playing in it and drove tractors across it to help plow fields and, in the newlywed years, moseyed into Abbotsford on summer nights to get Jeanette her chocolate éclair, which she'd hold up like a half-eaten passport to get them waved back through. "She's fine," he finally volunteered, not sure what the professor knew about his wife.

Wayne nodded. "Best of luck with that."

"Thanks," Norm grunted, hating his reflexive manners. He knew he should ask about his health, but he'd never understood MS—sounded like some electrical problem—and had let it go for too long to ask about it now without sounding idiotic. Part of him suspected it was a scam to get high anyway, though if you looked hard at Wayne, and got past the youthful hair, the playful smirk, the disrespectful eyes and the commanding voice, you saw there wasn't much left but an assembly of dry twigs easily snapped.

"Your cows getting any better?" Wayne probed.

"Not all of 'em." Norm back-shuffled from the ditch, alarmed he knew anything about his ailing herd.

Wayne winced. "Maybe you should lay off the antibiotics, huh? Kills off the good bacteria and messes with the stomach, isn't that right?"

"They're cows," Norm said, not bothering to point out that mastitis is usually treated with antiseptics, not antibiotics. "Their stomachs are different."

Wayne smirked through his exhale. "Can I ask you one question, my friend? Why do you think twenty million Americans smoke pot every year?"

"Think we've had this discussion before, Professor." This lecture usually digressed into the *irony* of Holland's *progressive* drug laws in light of the valley's uptight Dutch immigrants, which left Norm feeling obliged to condemn or defend some flat old country he couldn't care less about. Seemingly everyone but Norm had visited Amsterdam and returned to tell him about the hookers in the windows, to which he'd offer knowing grunts without admitting he'd never been there. Even the sight of the vowel-happy Dutch language made him uneasy. He felt the cobbled pavement beneath his left boot. Another step back and he could pivot on his good heel and go.

"What about the two million Americans who smoke it every day?" Wayne's voice climbed steadily higher. "They belong in prison? Cannabis isn't some wicked invention by socialists or Muslims or gays, Norm. It's organic, for God's sake. An or-*gan*-ic weed growing wild in every single one of your states. Washington and Jefferson grew it, okay? Washington and fucking Jeff—"

"Like I said, seems like I've heard all this before." Norm tried to exit on an agreeable tone. "I think it's illegal down here for a reason, that's all."

"You're right about that, and the reason is your leaders are cowards, your drug czar's an audacious moron and most of you are not only homophobic and xenophobic but euphoriaphobic too."

"I see." Norm sighed, folding his arms across his chest, rolling his hands into fists. He saw three birds settle on the telephone line above Wayne's head and stared at them, willing them to shit. "Sorry if we make you feel uncomfortable about your habit, Wayne, but—"

"Medicine. Understand the word? And it's *legal*—up here—when a doctor, like mine, prescribes it. It's med-i-cine. Can I ask you a—"

"It's more than that." Norm heard himself start to pant. "It's your new economy, isn't it?"

Face darkening, Wayne sucked hard on his shrinking joint and pointed toward Norm's back barn. "How's that monument to your ego coming along in there, anyhow?"

Norm was surprised his voice remained steady. "Ain't a barn big enough to build one to suit yours." He turned and shuffled away from the ditch, mumble-cursing himself for losing his temper, his throbbing knee adding to the ruckus inside him. The hell with Wayne Rousseau and his half-cocked—

"You people used it in cough syrup until you saw the Mexicans having so much fun with it!" Wayne shouted.

Norm popped two sticks of Big Red into his mouth to give his jaw something besides teeth to grind before glancing up the street and seeing Sophie Winslow in her yard. Of course. Now the professor had an audience.

"I see where your son's protecting the United States from us dangerous Canadians these days," Wayne yelled, louder still. "Called me twice last night *while* on duty. So I suggest you inform him," he continued, his voice still climbing, "that he best get a better understanding of his jurisdiction or someone like me is gonna sue the holy hell out of the U.S. fucking Border Patrol."

Norm turned and glared, pulverizing his gum, its fake cinnamon overwhelming his taste buds, then marched back to the ditch and glared down at him. "Don't talk to me about my son," he said, barely louder than the trickling snowmelt.

"Just offering some neighborly advice," Wayne replied in his emcee voice. "Just trying, as always, to help you see the big picture."

Norm set his feet wider to weather a swoon until the scenery swung back into focus, brighter than ever. Glittering patches of melting snow. Twinkling greenhouses. Fields rising into dark trees. The rest of Canada lurking over the hill. Norm looked down at the shimmering ditch between them, then at the tiny, smirking professor. The big picture? How big do you really wanna go? His wife was losing her mind.

His son was in danger. A third of his herd was too sick to milk. And his sailboat was a pipe dream.

Wayne sucked hard on the final half inch of the joint, smothered a cough, then flicked the last of his roach into the silvery light. The two men watched it ride a gust and arc surprisingly high, a fading spark twirling over the ditch from one country into another.

4

"East Indians are the best liars," Dionne told Brandon. "A good Mexican lies for no more than two hours, then gives up. A good Hindu can lie until the second coming of Christ. I've never seen such perseverance. And Nigerians? Keep your hand on your wallet. They're charming and polite as hell. 'Any-thing-you-want-to-know,' " she said, mimicking their rapid diction. " 'I-have-nothing-to-hide.' And it's the exact opposite."

"Did you take that ethnic-sensitivity test?" Brandon asked.

She yanked on the shoulder strap to give her lungs more room. "Fuck you, okay? Seriously. *Fuck you*. It's my job to prepare you for scammers. God knows the academy didn't. Yes, you will meet some of the honest little people of the world hoping for a chance to bust ass for a buck, but most of the ones you'll encounter—welcome to the Border Patrol—will be lying shitbags. And there are patterns to the shit, okay?" She spoke with hands, shoulders and eyebrows, aping his every gesture and flinch. "It ain't written down, and trust me, everyone will believe that I instructed you, just as I'm telling you now, to treat them all fairly and humanely and to remember they're all innocent until proven otherwise. We clear?"

"What about the Chinese?" Brandon asked, noticing the flaming pompadour of a pileated woodpecker—*nine*—flashing from one fir to another.

"Chinese like to play stupid, but they're among the smartest. Most of 'em are scamming bastards carrying some letter from some bogus

24

U.S. company inviting them to come share their business secrets. Of course, that's complete horseshit."

She had him troll through downtown Blaine and then turn toward the border, past peeling and abandoned houses. The plucky bayside town was the end of the line. Known for its sunsets and porn—even though the theater had long since closed—as well as its rumble of eighteen-wheelers, Blaine was the busiest northern portal in the West.

Brandon puttered around the backside of the Sunrise Apartments, a bland three-story box ensconced by overgrown firs. Unsupervised toddlers swung on a rusty aluminum swing set while Canadians whistled by at 'sixty just ten yards away on Zero Avenue. Brandon lowered his window in time to hear the dry chip of a fox sparrow, *ten*.

"When I first came up here," Dionne said, "I'd look at places like this and say, 'No shit you've got problems. The border's wide open!' I couldn't believe it."

She reminded him again to forget everything he'd learned at the academy, which was easy enough. He'd known just enough Spanish and guessed right just often enough on the multiple-choice tests to become the first trainee ever stationed in the Blaine sector, which Dionne told him the chief did as a favor to Brandon's father.

"You won't see roadies doing lay-ins like you did yesterday," she said. "They don't hide and wait. They park where everybody can see 'em so they don't have to actually confront anybody. Some pull up by houses with wireless and surf for hours in their rigs. Or they'll read James Patterson novels and count the days until they can go fishing in their canoes with a cooler full of Coors. And a whole lot of 'em spend most of their shifts watching movies on those mini DVD players. Greatest invention since the leaf blower. Just ask McAfferty. Met him yet? Can't miss him. Never stops talking. I mean, *never*. Talk about a roadie. His screen saver counts down the days till he can retire."

"What's a roadie?" Brandon finally asked, his eyes scanning trees and sky for something other than blackbirds and crows.

"*Retired On Active Duty*. When a roadie responds to a sensor, it's always a deer. They see more deer than Jane Goodall saw monkeys.

I've seen a dozen in the thirty months I've been here. Guys like McAfferty see a few every day. And if they actually have to chase somebody, they like nothing better than to be told to abort their pursuit. But that's for them to sleep with, okay? It has nothing to do with you. Don't let anybody ten-three you unless you have to. They'll want to ten-three anything that might get messy, which means just about everything. You gotta learn to tell them *too late.*"

They pulled into Peace Arch, where eighteen Canadian homes flanked the park's northern rim with a view of every picnic, Girl Scout festival and international drug deal. Brandon recognized the blue swoop across a curtain of poplars before he heard the signature heckle of a Steller's jay, *eleven.*

The park rolled west toward the bay, past the massive toothlike arch looming in the green expanse like a misplaced monument from some Parisian boulevard. Canada seemingly cared more about appearances, the U.S. side ratty and unimaginative compared to the sculpted shrubs and greener grass on the northern half of this shared space where citizens of both countries could mingle without consequence or scrutiny—although that notion felt increasingly dated, as did the arch's feel-good etchings that called the two countries "Children of a Common Mother" and "Brethren Dwelling Together in Unity."

"There are agents who haven't made a bust the entire time they've been here," Dionne said, and left that dangling.

They crossed rusty tracks so shabby that Amtrak barely used them anymore toward the marina and the defunct canneries where the continent unceremoniously tumbled down a modest bluff through dormant blackberry vines into Semiahmoo Bay, which the tugging moon transformed daily into a vast acreage of gleaming flats that turned to quicksand the farther out you strolled, and where Dionne had caught five Korean hookers—two of them stuck—one Sunday night when she first arrived, and where Brandon noticed three chevrons of water birds escorting an exiting tug.

"Some of these guys are just flat out nut jobs. You met Larabee yet? Had a couple disks fused and got hooked on painkillers, so he keeps having what we call 'OxyContin moments.' When he saw me last Wednesday he *introduced* himself. Seen him almost daily for two and a half years and he acts like I just transferred in from San Diego. 'Larabee, it's me!' 'Ohhhh, Dionne. Yeah, you look different.' Then we've got a couple gun freaks, which makes for great PR. Agent Talley shot a twelve-year-old Lab on Delta Line a week before you showed up. Didn't yell 'Sit!' or 'Stay!' Just, *boom!* Shot Old Yeller in the head. 'Greetings! We're with the government!' And three of our esteemed agents were arrested in the past year for getting hammered and assaulting somebody, usually their wives' boyfriends. The standout of that bunch would have to be Buzzy. Is there a better name for a fuckup? There were even odds in the Yuma Sector on whether he'd make it a month without getting arrested. Well, Buzzy made it a grand total of sixteen days before he hospitalized some dude with a chair. You gotta understand that half of these guys are bored shitless transplants who haven't adjusted to patrolling up here. Down south you just react. Up here you have to think. The tracking is different. The soil, the weather, the scams, the drugs—everything's different." She smiled wide enough for him to notice a chipped incisor and five silver fillings. "But hey, you're from here, and you're plenty different too."

Brandon's mother had been the first to help him understand just how different. "You think in pictures, don't you?" she'd asked when he was nine. Until then he'd assumed everyone did.

He picked up the binoculars, afraid the tug would scare them off. Buffleheads, *twelve*. Common loons, *thirteen*. And horned grebes, *fourteen*.

"See, that's what I'm talking about," Dionne said. "Not many agents would've even thought to take a closer look at that tug. Who knows what you're gonna see, right? And if you don't look, you won't see. That makes life a whole lot easier now, doesn't it?"

She directed him back into Blaine to the Border Brew drive-thru where he heard a European starling mimic a cell-phone ring, *fifteen*. "All that shit aside, most of these guys are brave and smart," she said. "And you're lucky to have 'em on your side—even the roadies."

Brandon started to ask questions as they rolled off with Dionne's triple Americano, but she talked right over him. The same thing happened at the academy, others rattling endlessly about golf, girls or cars, but whenever he started talking they eyeballed him as if he'd recited some obscure passage in a foreign tongue. And if nobody pointed out his misspeaks—such as *angel* for *angle*, *awesome* for *assume*, *aminal* for *animal*—he wouldn't notice until the giggling started.

His goal with Dionne was to keep his comments and questions as brief as possible. Danny Crawford taught him years ago to set an internal alarm that sounded whenever he heard only his voice for more than a couple minutes straight, and to watch for twitching eyebrows and curling lips that signaled he was talking too much or making no sense.

"Iranians are screamers," Dionne was telling him. " 'I'll be killed if I go bock to Eron!' Oh yeah? Well, it says here that you went back in the spring? 'That was chust do see my family!' And Koreans show up in huge groups of women stinking like kimchi and looking like prostitutes because they are. We get shitloads of Korean hookers."

"What about Russians?"

"Some of the most violent people you'll ever see. There's nothing you can do that better professionals than you haven't already done to them back in Russia. They don't bother to lie, just tell you to fuck off to your face."

They glided east over the H Street hill through a tunnel of alders and firs and real estate signs pitching new subdivisions—RIGHT ON THE BORDER!—until the landscape broke into undulating pastures where glacial ice had rounded the hills into green and gold dunes before everything fell into a valley as flat as a pool table. Brandon felt familiar relief as the scenery opened up and they cut through the soothing geometry of farmlands toward Lynden.

The sector was responsible for the thirty-mile stretch between the mountains and the sea, and the agents were free to patrol all of the terrain and the smattering of towns within twenty miles of the line. Lynden, the largest of these burgs, sat just five miles south of the border, yet seemingly considered itself closer to Holland than Canada, touting its Dutch roots with everything from windmills to an annual Dutch Days festival. The other towns were smaller and simpler, clinging to their fading cowboy, ranching or family-farm credentials.

Brandon turned north on the Guide Meridian, the valley's main north-south drag, then wound toward the border through dairies and berry fields drained by large ruler-straight ditches deep enough to kayak through. He tuned out Dionne's complaints when they got stuck behind a tractor pulling a dump wagon and watched the kitelike glide of a juvenile eagle, *sixteen,* the loopy trajectory of a northern shrike, *seventeen,* and the menacing hover of an American kestrel, *eighteen.* He scanned the sky for flocks of incoming songbirds. He'd heard of as many as a thousand exhausted barn swallows arriving at once from Panama or wherever they'd wintered. It had always dazzled him, the notion that boys near the equator considered his swallows theirs. The same acrobatic birds that made him feel like a Wright brother just watching them spent the colder months entertaining boys thousands of miles to the south, who as April approached looked up in the sky and asked, *"¿Adonde fueron mis pajaros?"*

They rolled past small houses and the escalating indignation over the ongoing construction of the tribal casino within a mile of the border. A NO CASINO! placard was followed by a CASINOS RUIN FAMILIES! yard sign only to be topped by a ranch billboard that shouted GAMBLING KILLS! Brandon watched seven mares staring in unison at a stallion being led down a trailer ramp on the other side of the street as Dionne griped about her daughter always being sick. "I've stopped letting her drink the milk around here. Already heard enough stories about girls starting their periods as eight-year-olds to make me want to move. Imagine explaining that to a girl that age? She'd think she was dying."

Brandon was staring at the horses and worrying about how strange Madeline Rousseau had sounded. Was she all right? She was the only girl he'd ever really known. So whenever he'd been approached by others, he'd always assumed they were probably similar to her, though they never were.

Dionne finished her coffee and shouted, "Where are you, two-zero-five?"

He knew he was on Trapline, but forgot the cross street, and stutter-mumbled a response.

"Know where you are at all times!" she scolded. A moment later, she slumped in her seat, shut her eyes and screamed, "I've been shot! What're you gonna do?"

After he stopped the rig and bumbled through that exercise, she sprang outside and pretended to be an illegal he'd just apprehended. "Watch my hands. Always watch my hands. My face can't kill you, but my hands can! Assume everybody is shit and let them work their way up." Chastising him further, she circled back to broader maxims: "Always look for what doesn't belong; always watch their hands. And no matter what happens, Brandon, always tell yourself: 'I'm coming home tonight. I *am* coming home tonight.' "

He pretended to listen while his eyes surveyed maples stenciled against an aluminum sky and the violet-green swallows on the telephone line. *Nineteen.*

He felt a sustained quake he estimated at magnitude 1.8, followed by a brassy clamor in the mattress-flat field behind the trees and the horses. How had he missed the trumpeters? *Twenty.*

"Brandon! Look at me."

He tried, but he couldn't. "Watch this," he whispered as the flock lifted in unison, their garden-hose necks extended and resonant, their jumbled music rising like clown horns. He counted more than a hundred of the world's largest swans separating themselves from the earth like a noisy snowfield returning to the sky.

Brandon imagined his own bones hollowing, his legs disappearing, his neck stretching, his pectoral muscles thickening, his brain shrinking to fit into a tiny soft skull, his 17,238 feathers working as one to catch up with the others. He twitched his butt muscles, steering with his tail feathers, and raised his arms, fully extending his seven-foot wingspan until his right hand was six inches in front of Dionne's face, obstructing her view.

"Brandon," she said calmly, "what *the fuck* are you doing?"

5

NORM HAD to wait until Jeanette got back from aqua aerobics to vent about the professor. And by the time he stomped inside, he found his wife clutching her chest and cooing as if soothing an imaginary infant. "Coca-Cola was originally green," she whispered, then followed that with "Astronauts can't whistle on the moon."

The last time they'd made love her unfocused expression made him worry that nothing was registering. The sensation of multiple alarms ticking at different speeds left him dry-mouthed, a loose wire flickering in his chest. How long before her mind misplaced the yellowing image of him that had attracted her in the first place? Then what? Even with Brandon helping with the bills, he still didn't know if he could finish the boat in time for Jeanette to remember anywhere they went on it, no matter how hard she exercised her mind memorizing strange facts or how optimistically she pumped herself full of ginkgo, choline, garlic, flaxseed oil and apple-cider vinegar.

Norm spent the rest of the day Wayne ruined worrying about his wife, his son and his cows, and dwelling on the rumor Sophie Winslow shared that Chas Landers found a duffel bag stuffed with $68,000 on the corner of his cranberry bog. Chas apparently assumed it was smuggling money, the masseuse told him, so he turned it over to the sheriff's office. That's right: Money fell from the sky, and Chas gave it to the county.

When Norm wasn't moping about all that, he was lamenting his own miserable luck after finding four more cows with inflamed teats.

Almost a third of his eighty-one Jerseys and Holsteins had it, according to the latest round of milk stats. Next month's cell count would tell the whole story. Even with a closed herd, mastitis rarely spread this fast and was simple to treat. Iodine and more iodine. So what was going on? And exactly why had the last six calves aborted? Still, he resisted ringing his surly vet, given the expense and scolding that came with that. He led the four cows into the sick barn with the others, then reluctantly grabbed his sharpest blade and lopped five gangrenous teats he'd rubber-banded off the day before. That was another difference between him and the big boys. They didn't bother numbing anything, just strolled up and whacked away like they were pruning trees. Norm was cleaning the knife when he heard the cattle trailer rattle up. Damn. He'd forgotten about the livestock auction. The entire day was wobbling off its axle.

Norm made sure Roony knew which two unproductive Jerseys to haul away, 29 and 71, then stepped out of sight of it all behind the barn for a smoke. Pushing sixty-three and still sneaking cigarettes. Copenhagen wasn't killing him fast enough? He carefully positioned his body and clothes upwind, smoking arm extended, as if pointing out land through fog. Jeanette had troubles recalling some yesterdays, but her nose missed nothing. He inhaled deeper when the cows started their mournful bellowing. "It's not that they know their cousins are gonna be butchered," Brandon reassured him once, as if he'd recently chatted with them. "It's just that they hate change."

Norm faced Canada and glared at the glitzy hills east of Abbotsford, where enormous windows twinkled like vertical swimming pools. Every third house was growing pot up there is what people told him. True or not, it fit into Norm's growing sense of an upside-down economy. While he squeezed a living from sickly cows, Canadians made millions selling drugs and Seattle kids earned fortunes in Internet and wireless worlds Norm didn't need or understand. *Microsoft millionaires?* Sounded like an Amway scam, yet he kept hearing about kids retiring in their thirties. Meanwhile, he didn't have the slightest control over the cost of his product. When milk prices rose, the big boys expanded and prices fell while the cost of everything else went nuts. Property tax. Insurance. Farm equipment. Everything. Feed costs had almost doubled in the prior two years alone, but the cost of milk hadn't changed much in decades and in fact was lower than it was in '84, when over half the dairies in the valley lunged at the government buyout. Norm should have too. Nothing was more obvious than that now. Could have sold his herd at fourteen dollars per hundredweight, then converted his fields into raspberries, hired himself a few illegals and taken winters off—as long as he could bend his morality and patriotism around all that. But what pissed Norm off even more than dairies turning into berry farms was dairies turning into cul-de-sacs or toy ranches for the rich. And worst of all was when the rich left the barns and silos standing out of some do-gooder nostalgia for an America they never knew. Almost half the silos were no more genuine than the false storefronts in those back-road towns still sucking on the Old West titty. How long would it be before the valley's dairy scene was nothing but the big boys and a few bedraggled family farms to amuse the tourists: *Look! There's Norm Vanderkool still milking cows on his bum knees.*

Norm could hear the clock ticking but dairy farming was every day, twice a day, until you die or sell, which left little time to rethink much of it. And if you were stupid enough to pass on the buyout and simultaneously attempt to build a thirty-eight-foot double-ended ocean-worthy sloop, well . . .

He strolled the western perimeter of his property, absently noting where the fence needed the most mending, futilely trying to picture his son chasing aliens into the Crawfords' back twenty. Does imagination fade with age to the point where you're eventually reduced to only what you can actually see? Norm squatted as low as he could to get a different view of his land, reluctantly admitting to himself that he was looking for sacks of cash.

Sixty-eight thousand dollars! How does anyone leave, drop or misplace that much money? The mast and boom, unassembled, would cost six thou. Three tons of lead would still run him a grand if he melted it down himself. The sails could soak up another ten. And he was out at least eight for an engine, even if he went with a two-cylinder Yanmar instead of the four-cylinder Volvo he wanted.

The boat had already swallowed eleven years. *Eleven.* Why hadn't anyone warned him about wasting what time remained on a project he'd never finish? He was thirty-five short, probably forty. And that left the cabin rough. Homey, isn't she, Jeanette? He glanced around his darkening farm. Could he blame Washington Mutual for balking at a loan? Who wanted to gamble on a snake-bit dairy? His eyes settled on the boat barn. A monument to his *ego*? No. To his incompetence? Probably. To his insanity? Definitely.

Norm lit another Winston and shuffled back toward the barns, sucking it down so fast he burned himself. He knew he'd have to raise Professor Rousseau's lecture with Brandon, though he could already picture his puzzled response. The patrol, of course, was Norm's idea. It was high time Brandon learned how to interact and have a life beyond the farm, even if he continued to live in the basement with his dogs. Sure, his rent checks would help with the bills, but Chief Patera had convinced him that the patrol could pop Brandon's bubble. Hell, he'd said, the kid's in his twenties and still searching for something in the moment that nobody else sees, which sounded as accurate as any diagnosis Norm had heard. What he hadn't expected was for Brandon to look like such an easy target, and wondered again if he'd pulled strings for his son or for himself.

Norm had put on thirteen pounds since Brandon took the Greyhound—there was no talking him into flying—to the academy. Thirteen pounds, Brandon's birth weight. They'd tried for almost five years before a somber doc pointed at an ultrasound of Jeanette's pinched tubes. They were filling out adoption forms when she missed her second period and her belly ballooned before their eyes. Gotta be twins, right? Norm had twins on his mother's side, and Jeanette's sister had identical boys, but the doc heard just one heart. Then came the whopper C-section.

Norm knew women obsessed over babies, yet in Jeanette's case it never passed. He came to see his son as an intruder sent to drive his wife crazy. She dismissed his speculation that Brandon's early peculiarities were side effects of spoiling. And she resisted efforts to diagnose him, withholding information from doctors such as the fact that he didn't speak clearly until he was three. Still, one pediatrician suggested Brandon's mannerisms and obsessive tendencies pointed toward mild autism, which meant he'd likely struggle with school, friendships and intimacy. Jeanette suggested the doctor was an idiot and demanded another. By second grade, it became alarmingly clear that Brandon couldn't read, that he was guessing and thought everyone else was too. Norm remembered Jeanette writing a sentence: *The boy made a bird out of clay and put a fish in its bill.* When Brandon read it aloud it came out: "The boy made a bed out of clay and pet a frog in its bill."

Jeanette patiently tutored him on the sounds of letters and drilled him on the tricky in-between words—*was, saw, is, as*—he kept tripping over until she concluded that the harder he concentrated, the worse it got. Meanwhile, birds came easily, and Jeanette fed his fascination as if both their lives depended on it. He memorized *Birds of Puget Sound* before he turned ten. Your son has a gift, Jeanette told him, for birding by ear and for mimicking their voices. Terrific. It never struck Norm as anything to boast about. You should hear my son's duck call! Next came his bird-rescue phase—he turned half the basement into a bird ER—and then his bird-art binge. He wouldn't paint from photos, preferring instead to paint from *memory*—usually in-flight smudges of color and motion with a floating beak, an oddly detailed wing and a yellow eye in there somewhere. By his early teens he had a body that could jack a Honda onto two wheels, yet all he seemingly wanted to do with it was play with the cows, build strange forts and paint more birds.

Strolling back to his sickly cows, Norm tried to comfort himself with the fact that the big boys would've long since slaughtered half his *burger cows* and put Pearl down a decade and nine calves ago. They demanded eighty pounds of milk per cow per day, whereas Norm asked his for forty or fifty. Pearl gave sixty, and never spent a day in the sick barn. She was so old and remarkable that Norm made an exception he regretted and let Brandon name her.

Truth was, for the most part Brandon was great with cows, particularly at noticing things Norm and most dairymen missed—the beginnings of swollen joints, split hooves or eye infections, and the potentially agitating shifts in lighting, texture, colors or sounds. The problem was he crossed the lines. Always had his hands on them, especially when comforting mothers who'd just had their calves taken away. He even got down on the ground and let them lick his head and neck with their long, rough tongues—something Norm desperately hoped nobody else ever saw. Plus, how long could he watch his enormous son crouch beneath cows? Milkers should ideally be five feet, like Roony, not pushing seven.

Norm heard voices ringing from Sophie's house and pictured clinking crystal, bubbled drinks, cream-filled sweets and sensual odors. She entertained so often it was as if she were running for something. Norm increasingly felt like the only man in the valley who hadn't gone for a *massage*. Her clients, based on the succession of cars behind her hedge, included Blaine's deputy mayor, Lynden's assistant city manager, First American's veep, the head of the BP and many, many others.

It amazed Norm how little he knew about her, even though they'd talked at least weekly since she inexplicably moved into the house she'd inherited from her aunt. A week later she'd placed an ad in the weeklies: *Give your body the gift it craves.* It felt like a brothel had moved in next door.

But it was more than that. She read him like a relative who'd heard about him for years. Without warning, she asked if he was worried about running out of time. No explanation, just the question, as if his fears were stenciled across his forehead. Then more questions, as if what he said mattered, as if she were interviewing Moses.

Norm heard dozens of rumors about her. She rocked preemies at the hospital, led aqua aerobics classes at the YWCA and ran current-events discussion groups at retirement homes in Abbotsford, which was probably what sparked the speculation that she was a Canadian spy. And she was definitely either independently wealthy or selling more than massages. How else could a single masseuse afford such an extravagant home renovation? She was a former stewardess. No, a dental hygienist. She came from eastern money, right? Actually, a horse farm in Indiana. Or was it Austin? She had an accent, but it wasn't exactly southern. Chief Patera insisted she'd been divorced at least twice and attempted suicide at least once, but it sounded like he was guessing. Others claimed she was a widow whose husband died suspiciously. And getting clear answers from her was impossible. She'd *moved around a lot,* and had some relationships end poorly. When she did offer something specific, it was oddly personal.

"I had an unusual mother. When I was thirteen, I invited three friends over for the first slumber party I was ever allowed. Cleaned the whole house myself and filled the basement with balloons. I was so excited it was hard to breathe, and I had asthma, so I was hitting the inhaler. My mom was yelling at me to calm down, and my dad was yelling at her to quit yelling at me. Well, none of my friends showed up. They all forgot about it. That's what they said, anyway. I couldn't stop crying, which led to more yelling. So my mother left the house and brought me home a cake that had a miniature gravestone in the middle of it."

Usually, however, Sophie simply redirected Norm's questions. And when she leveled her gentle green eyes on you, it was like your favorite sister asking you to please respect the privacy of her diary. Then she'd whisper a question, pull you closer, cock her chin and make you want to spill whatever guts you had left.

Did her massages have *happy endings?* Norm wondered. Of course they did. He heard a crane in the distance stacking steel girders at the corner of Northwood and Halverstick. Yes, a brothel next door and—coming soon!—a Las Vegas–style casino a mile down the street. What would life feel like if it were built around pleasure and temptation? What would it feel like to not second-guess yourself at three fifteen every morning? Something beyond Sophie's sympathetic eyes made him want to tell her everything and, worse, anything. Maybe it was as simple as those shapely lips, which he'd seen elicit whatever the moment called for—arousal, compassion, confession. Or perhaps she sensed he was that easy to split, like a roast so ready you could carve it with a fork.

Norm heard more women laughing freely, as they often did when men weren't around, and pondered again whether Sophie passed along what he told her. People blew through her house all day long getting what their bodies craved. Did she share his words?

He kicked lumps of snow walking back to the barn, hoping for the thud of cash, delaying thoughts about his sick cows as long as possible, wincing at laughter that reminded him of ducks.

Of course she did.

6

AN HOUR LATER, Sophie Winslow's living room windows were still vibrating with laughter from her party. Alexandra's rapid-fire cackle—*hack-hack-hack!*—sounded like an animal trying to scare predators off. Danielle and Katrina were drinking more aggressively than usual, lipstick gleaming, consonants softening as they bullied the others to play *faster, fasder, fasda*. The only two who weren't already somewhat belligerent were Ellen—who kept saying "That's so funny" without smiling so as not to deepen laugh lines—and Wayne Rousseau's younger daughter, Madeline, which made sense. Everyone had at least twenty years on her and she was the lone rookie, filling in for one of three Canadians who helped give Sophie the dozen players needed to keep her international bunco game alive for a sixth straight month.

Danielle yakked about the upswing in Americans lining up for cheap Lipitor, Zoloft and Prozac at her Abbotsford pharmacy while Sophie waded through the gathering, inhaling the chatter. A new over-priced subdivision popping up north of Lynden. A fired middle-school teacher suddenly driving an Escalade. A stone mansion being built on a bankrupt dairy by a former rock star.

Sophie's game plan was simple: Assemble the best-connected gossips she could find—bankers, nurses, pharmacists and others—and engage them in mindless gambling, then add liquor, and type it all up later.

Danielle asked if anyone else had heard the rumors about the linguistically gifted Abbotsford prostitute who could fake it in four languages, which led Alexandra to fake one in German—"*Ja, ja! Das ist sehrrrr guuuut!*"—and another in breathy French: "*Oui, oui! Magnifique!*"

"That's so funny," Ellen insisted as Alexandra popped eardrums with her machine-gun laugh. Madeline remained as contained as a house cat. The more everyone drank, the younger she looked: teenager thin, finger-combed bangs, mischievous eyes. It didn't take long to explain the game to her. The women took turns rolling three dice at three different tables. First they rolled for ones, then they switched partners and tables and rolled for twos, and so on. They scored points every time the right dice popped up; three of the right kind was a bunco. The regulars were eyeballing Madeline not just because she exuded youth, but also because her dice seemed to be listening to her. She rolled two buncos in the first three rounds.

"So how many of you would've done what Chas Landers did?" Sophie asked as the gamblers switched tables and prepared to roll for fours.

"Cranberry Chas? What'd that old fart do?"

Sophie told them, then waited for the disbelief and questions to settle. "Don't know exactly when he found it, but I do know he gave it to a deputy early this morning. Offered it first to the Border Patrol, who sent him to the sheriff's office."

Gasps and murmurs were followed by quips about brain-cell-killing pesticides. But beneath the tittering, Sophie sensed a new fantasy emerging in which clumsy smugglers drop or even plant sacks of cash on your property. Every month she sensed more excitement, as if the ever-escalating smuggling made everybody feel younger.

"Didn't Chas roll his tractor and bonk his head a few years back?" Katrina asked.

"A cousin of mine," Sophie said, "hit his head skiing and lost all his inhibitions. It damaged his frontal lobes, and he didn't know what was appropriate anymore. He started walking around the neighborhood with his pants off, in an obvious state of arousal."

"I live near Chas," Katrina said, "and I think I would've noticed if he'd strolled by with an erection."

"The money technically belongs to the county," Sophie explained. "Same as dope to them, so I guess he did the right thing." Chief Patera had told her earlier, though, while she loosened his left hip, that smugglers typically carry $40,000 bricks, which meant "dumbass" Landers probably had twelve grand in a drawer—or perhaps fifty-two.

"Don't think he's the only one finding money these days," Alexandra offered. "There's plenty of locals depositing stacks of hundreds." She wiggled her eyebrows amid cries for names before reminding them of her bank's confidentiality pledge, which she'd later break for Sophie.

Madeline casually asked whether the stakes could be doubled for the fives and received nothing but laughter.

Sophie found another opening while topping glasses at Madeline's table. "Saw your father get into it with Norm Vanderkool out at the ditch this morning."

"That's how they get their exercise, isn't it?" Madeline said, eyes on her dice.

Alexandra blurted a recollection of Wayne countering Norm's RIGHT TO BEAR ARMS bumper sticker with his own RIGHT TO ARM BEARS.

"Seems they were arguing about Brandon this time," Sophie said, then repeated what Dionne had told her about arriving at the Crawfords' field in time to witness Brandon's flying tackle.

"He's always been a freak of nature," Katrina said. "Once saw him climb out of his father's truck to help a night crawler across the road."

"A worm?"

"Is there any other kind of night crawler?"

Alexandra did her best impression of Brandon's snorting laugh. "Gotta admit he's kinda handsome though, in an overgrown, innocent kinda way." Then she broke into an off-key rendition of "Super Freak," growling, "the kind you don't bring home to mo-therrr . . ."

Sophie waited for a lull, then recounted Dionne's full rendition of how he'd chased five illegals into her arms, and how the nationality of the injured couple remained a mystery. "They put them on the phone with AT&T translators and passed the call around, but nobody could place their accent. Can you imagine?"

She was mentioning that the woman Brandon caught had been wearing clothes made of silk and lamé when Madeline volunteered, "He called me."

"Who?" Sophie asked, sensing that Madeline was drunker than she looked.

"Brandon."

"Last night?"

"Uh-huh. He wanted to know if we'd seen anything. Needed to talk, I think."

Sophie waited out the commentary. "So that was it?"

"Said the most interesting people he meets these days are criminals."

"Out of the blue?"

Madeline smiled. "Completely."

"He is the strangest," Alexandra began over the rising gabble. "I mean, have any of you actually—"

"Speaking of strange," Danielle interjected, saliva whistling in the corners of her mouth, "I hear you had a date with some foot-sucker, Madeline."

Madeline's head fell, and Sophie leaned forward as if to catch it. "Dessert anyone?"

She then glided toward the kitchen, blocking out the chatter and reimagining Brandon's tiny, nameless couple flying into Vancouver, and waiting a few anxious days until some overpriced stranger they couldn't understand coaxed them across the ditch. *Is this America?* The air, soil and trees looked and smelled the same. *Are we really in America?* And then—YES!—to be in the land of liberty for all of three electrifying minutes before getting chased and crushed by the largest, most unusual agent in the history of the U.S. Border Patrol.

Welcome to America, whoever you are.

7

NORM WATCHED his son lope up the stairs three in a bound, still resembling a giant Boy Scout in that silly uniform, ducking beneath the beam and looking so alive and powerful that if he inhaled too deeply everyone else in the room might pass out.

As usual, he seemed to see everything in a glance, his eyes sweeping from the ice on his father's knee to his mother hunched over stacks of photos on the sun-faded couch that her husband had promised to replace years ago. She'd written the names of friends and relatives on the back so she could flip through the prints like flash cards. From what Norm could tell, this exercise only complicated matters; the images were so meshed with memories it was like separating salt from sugar. At what click of the second hand, he wondered, would those names become meaningless jumbles of letters?

Until the past eight months—yes, it began when Brandon went away to the academy—she'd been their memory, their crossword whiz, their *Jeopardy!* champ. Norm had never read much except *Hoard's Dairyman* while she inhaled everything from *The Economist* to Darwin's original essays to *National Geographic Kids*—a holdover from Brandon's childhood—and armed herself with believe-it-or-not facts she nimbly recycled into conversations. Now these tidbits were part of her daily memory exercises and came out like meteors, if they came at all. "When you're one in a million in China," she'd told him recently, "there are still fourteen hundred people as good as you."

The dinner table was covered with clashing flavors and odors, braised lamb chops, red potatoes, spinach salad and a cod chowder made with coconut milk. Meals had become adventures. Nothing tasted the same twice anymore, and Jeanette was always adding some miracle food like kimchi, roasted garlic or pickled beets on the side too, as if her memory slump, as she called it, was just one healthy meal away from ending. But at least tonight she hadn't botched another recipe she'd known by heart.

As usual, he'd almost finished before she got started, and he spent the rest of the dinner picking through his salad, sipping the lone Pabst he allowed himself and watching Brandon plow through a second and third serving. Norm stopped nibbling on the rabbit food once he realized the dressing was pure vinegar, then studied Brandon's smooth face. "You all right? Lookin' kind of pale."

"Me?"

"Who else?"

"It's March," Brandon said, not looking up from the precise teamwork of his knife and fork. "Don't we all look pale?"

"You know what I mean. How do you—"

"What?" Brandon asked, still eating, avoiding eye contact.

"I'm getting my fillings pulled." Jeanette smiled. "And no, Norm, I don't know, or care, how much it'll cost."

He waited. "Where'd that come from?"

"Every time you bite into something a little bit of mercury gas squeezes out of your fillings." She hissed through her teeth.

"I see," Norm said, gambling the issue would pass if he didn't contest it. It was impossible to concentrate. He desperately wanted to tell them about the mastitis outbreak. That was the word he'd been flogging himself with for the past hour, *outbreak,* but Brandon would overreact and demand that he call in the doc even though nine out of ten times these things cleared themselves up no matter what you paid the vet.

"What's the problem?" Brandon asked, as if Norm had been thinking aloud. "Need some help?"

"You've got a job. If I need somebody, I'll call Roony."

"We could go out after dinner," Brandon offered. "Something happens, they'll call."

"Thanks, but I got her."

His son cocked his head, then shrugged his eyebrows and dished himself more lamb before pointing his fork at his mother. "Saw a hundred and twenty trumpeters leaving today. Least I assume they were leaving."

"Saw a snowy owl on the Moffats' fence," she replied.

Brandon looked to his father, then back to Jeanette. "Another one?" he asked hopefully.

She looked past him, her eyes going glassy in her broad Scottish face.

It would be so much more just, Norm thought, if he were the one losing it—a blessing, actually. No memory meant no regrets and no cover-ups. "Think you already told him 'bout that one, Jen."

She refocused and threw Norm a clearheaded smile that made him blush. "Don't I listen to your stories no matter how many times you tell them?"

He nodded, exhaling, then asked if they'd heard about Chas Landers finding all that cash in his field. Jeanette's eyes sparkled, but Brandon didn't seem to care. Money had never interested him, which Norm saw as further proof of his botched parenting. "So how'd it feel last night?" he finally asked.

"What?"

"You know what."

Getting Brandon to talk was sometimes like starting a chainsaw in the spring; you never knew how long it would take to get him going or when he'd shut off. He had the FM voice of a man but the jumbled rhythm of a child that made people turn to Norm for translation. He's got his own take on things, was all Norm could often offer. He now sucked the last drops of his Pabst, waiting out his son's silence.

"Like when I'd hurt somebody by accident at recess," Brandon finally said.

For a moment Norm thought that was it, but then came a torrent of words, as if he were talking to the blind—Crawfords' field unrolling like white shag, swirling snowflakes the size of chicken feathers, watching his own flying tackle *from above* . . . Norm hoped like hell he hadn't shared that version with the chief or anyone else. His son's face darkened with concentration as he described the injured "princess," her cartoon-big eyes, her clever purple lips forming words nobody could understand. "All right," Norm grunted, trying to rein him in without sounding impatient.

Brandon mimicked her birdlike accent. Birds, birds, birds. It was almost cute at first. "Birds are easy to talk to," Brandon used to say, which had always embarrassed Norm, but at least then he was a child.

He forced himself to listen to his description of the black hair blooming from her head and her regal clothing. "All *right*," he grumbled again, but it was obvious Brandon wouldn't stop until he was finished.

Norm groaned, his thoughts funneling toward doom. What if the herd had contracted something deadlier than mastitis? He'd read in *Hoard's* how seven huge British dairies had to slaughter every last cow. A few caught foot-and-mouth and six thousand animals had four-inch steel bolts plunged into their skulls. His chest tightened. He knew he should call Doc Stremler, but that involved a minimum of $300, a dozen told-ya-sos and at least one wisecrack about his boat. Stremler would lower his glasses, glare at Norm's duct-tape-and-baling-wire repairs and tell him that he desperately needed some experienced help. Then he'd glance around and say things like, You want your cows chewing cud and feeling good about life. As if Norm had gotten into dairies on a lark. You want them laying down, Norm, not walking around on concrete. Cow joints weren't designed for concrete, you understand?

Brandon was still talking, but his words were starting to swerve. "After she gets out of the hospital, they'll take both of them to this center detention where they'll stay in Tacoma till they can figure out where they should go. Chief said sometimes stay people there for months, even years, before—"

"I had a dream," Jeanette interrupted, "in which I woke up and nobody understood anything I said. Not a word. That was all in the same dream, the dreaming and the waking. At least I think it was. Was that last night?"

"You were doing your job," Norm said.

"Nightmares are my job?" Jeanette said hesitantly.

Norm shook his head. "Brandon was."

"They're Brandon's job?"

Norm wanted to tell his son that everyone kept telling him what a terrific job he'd done, but he knew that if he started into that he couldn't resist asking why he'd left his gun and flashlight in the car with the engine running, knowing that, as usual, the end result would sound like an ass-chewing. Plus, there was the matter of his taking ten times longer than normal to file a report jammed with so many misspellings and absurd time estimates that Patera wondered aloud how Brandon ever passed the academy. Still, Norm couldn't avoid everything. "Gather you talked to the professor."

Brandon looked up, curious. "Madeline. I talked to Madeline."

Norm scratched his scalp. "You talked to her father too, right?"

"Nope."

The sanctimonious bastard.

"Left a couple messages," Brandon noted.

"But you *did* talk to Madeline?"

"Didn't I just say that?"

"What'd she say?"

Brandon shrugged and squinted.

"You don't have any authority," Norm said, more officiously than he'd intended, "to question Wayne or any other Canadian."

Brandon looked to his mother and then back at Norm, as if gauging how much trouble he was in. "Was just," he whispered, "asking . . ."

Norm was about to explain that intent didn't matter when his wife said, "The only first lady to carry a gun was Eleanor Roosevelt."

Brandon tried to smile, but Norm could tell he'd shut the boy down.

"Ostriches are looking for water when they stick their heads in the sand," she continued. "And all polar bears are left-handed."

"Me too," Brandon whispered, reaching for the jug of raw milk.

Norm scrambled for a neutral subject. "Madeline still racing?" The thought of her sailing was one of his favorite images for reasons he couldn't place, but there it was—little Madeline Rousseau, shifting her weight to rock her boat and create her own wind, arriving at the marina a mile ahead of her becalmed competition. "She still racing Lasers?" he pressed when Brandon didn't respond. "One hell of a sailor," he added, as if defending the question.

He decided right then not to tell anyone about the mastitis just yet. The longer he kept the severity to himself, the less real it seemed—even if it coiled inside him like a scream. He imagined his herd, led by old Pearl herself, marching up the slaughter chute. Then Norm too, the steel bolt crushing the thumb-sized notch at the back of his skull, birds scattering at the pneumatic hiss.

8

MADELINE KNEW the guard ducks wouldn't shut up until long after she'd closed the trapdoor beneath the garage of the well-kept rental house nobody lived in on the western outskirts of Abbotsford.

The ducks were Fisher's brainstorm. A dog they'd have to feed, train and walk, but if they built a shallow pond and planted barley and buckwheat, the mallards would come. And there was no more delicate or reliable alarm system, he insisted, than nervous mallards.

She felt the familiar rush of fear and excitement as the hatch clanked into place above her and muffled the quacking, leaving her with the ruckus of rustling PVC pipes, humming lights and a hissing CO_2 generator. It was sweaty-hot, the moist air ripe with too many plants growing and exhaling in too small a space.

When Fisher first led her into this dungeon he'd acted like he was showing her some sunken treasure. The cockiness of pot growers astounded her, everyone was so self-congratulatory about growing hearty weeds that would stand five feet in September if you tossed seeds behind the barn in May. Still, they fawned over their homely shrubs and sticky flowers as if they were purple orchids. *Please*. Even the most spectacular buds looked like glorified sedge or burweed. Yet pot apparently brainwashed people into thinking it was not only breathtakingly beautiful and smelled heavenly but also channeled the supernatural—hallelujah!—and was worth, pound for pound, more than gold. So they grew these pumped-up clones that maximized speed and potency such that if you lit one on fire you could forget your name in the time it took for one long inhale.

Theoretically, there wasn't all that much for her to do other than prune, harvest, clip and cure. Timers and pumps watered and fed the plants the nitrogen, potassium and phosphorus they would've absorbed naturally if they'd been rooted in soil instead of rock wool. And six-hundred-watt bulbs delivered as much fake sunshine as the plants could handle. Still, there were so many things that could go wrong. If the power failed, everything died within twenty-four hours. Too many nutrients? The plants suffered heart attacks. She studied watermarks in the low ceiling. If water dripped onto the sodium lights, they'd explode.

Madeline hadn't been here in five days. It didn't look like anyone else had, either, except to cram more plants inside. Fisher had promised a max of four hundred. Right. There was barely enough room to get around the tables. After counting more than five hundred wide-leafed clones quivering in a fake two-knot breeze, she considered climbing out for good instead of being trapped inside when the trigger-fingered Mounties showed up wired on bad coffee. Fisher admitted he was juggling more than ten grows, which probably meant over twenty. But he insisted this was their baby, their safest op. Sure.

Dozens of baby clones—still trapped beneath humidity domes—should have been replanted days ago. And half the plants in the vegetation room belonged in the flowering room. She checked the thermostat: ninety-three. Far too hot, particularly considering that the rooms weren't adequately divided. She was supposed to harvest quadrant four, but most of quad three had slid into reproduction, which meant the plants needed darkness. Even a kid's night-light could ruin them. She studied the gray speckles on the harvest buds. Mold? Even worse, gnats! It was too late. A cloud of them drifted in her direction. She gasped, inhaling the tiny bugs, fanning her Expos hat and backpedaling until she bumped into the concrete wall. Once they scattered, she rubbed her face, coughed and blew her nose. When she risked opening her eyes again she saw a dozen greenhouse whiteflies, then dozens more. She fanned another gnat cloud while snipping and bagging buds as fast as she could.

Was this the double or nothing she'd been craving—this chance to rise above the oncoming rut of credit cards, mortgages and meaningless jobs? And do what? Travel! Yes, travel. Maybe she'd start in Indonesia—Bali!—and then crew on some exotic schooner headed even farther south. Sydney, then what? The exhilarating unknown. That's what. But the only daydream she could sustain in this hot, buggy hole involved prison.

She'd received only two U.S. hundreds—real convenient—for her prior six visits. Today, Fisher promised, she'd be paid in full, including her cut of the successful run the night Brandon's call rescued her from the foot freak.

Her intuition kept screaming at her to climb out. Now! But she was still furiously clipping and bagging buds, fending off real and imagined insects, when the ducks fired up again, first in random solos, then in riotous quacking unison. Shit! She turned up the baby monitor and panted until she heard Fisher's familiar mumble into the microphone stashed behind the bicycles: "Jus' me, Madness."

He had a nickname for everyone, and apparently there was nothing you could do about it. But he was easy to like, and while he didn't look like the sort you went into business with, he wasn't the type you worried about either. When she climbed up, he appeared to be staggering from some joke. Lizard-thin in expensive jeans and green fleece, he had a smoked, wrung-out look, his skin as dry as jerky. What startled her was that he wasn't alone.

She'd made it clear she didn't want to meet anyone, which of course was another part of the deal that had already been broken, although he'd apologized so profusely about sending Monty to her nursery that she'd asked him to drop it.

"Who the hell's this?" she said, not caring how it sounded, twitchy from her fingertips to her lips, heart hammering, jaw wiggling, ready to shout.

"Easy, Madeline. This is Toby. And this is . . ." He laughed awkwardly. "Well, this is his show."

Toby bowed slightly with the confidence of a senator in his gray T-shirt, corduroy shorts and sockless slip-ons. He wasn't all that large, but brawny, with neck muscles that angled up like rebar, and his bright, deep-set eyes looked as if they'd been screwed in too tight.

"If it is," Madeline snapped, "your show sucks big-time."

Fisher patted the air in front of him until Toby held up a palm as if testifying. "Thanks for all your work. Really. You are very good. And yes, this one has a ways to go."

She ignored his calming, pilotlike tenor and unloaded on Fisher. "You got fucking gnats down there like I said you would. And you've got too many plants on too many schedules and the whole thing's way too hot. And, if you haven't noticed, you've already waited too long on replanting half of—"

Fisher shushed her. "That's one of the reasons—"

"She's right," Toby said before Fisher could finish or she could reload, "on all counts." He handed her a tiny tube of aloe vera. "It's new. Keep it."

She opened it, dabbed some on her face and slid it into her jeans without thanking him. "You've got whiteflies down there too."

Fisher wondered aloud which pesticide would do the trick.

"Can't use insecticides on anything you smoke," Toby told him, "especially when you're calling it organic." He rocked his shoulders, and slabs of muscle shifted beneath his shirt. "Seeing how the room is sealed, we can up the CO_2 levels to ten thousand parts per million for forty-five minutes. If that doesn't work we'll bring in ladybugs."

"Beautiful," Madeline said. "Then you'll have another infestation."

"They're easy to vacuum." Toby grinned. "Then you just seal the bag and store them in the fridge till you need 'em again."

"We cool, Madness?" Fisher thumbed through a roll of hundreds. "It's my fault," he said, lip-counting to twelve. "We'll get you everything you need by Wednesday. Cool?"

She didn't concede anything, though her anger was dissipating faster than she would have liked. What she desired now was a peaceful exit, without telling anyone off, without even admitting she was *out*.

"What do you think of Fisher's ducks?" Toby asked.

"Ingenious."

Fisher turned to Toby. "You said you loved the idea."

"A few ducks, sure." He carefully applied ChapStick. "But you got a marching band out here."

"You start harvesting yet?" Fisher asked Madeline.

"Uh-huh."

"Pretty sweet buds, eh?"

"Not really."

Fisher acted like he hadn't heard. "Toby handles all the loads."

"Yeah?" Madeline slid the thick fold of hundreds into a back pocket and inched toward the door.

"Fifty-nine by land," Toby said, "eighteen by air, six by sea. And I've overseen three times that many."

The more specific the details, Madeline's father had taught her, the more thorough the lies.

"Any close calls?" Fisher asked.

She wanted to spare them the recruitment routine but couldn't bring herself to interrupt.

"People only get caught if they're reckless or wasted." Toby raised a thick eyebrow. "It's not something you do stoned or out of shape. Fact is, even morons usually don't get caught unless they pull up to Peace Arch when the drug dogs are out. Then anyone's screwed. Their best dogs can smell a seed beneath your floor mat when you roll by at twenty."

Madeline liked his voice. Maybe she was overreacting to a few gnat bites. Who knew better than her that only dumbshits got caught crossing a ditch she'd lived alongside most of her life? And she *did* just get paid, didn't she? And when you compared it to nursery money . . .

"There are always risks." Toby bounced from flexed quad to flexed quad. "But do you think the guy who buys a 7-Eleven or opens a bar doesn't have risks? Or the logger? The crabber? Think they aren't gambling? I've got my worries, but I own three houses outright and I've got two good lawyers if problems arise."

"If you've already got three houses," Madeline asked, "why still mess with all this?"

"It's my profession. I take pride in mine just as an engineer or carpenter or doctor takes pride in his. I drive this stretch of the border ten times a week. I talk to hunters, hikers and tugboat captains. And I probably know enough about dairy and raspberry farming to pinch-hit at either. I also know the names and habits of at least half the residents—their dogs, too—along Zero and Boundary."

She noticed that his tiny teeth looked out of place on his broad face, and realized she was taking mental notes for Sophie Winslow. What an odd request—Sophie pulling her aside after that bizarre bunco gathering to ask her to help keep her informed. About what? "About everything, hon." She got so close Madeline could smell the wine on her breath. "What you see and hear. I collect all the details." Then she'd cupped the back of Madeline's skull and kissed her nose, as if blessing her.

"I chart the weather and the tides and how bright the moon's likely to be on any given night," Toby went on. "And I use spotters with Gen Three night goggles and surveillance scopes. When there's no BP within fifteen minutes of our location, we go. It used to be as simple as waiting till midnight, but the sector has eighty-two BPs now and night shifts too. So you gotta know the agents, which isn't easy because a third of them are new. Still, I could spot most of 'em out of uniform from thirty yards, and I've memorized the sounds of their rigs, and I know where they like to park and how they burn time—which ones spit seeds, which ones smoke, which ones play the deterrence game, which ones do their best to see absolutely nothing. I've done well, but I'm not in it for the money. It doesn't work like that. You've got to feel it here." He patted his chest with an open palm and sucked air through his little teeth. "The way I look at it, I'm delivering a medicinal herb to a neighbor who desperately needs it."

She smothered a laugh.

Toby studied her face, as if measuring it for a mask. "We need more capable people willing to hump it across the water, because that's the safest route."

"Yeah?" She glanced at Fisher.

"I'm willing to pay extra for skilled people willing to deliver by boat, especially by sailboat."

She caught Fisher grinning, his eyes glittering.

"Understand you sail," Toby ventured.

"No," she said.

Toby slow-eyed Fisher, who instantly reddened.

"I race," she said. "There's a difference. So, what do you know," she couldn't resist asking, "about that new agent who tackled those illegals just over the border a week ago?"

Toby hesitated. "The big guy?"

"Uh-huh."

"Well, I'm told he spends a lot of time in the woods, but do I know his name? Is that what you're asking? I know he's been in the sector since—"

"Brandon," Madeline interrupted as several ducks started squawking.

"That's his name?" Toby leaned toward her, his eyeballs straining.

"Brandon Vanderkool. Got homeschooled his last few years of high school and somehow passed the GED. Helped out on his dad's dairy until last fall. We used to play together, seeing as how our folks lived across from each other back when nobody cared about the border."

Toby stretched his neck, tugging gently on his curls. "You used to play with him?"

"You could call it that."

"He's huge. Much of an athlete?"

"Could hit a baseball a hundred meters but didn't know his right from his left, so occasionally he'd run straight to third base instead of first."

Fisher laughed. "What else?"

"He carries flies and spiders out of his house in his hands."

"A Buddhist?" Toby asked.

"No."

"A gentle giant?" Fisher asked.

"You could say that. An artist too."

"Yeah? What kind?"

She grinned. "Paints, sculpts, all sorts of things."

"Is he any good? What's it like?"

Madeline blushed, suddenly uneasy about volunteering so much information about Brandon. "It's hard to describe."

9

THE ROBIN sang first, even before the Moffats' rooster, followed by eight other species politely waiting for their sunrise solos while Brandon sorted mating songs from territorial songs—*handsome-and-available, handsome-and-available* versus *this-is-mine, this-is-mine*—until a song sparrow embarrassed them all with three different renditions of his manic ballad.

A jolt of spring had followed the surprise snowstorm and stunned the valley all over again as trees, bushes and grasses strained to greet the long-lost sun and horses, goats, cows and deer browsed drying fields amid sudden insect hatches and incoming throngs of skinny, jet-legged birds from the south.

Brandon didn't have to work until late afternoon, so he rattled east in his father's junker pickup after daybreak to see as many birds as possible. He heard a black-headed grosbeak, *twelve,* in the alders near the massive foundation of the new casino, then turned off Halverstick onto Holmquist and pulled over at its high point. From there he set up his Bushnell scope and zoomed in on little Judson Lake. He spotted a hunched green heron, then a fully extended blue heron and a smattering of ducks, including a cinnamon teal, *eighteen,* the color of clay. He surveyed the water again, then stepped into the woodlands, making *pishing* sounds until some curious chickadees, warblers and juncos flushed to be counted. He strolled deeper into the forest and patiently went through his owl calls. First the northern pygmy, then, after a pause to clear the air, a screech owl, followed by a barn and a great horned, all the while scanning branches for football-shaped bodies. After giving up on owls, he sped into the brightening valley toward the Mount Baker Highway to see what he could find before hitting snow.

The highway followed the foamy Nooksack up through cathedrals of cedars and birch and young hemlock as graceful as ballerinas. He watched treetops for incoming flocks and took side roads and quick strolls, drawing out a red-breasted sapsucker, a MacGillivray's warbler and three different sparrows. He spotted an American dipper, *twenty-seven,* popping its signature knee bends on rounded river rocks, then sped higher past fake Bavarian lodges and steep green hillsides with firs angling skyward like arrows. When the road snowed out he parked and strode swiftly until he broke into a bright thawing meadow and stood there to listen. He heard the mock battle cry of a pileated woodpecker, then the chimelike mountain bluebird and a Townsend's solitaire compensating for its drab appearance with its catchy mating riff: *Doesn't my song sound great to you? Doesn't my song sound great to you?* Then a ruffed grouse in the bush somewhere drumming louder and louder until a red-tailed hawk glided through, low and fast and effortless, shutting everyone up with an irritable scream that sounded like an incoming Piccolo Pete. Before leaving, Brandon heard the one-note song of the varied thrush, *thirty-three,* its long tone setting off a series of other peeps, trills and warbles just as one clear flute tunes a concert band.

He followed the Nooksack out of the hills and felt the blush of exposure that came with rolling out of Baker's cool canopy into the low, blinding valley. The stench and heat intensified. Time slowed. There was little shade and few hiding places. Everyone saw what you were up to, and the smarter ones could tell how well you were doing it. Brandon sped past Dirk Hoffman's latest political statement— hundreds of shin-high crosses in orderly rows like a miniature Arlington National under his exhortation to: STOP SLAUGHTERING THE UNBORN. Farther west, cows were bounding in pastures like rambunctious calves. Seeing them play relaxed him, just as it enraged him to see them bullied. How could anyone be cruel to animals that were powerful enough to walk through walls yet hated to be alone and balked at stepping over hoses, puddles or even a bright line of paint?

Brandon roared out of the valley along back roads toward Tennant Lake, where he spotted widgeons, coots, mallards and canvasbacks before climbing out of the truck. He heard a marsh wren trill as soon as he stepped on the boardwalk, then a gadwall burp. He strolled past a bittern without blowing its cover, its eyes on the sky, its streaked vertical neck blending with the reeds. He saw common yellowthroats and heard nine different songbirds. Heading back out, he lobbed rocks into the reeds until he was rewarded with the unmistakable whistle and croak of a Virginia rail, *fifty-one.*

Brandon was eleven when his mother introduced him to the secret society of people who knew more about birds than he did. Most of them seemed like fussy librarians and doctors, but he looked forward to their Christmas bird counts more than Christmas itself. And they soon fought over him to boost their counts, especially after he won the twenty-four-hour birding contest, despite grumblings about insufficient documentation on 5 of the 118 species he'd claimed to see or hear. The problem was he never saw these people any other day of the year. And he never found anybody, much less anyone his age, who wanted to count birds every day.

He pulled up at Semiahmoo Bay in time to see western and glaucous gulls, Canada geese, marbled godwits and two western sandpipers feasting side by side, like some Noah's Ark spoof, along the banks of the creek winding down the flats. He coasted past all that onto the heavy-timbered pier and heard the *cooo-ooo-ooo* of mourning doves before finding them in the rigging of fishing boats, and beyond them the common murres, pigeon guillemots and even a few marbled murrelets diving for breakfast in the melon-green water. When he stepped onto the pier, a ball of dunlins flashed into view, following their leader, and shifting direction in unison, their white bellies flashing like aspen leaves while a low flock of eleven tundra swans soared overhead in subdued exile. Brandon sat down on the edge of the pier, overwhelmed.

A black-and-white belted kingfisher with Elvis hair, *sixty-three,* rattled out from beneath him and hovered fifty feet above the bay, started to fall, then aborted its dive to hover and wait. Brandon watched it hunt for fifteen minutes before realizing the whitened expanse of water a mile out wasn't one of the bay's reflective tricks but one of the largest flocks of snow geese he'd ever seen. They wintered a couple counties to the south and rarely assembled in large numbers this close to the border, but this congregation had apparently taken an early pit stop on its return flight to Siberia. He heard the wings and squawks before he saw the first eagle circling. Once the second eagle buzzed them, the birds began lifting, fear spreading like electricity from wing to beak to wing, until this impossibly loud white curtain blotted out half the sky.

And the sound! A solo snow goose flying overhead sounds lost and pathetic. *Hel-lo?* But with thousands honking simultaneously it is a wildly different noise, like the tribal roar you hear in stadiums, yet even greater than that, beyond animalistic, more like an enormous avalanche or the howl of the earth itself, the high-pitched hum of the sphere, if you could actually hear it, hurtling through space at sixty-six thousand miles an hour. Brandon tilted back and joined in, honking along with the flock until it split into long loose *V*s and the bedlam faded to an industrial squeal, then to an ambient wail as the skeins turned to threads before fading to blue.

THAT AFTERNOON, Brandon blew past Big Tom's raspberries where two Mexicans were clipping and restringing canes. He was supposed to run farm workers' names and DOBs through the computer whenever they stepped onto public streets—yet another part of the job he couldn't picture himself doing. He waved but got nothing but twitches in exchange. Seemingly everyone treated him differently or didn't even recognize him in uniform, as if it blurred their vision. He finished his rounds in less than an hour and strayed east toward the Sumas River, which shimmered diagonally through the valley. He slowed at its bends where debris gathered, drivers idling respectfully behind him, craning to see if he'd spotted drugs or bodies before signaling hesitantly around him and glancing back at the enormous BP—Is that the Vanderkool boy?—who was out of his rig now, squatting next to the slow water like a golfer studying the tilt of a green.

He plucked and overlapped two salal leaves and tried stitching them together with a pine needle. It took a while to find leaves supple enough and needles sharp enough, but within fifteen minutes he'd strung together an eight-foot garland. He lowered it delicately into the stream and watched the lazy current carry it over submerged stones into swifter water. Brandon scampered alongside his leaf snake, his ears sorting birds in the trees and bushes behind him, the *ohhh-so-sweetly* of a hermit thrush, *sixty-five,* and the *yaank-yaank-yaank* of a red-breasted nuthatch, *sixty-six.* He caught a cottonwood branch in the cheek, snagged his pants and stumbled as his creation broke into three smaller snakes that no longer undulated with life.

"Seven-eighty to two-oh-five."

"Two-oh-five, copy," he murmured once he got over being startled.

"Sensor at Markworth."

"Copy," he mumbled. "Be there shortly."

He sped along Garrison, then Badger and finally H Street, hurtling west out of the valley into the hilly woodlands like he'd seen Dionne drive, faster than he figured was safe. Once on Markworth he parked quietly, then loped across a clearing toward the woods and the trail sensor, the windblown spruce groaning like settling houses. He was noticing how the exhaust of a Vancouver-bound jet split the blue-black sky when he stubbed his boot on a root, and during his fall he heard, then saw, a doe and its fawn leap over ferns like cartoon reindeer. He rose, brushing dirt and needles from his thighs and chest, inspecting wrists and shoulders, before noticing his gun, planted cock-eyed in the dirt, the barrel pointed at his chest as if the earth itself was holding him at gunpoint. He'd barely passed the range test; his shots usually flew high, as though he thought he had to arc the bullets. He picked up the

Beretta and waited for his breath to stabilize before calling it in with his best murmur. "Seven-eighty, this is two-oh-five."

"Go ahead, two-oh-five."

"Least two deer down here."

"Ten-four, I'll mark it down as animal."

Brandon followed some tracks into a mossy meadow with surprisingly powdery dirt, which was where he saw the first large raindrop splat. More big drops splashed his hair and nose before he glanced up, then studied the dirt again for the smoothest, driest patch and carefully sat down, slowly reclining until his legs were spread-eagled and his arms perpendicular to his trunk, as if he were strapped to an imaginary wheel, his gun extended in his left hand for artistic purposes.

Rain continued falling in random splats, then in grape-sized drops and finally in noisy ropes that silenced the birds. He let it wash his face and soak his uniform. He lay there trying to come up with a good excuse to call Madeline Rousseau again, until the rain subsided. After it completely stopped, he lurched upright, his gun arm swinging forward with the exertion, and then heard gasps and curses thirty feet in front of him.

Brandon yelped like a dreaming dog as his mind sorted the visuals. Three men. Two in their twenties, one in his forties. Black duffel bags strapped to their backs like scuba tanks. The younger two bamboo-thin and pale; the older one larger and calmer, hooded eyes, long goatee. Brandon glanced repeatedly at their gloved and empty hands—*always watch their hands!*—until they began to rise, holding their palms up, like hesitant students.

"P-please," stammered one of the younger ones.

"Shut it," the old one mumbled, his eyes fixed on the forty-caliber gun in Brandon's big left hand, which he self-consciously dropped to his side.

"Let your hands see me."

Luckily, they seemed to know what to do.

"Where you coming from?" Brandon asked, simultaneously trying to catch his breath and remember the sequence of what to say when and what not to say at all.

"Just passing through," the old one said as convincingly as any hiker sharing a moment on a trail.

"What's in the bags?" Brandon asked, remembering his line.

"Food and clothes," the man answered in a bored singsong. The other two looked like they'd been bit by snakes.

"Mind if I take a look?" Brandon asked, sticking to the script but increasingly feeling he was harassing them. He wasn't sure what to say when they didn't respond or run. "Lock your heads on top of your fingers," he said, worried he'd skipped a step.

He unzipped the first bag and saw clear pouches of green and gold buds the size of pinecones.

Brandon couldn't remember whether to read them their rights or exactly when to call for backup and didn't trust himself to get the wording right on any of it. So he said as little as possible, then frisked each one. Two cell phones, one GPS, one ID with an Abbotsford address, no weapons. He only had two sets of handcuffs, so he used a plastic cable tie on one of them. "Too tight? You okay?"

When they turned to face him, he saw the old one, then the other two, straining to see the unusual pattern in the dirt behind him. He stepped aside to give them a full view of what looked like the outline of a huge crime victim, the gray silhouette of his body surrounded by black, rain-soaked dirt. The men looked at one another.

"Got buds and bodies," Brandon told the dispatcher in a bored mumble. "Three on the ground." He directed them out of the woods, afraid he'd already screwed things up somehow, three heavy bags slung across his shoulders. He tried to relax by *pishing* for birds. When they turned around, he asked them to please keep walking and resumed *pishing,* which flushed nothing but curious chickadees from the wooded fringe.

Fifty yards later, however, glancing back and forth from the smugglers to the treetops, he saw the high curling swoop of a raptor. The creamy underwings looked like a red-tail's, but the body was more like a rough-legged, though the wings weren't long enough and the tail wasn't quite right. Once its wings flapped the mystery was solved. A short-eared owl, *sixty-seven.*

"A short-ear!" he exclaimed, pointing at its angular glide back into the treetops.

The smugglers spun and craned awkwardly to see what he was pointing at but saw nothing at all. They glanced at one another, then back at Brandon, who dropped their bags so he could demonstrate the owl's exaggerated mothlike wing strokes, which was what Dionne and Agent Talley saw as they jogged around the bend toward them, flashlights and batons jostling on their hips.

IO

BRANDON DIDN'T have to attempt to lie. He was doing a lay-in, of sorts, got soaked in a squall, then got lucky. He kept his words slow and under control, imitating Dionne's tone and syntax. Everyone was focusing on the stats anyway. A hundred and twenty pounds of B.C. bud worth $310,000 in Seattle and $360,000 in L.A. if the DEA knew what it was talking about, which Dionne, of course, said it didn't. Within an hour they were calling him shit magnet. All of them. *Shiiiiit Magneeeet!*

Dionne led the interrogation, grilling each mule separately, repeating her questions with slightly different words, aping their every arm cross, collar pull and nose scratch, invading their personal space, willing them to speak, then talking for them and adding a question mark at the end so that a nod could turn her words into theirs. Then she came at them again, closing in without making it obvious, just as good birders approach birds without ever walking directly at them. When none of that worked, she got close enough to make their eyes water from her spearmint gum and pointed at Brandon. "You really want to piss him off?"

She asked each of them about "an Angel named Manny" and another guy named Toby, scanning their faces for flinches of recognition. "You're running dope for Manny, aren't ya?" Their responses were nearly identical. They didn't know what was in the bags or the names of the men who'd hired them. Their job, they said, was simply to leave the bags where Brandon found them. They had no idea who

65

was picking them up. None. They were all Canadians and apparently first offenders, which helped explain the older man's calm.

Dionne showed Brandon how to download cell contacts and log GPS waypoints, then stranded him to type up the report. As the shifts switched, agents crowded his desk to listen to Agent McAfferty mimic DEA agents officiously taking custody of the buds, rolling joints and talking on the inhale with the same robotic diction. "This tastes a bit like that Matanuska Thunderfuck, doesn't it, Walter?" Agents egged him on until Chief Patera squeezed through. "All right, people, only those of you who need to be here."

McAfferty waited Patera out to tell another story to Brandon, who bobbed his head politely, half-listening, eyes aching as he ground through the computerized paperwork, the simplest questions baffling him.

"Yeah, yeah, we'd do lay-ins like you did here—but at night," McAfferty began. "We'd hang in the dark with our hearts popping waiting for these illegals, then we'd jump up and say, 'Surprise!' Could be quite the rush, if you had company, but I was never big on solos. Know what I'm saying? An owl says hello and I shit my pants if it's dark enough. Ever see *The Blair Witch Project*? Movie scared the shit out of me. But the lay-ins down south were nothing compared to the war-wagon shift. You've heard about the wagons, right? Brandon, ya with me here?"

"Uh-huh." It was a high-wire act for Brandon to spell and type even when he wasn't distracted by McAfferty's needy nonstop chatter or the siren of house sparrows—*sixty-eight*—outside the door that only he seemed to hear. He tried whispering the words as he typed them.

"Either ya know or ya don't," McAfferty pressed. "Gotta picture this to appreciate it. You got thousands trying to cross each day. Thousands, know what I'm saying? So they'd try to overwhelm us. If enough of 'em run all at once, most of 'em'll make it, right?"

Brandon nodded aimlessly, exhaled and refocused on McAfferty's flabby face, twitching mustache and sideburns shaped like Nevada.

"So if you just sat there long enough, they'd eventually all run for it. There's a whole lot of courage in numbers, know what I'm saying? And you could tell when they were gonna go for it too. One of them would hurl a rock, then a few more. Suddenly it's raining rocks. Ya with me? That's their cover, see, because no matter how big a weapon you come out the door with, you still don't want to catch a rock in the face. A sawed-off won't stop a rock, follow?" McAfferty winked, paused, then continued. "So after we'd replaced our fifteenth windshield, our supe, this lifer who hadn't left his desk more than twice since the Kennedy assassination and who'd never once had a rock tossed at his bald head, came up with the brainstorm of these *war wagons*. So five of our trucks got customized with steel cages over the windows. Made them damn near rock-proof. Fantastic, right? Wrong. It just upped the ante. So now you'd get these spics—and I use the term lovingly—hurling rocks at you for hours, having the time of their lives, while you're playing it cool like you don't give a shit, like this is the sort of crap you do on holidays, sitting there reading the same paragraph, again and again, while you're literally getting stoned. *Thud! Womp-womp-womp!*" Brandon flinched. "Could go on for hours while you'd wait for 'em to make their move. Then you'd jam the truck into drive and cut 'em off, right? You listening? Think about it! What would *you* do when they made their move? Jump out and risk getting stoned? Let me ask you a question, Brandon: Does that sound like a good idea?"

Brandon waggled his chin, unable to focus on the computer screen or McAfferty, an ache sliding down his neck into his shoulder blades, the room losing oxygen and color, the paralysis spreading.

"All right. But see, this is what I'm heading at here. We had an agent there who was just as aggressive as Dionne." Another wink caught Brandon before he could look away. "And this daring fuck would wait, wait, wait, then fly out of his wagon and round 'em up single-handed. And keep in mind, this genius is making twenty-eight gross, but I'm tellin' ya he'd hop out and corral 'em like some cowboy on meth. And he was excellent at it. I'll give him that, but one time he caught a rock the size of a peach just past the temple. Right *here*."

McAfferty laid an index finger on the side of Brandon's left eyebrow. "With a whole lotta luck, and some timely prayers, the dumbass lived. But he was left with one hell of a souvenir—a two-inch metal plate in his skull." He clucked his tongue and tapped his own temple. "Wanna feel it?" He bent over, beady-eyed, as Brandon reached up in open-mouthed awe and pressed two hesitant fingers into his bristly hair.

McAfferty giggled, then stepped back and shadowboxed, jabbing the air with his little fists. "Do I look like a dumbass? I never once left the cage! Not *once*! And that's my point, Rook. I mean, what are we really doing? Stopping people from getting work or—God forbid!—getting high. Know what I'm sayin'? You do what ya can, but always wait for backup and don't try to show anybody up. Gotcha, didn't I?" He winked, tapped the imaginary plate in his temple and shadowboxed again, his gut jiggling with each lunge, until Patera showed up with a frown and cocked eyebrows.

"Don't you have somewhere else you could be, Mr. McAfferty?"

Patera examined Brandon's report through the lower halves of his bifocals, eyes drifting between the screen and the rookie, sighing as he scrolled down through blank pages, then groaning.

THREE HOURS LATER, McAfferty bellowed over the roar of the bar: "Pour the shit magnet another beer!"

Brandon felt like an exhausted child trying to prove he could stay up until midnight as the roadies vied for his attention. He took in the growing mob behind him through the slanted mirrors above McAfferty's head, wet-lipped, glossy-eyed locals staring from every angle as if he were a circus bear in a tuxedo. There was too much going on at once. He'd always felt more alone in a crowd. And he avoided chaotic gatherings, especially bars. He tried to focus on the rhythm of voices at his table like Danny Crawford had taught him—so he might know when to talk and when to laugh.

After another pitcher, Agent Candido warned him about getting overconfident. "Can't do anybody any good if you get hurt."

"C'mon," McAfferty said, "admit it, Candy. You're afraid he's gonna be another Dionne and make you look even worse than you already do." He slid into a Patera impression: "I believe we all should strive to make arrests like the one Mr. Vanderkool made here a daily occurrence."

"So we can stop six percent of what's rolling through instead of three?" Agent Talley groused. "It's all cat and mouse, and there's more mice every day."

"What does the DEA really do with the buds?" Brandon mumbled, then repeated it louder when he realized nobody heard him.

"The first thing," McAfferty said, "is they're gonna write it up quick so it shows up in the stats as their bust." He made a steeple with his fingers. "And after they take credit for your work, they'll burn the buds in their inferno and stand outside and watch the seagulls get stoned." He lowered his eyelids and flapped his fingers like mini-wings near his shoulders.

The more Brandon glanced around, the more people he caught eavesdropping or staring at their table and its five uniformed agents.

"There's no denying the Holy War is great for finances," McAfferty said. "But of course"—he lowered his voice to a whisper—"we're not actually stopping any terrorists, just helping Canuck drug dealers jack their prices by driving up the value of their merchandise." He raised his mug. "To the Border Patrol!"

"Personally," Dionne interrupted, "I feel pretty good about keeping the Hells Angels from selling drugs to elementary-school kids."

McAfferty shielded his mouth from her and whispered, to the other agents, "Hero complex."

"Why don't you quit, Mac?" Dionne's lips stretched across a cold smile. "If that's all I thought I was doing, I'd quit tonight." She took a long swallow, giving her face a chance to lose its color.

McAfferty laughed. "Don't worry, Dionne. I've only got two hundred and ninety-one days to go. See if you can put up with my honesty until then."

"Honesty?" She grunted, her face softening. "Bullshit's the word."

"Show me the terrorists we've caught, Dionne. Name them, please."

Brandon felt all eyes on him as he rose.

McAfferty interrupted himself to say, "You ain't leaving yet, Rook."

"Going to the bathroom." Brandon left the laughter behind him and stooped toward the rear of the saloon, trying to make himself appear smaller, ignoring Eddie Erickson's come-over wave—"Hey, Vanderfool!"—and absorbing all the smirks and stares, the how's-it-goings, the lookin'-goods, the wolf calls. He was used to the attention that came with being the biggest fish in the tank, people's eyes automatically following and measuring him. Danny Crawford had taught him to mimic other kids' behavior and emotions so his own stood out less, but he had no experience at trying to blend in with this much commotion, especially in a uniform. He tried to study the bar language anyway, how friends and lovers touched, how they cut insults with affection. *You're all right for a dumb SOB.* Or, *I love your sorry ass.* He'd watched McAfferty swing a clumsy arm around Dionne two beers ago and say: "Not to get mushy on you, my friend, but you are well above average."

He tried to block out the music and the crescendo of voices and just take in the beer-brightened visuals, everyone in their loudest garb like songbirds in spring. Milt Van Luven in baby-blue suspenders *and* a purple belt, even though his Wranglers were already too tight to button at the top. His younger brother, Lester, in electric-green trousers rolled to his ankles as if his legs had shrunk overnight, his left palm just above the right knee on the long bare leg of his wife, Julia, in a blouse so blindingly red it could provoke a bull. She covered her mouth at the sight of Brandon, though he assumed she'd been blabbing about him ever since she'd tried to seduce him three long summers ago.

Sophie Winslow and her flamingo-pink lips stood between him and the restroom. He heard conflicting speculation every time her name popped up. What he knew for sure was that she was remarkably easy to talk to.

She cocked her head to take him in. "You doing all right?"

"Me?"

"Look a bit wiped."

"I'm just—"

"Congratulations about today," she said. "Heard you were laying down."

He looked down at her looking up at him.

"When you caught them: You were laying on the ground, then popped up, right?" She grabbed his forearm and pulled him slightly to see if dirt on his backside could prove her case. He looked down at her upturned wrist and saw a scar angling across her veins like a purple seam.

"They call 'em lay-ins," he said. "I was doing a lay-in."

"Making what kind of art?"

He hesitated. "Where'd you hear that?"

"I didn't."

Her lipstick ran slightly wider and longer than her lips.

"They call 'em lay-ins," he said again.

She grinned. "Yeah, but . . ." She pointed an index finger at her forehead.

He shrugged, palms up, baffled.

She set her hands séance-style on top of his as if channeling the dead. They were so warm he wanted to lie down. "How's your mom?" she asked.

Brandon hesitated. It was impossible for him to respond quickly to complicated questions. *How's life? You believe in God? How's your mother?* Instead of answering, he made a mental note to ask people how their family members were. It seemed to be expected.

"I didn't know you were friends with Madeline Rousseau," she said.

Brandon studied her grin. "Did you see her? Did she say that?"

"I could tell by the way she talked about you," she said, her eyes fully dilated.

He reluctantly let go, aimlessly thanked her, then stood at a urinal so low it required a deep knee bend to avoid splashing. Madeline was talking about him?

The bar volume rose with more belly laughter and shouting. He saw Chas Landers in Sophie's gravitational pull, his chair cocked onto its forelegs, leaning across the round table toward her, practically shouting to be heard, his smile impossibly white for a smoker his age. And Brandon noticed four more distracted men, their eyes following the hypnotic swing of Sophie's bare foot in and out of her heeled clog.

Another foamy pitcher was getting divvied up as Brandon filled his seat, wishing he could just go home to his dogs and sleep. Yet he forced himself to try once again to learn the language between and beneath the words that everyone else played off.

"They can blame the exchange rate or the border lines all they want, but in my opinion they need to get more creative," McAfferty was saying. "I had an entrepreneurial brainstorm yesterday, for example, which I'm perfectly willing to share." Brandon studied McAfferty's delivery, sucking everyone in, and then slowing down. "Anyone else notice the new barista at Border Brew—the one with the infant? Well, she was breast-feeding when I rolled up Wednesday, which isn't something that typically moves me. Not that I'm prudish. But it's not one of my fantasies, is what I'm saying. However, in this case I confess that I had a spontaneous desire for a breast-milk latte. Follow?"

Brandon tried to join the laughter with some timely snorts, noticing Dionne's eyes roll and conversations stalling at surrounding tables.

"If she just breast-pumped her titty—pardon me, Dionne—into that metal pitcher they use, then steamed it until it's good and foamy? Brrrrrr!" He vibrated his upper body. "Then she could pour in the espresso, hand you your latte, take your ten-dollar tip, slip back inside her halter—and voilà! Exploitative? Not in the slightest. Showmanship? Definitely. And seriously, what could appeal to health-conscious, boob-loving customers more than that?"

Agent Talley bit his lower lip, and Canfield stopped laughing long enough to say, "C'mon, Dionne. Gotta admit there's some humor there." They smirked, tittering, waiting, while she futilely tried to tuck short bangs behind her ears.

"I'm drunk," she said, "and it's still not even close to being funny."

That busted them up even more. Talley topped his laughter with a belch followed by a giggling apology. Dionne belched back even louder while Brandon waited for another conversation to take hold so he could exit without getting heckled. But nobody had anything to say.

"Thanks, everyone." The room twirled slightly as he rose amid flashes that took him a beat to realize were coming from Sophie's camera.

"Where's the magnet going?" Talley demanded.

"Let him get some rest." McAfferty was sipping port from a tiny glass. "It's exhausting being a hero, isn't it, Dionne?"

"I'll follow you out," she said, ignoring McAfferty's "Uh-huh" and Talley's giggles as she flung a ten toward her empty mug and sauntered out into the clearing night.

"They're just jealous." She started toward her car, then strolled back and grabbed his elbow. "You did great today. Really. Most of them couldn't have brought those three in by themselves, and most trainees would've fucked it up somehow. You did great."

Great? What Brandon couldn't get past was how terrified the young smugglers were of him. That's what stuck, that and the fierce reek of piss in the backseat of his rig.

Brandon noticed she still hadn't released his elbow. "How's your daughter?"

"That's what I'm doing with my day off." She took a step away, turned and faced him. "Taking her to some Bellingham doc McAfferty recommended. He's not as much of an ass as he'd like you to believe."

"Is your spine straight?" Brandon asked.

She half-laughed. "Where'd that come from? As a matter of fact, last anyone checked it curves twenty-one degrees to the right—not that anyone has noticed it, or at least said anything about it, in the last twenty years, but thanks for asking." She tilted her shoulders and gave him a crazed expression. "Now you know I'm not perfect."

"If the earth wasn't tilted we wouldn't have seasons," Brandon said, pleased with himself for finding a spot for one of his mother's sayings.

Dionne smiled, then looked at the stars. "You can follow me home," she said, "if you'd rather not drive all the way to yours."

He missed her blush in the weak light. "Mine's closer, isn't it?"

II

HE DROVE with the windows down to revive himself, then pulled over a mile from home to see if he could spot any of the constellations he'd invented at the academy. That's what he'd liked most about New Mexico, a huge night sky that let him picture the whole universe, which his mother had told him was continually expanding, the stars like dots on an inflating balloon. True or not, it reinforced his growing sensation of standing on a shrinking planet beneath an expanding sky.

But tonight he couldn't even find Taurus or Cassiopeia. He absently listened to his radio and the dispatcher's monotone about three youths loitering in Peace Arch, a CI's report of helicopter smuggling in the Cascades and a blue Cutlass on some drive-thru a Canadian phoned in. He took in the silhouettes of silos and barns and the Abbotsford mansions flickering in the low northeastern sky like candles through beveled glass. The night air burped, whined and rang with frogs, mosquitoes and field crickets before yielding to the rising drone of an approaching vehicle. Brandon smelled manure in the fields, which probably meant someone was spraying excessively at night. Or perhaps it was just the forgotten stench of dairy country in the spring, the one season when realtors didn't coax out-of-town high rollers into their fields of dreams.

Brandon stepped around his hood into the headlights of a sedan that looked black or possibly midnight blue. The driver seemed to accelerate at the sight of him. Brandon hopped back inside, popped it in gear and leaned on the gas. "Do we have plates on the drive-thru?" he asked slowly after the dispatcher responded.

"Negative. No plates."

Brandon gave his coordinates and noticed he was drunker than he'd realized as he struggled to focus on the fleeing taillights. "I'm code two," he said, more eagerly than he'd intended and before he remembered what code two meant.

"Two-zero-five, this is Supervisor Wheeler. What vehicle are you driving?"

"Private."

After another long pause, Wheeler said, "Ten-three the pursuit, two-zero-five."

"Too late," Brandon replied.

Dionne had warned him that Patera didn't want to catch hell for chasing hooligans through family neighborhoods or scaring tipsy locals off the road. Still, if a blue Cutlass hopped the border and blew past him and Dionne was his trainer . . .

Brandon eased his truck up to sixty yet fell farther behind. Was it even a Cutlass? He could tell trucks from cars and sedans from compacts, but beyond that he was guessing. What he did know was that the Bender Road straightaway curled into a tight S-turn before crossing Pangborn.

"Two-zero-five," the supervisor repeated after the longest pause yet. "You have been officially ten-three'd."

"Copy that," Brandon said, accelerating to avoid falling farther behind. "But it's too late."

The sedan's smoldering taillights blew past the yellow sign warning drivers to slow down.

As Brandon rounded the first curve he noticed the lack of lights ahead. Then he saw why. The sedan's left rear wheel hung almost comically above the shoulder, its trunk sprung and gaping at the stars. The rest of it was stabbed diagonally, hood-first into the steaming ditch, as if the driver hadn't even attempted to turn. When he radioed it in,

Brandon abandoned his contained mumble for a near-hysterical and repetitive cry for an ambulance.

He slammed his right knee lunging from the truck, then galloped, vision pulsing, to the back of the sedan, trying to take it all in at once. The depth of the ditch, the height of the water, the pitch of the hissing steam, the diagonal posture of the *green* car, the manufacturer's name in raised gold letters below the popped trunk: *P-o-n-t-i-a-c S-u-n-b-i-r-d.*

It wasn't even the right car! His mind jammed. No pictures, no words, just that hissing sound, yet his body kept moving and he heard himself shouting into the ditch, though the words didn't sound like his. He used the cross brace on the telephone pole to help him climb down before slipping the final few feet and falling into freezing water up to his hips along the driver's side of the bowed and steaming hood. Amazingly there didn't appear to be water inside the car, but he wasn't sure that mattered. The driver was lying on the steering wheel, his face cocked awkwardly toward the passenger seat. Brandon couldn't see much beyond a thickly bearded cheek and dark hair buzzed close to the scalp.

The window was half open and Brandon shouted louder than he intended to that help was coming. He reached for the door handle, then realized he couldn't open it wide enough to pull the little man out without letting water in. He ransacked his memory for guidance in such situations, groped through the window, fumbled for the man's pulse and, finding none, slid a panicky hand beneath his armpit to palm his chest. After recoiling from the thumping heart, he unleashed a jumble of apologies and promises. His flashlight darted around the interior of a vehicle that looked as clean and impersonal as a rental car. "Gonna be all right," he told the man and himself, then straightened up in the ditch, the mud suction starting to control his boots. "Gonna be all right."

Brandon watched himself from above, climbing in slow motion out into his headlights, unsure about what to do next or how much time had passed, feeling severed from the moment, moving through air, his torso floating above numbed legs. Radioing in again, nauseous now, he pleaded for the ambulance that had already been sent, described the driver's condition and shared the vehicle's model and plate.

The supervisor's tone had changed. He slowly and clearly enunciated every word, as if for a jury. Brandon realized he was over-talking and began offering the minimum, chattering before cutting out and limping hesitantly to the ditch, pants heavy and sagging, body shivering, checking to make sure the water hadn't climbed any higher on the driver's side. Wanting to call his mother.

It wasn't until he shuffled around the back of the sedan again that he heard the reassuring wail of a siren. And it wasn't until the too-bright, too-loud ambulance stormed down Badger Road and turned up Bender that it occurred to him that he still hadn't looked inside the yawning trunk.

He didn't know what to make of most of the mess—mason jars full of dry powder and fluids leaking from tubes in a slotted Styrofoam case. But after helping his father blow up a dozen stumps he knew what blasting caps looked like. He held up his icy hands, as if surrendering, to slow the ambulance. A BP rig sped up behind it, doubling the light show. Three medics unloaded and charged toward his shivering figure and the cockeyed Sunbird, which was also when Brandon saw, behind and above the men, the faint, sprawling, nine-star, barn-shaped constellation he'd invented in New Mexico but never named.

12

THE LITTLE squawk box told Norm where to go after they beeped him through security. "Yeah, yeah, yeah," he said, but was immediately lost. The three bunkerlike buildings all looked the same. There didn't seem to be a goddamn entrance anywhere. The entire compound was rung with razor wire. Who, exactly, was the Border Patrol trying to keep out? When he finally came to a door that opened, he felt like as much of an outsider as he had the night he went prowling for one bourbon too many and stumbled into a hall full of grown men wearing antlers and exchanging moose calls. No animal costumes this time, just the corny green uniforms that made them all look like Smokey the Bear, but the noise was similar, everyone seemingly lit and talking simultaneously, yet with no sign of liquor *or his son* at 1:27 in the morn. The hubbub raged until the door shut noisily behind him.

Norm initially thought that Patera had called to tell him that Brandon had been injured in a bombing, though the real story wasn't much more comforting. The patrol had always looked like glorified security work, but now he felt as if he'd sent his son to the front lines of a war he hadn't realized was going on in his own neighborhood. If there was a worse crime than shoving your child into danger, he couldn't think of one.

Conversations hushed as faces swiveled toward him and a meaty uniformed woman with a courteous smile stepped from behind one of the fancy desks and pricey computer screens. "Mr. Vanderkool? I'm Dionne, Brandon's trainer."

Her shake made him wonder how often she had to prove her manhood. He followed her through agents stinking of beer who gave him the clumsy deference doled out to grieving parents. "Brandon has amazing instincts," she told him, without actually looking at his unshaven face. "It's rarer than you think to find a trainee with great instincts for this work, or, for that matter, even experienced agents." Her grin surprised him, as if they were sharing secrets.

"He's all right?" Norm said.

"A bit shook up, but that's to be expected, really. Totally normal."

"So when'd it happen?"

"Five after midnight."

More than an hour ago and he's *still* shook up? Why was Norm even called? If he was too shaken to drive, why couldn't someone give him a lift? Norm hadn't asked for any middle-of-the-night courtesies.

"Excuse me, Chief. Mr. Vanderkool is here."

Tony Patera held up a ringed finger as Dionne whispered an apology, not realizing he was talking on a cell phone clamped to his left ear. He was mumbling, but what Norm heard included something about how to word a release about closing the border.

"The border's closing?" he asked incredulously, but the woman agent had stepped into the hall and Patera was still yakking into his fancy phone and hadn't acknowledged Norm's existence yet.

He glanced around at the half-acre desk, the tidy in- and outboxes, the walls sagging beneath heavy plaques, certificates and photos of a grinning Patera with other similarly self-important men. Beneath the window were stacks of *The New York Times*, *The Seattle Times*, *The Bellingham Herald*, *The Vancouver Sun* and *Abbotsford Times*. He'd heard Patera boast that he read all five cover-to-cover every day, which told Norm he was either a liar or had nothing to do. He reminded himself to ask him if Washington and Jefferson grew dope. Patera never ducked a question. He'd make something up before admitting he didn't know.

The chief nodded gravely, said good-bye and retidied a stack of papers before hoisting himself to offer Norm his palm. He was as spiffy as ever, starched and tailored but going jowly, with walrus creases in the back of his neck. Norm counted four rings on manicured fingers. How had he missed that omen? He'd never had any luck with men who wore more than one ring, much less those who paid women to snip their fingernails.

"Thanks for coming down, Norm. Your *sonnn*," he said, stretching it out like he often did, one of his many tics that made his stories so exhausting, "may have just made the most significant arrest on the northern border in years. Well, truth is, we don't really know what we've got yet. Lots of IDs on this guy, but if he is who the FBI thinks he—"

Norm's patience had left him. "Where's Brandon at?"

Patera pointed to the door, and Norm followed him into a piss-colored hallway. "He's a little shaken up." Patera made it sound like a medical term. "Lost his cookies, so to speak. Very common. Hasn't thrown up since I called you, least I don't . . ." He looked to Dionne, who shrugged her manly shoulders. "Something else," he added. "Between us, without alarming people, I'd appreciate your help in spreading the word to tighten security at the dairies. You know what I mean."

"No, I don't know." Everything was moving too fast for Norm. Something important had shifted. Was Patera cashing in favors or viewing him as an ally or, worse, a minion?

"You know, like locking the milk tanks," Patera told him, "and not letting strangers past the house, that sort of thing."

Norm tried to picture suicide bombers hopping the ditch to blow up his milking parlor. "What do dairies have to worry about?"

"Well, you just don't know anymore, do you? Mad cow could be spread pretty easily by a saboteur with a spray bottle, couldn't it? Or what about botulinum, or whatever it's called. From what I'm told, one bottle of that in your bulk tank gets trucked to a milk plant and mixed in with product from other farms and suddenly a half million lives are at risk. The government values its dairy product, Norm."

"Who told you it's the government's product?" Norm felt like he was missing critical pieces of information.

"I think you know," Patera whispered as more beefy agents approached with questions, *chief* this, and *chief* that, adjusting sleeves and belts like batters fidgeting at the plate, rattling off updates and questions about how long the border should be closed for and what they'd heard from the FBI, HQ, RCMP and other acronyms, and how a multiagency release was coming along. Finally, Patera arrived at a room crammed with yet more people, including Norm's son in some undersized jacket, a dirty blanket spooled around his legs.

Norm was startled for the millionth time by Brandon's size. Even hunched in a stubby chair, his head was more than five feet off the floor, his face so white he looked like an enormous mime.

One agent was typing, another asking questions. From Norm's vantage, it appeared his boy was getting interrogated. Was he in trouble? He was definitely in spooked mode, mumbling, rocking slightly at the hips.

When Brandon glanced up, eyes fully dilated, Norm's heart skipped. Not *now*. Please.

Patera told the agents to give it a break. They sighed, smirked and moseyed from the room, readjusting belts and crotches.

"How're ya doin'?" Norm regretted his impersonal tone, but Patera and Dionne were still there and he didn't want his son to start ranting or bawling. He rarely cried, but when he did it was hard to stop.

He rocked faster, then blurted: "Ten-three'd have should I."

Dionne horse-laughed and Patera muttered, "What the . . ." as Norm watched Brandon recognize his gaffe, then carefully enunciate, "I. Should. Have. Ten-three'd."

It astounded Norm that Brandon hadn't grown out of these episodes. He rested a hand on his shoulder, gripped and released, then again. "C'mon," he urged, "you're all right."

"He's just like you'd expect him to be," Patera said. "Juiced." He winked knowingly, ambled bowlegged to the door, leaned his head out and called, "Linda!" Turning back to Norm he said, "He's got instincts. Too much to chalk up to beginner's luck. That's for certain."

Norm desperately wanted to grab his son and take him home before he shoved one more sentence over his lips or before Patera patronized him one more time and Norm shouted something he'd regret. "I don't want any media at the house," he grumbled.

"Not a problem." Patera looked puzzled. "Already an FBI matter, Norm. I'll handle what reporters we get. Nothing to worry about there. There's just some coaching that needs to be done on what Brandon should and shouldn't say in front of various officials and cameras, if and when we decide it's appropriate. If and when, Norm."

Driving home, Norm tried to fill the truck with the normalcy of his observations about the left-handed Japanese reliever the Mariners signed, Channel 4's prediction of record rain the following week and Uncle Wyatt's hip replacement. "Everyone says you got what it takes." He felt like he was trying to convince himself. "They can't stop telling me about your instincts."

"Pull over," Brandon said, lowering his window.

"What?"

"Pull . . . *over.*"

Norm straddled the shoulder between Dirk's reader board, which he couldn't make out in the dark, and Big Tom's Statue of Liberty, which for whatever reason had its torch illuminated tonight. Brandon sounded like a dog barking himself raw.

Norm leaned back into a swoon, recalling Sophie's most recent request for a dairy tour. She'd sauntered over to ask, this time in cowboy boots and a cotton dress. She had so many looks. She dipped in and out of decades and fashions, letting her hair tumble over her shoulders one day, piling it high the next or even slicking it back, all of which Norm assumed was designed to let you know that she could play whatever part you wanted her to play in whatever you had in mind.

His dairy looked grim even to him. Through her eyes it would probably look like a gulag.

Jeanette was waiting braless on the couch, sipping ginkgo tea in a nightgown so soft and faded it was impossible to know what colors it used to be. She listened silently to Norm, then patted her thighs after

Brandon reappeared in a robe. He draped his knees over one couch arm and rolled himself out until his head landed in her lap.

"Your latest paintings," she whispered, "are lovely."

"He just needs sleep," Norm said, feeling empty and invisible, pacing and muttering, "What can you do?" and other fillers. The dogs started yipping, and he knew they wouldn't stop until they'd seen Brandon. So he hobbled down to the basement and freed them before climbing into his milking clothes.

Nothing had changed while he was gone, other than the three strays had curled up within worshipping distance of his son. One of Jeanette's palms was on his forehead, the other on his chest, her eyes fixed to the TV as if it were on. When Norm saw an Alzheimer's headline at the 7-Eleven his first thought was that maybe everyone was getting it, like some sort of bizarre virus. He bought the paper and read as much of the article as he could bear.

"Intelligent people have more zinc and copper in their hair," she whispered now to their son. "The earth's temperature rises slightly during a full moon."

"Good job," he said, without opening his eyes.

Norm spread a light blanket across Brandon's legs. "Gotta go . . . ," he began, stating the obvious, then reluctantly stepped into the chill, late for his cows. He saw Sophie's kitchen light was still on. There'd be nothing he could tell her by sunup that she wouldn't already know. He looked across the ditch. The professor's lights were on too.

WAYNE ROUSSEAU WAS mumbling through another all-nighter. He'd progressed right through the tedious trials—although skipping over hundreds of failures, which seemed fair considering he didn't have a staff—before finally discovering the remarkable resistance he could get from horseshoe-shaped carbon-coated filaments. And then, for the past two days, he'd wrestled with bad vacuum seals and imperfect carbonization, which resulted in sputtering light or broken glass. His sleep amounted to short couch naps, and he no longer played music. In fact, he wore earplugs to better simulate Edison's hearing. He also smoked more cannabis than usual to feed the delusions and stay in character.

He clipped a perfectly baked and carbonized cotton filament into the tube, pumped out the oxygen and slowly lowered the switch. A bright yellow-white light filled his basement. Wayne squinted at the bulb as if it were an eclipse, waiting for it to flicker, shatter or both. And waited. Several minutes passed, then another ten without the slightest flickering. Think of it! The exact same bulb Edison burned for 550 hours in December 1879! The first bright steady light that wouldn't waver in wind! A practical lamp that could change the experience of night! And not just for the rich—for the masses!

The epic significance of his accomplishment swelled inside Wayne until he hopped around the brilliant bulb shouting and whooping his throat raw as if he'd discovered fire.

Part Two

13

AFTER BRANDON'S bust it rained all day every day, mercifully at first, then violently, punishing the land and turning streams into rivers, puddles into ponds, marshes into lakes. For ten days the valley woke and retired to the roar of a deluge manufactured by the Pacific rain factory. The relentless downpour added to the sense of siege by trapping people indoors, but there was no getting away from it. The moisture seeped through walls and dampened bedding, clothes and the pores of your skin as water overflowed on both sides of the ditch, swamping stretches of Boundary and Zero where BPs and Mounties hydroplaned along in record numbers, squinting at a landscape blurred beyond recognition.

The entire border, after closing for twenty-seven hours, remained in paranoid mode. Commuters with NEXUS passes were no longer waved through, and most southbound drivers were interrogated as if all thirty million Canadians had suddenly become suspects. Cars were randomly searched, their undersides scrutinized with mirrors on poles. And haggard Customs agents found mother lodes of Cuban cigars, fake IDs, untaxed cigarettes, weapons—brass knuckles, swords and grenades—and bins of counterfeit Rolexes, eagle feathers and a never-ending cache of undeclared fruits and alcohol. The unspoken message as you crept toward the booths? Expect to get grilled. Grannies were asked if they carried mace in their purses. Children were questioned about their parents. Arabs were strip-searched, especially if they had accents.

When Customs claimed it had detained several "people of interest" at the Blaine and Lynden crossings, the anxiety escalated. Local BPs went to twelve-hour shifts, and Patera was assured that a dozen incoming transfers were being processed.

The media struggled with this vague and confusing story. The few juicy particulars were repeated endlessly: A trunk full of RDX, described as a relatively stable cousin of nitroglycerin. Three pounds of B.C. bud found stapled behind door panels. The suspected dope-toting terrorist still hadn't been identified. There was no photo, no name and no information released about him other than that multiple IDs were found in the vehicle—stolen in Vancouver—along with a map of Seattle Center and the Space Needle. The mystery of his identity, according to the FBI, was compounded by the fact that he remained in a coma of sorts. Beyond that, the FBI would not discuss its probe until it was done. However, *The Seattle Times* asserted several days later that the FBI was ninety percent certain the unconscious suspect was Shareef Hasan Omar. Reputed to be a twenty-nine-year-old Algerian jihad trainer, he was suspected of recruiting in Toronto under multiple aliases, including one found on a fake passport inside the crumpled Pontiac.

Patera had kept Brandon's identity hidden from the media. Part of it, he told Sophie, was that he had no idea what Brandon might say; the other part was those credit-stealing *Feebs* demanded complete control of the story. But his name leaked anyway, and reporters bombarded the Vanderkools' answering machine, pleading or wheedling for return calls. The pursuit fizzled once the AP ran his sophomore class photo, which looked like a mug shot, alongside comments from his art teacher that Brandon possessed a "unique vision," which amused locals and inspired this headline: SPACE NEEDLE BOMBER FOILED BY ROOKIE AGENT'S 6TH SENSE.

Just as the coverage started to cool, another suspected Algerian terrorist, this one armed with two handguns, was caught bushwhacking across the border into Vermont's Kingdom County. Suddenly, for the first time anyone could recall, Americans were talking about the world's longest undefended border as if it were some government gaffe as ridiculous as the Pentagon blowing $2,315 on a toilet seat or the Agriculture Department bankrolling cow-fart studies at Washington State University.

Television crews fanned out to illustrate just how unguarded these 4,200 miles actually were, and *border* seemed like too big a noun for what they found. Most of the boundary was less momentous than a state line, less delineated than the average cul-de-sac. There weren't any fences, and many formal crossings were guarded after dark by nothing more than traffic cones. The border looked like a timid line drawn in pencil, especially west of Minnesota where it no longer followed the contours of rivers, mountains or lakes but simply traced the invisible arc of the 49th parallel out to the Pacific. People pulled out maps and globes and pondered the portion of the dotted line that turned into the ditch that was now in the news, a ditch like you'd see anywhere.

As the story lingered, reporters scrambled over one another for fresh angles, casting the western end of the border as a farmer's, retiree's and outlaw's paradise, or dredging up its rum-running days, and its historical ebb and flow of legal and illegal commerce. Papers ran fever charts showing recent spikes in bud seizures and alien captures, or highlighted the countries' differences in immigration and drug laws. Old stories were rewritten with more hype, particularly on the study that identified fifty active terrorist groups in Canada. Editorialists, bloggers and cartoonists piled on as the outrage swelled. While Mexican farmhands faced a gauntlet of fences and agents and vigilantes, terrorists were driving across the unguarded northern border with trunks full of explosives! Congressmen were demanding more studies and greater investments in security. Not to be out-alarmed, Washington's governor offered the state's National Guard. And the same Minutemen exasperating BPs along the southern border vowed to help seal the north.

Meanwhile, sales of deadbolts and canned goods surged in the valley, hardware stores ran out of ammo and home alarms, mailbox flyers suddenly touted security consultants and local paranoia mined the unknowable: How many other cars were hauling explosives through here? Dirk Hoffman offered his concise reader-board commentary: CANADA EXPORTS DRUGS AND TERROR.

North of the line, black-humor asides about U.S. tanks rolling north morphed into genuine fear after the President warned that any country housing "evildoers" would be treated as an enemy.

And just when Sophie thought people couldn't possibly talk more about Brandon, the chatter tripled. Most of the stories were exaggerations or fabrications, such as the claim that he broke arrest records during his first month, or, even more apocryphal, that he had a Spider-Man-like knack for sensing or anticipating crimes, or had suffered a breakdown after the bomber bust that made him speak backwards or—as Alexandra Cole kept claiming—in tongues. And then there was his art. Apparently he was making peculiar sculptures of sorts on public and private lands when he wasn't swinging Tarzan-style from trees to arrest smugglers, aliens and bombers.

Sophie told McAfferty to roll onto his back, then asked, "What do you make of Brandon?"

"The shit magnet? Great kid. Wouldn't want to stand too close to him in a lightning storm, but a great kid. Took him for an oddball at first, but he's even odder than the average duck we hire. Know what I'm saying? Rarely wears a gun, which is probably good, considering he might be the worst shot we've ever had. As a matter of fact, he can't even type. Hunts and pecks like something out of a Bogart movie. Dionne does most of it for him. What's worse is he's as gullible as a twelve-year-old. He'll bring people in and say, 'They didn't know what was in the bags,' or 'They didn't know they needed a visa.' It's all we can do not to bust up. We figured he was lucky at first. I mean *amazingly* lucky—though I still don't know what to make of his so-called bomber."

"What do you mean?"

"Well, for starters, who'd risk a dog hit on dope if you're carrying RDX? Dogs aren't trained for both, and most are dope dogs, not bomb dogs, so why risk hauling bud if your mission's to blow something up? I'm just saying this guy, whoever he is, doesn't strike me as any mastermind. But back to Brandon: It's like he expects something to happen at every moment, no matter where he is or what he's doing. And if he strolled through this room right now, I bet he could tell you almost everything that's in it and exactly what you're wearing and which of my bulging muscles you're rubbing and what's on the walls and the precise youthful hue of my skin. Most agents try not to see too much, know what I'm saying? Plus most of us have to puff up whatever courage we need. Brandon just *is*. And his eyes are really, really wide open. A sensor went off, okay, and he and Talley responded. Talley finds tracks and starts tearin' off before Brandon tells him they're old. Talley's the veteran here. Can track as well as anybody. But the big rook points out a tiny spiderweb suspended directly above a boot print and says it took at least an hour to build. See what I'm saying? So yeah, he's as strange as he is large and, yes, I worry about him getting killed. Next question?"

Sophie recorded her interviews and photographed her subjects. I'm just a nutty scrapbooker, she told some people. To others she hinted at some kind of oral history. The rumor soon spread that she had a publisher, that she was an accomplished author with multiple pseudonyms working on her quirky border-town version of *Midnight in the Garden of Good and Evil*. What was actually true didn't seem to matter. People lined up to gossip and gripe, to speculate and get rubbed, to confess their temptations and share their biggest worries.

Wayne Rousseau confided his: Madeline.

14

LISTENING TO the French station, watching herself speed, Madeline drove Zero Ave. knowing she should have taken the back roads with a hatchback full of pot. She passed hundreds of greenhouses and miles of raspberry fields before cutting through new pinot, merlot and chardonnay vineyards. Every third car on the other side of the ditch was a green-and-white SUV, but the groggy BPs never glanced over. Beyond them, the valley still looked awash, and if she squinted it turned into a massive bay, the farmhouses and barns anchored freighters, the vehicles and sheds leisure boats.

She jotted mental notes on the popular foot-smuggling routes Toby had marked. He was right. Even with doubled patrols, it took an idiot to get caught. She wove through queues of exasperated drivers at the Pacific and Peace Arch crossings and rolled west away from the border toward White Rock, where steep, narrow streets turned into toboggan runs in the winter and tall houses jockeyed for peephole views of the bay.

Parking at the marina, she watched a lanky couple necking against a phone booth, cigarettes dangling behind their heads. The northwesterly breeze looked perfect, but she was an hour early and considered rolling a joint to relax before recalling Toby's rules. She marveled uneasily at his growing influence. He'd said she needed to move out of her apartment here, promising to find her a better place closer to him. Could she say no to this man, no matter what the request? She rolled and smoked a pinner after convincing herself anything this skinny didn't count, then strode into the silver twilight and the briny reek of exposed flats. From this angle, the United States looked barely discovered, with only a towering resort hotel and a smattering of lights visible on the fringe of a grand forest.

White Rock's bayside strip of bars, restaurants, ice cream parlors and boutiques served as B.C.'s Riviera in July and August. In the off-season, it attracted an older set, like the graybeards Madeline found crammed into an oval alcove in Trudeau's beneath photos of the Beatles cavorting, Sinatra in a gangster hat and a shirtless, defiant Jim Morrison. Their conversation was too intense for anyone to notice Wayne's daughter order a margarita or to hear the bored bartender tell her the "gang of four" had expanded to the "gang of eight" over the past couple weeks and that the old boys were drinking twice as much as usual. She duck-flapped fingers and faked a yawn that turned real.

Madeline couldn't see more than the back of her father's head but could tell by his honking voice that he was flying on at least three vodka martinis. She eavesdropped on the laments about Vancouver's traffic, the lack of hockey and the idiocy of the premier. Halfway through her second margarita, she realized she was listening for Sophie. The masseuse had obviously briefed her father on the trunk bomber, because right from the start he knew more than the papers about the type and amount of explosives, the feud between the BP and the FBI, how Brandon had, at the time, been driving home from the saloon in his own truck after celebrating his first pot bust—which Fisher told her cost Toby & Co. almost 300 K.

She'd saved the two messages Brandon left her, semicoherent rants about how he should have ten-three'd, how he was drunk and didn't like to drink anyway, how impossible the paperwork was, how he'd talked backwards for the first time in years, then asking if she wanted to see his new dog and if she knew when Danny was coming back or—her favorite—how long "commas" usually lasted. His panicky voice triggered an old reflex to soothe him, though she couldn't even bring herself to dial his number. She'd avoided him ever since Danny C wasn't around to make his oddities so entertaining and endearing. He was the one she wanted to talk to, but after laughing over Brandon's fluky heroics they'd have to catch up, and that conversation was predictable.

How's med school? she'd ask.

Hard. *Very* hard. Still working at the nursery?

Uh-huh.

So, have you been looking out for Brandon?

Madeline sipped her cocktail and tuned in to her father's powwow.

"We could hold them off for, what, ten minutes?" his pal Lenny Ribes asked.

"Maybe twenty."

The men eyed the darkening bay as if checking for aircraft carriers or Marines crashing the beach.

"Whaddaya think England would do?"

"We've seen what she'll do," Wayne barked. "An enemy of the superpower's an enemy of hers. Ever since W. W. Two, the Brits have embraced their role as the junior partner in charge of European propaganda. They've mastered the double-talk of sucking up while feigning independence."

"Yeah, but—"

"Anybody else want more salsa?"

"Yeah, but it's never gonna happen. You think their conservatives want to add a fifty-first state as populous as California and as liberal as Vermont?"

"This place used to give us as much salsa as we could handle."

"Who the hell's this bomber, anyway?" asked an owl-faced man Madeline didn't recognize. "Seriously doubt he's a flag-wavin' Canadian. It's not like we've got lifelong citizens runnin' over the border to blow things up, is it?"

"Well, we're a staging area, as they call it," Lenny said, lunging for the wine.

"And that's our fault?" Wayne said. "Can we help it if they piss off everybody so much people start lining up in our yard to throw turds in theirs?"

"Yeah, it kind of is," Lenny countered. "We let anybody in. And by the time their lies are sorted, it's a little late to ask 'em to get the hell out. They're already here—or there." He nodded south.

"Gather the guy's an Arab."

"Thanks, Rocco. That helps a lot."

"Well, they say he's Muslim, right?"

"If he's still in that convenient coma," Wayne pointed out, "and if there's a bunch of fake IDs on him, how do we know whether he's a Muslim or a Baptist, a Jew or an atheist? Muslim blood a different shade of red, Rocco? Or is it the beard that gives him away? Does my lousy beard make me a Muslim?"

"Maybe."

"Personally," Wayne said, "I doubt the guy exists."

"They invented him?"

"That's right."

"Why?"

"I think that's obvious."

"What's obv—"

"This better blow over by the time that casino opens," Rocco interjected. "That's all I gotta say. Otherwise the lines are gonna—"

"Truth is," Lenny interrupted, "without the U.S. we'd be as irrelevant as seagull shit."

"What're we even talking about here?"

"That's our identity," Lenny said. "We're *not* the U.S. *That's* who we are."

"Not this again," Wayne grumbled.

"Am I wrong? Without them would we look so rational, polite and beautiful?"

The old men stared at one another.

"Seriously," Lenny continued, his voice rising to the challenge. "We're the rebound boyfriend after the hostile divorce. Women love us because we're not the violent, self-absorbed jerks they just dumped."

"Have some more wine, Lenny."

Wayne's agitated eyes then lifted and traversed the room before settling on the most unexpected of gifts. And in the moment before she felt his glance, he noticed how she slouched over her cocktail like a burdened woman twice her age straining against some invisible hand.

THE BORDER PATROL had installed a new night watch near Peace Arch in case anyone tried to traipse across the invisible line splitting the mud-flats and slaloming through the islands. But drowsy Rick Talley didn't notice the black Geary 18 gliding southbound across the bay, nor its captain in her black wetsuit, nor the jib she raised and filled with no more noise than a tossed bedsheet. And nobody except a rotund man pacing a gravelly shore just south of Semiahmoo Spit noticed the brief flutters when the sails fell forty minutes later.

Toby had bigger sailboats in mind than her dad's old plywood flattie, but she'd assured him the boat was built for beaching and she could pop eighty pounds across the bay without having to dock anywhere or needing another boat to greet her. But what if she got up on the flats and the man holding the intermittent white light in one hand held a gun in the other?

Fighting off the urge to flee while he was still too far up the beach to catch her, she towed the boat close enough to ground it. He was built like an umpire and introduced himself in such boisterous fashion Madeline immediately forgot his name. She unclipped the large foul-weather sacks from the mast and handed him one.

He took his time and shined his piercing light up and down her wetsuit, lingering on her crotch. "Cuter than the average mule, aren't ya?" He stuck the light in his mouth so he could hold the bag with one hand and fondle the pouches with the other.

Her eyes adjusted well enough to make out a thick fleshy face beneath a dark leather beanie.

"You haven't even told me your name, darling."

Her throat was too tight to tell him to shut up or hurry.

A short laugh caught in his throat and ended in a noisy spit. "The great Toby sent me a mute? Give me the other one."

She did, and he finally cracked open his money bag against his belly, forcing her to lean into his reek of armpits and burger grease. Seeing what looked like six plastic-wrapped bricks of U.S. hundreds, just like Toby said there'd be, she squeezed one to pretend she knew what she was doing. He held on to the bag when she started to pull it away, then let it go so she stumbled backwards, which triggered more laughter and spitting. She clipped the money to the mast and shoved the boat toward deeper water.

"Isn't that boat too big for a little thing like you?"

Once the water cleared her knees, she flopped her torso onto the stern and belly-crawled into the cockpit.

"What if the wind dies?"

She fanned the rudder to propel her out far enough to drop part of the centerboard, but a headwind rose up, knocked the boat sideways and shoved her back toward him.

"Can I help?" He started wading. "Need a hand, my sweet muffin?"

When she yanked on the main halyard, the wind grabbed the sail before it was halfway up and knocked the boat sideways again, back toward shore. Shit-shit-shit! She had to drop some board, but when she did it struck mud and the hull lurched onto its side, then popped loose again. Now he was shining his obnoxious light on her body and wading faster toward her. She shifted her weight leeward until she felt the sail tug well enough to ease the bow windward. After another ten yards of moving mostly sideways, she dropped more board and felt the boat track, then yanked the rest of the main up, dropped the entire centerboard and fell back with a sigh that sounded like a sob, her hand trembling on the tiller. She heard clapping but didn't look back.

Once free of the squirrelly land gusts, the wind steadied and her panic cooled toward blank exhaustion. She popped the jib, knowing she'd have to point higher or tack twice across the swath of bay where they'd dumped her mother, which brought back all the sweaty questions she'd never asked. If there were four in the tram when the cable snapped, how come her father and the other couple suffered only bruises and whiplash? Why was her mother cremated? How did they know those ashes were actually hers? And why weren't they stored in some quiet place where they could visit the woman who squealed on water-park rides and dressed up as a fortune-teller at her daughters' birthday parties and crawled into bed to snuggle even after they hit their teens? In the end, she looked like dried soup flung overboard no matter what fancy words her father blubbered before the boom swung silently across the cockpit. Nicole took it personally, of course. But even Madeline wasn't sure whether it was karma, a freak wind shift or her own volition that sent the wooden boom into her sister's mouth.

Madeline vowed again that she'd take her cut and get out—did she need any more evidence that she didn't have the nerves for this?—yet even while berating herself she couldn't ignore the sizzle that came with $240,000 strapped to the mast, $2,400 of which Toby said she could keep. Minutes later, as the wind shifted and allowed her to tack five degrees higher, she revised her pledge and cantilevered all but her shins beyond the rail, arching her spine and neck until her head was just inches off invisible waves, the main sheet in one glove, the tiller in the other, her eyes on the sky. Two more weeks. Four of her six ops hit their harvest dates by the first of the month. Two more weeks.

Then what? She'd climb aboard a southbound plane. Costa Rica, maybe Rio.

Soon she was simply sailing, not scolding or doubting or day dreaming, just sailing. A victorylike giddiness filled her as she crossed into Canadian waters toward the marina's steady green lamp. She heard herself mumbling, in part a celebration, in part a pleading, as she coasted toward the docks, sails flapping and falling, her mind skipping to images she still couldn't file: her father trying to save himself with reinventions, Brandon chasing smugglers and bombers, the oddly irresistible Sophie Winslow connecting the dots with neither judgment nor bias.

15

BRANDON AVOIDED the HQ banter he couldn't partake in and drove east into a valley that kept changing on him.

More retirement ranches were popping up with two-chimney cha-lets, stone facings, white trim and three-plank fences. Closer to Lyn-den, new cul-de-sacs sprouted alongside the bulldozed moonscape of the future Paradise Links and the corner gas station at Badger and Ben-der was turning into a neon destination with New York Pizza, the Maui Tanning Salon and the Nuthouse Grill. Closer to the border, bushy raspberry rows now doubled as potential smuggling lanes and the future casino's steel girders lunged toward the sky.

The people were changing on him too. Even his parents looked at him differently. And when he'd burst into the saloon looking for Dionne a while back, people started clapping. The attention jammed his circuits. He wanted to say it was the wrong car and the guy was still in a coma, but all he could do was stand there, wondering where to put his hands, until they started laughing.

Though he'd since tried to notice as little as possible that could lead to arrests, paperwork or acclaim, it was no use. He saw more than ever. He intercepted buds on Halverstick, then caught a smuggler on Judson Lake and yet another in downtown Sumas. And the increased patrols didn't seem to discourage the illegals he kept finding in fields and forests or sardined into muffler-dragging vans. He and Dionne appre-hended five Filipinos in a Voyager on Froberg Road. Two nights later he watched a Monte Carlo cruising Markworth on an obvious decoy run. So he left his rig, jogged up the street and saw four Cambodians crouched in the ferns, hands over their eyes like kids who didn't understand hide-and-seek yet. *If I can't see you, you can't see me.* The next night he caught four Romanians, then three weepy Mexicans who pleaded with him in Spanish until he would have let them go if he hadn't already radioed them in. They kept coming, as if racing to enter the States before the doors slammed shut for good. And nobody resembled the dangerous, lying scammers Dionne had warned him about. They were illegal—by definition, right?—but they didn't look like criminals. Most of them struck Brandon as exotic, even beautiful, though they weren't always endearing. Two Iranians lectured him in broken English about the Bill of Rights, followed by an indignant Sri Lankan couple who scolded him for ruining their honeymoon. Brandon stepped into the woods to pee later that night and nine Venezuelans surrendered. The shit-magnet razzing roared to new heights.

Brandon began to sketch all the illegals who stuck in his head, first by pencil, then with oils. A Moroccan with a flat nose and eyebrows like warning flares. A Frenchman with long, wide sideburns and swollen lips. An old Algerian with almond eyes and a creased mouth in a face as finely boned as any child's. So much about the job burned his stomach, but he'd always wanted to see the world without actually having to travel. And now, seemingly, amazingly, the world was coming to him.

He turned off Badger onto Swanson and tried to focus on comforting familiar sights: freshly plowed fields of dirt the color of powdered chocolate; pastures so thick with dandelions he saw nothing but yellow; pom-poms of blooming maples, crabapples and alders packing the eastern hillsides; rows of hand-tied raspberry canes flickering past his window. He wheeled past a rusty dozer 4 SALE and another handwritten sign, HORSE MANURE $1.50, before braking alongside a muddy El Camino with Arizona plates on the fringe of Gil Honcoop's sixty wooded acres, a border-straddling mix of trees, bushes and meadows popular with smugglers and songbirds.

As he approached the trail, a warbling vireo rushed its insistent mating riff: *It's-time-to-listen-to-me. It's-time-to-listen-to-me.* A chestnut-backed chickadee cut short its laid-back come-on, *heyyy-there, heyyy-there.* And once he'd entered the canopy, a brown creeper offered its odd plea, always ending on three impossibly high notes, as if straining to stay upbeat. Brandon was too distracted to count the birds. In fact, he hadn't been able to muster an accurate daily count for weeks now. He resisted the urge to call Madeline again as a know-it-all robin scampered nearby, letting loose its rising and falling *I know ever-y-thing. I know ever-y-thing.*

He followed fresh boot tracks, then veered off the path through the brush until he saw a Bewick's wren's sloppy decoy nest, which he doubted fooled anyone. He'd studied nests since he first watched barn swallows build mud igloos beneath every eave on the farm. He'd noticed that goldfinch nests are so tightly woven that the chicks often drown during big rains. He'd seen magpies weave nails, tin, tape, glass, rags and even barbed wire into their nests, and he'd happened upon an indignant robin incubating a Top-Flite golf ball and a dizzy cormorant sitting on a seventy-five-watt Sylvania lightbulb.

Back on the path he noticed the purple blooms of salmonberry and the white flash of Indian plum, then spent ten minutes cutting inch-long thorns off a black hawthorn tree and hacking the dried husks of last year's blackberry vines into foot-long sections. He used the thorns to tack five husks together, pinned one to a low maple branch and carefully added husks—one by one—to the fragile form until it looked like an asymmetrical spiral of sticks floating in the air.

Nervous chickadees were the first to warn him that someone was approaching, followed by juncos and kinglets all curious as to what the chickadees were fussing over. Their Carhartt pants, canvas shirts and camo hats all fit with the El Camino and the footprints. "Hello there," the larger one volunteered.

"Hi." Brandon kept his eyes on his form, which the mildest gust could destroy.

They eyeballed the web of suspended sticks, then gawked up at him—his shirt untucked, its buttons misaligned—as if waiting for an explanation. "How's this work?" the shorter one finally asked.

Brandon didn't respond, his ears tuned to the distant jackhammer of a pileated woodpecker trying to attract females by slamming its head against a farmhouse drainpipe.

"Some kinda decoy?" the other speculated. "Psy-ops? Messin' with their heads, right? When you're dealing with a large group, Marty, you want to have 'em all lookin' the same direction. Crowd control, right?"

Brandon connected another stick.

"So what would ya call this?"

"A form," Brandon said, distracted by the bossy whine of a hummingbird he couldn't see.

"Sir? I'm sorry, we haven't introduced ourselves, have we? I'm Buford McKenzie Strom, and this here's Martin T. Long, deputy state-chapter director of the Arizona Civil Homeland—"

"Minutemen," Brandon said, at the same time identifying the first two notes of an olive-sided flycatcher's call.

"That's correct, sir. Here to help y'all with the border. And from what we can tell, you need all you can get. We were just talkin' 'bout how we'd be happy to help build a fence of sorts from here to the water. In fact, that's exactly what we're gonna suggest when we meet with Chief Patton."

Brandon looked down at them. The smaller one had the longest eyelashes he'd ever seen on a man. "Patera."

"That's the one."

"He'll tell you nobody wants a fence."

"No kidding? So what is this, really?"

"A form."

"Like a trail marker for navigatin' in the dark?" Buford guessed. "Did you make that other form we saw up there? Kind of looked like a big nest, didn't it, Marty?"

"That would be one large bird," Martin offered.

"It's art," Brandon said.

Buford's laugh turned into a gasp and a harsh cough. "Wrong pipe," he hissed.

The fluttering and chirping rose to such a crescendo the Minutemen looked up too.

"May I ask how long it took you to make this?" Martin asked.

A whisper of wind wiggled the structure and Brandon's hands shot up, willing it to stay intact.

"Please explain this like we're mo-rons," Martin said. "I mean, from where I'm standing, just one taxpayer's opinion here, having someone your size just standing up on the border would do a whole lot more good than whatever it is you're doing here. No offense, Agent . . ." He leaned forward, squinting at the name tag.

"The reason I'm here right now," Brandon said, his eyes on his form, "is that Mr. Honcoop asked me to tell you to stay off his property."

Brandon heard "well, well" and some muttering about landowners who may have a "vested interest" in keeping the border wide open, but he was barely listening. Their upturned faces and gaping mouths reminded him of what he'd intended to do earlier.

The Minutemen stopped chattering to watch the giant agent step through ferns and salal to an alder, which he shimmied to its first branch and removed a nest wedged against the trunk. He fanned a hand over the top of it and flipped it upside down, straining water through his fingers before returning the nest and its four pale-blue eggs to the nook.

"What'd you just do?" Buford asked while Martin snapped photos.

Brandon was debating whether to tell them about goldfinch nests when he felt the earth shake and glanced at his form just as it quivered and collapsed. "Feel that?" he asked. The men glanced at each other, then stared at the disconnected pieces scattered on the ground before looking back up at Brandon's lopsided grin.

16

HE WAS expecting little Roony, so it took a couple beats to adjust to the sight of this imposing figure on the half-lit porch of his milking parlor at four a.m.

"Good morning, Mr. Vanderkool." The large kid stood too close, with the overly friendly eyes of someone about to try to sell him something he didn't need.

"Says who?" Norm grunted, widening his stance.

"How're we doin' today?" he said, his size and confidence vaguely menacing.

Norm's frown deepened. "Too early to know, isn't it? What is it you want?"

"I'm here, sir, on behalf of a small group of businessmen interested in leasing a path of sorts through your property."

Norm struggled to attach meaning to the words. He hadn't been able to sleep for more than fifteen minutes straight since the monthly milk-tank tests arrived the prior afternoon. After a frenzy of disinfecting and cleaning—just in case salmonella was also in play—he'd left a message for Roony to show up early so he could at least share the news that the dairy might lose its Grade-A status. "You a realtor?" he asked.

"I'm Michael." He stuck out a large right hand at an odd diagonal. Norm didn't register that the kid was offering a shake before it was casually withdrawn. "And like I said, we're simply interested in whether you'd be willing to consider a little side arrangement that

compensated you for allowing us to pass discreetly through your property on occasion."

"You want an easement," Norm said, a tick before the offer had
sunk in.

"Whatever you want to call it is fine with us." The kid's multi-
dimpled grin—the highest indents just below his eyes—had clearly
moved mountains before. "You'd receive a thousand dollars for every
time we came through but at any rate no less than ten thousand a
month—in cash. The crossings would be at night. And you'd never see
anything or have anything to actually—"

"Who's we?" Norm's voice squeaked, the audacity of the offer
snowballing inside him. It had been less than a month since the border
lockup and Patera's formal dairy warning—which, while greeted with
eyerolls, had resulted in security upgrades on perhaps half the farms.
And here came this kid strolling door-to-door before dawn, as if gathering signatures or selling vacuum cleaners. Norm wished like hell that
Brandon would amble up behind this hustler and trump his size. "And
who do you think—"

"Sir," the kid interrupted, "it's a business offer like any other,
which you, of course, have the prerogative to reject. What I can assure
you is that it will be discreet. You won't see or hear anything. Simply
check your mailbox on the twenty-third of each month, with the first
payment beginning the month after which usage begins and proceeding
every subsequent month that such an arrangement is utilized."

Norm examined the kid closely so he could describe him to Patera.
A solid six-four, slate eyes, Redford bangs, freckles near the temples.
"Get off my p-p-porch," he stammered, the offer clanging in his ears.

"I'll swing back in a month to see if you've changed your mind,"
the kid said with the confidence of a missionary. "Unless, of course,
enough of your neighbors have already signed on."

"Don't even think . . . ," Norm said, trying so hard to picture what
ten grand would look like in his mailbox that he couldn't finish the
sentence.

"I'll see if they might be willing to increase the minimum." There wasn't a glint of shame or fear in the kid's heel-dragging stroll from Norm's bug-swirled porch.

Norm started to follow him but it was too dark, so he waited for the metallic clunk of a car door that never came. He stood in the gravel, straining to hear and wishing he had a flashlight. The kid must have hopped the ditch. He was definitely Canadian. But wouldn't he have parked on Zero? Norm marched toward the house to report the outrageous encounter while his indignation was fresh. However, his pace slowed until he was rocking in place next to Aunt Mary's mildewed Winnebago and his brother-in-law's rusting jet boat, which hadn't moved in six years. Farms, his father explained early on, are great places for everyone else to store the crap they never use. He took in the buttery tease of sunlight to the east, then trudged back to the milking parlor with the sensation that his dairy was on some war map. Norm snorted. It was hard to imagine an easier target. He'd traversed the same ribbon of grass and gravel at four a.m. and four p.m. for thirty-eight years. Still, he felt exposed, and it unsettled him that this kid knew his offer was a tiny blade that would spin inside Norm's belly. *Prerogative.* A hustler who used words like *prerogative* and *discreet*? Was it a coincidence he'd shown up the morning after the milk stats came in? Norm had agreed to nothing but still felt like he'd already concealed something. He knew this information would thrill Patera, who was already giddy about some politicians supposedly flying out to tour his sector. Norm didn't mind not telling the chief, or anyone else, every last detail, though he wasn't sure he could shoulder one more regret.

He fended off a swoon with a three-finger clod of Copenhagen, then reentered the vestibule to finish disinfecting the pipes and hoses leading to the bulk tank. He flipped on the vacuum pump and heard the cows stir. Propped against the wall, his eyes watering from the chlorine, he saw how hopeless his parlor would look to an outsider.

The last tourists he'd let in were Helen Schaffer's third graders. He went the whole morning without chewing, as Jeanette had insisted, explaining as clearly as he could what he did and why, while they groaned and blanched as if they'd been forced to climb down manholes to learn where their piss and shit went. Brandon had scrubbed the place down beforehand, but it still was everywhere and eventually one of the tykes realized it wasn't dirt. "How does number two get on the walls?" Before Norm could finesse a response, diarrhea flew out of a milking Holstein on cue, inspiring one of the ponytailed gigglers to puke and Miss Schaffer to glare at him as if the field trip had been his perverted idea.

And now Sophie kept threatening to turn up at dawn to see exactly what he did for a living. Terrific. She wanted a tour of the boat, too. The truth was he didn't want to see his world through her eyes for fear he'd sleep through the next milking, torch the barns and drown himself in the Nooksack. At what point, he wondered, do you have to admit, at least to yourself, that you love somebody you shouldn't?

If Chas Landers gave his jackpot to the sheriff's office, then perhaps that's who Norm should call. But he didn't know anyone there anymore. No, he'd have to call Patera. Then there was the catch: If he drew attention to himself, he couldn't change his mind. He sighed and spat. And what if he was the only holdout, with Moffat, Crawford and God knows who else already pocketing their ten grand on the twenty-third of every month? Another thought ambushed him: Is that how Sophie financed her remodel?

"All right, all right," he said, approaching the gate where the big brown and white faces hovered patiently, with Pearl in front, of course, as if to reassure him they'd get through this together. He opened the gate, slid open the parlor door and watched six of his best producers lumber inside, lining up like large men at stadium urinals and sticking their heads into the trough. They ate noisily while Norm hooked up the hoses. Some got frisky during vaccinations or hoof trims, but it had been a while since one turned on him in the parlor; gentle cows were one upside to a closed herd, as was not having to mess with bulls. He reminded himself to visit Ray Lankhaar, who'd just had his ribs rearranged by his, though even the idea of conversing with the condescending dairyman was enough to exhaust him.

The downside of a closed herd, naturally, was the cows got sick in bunches, which meant that Norm had to be his own vet most of the time or else he couldn't make it. Squatting beneath Pearl, his knees quieted with Motrin, he soaked each teat in a rubber cup full of iodine before attaching suction hoses and slinging a light harness over her back to keep the hoses off the concrete.

He moved to the next, sanitizing the nipples, fastening the hoses, and likewise with the other four, relieved that the first six udders looked so healthy. He watched velvety milk swirl through the glass ball where the hoses came together on the way to the tank. The leukocyte and somatic cell counts could be misleading, he assured himself while stepping out to check the vacuum level. He knew his cows better than any goddamn computer. He back-flushed the hoses, then stepped back, rinsed his stained hands and packed another chew while the cows munched and milked before he coaxed them out, one by one, most of them moving to the chirp of his voice, a few needing a nudge in their flanks. *We can get through this,* he thought, then said it aloud.

Two of the next six had pinkeye. Norm hooked up their hoses, dripped oxytetracycline in their puffy eyes and checked their ribs to see if they were losing weight. Most of his cows had already calved at least four times. The big boys would have fattened them with malt and slaughtered them years ago. But how do you give up on cows that haven't given up on you?

After squeezing 212 gallons of four-percent from the healthiest half of the herd, he scraped manure out of the parlor with a snow shovel and found himself ruminating over Dale Mesick's "green-power project" to turn cow shit into electricity. What a genius! Three hundred kilowatts—enough power to meet the needs of two hundred homes! Even got grants for it, including a check from Paul Allen's philanthropy! Norm knew part of his resentment was that this *never* would have occurred to him. You make it to sixty-two and your limitations are posted on the wall. Yet he felt like he'd put his own hoax in play by shoving Brandon into the BP. The ongoing mystery of the bomber's identity—had he woken up yet?—only added to the circus, with everyone filling the blanks with speculation and Patera whispering in his ear, "Brandon has it. You don't see it often, but he's got it."

Microsoft millionaires. Shit-to-power. Brandon the supercop.

Norm knew it was just a matter of time before it turned to embarrassment, tragedy or both. Another ticking alarm. But it all bounced off his son like none of it had anything to do with him, as if his days were divided by dikes.

Jeanette, too, seemed increasingly disconnected to yesterday. A week ago, he'd seen her glance up at Brandon with an unspoken question on her hesitant lips: *What are you doing in that uniform?* She was barely holding it together, and it was like watching someone spackle over rust. "Norm, we need to talk," she'd told him one afternoon, after flapping her blouse and blowing into her cleavage to cool another flash. But when he sat down she'd already teared up, because she no longer remembered what she'd wanted to discuss.

He rested his knee before loading the Super Slicer with alfalfa bales, doubting he'd be able to nap that afternoon with the *easement* offer and all the grim cow care circling overhead. Was his dairy so forlorn that any Canadian glancing across the ditch could tell he needed cash? Or did someone like the professor tip them off? The list of people Norm trusted kept shrinking. He didn't discuss money with anyone anymore, including Jeanette. And it weighed on him that she didn't know they'd already sunk $38,750 into a partially completed sailboat he doubted he could sell for half that. She used to write the checks and cushion him from the daily panic, until the numbers started getting lost inside her. He half-envied her detachment. That's all he figured he'd have at the end, the *drip-drip-drip* of numbers. Fifty-year-old phone numbers of cute girls he'd never called. Seasonal schedules for ferries he'd never ridden. Dimensions of the sloop he'd never finished. The birth and death dates of his sister, parents, uncles and aunts. The Cialis flyer in yesterday's mail, which his mind instantly distilled to $1.49 per erection.

He spread more Clorox around the main barn. He'd noticed only a few cases of diarrhea, fewer than normal, but nothing was normal now. And where the hell was Roony? He felt dizzy and stepped outside for a smoke, the valley brightening with false hope. The rumble of the incoming feed truck—another two grand down the tubes—interrupted his second Winston and brought him back to business. He couldn't bring himself to check on the sick barn yet so he shuffled out to bottle-feed the calves, which he'd usually left to Brandon. This was the easiest way to get too close to your cows. The big boys didn't have that problem. They didn't bother raising calves and waiting two years for them to freshen. They just bought more heifers and sold the calves for meat. There were many reasons Norm never ate veal. For starters, Jersey calves were cuter than puppies, so curious and friendly he had to force himself not to play with them. Secondly, a cow's uterus is pretty much the same as a human's, something he liked pointing out to people; and if that wasn't enough he'd mention that their ovulation and gestation cycles were also about the same and that calves pop out with umbilical cords just like yours.

Unless they abort. Norm's herd had suffered more abortions in the past six months than in the prior three years combined, which reminded him of that article in *Hoard's* about dairies hit with forty or fifty in a row. They even had a ghoulish name for it: abortion storms.

Once he got to the sick barn, there was more bad news. After cutting off four teats he'd rubber-banded off the day before, he found six more that were newly engorged. Some of these cows were chronics he'd dried out before, which meant it was probably culling time whether he wanted to admit it or not. It had been two weeks since he'd caught Brandon inspecting the herd. After he finished haranguing him, Norm had agreed to call Doc Stremler so long as Brandon stayed off the dairy and focused on his job like he'd promised. But he hadn't gotten around to it, and the longer he waited, the harder the call was to make. He wanted to go over the latest milk stats with an optimist like Roony before the doomsday doc lowered his glasses and started lecturing: At a good dairy, cows like to be milked. It was Stremler who'd warned him that if he didn't replace his son with a quality dairyman, he'd be in dire trouble within six months. At first Norm thought he was joking, but he was as humorless as ever. Brandon was at the academy for two months before Norm saw what the vet meant.

He was rethinking the cheaper semen he'd been buying when the image of that kid on his porch swung back at him. If they knew Norm's habits and needs, they also knew who his son was, right? He tried calming himself by whispering to the sick cows, then returned to the healthy barn to see if any of the heifers he'd AI'd were pregnant yet.

"Norm!"

After wondering if he'd imagined the shout, he realized Roony must have finally arrived. "Back here!" he yelled, deciding right then that he wouldn't share the numbers with him just yet, given how misleading his relentless cheerfulness could be. Norm needed to feel this pain.

The second "Norm!" sounded shrill, possibly feminine. Jeanette, he assumed. But he was in the middle of a PT, feeling for that solid lump of new life. "Give me a minute," he shouted, "or come on back!"

The barn door swung, and a shaft of daylight pulled Sophie Winslow in with it. She was puffing hard, adjusting to the gloom, bangs dangling between her alarmed eyes.

Norm saw himself through them. Rubber boots caked in manure, his bib so stained you couldn't tell it used to be yellow, sweat and dirt and iodine smeared across his face beneath a ball cap so dingy Jeanette had begged him to trash it a decade ago. He watched the confusion cross her face. *Where's his right arm?* When it became obscenely clear where it was, she paled and turned away. He pulled out of the heifer's rectum faster than he should have, the suction sounds appalling even to him.

He was peeling off the glove when she turned back around, looking pasty as a clown. "Know how you said to let you know if I saw a cow down out back?" she panted. "Yeah, well . . ."

Norm galloped outside toward the medicine shed before she finished. He had four swollen cows in the field, and badly needed a healthy calf and a productive mother. They were good producers out there, too, all of them. Great producers, actually. And if the mother had already calved, the calf needed her right now.

He grabbed a bag of CMPK, then ambled—knee grinding, groin tightening—to his battered pickup. Sophie jogged alongside, babbling about how she'd been eating cereal when she noticed a cow struggling on the ground. He climbed inside and she did too, rearranging old Copenhagen lids with her clogs on the rusted-out flooring. Even now he was distracted by her smells, her wet hair, her peach-colored pants that fell just above the raised goose bumps on her tapered calves. His truck rounded her house with a mild squeal, then whined out Northwood to the entrance to his back ten. After a quick scan, Norm groaned.

"What?"

"It's the Holstein." He grimaced. "She's a great producer. A great, great producer. And . . ." The image of both 83 and her calf already dead or dying shut him up.

It didn't occur to her to open the gate, so he lunged around the hood, unwrapped the chain from the post and pushed the gate inward, then scrambled back behind the wheel without glancing at her. He stepped on it, the four cylinders squealing until he shifted out of neutral and lurched forward, rattling across the cattle guard. When he tired of high-centering on the rutted road, he braked abruptly. Sophie's pretty wet head swung toward the dash. He grabbed a coil of rope from the back and hobbled ahead.

He was relieved to see a wet calf the size of a Great Dane wobbling near the fallen Holstein, waiting for its critical first feeding. But the mother was spread on her side as if staked to the earth, moaning, head lolling, belly bloated well beyond any pregnancy bulge. Norm looked into her crazed eyes and felt behind her ears for a fever. "What's wrong, girl?"

He slipped a harness over her head, dug his rubber boots into the mud and grass and yanked her thick neck back toward her hind legs in hopes of coaxing the twelve-hundred-pound beast to her feet. She snorted miserably. He tried again and then gave up, gasping.

"She have twins?"

He'd almost forgotten Sophie—barefoot now, at a safe distance, clogs in hand, her face cadaverous, a camcorder hanging at her side, the red light on, filming.

"You see another one?" Norm glanced wildly about.

"Well . . ." She pointed hesitantly at the four-foot oval of pooled slime behind the Holstein's hind legs.

"Afterbirth," he grumbled. "Now put that damn thing down and hold on to the end of this."

He watched Sophie hesitantly wrap her lotioned hands around the rope and realized that asking her to help was ridiculous, but it was too late. He tugged until his wrists, shoulders and back hurt almost as much as his knee. The cow groaned again. Sophie slipped and shrieked, then straightened, seemingly too scared to tug on a goddamn rope. Norm couldn't compose himself. There were no more appearances he could muster, not with a calf stumbling around and its mother fading to black. Sophie was seeing him stripped and peeled, his calamity her drama. He wanted to shout questions at her: *What are you really doing here? Where'd you get your money? Are you writing a goddamn book? Did you murder your ex?*

Instead, he jabbed his Swiss Army blade into the Holstein's top rear leg. She jumped, and so did Sophie. Then he stuck the blade into the bottom leg and, getting no response, stabbed harder. Sophie yelped, but the cow didn't even flinch. He grabbed the CMPK, straddled her neck and pulled a needle from a vest pocket, feeling along her neck for her jugular and squeezing it until a vein the size of a garden hose bulged on the surface. A swift hammer stroke sank the needle, a red geyser misting his face.

"Hope blood doesn't bother you," he told Sophie. Actually, he hoped it did. He shoved the needle deeper, fastened a drip line to it and held the bag above the cow's head.

"What's that in there?" Sophie asked sheepishly, filming again.

"Calcium, mostly," he shouted over his own anxiety. "If I give it to her too fast it'll give her a heart attack, but, see, I can feel her heartbeat through my butt here." He paused until he felt it again. "So when it skips or hurries—like it just did—I pinch the drip line here and slow the flow."

"You can feel her heart through your butt?" Sophie asked incredulously, tiptoeing around the front of the cow as if it were a dragon. "What's wrong with her?"

Any number of things, starting with a broken leg and milk fever. She was obviously full of air, and that alone could kill her if she didn't belch. And she may have hemorrhaged. She was worth twenty-five hundred, easy. And that's all he shared with Sophie: "Twenty-five hundred bucks!"

He looked up in time to watch the calf drop in the field, then wobble back onto its feet. Norm groaned and sped the drip up again. After two thirds of the bag had been drained into her, she stopped moaning and stirred. Norm pulled the needle and stepped away as she tried to maneuver her hind legs beneath her. He told Sophie to yank on the rope while he shoved from the backside. She set the camcorder back down, then fell over twice. *Welcome to dairy farming, m'lady.* The Holstein finally had three legs under her. Norm shoved hard on her hip, coaxing her to adjust the leg that hadn't responded to the blade; it twitched finally, and with his grunting help she rose, the placenta falling from her and bursting open with a loud slosh of fluid that splashed up to his knees.

He heard a gagging noise but didn't turn to Sophie. His eyes were locked on the dazed cow, sturdier with each stride toward her stumbling calf, the rake of her rear and backbone as perfectly right-angled as any Holstein he'd ever bred. She licked her calf's umbilical cord, removing the newborn scent as fast as she could. Norm's mouth tasted metallic, but his gut loosened and he felt a sleepy gratitude as it occurred to him that both the mother and calf would be dying if Sophie hadn't come running.

He looked over when she groaned again, hands on her thighs and facing away as he took in her athletic backside. She wiped her mouth and tried to smile before staggering away. Norm sensed her recoil, her full-body revulsion. He glanced at his trembling hands, blood pooled and dried in the knuckle creases. What words could possibly make her stay? He suddenly wanted to tell her about the bribe he'd been offered that morning, slowing the story down whenever it got juicy, seducing her with the details. He started toward her as the old Chevy puttered into view with little Roony beaming out the window as if this were the grandest of days. Behind him came the clanging of the casino going up. Though Norm hadn't noticed it until right then, it sounded louder than ever, as if the tribe were racing to finish before some pious mob put a stop to it. He turned again to Sophie, who was farther away now and looking battered and bowlegged, as if she were the one who'd just given birth.

17

WAYNE WROTE through the night, his handwriting getting larger and sloppier the more exhausted and excited he got—reading, writing and rewriting until he crafted the last few pages from memory and the final crescendo of words felt like his own. "Gatsby believed in the green light, the orgiastic future that year by year recedes before us," he scribbled with throbbing fingers. "It eluded us then, but that's no matter—tomorrow we will run faster, stretch out our arms farther . . . And one fine morning—"

He climbed the stairs, buzzing with the beauty and wisdom of his prose until he glimpsed his reflection and remembered how little he resembled a twenty-eight-year-old F. Scott. He cracked the refrigerator, saw nothing but condiments and Bombay Sapphire—Fitzgerald was a gin man—and then searched for his medicine, feeling less and less like a daring young author.

Over the last few days, that little book had often struck Wayne as the most exquisite novel ever written. At other times it felt like an over-hyped novella about irrational love. Was it truly the great novel about American aspiration and self-reinvention? Or a melodramatic yarn about an eccentric's relentless obsession for a woman he couldn't have? What was so singular about that? How many men, he wondered, saw Sophie Winslow as the green light at the end of their dock? Maybe that was it, the commonality of Gatsby's misguided quest capturing what-ever irrational dreams we all harbor. Clearly, F. Scott knew he was writing a masterpiece; his letters proved it. He'd be dead before the critics and the masses concurred, but he knew. And perhaps such faith is essential for greatness. For several flickering moments that morning Wayne had felt the language thrumming through him. Now, though, it was gone. He lifted every newspaper and couch pillow twice before finding the half gram of skunk crushed beneath the next book on his reading list, *Ideas: A History of Thought and Invention, from Fire to Freud*.

He botched the first joint watching the Vanderkool boy drive his battered truck, erratically as ever, along Boundary Road, slowing to study something in the ditch before turning south on Assink. Wayne couldn't come to terms with the sudden fanfare. America loved a hero, any hero. But a kid who looked at you like he was trying to make a Picasso out of your face? Whose paintings gave you that same *good-for-you* sensation you got watching the Special Olympics? You might as well call every cloud, tree or wave a work of art. Every tweet, flutter and fart.

He messed up the second roll obsessing over Madeline. He'd never had the stomach to confront her directly. In fact, he'd almost encouraged her mischief because he was so delighted she wasn't as proper and predictable as her sister. And after Marcelle died, he'd let Maddy do whatever made her happy in hopes she'd stick around. But he'd never pictured this reckless apathy. When he called Nicole for advice, she'd grunted and said you can't help people who don't want help. She had volunteered, though, that she and her mannequin husband would make an appearance at his sixty-fifth. Beneath the words, it sounded like a chore.

By the time he finally had a serviceable joint, he questioned whether he should smoke it. His pain was mild, and he wanted a clear head when he called Maddy. He tended to get more philosophical with each toke, until he crossed some line and turned ridiculous. It was the same thing with wine, and he'd always made a point of never writing op-eds or art reviews with more than two glasses in him. He had a flame poised, his eyes on the Vanderkools' dinghy full of blooming yellow tulips, when he heard voices up the street and remembered Sophie's invitation.

WHEN TONY PATERA explained that congressmen were coming out for a briefing, she'd encouraged him, while oiling his arthritic toes, to do his show-and-tell in front of her house. Where better to make his case? But she was surprised he took her up on it, and even more astonished by the gallant mob that spilled out of BP vans in leather-soled shoes. Seeing as how there was nobody else to charm, the politicians all fussed over her, flattering and touching her. And when she brought out the camcorder, Sophie was greeted anew with warm smiles and improved postures.

She listened to Patera begin his spiel, stating the obvious as if it were revelatory. "Yes, this is, in fact, the border. Right here. And, yes, this two-foot ditch is actually one of the better barriers we have. A few hundred yards down the street"—he pointed toward the Cascades—"is where we now get drive-thrus on almost a nightly basis. All we have to guard our busy sector, ladies and gentlemen, is a small, dedicated crew of overworked agents and outdated motion sensors. So, as you can imagine, if we're not already in the neighborhood when some smuggler or alien—or bomb-toting terrorist—crosses . . ." He shrugged. "We frankly can't respond to more than half of the sensor alarms. That means we mostly catch the dumb ones, understand? Still, we're on pace to apprehend twice as many illegals as we did last year, and we've seized over twenty thousand pounds of marijuana over the past twelve months, up fivefold from three years ago. However, we're still probably intercepting less than five percent of what's rolling through. Keep in mind that two thirds of Canada's marijuana production is grown indoors in B.C." He wagged a finger to the north. "Unfortunately, the Mounties don't have the manpower and Canadian courts don't have the will to do much about it."

The politicians eyed their security expert for confirmation or skepticism, but the grim little bureaucrat in the gray suit ignored their glances and didn't veer from his melancholic pacing.

"When the Mounties do try to enforce," Patera continued, adjusting his Eagle Scout tie clip, "seizures usually involve basement operations with about five hundred plants yielding several one-point-five-million-dollar harvests a year. So we're talking real money. With ninety percent of their market down here, of course they get it across in every way imaginable. If they don't want to risk sneaking it through the ports of entry, they jump this ditch here or run it through raspberries over there or put a car on each side, make sure we're not around, then throw some hockey bags over, drive off and *poof*—gone before we can respond. Plus, they can paddle across the bay in kayaks, or use helicopters, snow-mobiles and remote-controlled planes."

"What about putting in concrete barriers like we have in front of the Capitol?" twanged a Tennessee congressman who later called the Canadian border *the Mexican problem squared*.

Grateful for the question, Patera smiled and paused for effect. "That was my first idea, and I'll tell you what I was told: Every civil-liberties organization would start howling as soon as—"

"They're gonna howl," the congressman interrupted, "no matter what we do, aren't they? If we made decisions based solely on who's gonna complain—"

"What about cameras?" asked a politician Sophie recognized by his grimace.

Patera bunched his lips, as if the gravity of what he was about to share warranted a moment of silence. "Cameras," he said. Then, after another flamboyant pause, "If we had about thirty cameras on fifty-foot poles at strategic locations, we'd have a level of deterrence I truly believe would be tantamount to tripling our force at a third the price." He cleared his throat. "As some of you know, this subject has been studied before, but its time has come."

"How much?"

That's when Patera rolled out a number half again as large as the one he'd shared with Sophie. While "fifteen million" echoed through the crowd, he evangelized about other surveillance options, including tethered blimps and unmanned drones and even a virtual fence made up of ground-based radars that could all serve as "force multipliers."

"As you well know, most of the bud is run by organized crime. And there's also evidence that terrorist cells in Canada are getting into the business to raise money, which of course means the war on drugs has, in fact, become the war on terror. And yes, sometimes, with a combination of teamwork and luck, we get a twofer like we did last month when we caught a suspected bomb-carrying, bud-smuggling terrorist." He talked right over a mumbled question. "This has become the border of choice for almost anybody trying to sneak into our country. During the past two months alone, we've caught illegals from Algeria, Bosnia, Bulgaria, France, Germany, Iran, Iraq and Mexico—yes, we increasingly catch Mexicans flying to Vancouver on Japan Airlines and walking across here because it's so much safer. Plus, there's Morocco, Pakistan, Romania, Sri Lanka and . . . I'm missing one." He winced, feigning concentration. "Oh yes, *Nowhere*. We caught two people from Nowhere."

Patera nodded while the politicians scrambled to catch up, but his clever little parable about the Prince and Princess from Nowhere was interrupted by a sudden drizzle and Wayne Rousseau scampering up to the Canadian edge of the ditch under a red umbrella.

"Greetings!" he called.

Sophie zoomed in on the exhausted professor, then panned as Patera's distracted audience prepared to meet a real Canadian despite the rain and the muddy ditch between them.

"As the interim spokesman for the great nation of Canada, I ask you to please not let my good friend Chief Patera persuade you that you need to throw more agents at this border or pay for intrusive cameras or whatever other placebos he's hawking."

There were chuckles and smirks in Patera's direction while the scrawny Canadian lit his homemade cigarette beneath his umbrella. The wind was drifting the wrong direction, so all they could do was whisper uncertainly, their nostrils twitching, sensing this might be the story from their border tour.

"Meet Wayne Rousseau," Patera announced, "retired UBC history professor, known for his frequent—"

"Political science!" Wayne corrected. "I taught poli-sci."

"—and colorful condemnations of the United States," Patera concluded grimly. "We're in the middle of something here, Professor, so if you'd please—"

"Anybody care for a puff?" Wayne asked jovially. "Come on." He hinged forward, readjusted his footing, extending his arm, smoke curling, eyes bulging, grin quivering. "Meet your enemy."

After a flurry of clumsy jokes and questions, Patera mustered a mumbling explanation of Canada's medical marijuana laws.

But Wayne didn't stop talking. "Jefferson and Washington grew this stuff. I mean, seriously, how can you get more American than that? Yet despite the wisdom of your founding fathers, you all keep climbing over each other to—"

"I must correct you on that point, sir," bellowed a stout Michigan congresswoman. "Washington and Jefferson did grow hemp, as did many colonists. However, the hemp they grew wasn't smoked, nor was its psychoactive potential known at the time."

Her colleagues shared grins and winks. Something else to recount: Miss Piss 'n' Vinegar sparring with one of Canada's pothead intellectuals.

Before anyone could praise her command or bluster, Wayne shouted, "Marijuana's medicinal and psychoactive properties have been known since ten thousand B.C.!" He shrugged. "Didn't you people learn anything from Prohibition? Oh, that's right. I forgot superpowers don't study history. *You spread freedom.*" He shifted into a folksier drawl. " 'Americans have freedom of expression and freedom of conscience and the prudence to never use either.' "

"Who are you misquoting now?" Michigan wanted to know.

"Twain." Smoke leaked from Wayne's lips. "Your very own Mark Twain, madam."

"Mr. Twain," she snapped, "never even graduated from elementary school. And no offense, Professor, but I personally don't find your country's peculiar brand of socialist monarchy worth emulating."

While Patera retreated toward Sophie's driveway, wheeling his hands like a coach calling for a huddle, Tennessee wondered aloud whether the retired professor was the ideal spokesman for Canadians. But Wayne's audience lingered until he flicked his roach into the wind and everyone stopped to watch it bounce off his umbrella. Then they began their retreat, exchanging glances and smirks. "Yeah, you all go back now!" he taunted. "You've been standing in Canada illegally this entire time anyway."

Michigan turned and pointed at the concrete pylon on the far side of the ditch.

"The border's at forty-nine degrees, correct?" Wayne shouted, then lobbed a pocket-sized GPS across the ditch.

Michigan stepped forward and snared it angrily. She squinted at the screen, wiped it with her sleeve and squinted again, three colleagues crowding her. "I'll be damned," she muttered, glancing again at the border pylon.

"What's it say, madam?" Wayne mugged for Sophie's camera, then broke into a lecture she'd heard twice before about the border being an arbitrary line agreed upon in 1846 by politicians in London and Washington, D.C., and how finding and defining the 49th parallel soon turned into a comic competition. Charged with divvying up the overgrown West, dueling teams of ill-equipped astronomers and surveyors felled trees as wide as houses and stacked cairns every twenty miles or so. Biased sextant readings resulted in multiple-choice borders, with incoming settlers discovering an American, a Canadian and a compromise in-between. In the early 1900s, intrepid border teams headed out on a Monty Python–like quest to find the original rock piles and establish permanent monuments along a still imprecise line that nature erases every few years anyway.

"And now it's your turn," Wayne shouted to the suddenly attentive politicians. "You all are the latest act in the ongoing comedy *to see what can be done, by God,* about securing this nonsensical border you know so little about."

The discussion that then broke out looked like it gave Patera a toothache.

18

THERE WERE too many cows on their feet. The scant and soggy beddings should have been replaced weeks ago, and manure was stacked in random gnat-swarmed piles. The parlor was a mess, too, with cow agitators everywhere.

Brandon stooped through the narrow passages, looking for what was injuring their right flanks, something sharp enough to bruise but not puncture. He noticed plenty of limps, too, that the cows weren't able to hide. And all that was before he went into the sick barn, which was where his father found him petting 89.

"What're you doing out here?" Norm demanded.

"You didn't call the doc, did you?" Brandon asked, without looking at him.

Norm hesitated. "What's he gonna say besides *iodine, iodine, iodine*?"

Brandon unshuttered two windows. Gnats and dust motes twirled in the trapezoids of light spreading across the floor.

"What're you *doing*?"

He opened a third window, and the barn brightened evenly. "How many got it?" he asked, dropping to a knee to examine 43's inflamed udder.

"Thought we had an agreement." Norm sighed. "A dozen or so."

"So what are the others doing in here?"

"Precautionary."

Brandon inspected more infected udders. "It's normal mastitis?"

"That's right."

"You back-flushing the—"

"Thought we had an agreement," Norm repeated.

"We did." Brandon looked away. "You were gonna take care of the cows."

"This isn't your concern for now, son."

"What do the tank numbers look like?"

"What did I just say?"

Brandon heard a chain jingling on the latch to the insemination box, strode over and tied it off on itself. "Where are all the calves?"

"Where they always are."

Brandon removed the rubber stop from a rarely used gate and secured it to the bare latch of the barn's busiest one. "I only saw three out there."

"That's right."

"Have some abortions?"

"A few."

"Quite a few? Lepto?"

Norm nodded. "Looks like."

Brandon glanced around for signs of rodents. "You vaccinating them before they're freshening?"

Norm nodded again, almost imperceptibly, as if his head were getting too heavy to move. "You saw the Holstein calf, didn't ya? She's as healthy as they come."

Brandon climbed a stepladder to shift the slant of a barn lamp, then tucked the ladder out of sight.

"Think I'm not concerned enough?" Norm asked. "That I'm not adequately alarmed?"

The question didn't register with Brandon, other than that it was loud enough to agitate the cows. He once felt a calf's heart rate double at the ring of his father's cell phone. "You're feeding calves milk from the sick cows, aren't you?"

Norm's jaw loosened and his palms flipped upward.

"Can tell by how the Jerseys are walking that they've got bacteria in their joints."

"So I'm not concerned enough," Norm said flatly. "Is that it?"

Brandon noticed half of the sick cows staring in the same direction. The slightest shift in texture, color or noise could spook them; something as simple as this bale wrap flapping halfway across the barn could drive them nuts. "Could I see your knife?"

"Well, I'm plenty concerned," Norm told him. "And I've got a few other concerns too, in case you haven't noticed."

Brandon cut off the loose plastic, wadded it into a ball, then folded the knife, handed it back and looked away from the deepening creases in his father's splotched forehead. "Either you call Stremler or I will," he said, surprising himself.

Norm took a deep breath as if gathering a shout. "I'll call him," he whispered. Then, after a pause, "We need to talk about your mother."

Brandon blushed. "Her mind's just in a slump," he said, repeating Jeanette's favorite theory.

"She couldn't even remember where she parked yesterday, Brandon. Walked around for an hour before she finally called."

"Menopause alone," Brandon said, rolling out another of his mother's lines, "can make women foggy."

"Not like this. I think we should get her to talk to somebody about it. We need to know what's going on."

"Some doctor putting a label on her won't help. Memory's a muscle, and she's exercising it every way she can."

"Well, I just think we need to encourage—"

"She doesn't have Alzheimer's," Brandon half-shouted, then strode to the near wall, snatched Norm's new red Darigold hat from its nail, flung it out of sight and marched from the barn.

AFTER DINNER, he drove out past Dirk Hoffman's reader board—SPEAK ENGLISH—and cruised East Badger Road before rolling up

Garrison to where the Sumas River curled around three oaks and dairymen dumped stillborns for roosting eagles.

He hadn't more than spun by since he'd returned from the academy, and he'd never seen so many bald eagles there, almost a dozen per tree, fixed to limbs and stoic as gargoyles. He watched them perch, fly and land, chatting in high, delicate voices better suited for pigeons. Their ramshackle nests were the size of satellite dishes, as if designed to look even larger than they were. What did a bald eagle have to fear? Try to find self-doubt in those pale yellow eyes that can discern a snow goose's limp from a couple miles away.

Brandon set up the birding scope he now carried everywhere, which Dionne touted as further evidence of his commitment to the job. He studied how amazingly comfortable the couples were with each other, then zoomed in on the largest female, her head a thousand miniature white feathers above a shimmering black vest and a bleached tail. She pushed off into effortless flight across the field and along the river before returning to the same exact perch, gripping it with talons as sharp as X-Acto knives.

When his gaze finally wandered, he noticed cottonwood seeds floating around his head like weightless snowflakes, then the snags, stumps, deadheads and boxy bales drifting down the muddy Sumas. The hay, with its bright orange twine, looked so fresh he figured it must have tumbled off a flatbed that morning, but he couldn't think of a bridge or even a farm upriver likely to lose bales to high water. He wished he hadn't spotted them in the first place because he soon counted six more. No telling how many he'd already missed.

The hay was followed by three conspicuously clean logs lacking the slimy green-black sheen they accumulate after a week in water. He glanced up at the eagles, reluctantly back at the river, then climbed inside his rig and drove down to the Lindsay Road bridge, where the water widened and shoaled amid stones the size of softballs. He parked and baby-stepped out on the slick rocks, slip-sliding to his knees in the central flow, to retrieve stranded or drifting bales. The weight of the first one felt about right, seeing how it was wet, but he felt plastic beneath the outer layer of hay.

He heaved seven bales onto the bank—at least one must have beached higher up—and ripped one open. Packed in thick plastic were compact buds the size of his thumb. He stalled for a moment, mumbling to himself before climbing the bank for a better view. Nobody was in sight, either in a car or on foot, and nothing but fields beneath the darkening clouds. Yet he knew people were despairing somewhere, the only glitch in their plan being that he'd decided to check out the eagles after dinner. "Got buds," he reluctantly murmured into his Motorola.

By the time Agent Talley joined him, his mouth full of sunflower seeds, Brandon had found two more corked logs—Rick called them "coffins"—and the missing bale, too. After inspecting a bag of buds, Talley started photographing everything. "Chief wants to e-mail pictures to some congressman tonight. He's absolutely loving this shit. You wouldn't believe how jacked up he was when you called this in."

Brandon was helping him stack buds photogenically in the back of his rig when Talley pulled a crisp newspaper from the cab and handed it to him. "Brought you something. Seen this?"

It wasn't the same woman Brandon had stored in his head. She was turning toward the camera with the ambushed surprise you see in Hollywood tabloids, her sprung eyes making her features even more dramatic. The photo was such a close-up that you could make out her individual hairs below the *Seattle Weekly* masthead and above the headline STUCK IN LIMBO HELL. "The Border Patrol calls her the Princess from Nowhere," Brandon read, read it again, then stumbled into the next sentence.

"Heard some Seattle comic held that up last night and went, 'Talk about the perfect date!' " Talley said, slipping into a stage voice. " 'No small talk. No past. No baggage. And we want to build fences to keep these women out?' "

Brandon read on, but the story wasn't actually about her. It was about how some illegals were put in a detention center, given blue jumpsuits and issued numbers; the princess was 908, just like Pearl was 39. Most of them, it said, would wait in cells for months, even years—if the government didn't know where to send them—before they ever got a hearing.

"You hear your bomber woke up?"

Brandon shook his head numbly, suddenly so queasy he had to sit down in the dirt. Rain started falling, abruptly and aggressively, as if the heavens were getting in on it, if a little late, trying to raise the river and help the smugglers float their weed.

"They say he's fine, but I guess they kind of fucked up on identifying him."

Brandon looked up into the rain. "What do you mean?"

"Just what I said."

"Well, who is he?"

"Fuck if I know." Talley pulled on a hooded jacket. "Gonna give me a hand with these buds here?"

19

MADELINE'S DRIVER pulled away from the maple-shaded split-level with blooming daffodils out front and a basement full of flowering cannabis. It was the fifth crop she'd tended to that day without a glitch, no longer feeling any relief that it had all passed without consequence. This illicit work still induced more adrenaline than nursing orchids and lilies but it had, as odd as it sounded, become a job, though a lucrative one.

The more she learned about Toby's empire, the less anxious she felt. Cars parked in front of every house. Bills paid in advance. Lawns mowed. Christmas lights hung through December. Even the birdfeeders were always full. The growing logistics, too, were reassuringly consistent: Tables and lights on wheels. Holes drilled through water-meter paddles, the power meters bypassed on any op with more than ten lights. Five to six crops a year. Fourteen to seventeen pounds per harvest. And not one of the twenty-three sites she'd nursed over the last two months had been busted or ripped off. Still, Toby grew clones simultaneously in different locations to guard against losing a popular strain all at once. And he only hired people without records, reasoning that first-time offenders got such light sentences they were less likely to turn on him. All of which made everyone more careful, especially because Toby paid better than the competition.

Her driver, Michael, a large UBC undergrad, chattered about his door-to-door recruitment efforts on the American side of the border.

She pretended to listen earnestly as the beige minivan navigated Abbotsford's rush-hour snarls until Essendene Avenue turned into Old Yale Road and ascended through suburbs, past freshly logged lots into neighborhoods of mock castles with vast stone decks, climbing still higher to where unique houses hung on blond cliffs and the hill narrowed to a rocky cone and the fresh asphalt finally ended in a broad, Lexus-jammed, clamshell driveway beneath a stilted glass palace.

The giggling woman standing by the door didn't appear naked until Madeline got close enough to see her gooseflesh and paint smears. She swapped smiles, then glided through a candle-ringed vestibule into a high-ceilinged room with glass-jeweled chandeliers and a long oval table shoved against a wall cluttered with appetizers. Michael offered his hand and guided her past two more painted women—one so skinny that her hip bones flared like handrails—and through dozens of conversations and past strangers with intentionally messy hair to an even smokier room with a ceiling higher still and a massive diamond-shaped window overlooking the checkerboard of American farms. Her hand felt lost in Michael's, tugging her toward a glass table behind which towered a loud, tuxedoed man with a gummy smile and a lime-green cannabis leaf stitched into his black cummerbund.

He spoke nonstop to four queues of people, interrupting himself with impersonations and asides, throwing his voice and answering questions with the agility of an auctioneer. Four tiny glass pipes billowed, the puffers smacking lips, closing eyes, wincing and squinting as if trying to remember something important.

"None of these are Vietnamese B-grade," he told them. "This ain't your father's schwag. These are all pedigreed triple-A sativas or indicas or some mischievous blend thereof, cured for at least a week and usually two. You won't see any freaky growths on these buds. No purple fungus here, my fellow stoners. Check out the crystal resin on these colas. You're looking at the Bordeaux of buds."

"Taste tests," Michael explained, pulling her aside so she could see the featured buds displayed on gold platters. "Marcus," he said, pointing at the man in the tuxedo, "loves these things." The chalkboard menu read:

Afghan Dream
Time Warp
Burmese Incredible
Love Potion #2

Marcus was coaching the testers now to notice the various flavors, the orange mango chutney of one bud, the bubble-gum fruitiness of another, and to differentiate between the swift body high one strain offered and the soaring cerebral rocker of another.

Once Madeline ditched Michael she explored the noisy house on her own, taking in the neon sculptures and erotic ceiling murals, repetitive reggae pulsing from invisible speakers in every room.

All Fisher had told her was that it was a Drug War Party and everybody who was anybody in the B.C. cannabis scene would be there. A retort, he explained, to a flurry of news flashes, the first being *Forbes*'s report that indoor pot was now B.C.'s largest agricultural export, followed by the U.S. drug czar accusing Canada of flooding the States with "the crack cocaine of marijuana" and citing the Space Needle Bomber as proof of the link between drugs and terror. "If you buy B.C. bud," he concluded, "you are sending a check to the terrorists."

Madeline wished she'd showered and changed. Nobody else looked like they'd just come from work. Searching for a bathroom, she stepped into a den and found six men and one woman slouching on green leather couches and loveseats, listening to some mohawk in a wheelchair. "We're all just animals," he said, his voice reminding Madeline of pull-cord dolls. "I mean, we're essentially advanced squirrels, aren't we? Not as agile, but smarter. Or maybe glorified possums with big brains? Well, pretty big." He cocked his head toward the lanky redhead sucking gently on a bubbling glass bong, smoke rising toward her exaggerated lips.

"Actually, we're fancy monkeys," said a man with a braided beard and an eyebrow ring. "Fancy monkeys clinging to an average planet orbiting a dying star. Who said that, anyway? Chomsky, or was it Leary? Whoever. Doesn't matter. It's as true as—"

"Hey!" Fisher crossed the room, smoke curling from his fingers, the spotlight swinging from him to her. "How ya like Marcus's crib?" He unfurled his spindly arms as if to hug her, but to her relief simply passed a joint. She inhaled hot smoke while Fisher introduced her as "Dahlia," as he'd said he would. To her unease, they all nodded knowingly, including the big-lipped redhead who walked the loaded bong over. Madeline wasn't interested, but didn't want to seem rude, so she sucked the flame into the bud-packed bowl and gave it a steady pull until the ashes plunged. Her vision blurred on the exhale as she strained to read the sign on the wall: OVERGROW THE GOVERNMENT.

"Toby here?" she asked once Fisher escorted her out.

"Doesn't usually show up at these sorts of things," he whispered. "But he's got business here tonight, so we might see him."

He led her upstairs into what felt like a trade show, complete with T-shirts, banners and bumper stickers for sale. In one corner, a television was replaying drug-czar sound bites. In another, a manic bald guy was barking out the virtues of vaporizing hash as an "alternate ingestion strategy." People lined up to get vaporized while a gap-toothed, green-haired woman sold grams and seed packets with the bored efficiency of a blackjack dealer. Another woman was pushing a petition. "Decriminalizing isn't the answer," she insisted. "It still forces everything underground." Men bobbed in agreement, lost in her cleavage.

Fisher pointed out a refugee from the U.S. drug war and veterans of the B.C. drug courts, including an old attorney milling around like a proud grandpa. The King of Cannabis himself floated up the stairs a moment later, his head tilted back and nostrils flared. The visionary who'd invented the Marijuana Party and recruited candidates to run for everything from premier to the Vancouver school board had an entourage that included Toby, in corduroy shorts and a bowling shirt. His tanned forearms rippled as he opened a bottle of artesian water and handed it to Madeline. He'd barely made eye contact before he laid his left hand on the small of her back, gently steering her away from Fisher.

People rose from couches and beanbags to meet "Dahlia," whom Toby introduced as one of his top growers. Poached eyeballs settled on her respectfully, as if his flattery made her not only famous, but also desirable. They asked cloning and curing questions and whether she agreed that seabird shit was the best fertilizer until Toby grabbed a decorative sword off the wall and whirled it around with such grunting intensity and precision that it left Madeline sweating and others cheering. He put the blade back, his sword hand returning to the skin right above her belt, a disconcerting numbness creeping south from his fingers. He suddenly excused himself and stranded her with the king and his acoloytes, who took turns speculating on what effect the drug czar might have on local and federal politics and their legalization crusade.

The king offered no opinion until he finally decreed: "It's Prohibition all over again. That eventually ended because it was impossible to enforce, because alcohol was everywhere." He lit a joint the size of a breakfast sausage, and everyone waited for him to finish popping smoke rings. "A year after legalization, every stoner will grow an assload of weed and stick it in pickle jars like they used to." He held the joint at eye level, rolling it between thumb and forefinger as if focusing binoculars. "And people won't be able to smoke all they grow. It'll go moldy long before they can suck it down. And they won't be buying pot, either. Please get that through your heads. They will not be buying pot. Maybe one percent of the Canadians now making a decent living at it will still be in business, okay? The best will survive, yes, but nobody will be building these McMansions—not that I don't love yours, Marcus. Trust me, this gold rush will pass, and that's a good thing. Yes, there eventually will be Amsterdam-style coffee shops on every block in downtown Vancouver." A cheer rose up. "And yes, people will be cooking with cannabis, breaking up buds, sprinkling them on salads and smothering them with balsamic." He licked his dry lips, and everyone but Madeline laughed on cue. "And the persecution of people who enjoy cannabis, my friends, will finally be over. It's not if,

it's how fuckin' soon. And you know the biggest reason it won't happen soon enough?"

"Parliament's fear of pissing off the U.S.?" Marcus suggested.

"Not quite," he replied. "It's the U.S. government's fear of its own
pharmaceutical companies. Follow? That's the real cartel that needs to
get busted up. For now, Uncle Sam does the 'ceuticals' bidding by
demonizing this sacred plant and keeping citizens from realizing they
could grow this medicine in their backyard and not have to pay Pfizer
and the others for Vicodin, Vioxx, OxyContin and the rest of that hill-
billy heroin that's killing people faster than any natural drug ever has
or will. Am I wrong?"

After a respectful pause, a man with teeth the size of thumbnails
said, "Word."

Madeline smothered a giggle, excused herself around Marcus, then
glided downstairs and outside into a Zeus-like view of the valley. The
farmlands were spiked with almost as many steeples as silos, and out to
the west the spangled water broke free of the islands toward the smoldering belt of orange clouds and the rest of the world. There was no
sense of any border, no visible line of tension other than the narrow
clear-cut in the sloping foothills north of Baker's glaciered belly.

She had no idea how long she'd been standing there when she
remembered promising to make her father dinner. She'd dumped everything she owned into his tiny guesthouse again after Toby's promised
alternative never materialized. Her father had stood long-faced in the
doorway looking at her mess, then told her about Mrs. Vanderkool.
Why had it taken until now to think about what he'd said? Perhaps
because Madeline couldn't imagine that the elegant lady who knew
exactly what to say when it mattered most was actually losing her wits.

She'd pulled Madeline aside a month after her mother's funeral,
when everyone was still avoiding her, and said, without preamble, "It
may get worse before it gets better, but I promise you that the older you
get, the more strength and comfort you'll draw from knowing that
such a beloved woman absolutely worshipped you."

Once her weepiness passed—*Jesus, I'm high*—Madeline felt relieved that she hadn't driven. She moseyed inside looking for a friendly face, then got wedged against the diamond-shaped window alongside a painted woman gnawing through a box of chocolates. "That paint hard to put on?" she asked, desperate for conversation.

"Ya don't put it on yourself," the woman drawled. "Least I don't. Maybe you could."

"All right," Madeline said, not sure if she'd been insulted. "Next party, I'll come painted and you can show up in this boring sweatshirt." She edged away, but the woman started talking—and it could only be to her—about all the shitty job offers she'd received that night and how she'd recently dumped an abusive boyfriend hooked on blow. Madeline nodded knowingly, as if she'd been slapped around by her share of cokeheads.

"First few times I did this I felt ridiculous," the woman admitted. "Now I don't even notice the looks."

"I once snuck Cuervo into a concert in Ziploc bags inside my bra," Madeline told her. "I've never gotten looks like that before or since."

The woman yawned. "You like tequila?" She reached behind her and handed Madeline half a pint. "Whaddaya think of the toilets?"

Madeline chugged, her mind racing for context.

"Haven't gone? They don't make *any* sound. I flushed twice because I thought there's no way it was that quiet." She looked at her earnestly. "Best job I ever had was as a hairdresser. I can cut hair, 'specially men's."

Madeline spontaneously offered her a job as a bud clipper at twice the going rate even though she didn't do the hiring. Luckily, the offer simply triggered more disjointed stories. When Madeline couldn't scare up a single thought worth sharing, the woman half-yawned and swiveled away, blue paint smearing and bubbling along the muscled groove of her spine.

Once again, Madeline realized she was getting even higher. She hadn't noticed the music in how long? "I-I-I-I seeeeem to recogniiiiize your faaace." She went looking for Fisher or Michael or anyone who could haul her away, trying not to look too alone, wondering how much time had careened past. She roamed up the stairs, needing the railing and hoping Toby wasn't around to see her in this condition. Amazingly, all that remained of the trade show was a smattering of stoners and a couple pressed passionately against the floor-to-ceiling window.

She followed snorting giggles downstairs into a room where three strangers were sprawled on a round bed and two others draped across couch arms, everyone smirking in the same direction. She leaned against the doorjamb and slowly placed the cartoon faces on the large flat screen. *The Simpsons.*

Had the party adjourned to some secret room? She peeked into the bonging den where she'd first seen Fisher and saw an ensemble of sober-looking young men—many of them teenagers—listening to Toby's thoughtful murmurs while he secured a map with ceramic bongs. It was too late to retreat, though his attention was the last thing she wanted. "She's with me," Toby said, nodding toward an open chair. Then he began pointing out where the thirty-two cameras were going in, one by one, as if they were military targets, everyone crowding in, mumble-cussing.

An older guy with a swashbuckling mustache was eyeballing her. She felt her stomach roll and jerked her sandals beneath the chair, looking everywhere but at him.

Toby crossed the den and examined her pink eyes. "You okay?"

"Where's Fisher and Michael?" Her lips felt numb.

"I'm your ride," he said. "We're almost done."

"Maybe we go back through the main portals?" someone asked as Toby returned to the table.

"No way." Toby snorted and shook his head. "They do randoms now. They'll search thirty cars in a row if they feel like it. And if one of those dogs signals, they'll pull you in for a secondary and you're toast."

"What about the truck routes?"

Toby bobbed his head. "They X-ray every load, and bud jumps out unless it's packed with something of identical density. I've got somebody working on that, but we're not there yet. So for now we've just gotta do what we do better than we're doing it. Once those cameras are up, we'll reevaluate."

Madeline listened to Toby's money-handling tips and watched him hand out business cards of realtors, car dealers, insurance agents and bank tellers who took cash without questions, all of which made her worry about the awkward bricks of U.S. hundreds stacked in the bathroom closet of her father's cottage.

Spiraling downhill in Toby's restored Impala, she tried not to look at the fuzzy lights, but every time she closed her eyes her belly moved. He lowered her window from his side, and she heard her head bounce off the frame. "Sip this." She felt a cold plastic bottle in her left hand and brought it to her mouth. Pepsi.

Toby was talking again, but it might as well have been a baby babbling. She had a vague sense he was following the speed limit, using blinkers, staying in his lane, but when they got to Highway 1 they didn't head west. "You've got an hour or so, don't you." It wasn't a question.

She nodded helplessly, wishing she could go home, afraid she would now be expected to perform.

"Wanna show you something."

"What?" was all she could muster. She tried to raise the window, but either he child-locked it or she was pressing the wrong button. "I'm cold."

"Have some more Pepsi," he said.

A sip steadied her right before his first question about Brandon Vanderkool.

"Do you think your large Border Patrol friend would've known anybody at that party besides you?"

She hesitated, thinking she'd misheard.

"Well, he must have a mole, don't you figure? How else would he know to hang out on the Sumas on the one day we try to float a big load?"

Madeline sorted his words and waited.

"Sure you didn't see anyone he'd know?"

She shrugged warily. "He's not my friend," she said, trying to focus. "He's just a kid I knew who never figured out how to . . . act normal." She suddenly pictured him painting furiously. "He's an innocent."

Toby clucked his tongue. "An innocent who's bad for business."

Stars brightened the deeper they drove into the valley on dairy-lined Chilliwack Lake Road. Finally the pavement surrendered to gravel, then to dirt, and the Impala ground to a noisy halt. When Toby killed the lights, Madeline realized they were far beyond the last farm-house, where any scream would blend with the whine of coyotes. She thought she saw meteorite showers, but couldn't be sure. Toby stepped out and hustled around the hood to open her door. Her legs balked, as if warning her to stay in the car, though suddenly she was standing in mud beneath stars that quivered like fireflies. The only weapon she could think of was her keys.

He popped a heavy shovel from the trunk and shut it with a violent *thunk*. He handed her the flashlight, his thick fingers settling on her spine, a couple aggressive notches lower than at the party. They walked thirty yards, the beam illuminating a prior stampede of boot tracks. "See anything?" he asked.

She wanted to plead her case—I'm not a mole!—but instead looked for somewhere to run.

"Look around. Where do you think we're going?"

Her small circle of light bounced uselessly across a grim field of mud, orchard grass and tangles of scrapped barbwire. Her mind raced. He had to have more than a hunch that she'd tipped off Brandon. Had she talked out of school? She'd blown it somehow, that much was alarmingly clear. She poked keys between the fingers of her left fist and held the flashlight in her right, gauging its heft. Was all his affection at the party designed to make his grieving more convincing? Her heart wasn't racing so much as missing.

"Hear anything?" he pressed.

About Brandon? She tried to shake her head, but then . . . "Yes!" she exclaimed, as if the right answer might rescue her. "A humming sound."

He told her where to point the flashlight, then began digging what she tried not to think of as her grave, skimming dirt until it sounded like he'd hit a rock. She flinched when he peeled back a long rug and flung it aside, clods flying. The hum was louder now, sounding like a muffled motor. She focused the flashlight on what looked like a flat handle welded to a rounded plate of scratched yellow steel.

Toby squatted and tugged at the handle until the three-by-two-foot hatch popped upright, unleashing a nimbus of white light, as if the earth had opened to its bright core.

She staggered back until the six-hundred-watt halogens and the reek of blooming cannabis rendered her nightmare harmless and familiar.

"Holy," she managed. "What is—"

"We dug a hole with an excavator," he explained, "then lowered a gutted school bus down there and filled it with lights, tables, plants and a generator. You like it?"

Her giggles sputtered into tears, but Toby pretended not to notice. "Not a great producer by any stretch," he said, "but a worthwhile pilot. Least I think so. Not everyone agrees. I'll take you inside some-time when we're not messed up." He dropped the lid back in place, replaced the rug and dirt, then guided her back to the car, telling her where to step, his hand sobering now, the stars returning to fixed pin-pricks of light.

"Something came up tonight, an opportunity I'd like to offer you if it comes together," Toby said neutrally. "But for it to work, I can't have you showing up at parties like this, understand? What about the oth-ers? you might ask. Well, they don't matter to me. You do. And I need you to come off as a young woman who has a real job and takes care of her dad."

A new fear rolled through her: She already knew too much to ever get out. That's what this was about.

He locked her elbow inside his. "How would you like," he asked, now as gentle and solicitous as a department-store Santa, "to live in a nice house less than a kilometer from your father, right there along the border?"

20

NORM MADE himself wait, not knowing if he should check his box before or after the postal truck came, finally deciding he couldn't stand it any longer. What if the postman saw the money? If there was any, of course. He knew it was the longest of long shots, but he craved a shot, any shot, the image of free money rushing through him. Norm had clearly said no, hadn't he? By now, he had reworked the conversation so many times—including all the kid's insinuations and *discreetly*s and *prerogative*s—that what he'd said and what he *wished* he'd said were getting jumbled. He hadn't agreed to anything, he knew that much, but who knew how it was interpreted? And what if they wouldn't take no for an answer?

A minimum of $10,000 on the twenty-third day of the month? He had no idea what *that* would look like. Rubber-banded stacks of hundreds in a manila envelope? With a note, maybe: *Appreciate your business, Mr. Vanderkool.*

Wasn't he due for a break? Doc Stremler would be there within an hour to lower his glasses and hand him a verdict, a lecture and a bill. Most of the night, Norm had been straightening and cleaning the barns until he had to ice both knees, his mind circling to Sophie's recurring suggestion that he let her "work" on his legs. His curtness with her in the field seemingly hadn't dented her desire to get to know the savages. She'd waited a couple days, then swiveled over and crawled right back inside his head to remind him of her "good-neighbor discount."

He shuffled toward the end of the drive, glancing up Boundary

Road at the new motion-detecting video camera on the fifty-foot pole. It was hard not to take it personally. Everyone heard the cameras were coming, but they went from rumored to ordered to installed practically overnight and felt twice as intrusive as Norm expected. They'd be watching if he took a leak in his back ten, or if he strolled over to Sophie's for a good-neighbor special. . . . And there were more coming, including one right on Northwood. He took a breath and shuffled toward the box, simultaneously hoping the money was there—so he could breathe!—and that it wasn't, so he wouldn't have to plumb his weaknesses any further. He'd clearly said no, so it wasn't as if he'd been compromised, right?

"How're the cows?"

Christ! He looked up to find Wayne leaning against the shady side of a telephone pole on Zero Ave. "Just great," he snapped.

"Excellent." The professor matched his sarcasm. "What about your boat? When do you launch that cruise ship?"

"Don't know, Wayne. When're you gonna patent that lightbulb?"

Wayne laughed. "I had no idea you knew about that sort—"

"I find it interesting," Norm said, breathing harder, "that Edison's father was run out of Canada." He scrambled to recall what Patera had told him, bungling the details right out the gate and wishing he could start over.

Wayne grinned and waited.

"He got ousted from Canada," Norm said, "as I recall for—"

"As you recall."

"For rising up against a government that wouldn't even stand up to the Brits."

"Did someone read that to you?"

"Seemed pretty well documented," Norm said, the insult sinking in.

"Oh, let me guess, you're gonna tell me Edison was an opportunistic bastard who stepped on everybody for his own glory."

"He sure doesn't sound like your kind of hero."

"Who stands up to that sort of test, Norm?"

"What?"

"Who looks like a white knight after all the historians and gossips get done with him?"

"I think Thomas Jeffer—"

"Banged his slaves."

"We don't know that."

"Yes we do. A smart guy who knocked up Sally Hemings."

"Well, I think it's safe to say that perhaps Jesus has withstood the test of—"

"*Modern,* Norm. Someone we actually know something about."

"Well, I'd argue—"

"We are not gonna have that discussion. Who stands up—musicians? Mozart was an ass. Wagner hated Jews. Sinatra was a mobster. Edison was just fine, Norm. Brilliant, actually. Can we just admire the guy and accept his imperfections as part of the inev—"

"You're defending Americans. Now, that I like."

"Not at all. I'm saluting greatness and originality without pretending to know or to judge anybody's integrity."

Norm didn't even know what he was arguing. One potshot about Edison and he was suddenly trapped in Wayne's dissertation. "What about Ripken?"

"Who?"

"Cal Ripken," he snapped. "The shortstop! Retired now, but he played in over twenty-six hundred straight games with—"

"The help of steroids."

"Bullshit." Norm turned to leave, furious with himself. "Ben Franklin!" he bellowed over his shoulder.

"Ah, Franklin!" Wayne exclaimed. "A great man, an amazing man, but the first great American xenophobe, eh?"

"Whatever you say." Norm headed toward the barn, waving off further objections. He watched through the slats until the professor hobbled home, then stepped into the light as a baby-shit-beige Mercedes puttered into view. Unbelievable. He'd forgotten Stremler always arrived a half hour early.

The vet didn't acknowledge his wave, just parked in the shaded grass beneath the willow, pulled on rubber boots and organized the supplies in his trunk like a fussy angler preparing to fish a river. He responded to Norm's warmest "Hello there" by asking, without even a glance, why he didn't have any casino signs up, especially considering the proximity. That was another thing Norm had forgotten about the doc, that he'd started the anti-casino crusade.

"You in favor of gambling, Norm?" Still no eye contact.

"Of course not."

"Then why don't you let folks know?"

"Because I don't see how putting up signs changes a damn thing."

Stremler finally eyed him. "If you don't believe in democracy, why don't you move somewhere you don't have to participate in one?"

The old vet loved words like *democracy* and *proximity,* and if there was a four-syllable synonym for a one-syllable word he'd brandish it. "I think that might be a slight overreaction, doc." He took a breath. "The casino's already half-built in case you haven't noticed."

Beet-faced, Stremler marched toward the parlor at a pace Norm couldn't match. As usual, he insisted on seeing months' worth of records before cocking an eye at the first cow. He studied the daily milk temperatures and yields as well as the monthly stats on somatic cell counts, leukocytes and production, zeroing in on cows that had calved in the last year.

Norm had downplayed the situation, not wanting it to sound urgent. There was a little mastitis issue the doc could check out whenever he had the time. No hurry, he'd said, but he hadn't expected it to take three weeks for Stremler to show up.

The vet reshuffled the papers, agitated. "Where are the other culture tests on your bulk tank?"

"You've got 'em all there."

"This is January and April, Norm. We're in late June here."

"Those are the most recent ones I've got."

Stremler pulled his glasses off, baring eyeballs with too much white around the edges. "Hey, you need to wake up here. This isn't going to just spontaneously rectify itself. You need to pay for a culture test and a staph antibody test so you know exactly which animals to segregate. You can't ballpark this sort of thing. And if you've dried some of these chronics twice already and they're still carrying and their production's still low, you've got to cull them. Understand?"

"You want to actually look at the animals," Norm said, "or are the numbers more important to you?"

Stremler put his glasses back on to gauge this insolence. "I'd have been out here weeks ago if you'd told the truth about how bad it was." He started toward the main barn, explaining that while he'd skip lunch he most certainly wasn't about to be late for an appointment at an Abbotsford dairy.

Norm remembered that Stremler fancied himself an international businessman, seeing as how he stuck his arm inside some Canadian cows and rolled so freely over the border with his fancy NEXUS pass.

After inspecting a dozen scabbed udders, the vet looked up as if he'd just caught Norm mounting one of his heifers. "Some of these definitely have staph. The carriers need to be milked separately *or not at all*, and a few need to go on antibiotics immediately."

Moments later, he jabbed Norm with another glare. "Your bedding's atrocious. They need *dry* wood chips or, better yet, sand. Your cows are disconsolate, Norm. You need Brandon, or someone who understands them, out here full-time."

Norm forced a laugh. "He's a little busy these days, if you haven't heard. I've got Roony helping me out."

"Roony Meurs," Stremler said like a prosecutor calling a witness, "is the only dairyman I know who's contracted both farmer's lung and salmonella *twice*." He inspected another udder. "That boat of yours still taking up prime barn space, Norm?" He didn't wait for an answer. "The security around here looks nonexistent. Anyone could walk right up to your bulk tank."

"Yeah, and who, exactly, would want to?"

"Don't play dumb, Norm. You read the papers, I presume. Ever hear of botulinum? Someone empties a bottle of that in your tank, it gets trucked away and mixed with the rest of the milk supply and half a million lives are at risk."

Of course, Norm thought. That's how the chief got his little speech on the subject. Patera and the doc had a weekly chess game, and he couldn't imagine anything more excruciating.

"You consider selling, Norm?"

He snorted. "Who'd want a dairy in this shape?"

Stremler curled an eyebrow. "Developers."

Norm grunted, amazed. "You're asking if I'd sell to a developer?"

"Suit yourself." Stremler crouched beneath one last cow. "My farm looked like this, I'd off myself."

Norm hesitated, speechless. Did he hear the doc correctly? It was barely more than a whisper, so maybe he missed a word or two. "You'll send me a bill?"

"No, you'll write me a check right now." Stremler glanced at his Rolex. "Two hours, so four hundred."

"Nice big number to round up to," Norm mumbled, his gaze just low enough to miss Stremler's eyes. No matter what the bill, the vet always acted put out when you paid up, as if you'd stiffed him. Norm fumbled for his checkbook and did the math, multiplying two hundred by forty by fifty-two; at this rate, the doc collected more than four hundred grand a year belittling bankrupt dairymen.

By the time Stremler's Mercedes left a diesel fart for Norm to stand in, it was midafternoon and he realized that he needed food and a nap or he'd soon collapse. But before heading to the house, he lit a Winston, scanned the ditch for Wayne or any other voyeurs and revisited his mailbox fantasy, shutting everything else out—the vet's warnings, his own worries about Jeanette and Brandon—to indulge in a moment of uncluttered hope. He took a long drag, bent at the hips and peered inside the box at a stack of envelopes and colorful flyers, then lingered in the unsympathetic glare, his heart slowing as he clumsily flipped through them, the only one with any girth returning canceled checks. He opened a letter from the Dairymen's Association and scanned the bold type until he came to: "In the hands of a terrorist, a dairy is every bit as deadly as a chemical factory or a nuclear plant." Norm grunted and, out of habit, thumbed through the junk—flyers for home security, farm equipment scams and another E.D. pitch even cheaper than the last. Pretty soon they'd be giving erections away in the mail. He felt around the sides and top of the box, in case something had been taped to the interior, but his hand came out empty and black.

Could the postman have considered the money outgoing mail? Not that Norm could do anything about that. Excuse me, did you happen to find ten grand in my box? And what if he was the only one on Boundary Road *not* getting paid? Didn't the hustler say he'd come back if more of his neighbors didn't sign up? It occurred to Norm that he was probably being watched right this minute by people laughing their butts off. He glared into the glassy reflections in the Canadian hills until he felt something crawling on his free hand and glanced at a large honeybee that flew off when he flapped his fingers. He didn't see where but didn't have to wonder long, because something brushed his right cheek and left a burning pinch below his eye. He squealed, dropped the mail, spiked his cigarette and lurched around, one hand holding his face, the other whirling spastically.

Had to be Dunbar's goddamn bees. He brought crates in every spring to pollinate his laser-straight raspberry rows and—surprise, surprise—the bees stuck around all summer to repeatedly sting Norm, who was more than mildly allergic. Big Tom slipped out of dairy farming into berries and out of an old wife into a young one as easily as most people changed clothes. Then, without a flicker of shame, came his platoons of illegal workers.

Norm was cursing Tom and patting the swelling pouch beneath his eye when a Plymouth sedan rolled to a stop in front of him as if God had hand-delivered somebody for him to yell at.

A stout woman with hyper-blinking eyes and a raised birthmark on her neck rolled down her window and looked at him. "Mr. Vanderkool?"

"What?" he barked.

"I'm pulling over." She parked precisely on the narrow shoulder and walked toward him slowly, nervously. A young man popped out the other side, straightening his collar and hurrying to catch up. Were they from the Ag office? Had Stremler already spread the word? But the woman's stricken expression made Norm suspect it was far worse than that. Picking up his mail, he braced himself for the worst news a parent can hear. He stood there already feeling guilt and loss and Jeanette's delayed reaction and the burden of meeting everyone else's expectations about how a parent should grieve. Though by the time the woman closed in and said two words—"Rebecca Wright"—he recognized the diction and body language of a regulator.

"I'm with the EPA," she added, polite but hardly friendly. She'd no doubt learned that a sense of camaraderie is the last thing you want to conjure with someone you'll likely have to punish. "We're here to inspect your compliance with the Dairy Nutrient Management Plan," she said, handing him an envelope like she was serving a warrant. "We've been recording high levels of nitrates and algae growth in Fishtrap Creek. So we'll need to take a look at your waste repository."

"Lots of dairies in this valley," he bluffed, an ache spreading across his chest.

"Not upstream from where we sampled, Mr. Vanderkool." Her eyelashes were fluttering so fast that Norm worried they'd fall off. "And with tribal shellfish and salmon protections being what they are, sir, we're required by law to take action if we find low dissolved-oxygen levels . . ."

He wasn't listening, wondering simultaneously how much chest pain could be chalked up to indigestion and whether this was a warning or a raid. He'd heard about the EPA showing up with aerial photos that left no doubt about who was polluting what. "What about all those new cul-de-sacs?" he asked, hating his petulant tone. "You policing them, or just going after the lowest hanging fruit?" He'd heard Morris Crawford deliver this argument much more diplomatically, but now he had to finish it. "We can't regulate ourselves back into yesterday, Ms. Wright, can we?"

Her lip tremor made him feel like a monster. "We're here to inspect your operation from the parlor to the pond, Mr. Vanderkool. The sooner we begin, the quicker it will be over. Depending on what we find, we might issue a warning. This would put you on notice that there appears to be a problem, in which case you may want to contract with someone to figure out a better site for your lagoon."

He snorted and then glared at her with his good eye, the other swelling itself shut. She took another collarbone-heaving breath and looked away. Norm turned his scowl on the trainee, who reared back as if he'd been slapped.

Beyond them, Jeanette was standing beneath the green willow in the driveway, her hands clasped. Across the ditch, Wayne Rousseau was propped against a railing, blowing smoke, his slender shadow falling over the deck. Norm pivoted on his good knee until he saw Sophie, in turquoise shorts, pinning colorful wet panties to her clothesline.

Nobody wanted to miss this hanging.

21

BRANDON FOUND it hard to track what Patera was saying. We need to be on full alert, as usual. Nothing has changed, understand? So be ready. His words seemed secondary to the urgency he radiated to seize the moment and show—ASAP!—that these new cameras were worth every penny. The sooner their benefits were proven—no pressure!—the sooner the people who listen to us (him) and believe in us (him) would be rewarded. See what I'm getting at?

In other words, as McAfferty later summarized, it was a pep rally to jack up the stats and justify the border cams, preferably right away but definitely within the next reporting period. Not that the chief was suggesting they do anything differently. No, everybody was doing *great* work. Best sector in the country—if you factored in the complicated terrain and mandate and the sophisticated smuggling and, well, there's just no doubt about it.

Patera then packed the agents into a dark command room where he beamed like a game-show host in front of thirty-two wall-mounted screens, fourteen of which were already connected to video cameras. He asked the technician to demonstrate what Charlie 1 through Charlie 14 were providing beyond live views of vacant trails, empty fields and desolate streets, including, Brandon noticed, a stunningly familiar strip of Boundary Road.

The technician panned, tilted and zoomed Charlie 1, showing how it could read license plates or detect motion more than a mile away. Not even McAfferty's Big Brother cracks could dent the chief's enthusiasm. "Think of it," he gushed. "This sector's first HQ was a farmhouse on Double Ditch Road, back when agents were called Mounted Watchmen and the focus was bootleggers and a potential Chinese invasion. An agent's qualifications were somewhat less stringent then: You had to be six feet tall, of good moral character and own a horse." He waited out the polite chuckles and McAfferty's audible yawn, then asked the tech to show how video could be instantly retrieved, explaining as she did so that the cameras tape in forty-eight-hour loops, with infrared lenses kicking in at night. "This is completely different than a sensor call." He balled a fist and pointed aimlessly with his other hand. "We'll know the difference between a deer, a smuggler or local traffic— if not immediately, then shortly thereafter. So we'll need prompt responses, understand?"

His eyes flitted across the room, skipping over the gum-smacking roadies, lingering on the seven new agents transferred from the southern line and finally settling on Brandon, a full head above the others, his eyes fixed on Charlie 7. "We're here to stop terrorists," he said, as if for the first time. "That, of course, is our foremost responsibility. And it is with considerable unease that I must inform you of interagency warnings that something may be plotted for right along our sector in the near future."

"Chief?"

"Yes, Mr. McAfferty."

"Could these warnings be any more vague?"

Patera attempted to grin. "We all wish they were more specific, but the fact is we have to be prepared for everything from armed terrorists and smugglers to an attack on the food supply."

Brandon couldn't believe what he was watching: his father—at a distance, but clearly his father—limping out to their silver mailbox, glancing around, then opening the box and apparently trying to fit his head inside it.

"Has our so-called Space Needle bomber woken up yet?" McAfferty asked.

"Yes, I'm told he has," the chief said briskly. "But I'm not sure of his faculties at this point, nor where the FBI stands with its investigation."

Brandon tuned out the murmurs and watched his father thumb through the mail, then stick his arm in the box again.

"So is he that Algerian the FBI claimed he was?" McAfferty pressed.

"I don't believe so, but I can't say much beyond that." Patera pointed at the screens. "As you all also know, we are increasingly considered the front line of the drug war, so . . ."

Brandon jerked upright when the bored tech, awaiting further instructions, zoomed Charlie 7 in until the man practically filled the screen. *Dad smokes?* He angrily flicked his cigarette, as if he'd read Brandon's mind, then threw the mail on the ground and karate-chopped the air with his left hand while hopping around on his good leg.

"B.C. bud has become so lucrative it's attracting people who don't fit any profile," Patera warned. "Grandmas in RVs are potential smugglers. Everyone's a suspect. So we need to make the risks greater than the rewards, understand? And not just for smugglers, but also for local accomplices."

Before Brandon could figure out how to point out his dad's seizure-in-progress, a car rolled up and an erect lady and a little man popped out to help. Suddenly his father was himself again, bending stiffly at the waist to scoop up the mail and talking with his free hand. The camera angle widened until not one of them could have been recognized or identified.

"So we've got to ramp up to meet these challenges, just like we always do. Nothing has changed. But please realize that not only are we watching *everyone*, everyone's watching *us*. Continue what you're doing, but use these cameras to your advantage. I thank you all in advance for your ongoing vigilance."

Brandon was shuffling out of the station, feeling drained and as out of place as ever, when McAfferty broke into another impression. "Don't ever change, Dionne! Understand? That's not to say that the right kind of change can't be just what the doctor ordered, but I'm talking about a completely *different* kind of change. A *changeless* change!"

She wasn't laughing. "I thought this was gonna be a safe, quiet place to raise my daughter."

"It's the same place you thought it was," McAfferty said. "Bad shit has always passed through here, but now we're watching so closely that we see way more of it. You can't blame the colon for the shit, is what I'm saying." Then he waved Brandon over to his rig, where he pulled out two large color photos. "Don't ask me why, but intel's wondering if you can ID this woman."

The first picture was a low-angle shot of a beefy, curly-haired man in shorts, his right hand on the back of a slender woman, her face angled away. Brandon focused on the man's brutal forearms, carnivorous jaw, dimpled chin and meaty lips. But what alarmed him was her captive expression, her tight lips, her strained posture twisting her spine away from his touch. She didn't look like herself, but she didn't look like anyone else either. "Who's that guy with Madeline?"

"So you do know her," McAfferty said. "Easy to underestimate a plain-looking broad, ain't it?"

"If you saw her laughing, you wouldn't say that."

"Huh?"

"Plain."

McAfferty studied the picture again. "Whatever you say." He shuffled the photos. "Here she is with her boyfriend again."

Brandon felt his face heat up. They were both smiling this time, though not at the camera. She still didn't look happy. "Who is he?"

"Tobias C. Foster." McAfferty flicked the man's forehead with a fingernail. "World-class douche who's in with the Angels and arrogant as a senator. Trolls the border like he owns it."

"Where is this?"

"Looks like a party to me. Date's in the corner there."

"How'd we get these?"

"What, you worried about her privacy? Evidently the Mounties finally turned somebody."

"What am I supposed to do about it?"

"You just did it. Beyond that, hell if I know. She doesn't have a record, and the fact they needed your ID says they don't know shit. It's all part of this new international kumbaya we got goin'. You know, sharing, collaborating, circle jerkin'. Gather they heard you grew up next door or something, and seeing as how you're the new James Bond they probably hope she'll tell you where all the weed's coming across—not that the Canucks'll do jack about it. Just talk to her if you get the chance—not officially, for God's sake. You know, get caught up on when you two used to play doctor."

It was all Brandon could do to resist blurting that she wouldn't even return his calls. "She's real nice."

McAfferty smiled his mustache straight. "I'll pass along that too. Yes, it's Miss Rousseau, and she's a sweetheart with a beautiful laugh."

HE SPENT the warm afternoon trolling Blaine's simple grid for anyone who didn't belong, illegals slipping into idling cars or mules trying to blend into a city so small it was hard for strangers to loiter convincingly no matter how disinterested they seemed. Clothes air-dried over railings on the forlorn apartments abutting Zero Ave., where three young men were smoking in the shade and trying not to look spooked when Brandon wheeled into the lot. A block away, a shirtless red-haired boy with a fishing rod stepped out of an abandoned school bus into an overgrown yard. He gawked but didn't return Brandon's wave, then began casting into the dandelions.

Within minutes he was cruising spiffier cul-de-sacs, past happy children in bright shirts riding pricey bicycles on hosed sidewalks. He pulled over, opened his cell phone, scrolled down and stared at Madeline's number as if it were some code he needed to crack. Danny Crawford would just dial her and the right words would pop out, but what would they be? He pulled out McAfferty's photos again. It looked to him like she was in danger.

He hated the claustrophobia of the Blaine beat, the lack of open space, the recurring sensation that he was hassling or scaring people. He breathed deeper after rolling across the railroad tracks onto the pier, with the windows down, taking in the low-tide stink of diesel and clam spit. The BP shared responsibility for policing border waters with the Coast Guard and Customs, but owned just one leaky Bayliner. That was something else the chief was working on, McAfferty told him, a navy to go along with his two-chopper air force, his growing army and his Big Brother cams.

Brandon swept the harbor with binoculars, finding only year-round cormorants, hybrid gulls and a few mourning doves. Birds always were scarce when the heat rose, though he couldn't remember it ever being this bad by late June. He was scanning the tidal flats, desperate for a sandpiper or godwit, when he noticed, midway out, a large tangle of marooned driftwood. He spent several minutes surveying the midsized logs, branches and what looked like curved planks, then reluctantly drove back into town.

He feared he'd missed something important when he saw the overflow of BPs and Blaine Police at the Chevron, but so far as he could tell the only thing going on was a bloated city cop soliciting compliments on how much weight he'd lost. "You guys are killing me. Had to go down a shirt size here, in case you haven't noticed. Where's the love?"

Brandon lingered in the laughter with his lopsided smirk, then slipped away unnoticed to ask the breast-feeding barista a question: "If you had an old friend who wanted to see you, but didn't want you to think it was a big deal, what would you want him to say?" He took in her nearly invisible mustache, her askew eyes, her raspberry tongue flicking the chapped corners of thin lips.

"Lunch," she said. "Nothing intimidating about that. Dinner's a date. Lunch is more like, 'What ya been up to?' But you can't just call up and ask her out for lunch. That would sound like a date—and a boring one." Before he could ask her to explain, her baby started warbling and she waved in her next customer.

Now strolling through Peace Arch, Brandon tried practicing chit-chat with strangers, though everyone he approached acted annoyed. He asked a backpacking drifter what stood out from his travels, hoping for an exotic image. "Nothing, brother. Nothing" was all he got. The only people willing to talk were the aspiring derelicts who'd chime, "Hey, big man," as if they were pals because he hadn't busted them yet. But he couldn't sustain those conversations either, even if he parroted Dionne's effortless queries about where they'd had lunch or if they'd seen a decent flick lately.

He sat at the picnic table closest to the jungle gym and watched couples sprawled on blankets in the grass, chatting, touching, smooching or reclining in each other's armpits, baring their smooth stomachs to the gentle sun. He finally dialed Madeline and froze after the beep. "It's me," he said finally. "Brandon Vanderkool again. You will call me. . . . Okay?" Another pause. "Bye."

He bolted from the table, furious with himself. *You will call me.* He heard a mother and her screeching toddler in the bathroom and saw two Mounties lazily smoking near the Canadian gardens. Beyond the arch, a line of southbound drivers gazed at him across the sloped greenery, his size pulling them in, some pointing him out as if they'd spotted a moose.

He couldn't stand patrolling the park a moment longer. The only significant smuggler he'd ever caught sneaking across there was a man in a wrinkled suit trying to use a wedding party as cover. So Brandon strode at a determined diagonal past the weathered concrete arch, which needed grass seed along the worn patch where tourists stood to get photographed, and cut briskly through the jammed lanes without looking at the drivers, then hurdled the blackberry brambles down the small bluff to the flats.

Once he got his bearings he loped toward the storm debris beyond a dozen black-haired people, most of them shorter than swans, the smallest ones playing chicken with the waves, their black-and-white outfits flapping in the wind. Asians, probably Japanese or Chinese. He didn't care if they were illegals carrying buds or nuclear devices, yet one by one they stopped whatever they were doing and faced the enormous uniformed man jogging up, his massive boots sinking well above the soles.

Brandon waved and slouched, but it was no use. Whether tourists or illegals, foreigners always panicked at the sight of him. He pointed at the debris line behind them as they bunched together like swallows being chased by a falcon. After he slowed to a swift walk and offered his friendliest wave, one of the men raised his passport in surrender and started timidly toward him shouting, "Posspolt!"

Too anxious to smile, Brandon waved off the eager little man without slowing or changing direction. He heard confusion and relief in what sounded like Japanese, then blocked them out altogether as he took in the trove of surf-rounded logs the size of his legs, waterlogged boat planks, several head-sized boulders and tangles of snapped branches and boughs, as if a ship and several firs had been mauled, milled and spindled by the sea.

Almost everything would be floating again within an hour, so he quickly braced the heaviest, flattest logs with boulders and built a six-foot circular base on which he balanced more logs, filling any gaps with branches, and then stacked ship planks, their uniform flatness steadying the structure. Working faster now, the bigger waves closing in, he piled more logs, tucking and weaving branches and boughs vertically to tie them together, snapping them by hand and foot to get the sizes right, mixing ship planks with logs. There was plenty of driftwood to stack higher still, though on the water side he was already wading. Soon the tower was almost up to his shoulders, which were beginning to ache. When he next looked around, the Japanese were gathering driftwood at the lacy edge and handing the pieces to the *posspolt* man, who cradled them and waded above his knees to pass them to Brandon with an odd mix of urgency and gratitude.

Waves lapped against the base, the structure—now over six feet tall all the way around—was creaking but holding. A child got stuck in the mud, but there was no commotion beyond an efficient rescue Brandon was only dimly aware of. Then came a sharp cry, and he turned from his project and focused on the tiny people below him on the flats. The man who'd helped him was bowing, then the others, even the women and children.

Suddenly his radio blared. "Two-zero-five? You read? Two-zero-five?" He looked at the wet radio on his hip, back down at the Japanese, then up high to picture what it all might look like from above. Meanwhile, cameras were clicking. "Two-zero-five!" the radio barked. "Do you read?" White people were snapping pictures, too, and where'd they come from? Two of them looked familiar, though it would be hours before he remembered their names were Buford and Marty.

Looking into the brightening sky, Brandon saw a stout black-and-white bird flapping toward him. Given its rounded, low-aspect wings, it was definitely an alcid, yet too hefty to be an auklet or a guillemot. As it passed overhead, he saw its dark belly and its long orange and yellow bill. A puffin—this far from the open sea? His mind flashed to images he'd seen, from above and below, male and female, mature and juvenile, breeding and nonbreeding, in the Peterson guide, Pyle's guide and the *Field Guide to Birds of North America*. It definitely had the multicolored bill and bright orange legs, and as it banked back toward the bay, the blond hairlike pigtails on either side of its head swung into view. A tufted puffin! He pointed out this marvel, and the tickle in his throat morphed into a melodic humming.

22

NORM FLIPPED on the French station for his cows, though he doubted, regardless of what Brandon claimed, that this music relaxed them any better than country or classical. Insomnia had lightened Norm's worries because he couldn't keep his mind on a single fear long enough to generate genuine desperation. He'd played the freak rainfall alibi with the EPA lady, claiming his lagoon possibly had overflowed during the deluge. This wasn't true, but was plausible enough to make her hesitate, which bought him another month of monitoring that might include aerial photography. She left him with a straight-faced warning that if her agency concluded his manure pond was leaking into the creek he'd have to patch it or build a new one or face fines up to twenty-five grand a day. He'd muttered his solemn acknowledgment, though it was hard not to giggle, his mind calculating that $175,000 a week meant $700,000 a month and $8.4 million a year.

By the time Dirk Hoffman called mid-morning, firecrackers were already jolting the valley. Norm expected, once again, to be bullied into whatever Independence Day bluster his neighbor was pushing—a tractor parade, a hundred-dollar donation to the VFW or another invite to one of those parties where Dirk and Tom Dunbar dressed up like Founding Fathers to recite the Declaration. Instead, he was blindsided by Dirk's observation that he hadn't realized his tax dollars were paying Brandon to build forts on the beach, until he'd seen the paper. Norm yeah-yeahed through the accusation as he rifled through the mail for the weekly, flipping pages one-handed until he found the "photo of the week" on the next to last page. *Christ.* Dirk, tired of waiting for a reaction, shifted into bully mode. Would Norm care to join him and Big Tom in digging trenches along Boundary Road to stop the damn drive-thrus?

"Love to, but I can't," he said, his humiliation rising the longer he looked at the photo of Brandon, in uniform, standing by a chin-high column of driftwood. No headline or words accompanied the picture, as if it either defied explanation or didn't need any. When would the insults stop? Stremler assailed his cow care, the EPA doubted his honesty, the newspaper mocked his son and now his patriotism was being questioned. "I've got some calving ahead of me this afternoon," he lied.

"Can't those cows reproduce without you, Norm?"

Too worn out to work, too strung out to sleep, he wrote Jeanette a note and found himself in the boat barn for the first time in weeks, the drills, hammers, Sawzall, epoxy and varnish scattered exactly where he'd left them. He dusted off his rationalizations for the project, the most amusing of which was that it might give him honor. He picked up the bronze prop, feeling its heft, marveling once again at how the three blades retracted like wings on diving birds. He'd purchased it at his delusional pinnacle, thinking that if he used the best materials—$982 for a propeller!—he'd end up with a masterpiece. Now the fancy prop—a fixed three-blade at half the cost was more than adequate for any nonracer—felt like proof of his foolishness.

The bare hull sat inside the thirty-by-fifty-foot barn like a ship in a bottle, with barely enough room for scaffolding. The dark, curved fiberglass shell had been intimidating at first, as if it were some massive black Buddha to worship, not hammer, glue and screw. But eventually he'd found a rhythm. The farm was stable those first several years when he'd committed two to four hours a day to her. His mentors were Chapelle and Steward, whose books taught him how to turn plywood, fiberglass, epoxy and teak into decks, cabins and bunks. Those days he woke up proud and excited about his secret—talking about it might jinx it—that something magnificent was emerging, this eleven-ton jewel inside his shabby barn.

He gawked at the glossy hull from several angles, his thoughts merely fragments and splinters of larger worries and embarrassments until he settled on his latest vision of Sophie's good-neighbor special. He reached up and slid his hands along the aft of the hull, caressing the flawless gelcoat, his mind going dizzy and pornographic, closing his eyes as his palms slid over the stern.

"Hey!"

Startled to the point of gasping, he stepped back and watched Jeanette examine the hull herself, holding her arms behind her like a polite waitress. His belly told him she was *finally* grasping just how selfish and delusional it all was. Then she turned and said, "I forgot how gorgeous she is."

He coughed mid-swallow.

"Even unfinished. Really, Norm, I know you worry about how long it's taking, and what your parents would've said, but none of that matters. Your mother never liked the way I prayed, remember?" She closed on him, her hands still behind her back, and he smelled the Samsara she used to wear to distract him. "How could there possibly be a wrong way to pray?"

She pulled a magnum of Brut and two slender glasses from behind her back, then dropped her chin and peered up at him from beneath dark eyebrows, looking so gentle and forgiving that he swayed toward unconsciousness.

An hour later, he leaned on an elbow above his wife. Her skin draped past her jawline but her expression, smile and whisper were all timeless.

She'd picked him. That was the incomprehensible part. Cornered him with a smile on a random bar-hopping night in Bellingham. And even back then he was talking about building a sailboat that could go anywhere. Just saying it made Norm like himself more. Even his killjoy father called her a catch, despite her being a Volvo-driving, bra-less Bellingham environmentalist.

Norm blocked out Dirk Hoffman's afternoon fireworks and tried to enjoy the splendor of his youthful wife. But against his will he slipped ahead ten years to a vista from which he was looking back on this sliver of time, already wistful for now.

BRANDON TRIED to ignore the red cloth flapping beneath a fish truck as his least favorite day of the year crackled and thumped toward dusk. It could have blown off the road and wrapped around the axle, right? But now that he'd seen it . . . He reluctantly put his rig in drive and passed a VW pop-top, a produce van with *Playboy* mudflaps and a Ryder truck until he was tailgating the fish wagon.

His goal for this holiday shift had been to hide out near the Sumas border crossing and avoid talking to anyone. He didn't want to hear any more gripes or jokes about the border cams or the beefed-up patrols or *that thing* he'd made out on the beach. The flatterers and suck-ups, as Dionne called them, were just as annoying, buttering him with praise then sharing suspicions that were none of his business. Milt Van Luven pointed out how plenty of half-assed farmers suddenly could afford new tractors—"not to name names," which he then did. Almost everyone, it seemed, was turning into a griper, a gossip or a suspect. Even Madeline.

Before Brandon's beach art hit the paper, Patera had called him in for a confusing chat about being more careful about how he passed his time. "You need to find things to do in the vehicle. People are watching you, understand? They've seen you strolling around graveyards in uniform. What am I supposed to tell 'em?"

"Owls like cemeteries," Brandon said.

The chief exhaled through his nose. "Find things to do inside your vehicle. Listen to ball games."

"I don't like sports."

"What about crosswords?"

"I'm dyslexic."

"Spend more time in your vehicle."

Brandon stared at the flapping red cloth, which definitely wasn't signaling an oversized load. He called Sumas Customs and was transferred to the truck window, then got cut off. He didn't redial. It was almost certainly nothing, but now he had to check it out. Yet to do that he had to flip on his obnoxious lights and stroll up to the truck while the driver studied him in the side mirror.

People routinely went pop-eyed on him, so he didn't think much of the sweat bubbles on the man's forehead when he stopped behind the driver's window, at the don't-get-shot angle he'd been taught, playing his part and forcing the bulky man to twist his ruddy neck. "Can I see some identification, please?"

"What's the problem?" the driver whined. "I just went through all this."

"Where you going?" Brandon asked, following Dionne's advice to always ignore a suspect's questions.

The man snapped that he was headed to a couple grocery stores in Bellingham, that it was bad enough having to work on the Fourth without getting hassled.

Recognizing something in his pout, Brandon read the name on the license again—Gregory Olin Dawson—and pulled up the image of a slender, effortless golf star who was nicknamed "God" and sauntered the halls like a man in slippers, talking to girls with big teeth. "You went to Lynden High."

"That's right!" The sulk turned to jubilation. "And you're Brandon, aren't you? Couple years behind me?"

"Until I was homeschooled." Brandon handed the license back, wishing he hadn't pulled God over and dreading what was left of this conversation.

"Well, hey, good for you!" Dawson said.

"How do you mean?"

"Getting on with the Border Patrol and all. That is so cool. *Good for you.*"

Brandon considered the tone, the words, the coffee-stained smile. "Would you let me show you something?" he asked, back on script.

"What's that?" Dawson grimaced again, mouth-breathing. "Got a truck full of salmon here, and I'm already running behind."

"Grab the keys and step out for a sec," Brandon said, as casually as he'd ever delivered the line.

Dawson slid reluctantly onto the street, looking twice his high-school weight, his khakis stuck to his thighs.

"You've got some cloth dragging under here," Brandon told him, pointing.

"I do?" Dawson half-squatted to see for himself.

"I'll get it for you." Brandon dropped to the pavement, leaning on one hand, and saw the cloth was actually a dangling sleeve and above it was a plywood platform wedged below the axle. He craned his neck to watch Dawson's restless sneakers, then yanked on the sleeve. Hearing gasps and whispers, he slapped the board hard, twice. "Everybody out."

"Who the hell are they?" Dawson sputtered as Brandon brushed the dirt off his uniform and radioed it in. "I mean, really. Really! What the hell are they doing under there?"

Brandon asked him to stand behind the van on the shoulder, then helped four thin Chinese women emerge from their hot little shelf. They squabbled at a volume that could be heard for blocks, their noisy anguish focused on the flush-faced golfer.

Dawson started babbling even faster. "Seriously, I don't have any idea who these people are. Not a clue! I drive the van, okay? That's what I do. I don't look underneath it, ya know? Can I call ya Brandon? I mean, why would I look under there, Brandon? Who would . . . I'll be damned!"

Brandon handcuffed two women and cinched PlastiCuffs on the others. He didn't know what to do with Dawson, who was rattling off the details of his route and where and when these women might have snuck in there, stressing repeatedly that he'd never driven this particular van before. The longer he talked, the more believable he seemed, so Brandon tuned him out, flinching along with the percussion of nearby firecrackers until McAfferty rolled up, his spinning lights adding to the spectacle.

Mac listened to Dawson's increasingly breathless alibi, grunted sympathetically, unhitched a pair of handcuffs and said in his most understanding tone that there'd be plenty of time to discuss everything at HQ.

The women continued shouting at God in Chinese as he ducked into McAfferty's rig, their stretched faces, slit eyes, childlike bodies and odd vocal rhythms filling Brandon's memory banks.

SOPHIE POURED MORE WINE. "Still worrying about Maddy?"

"Oh, Lord."

"Have you always worried about her?"

"Ever since she declared war on normalcy."

"When'd that start?"

"A year or two after her mother died. Her sister just got more cautious and selfish. Went into the *investment* business and married an anesthesiologist who makes me yawn whenever he walks through the door."

Sophie emptied three envelopes full of photos onto the table. "And Madeline?"

"Opposite story. I don't know, maybe she needed a mother more. But suddenly she got extreme about everything. Wouldn't go sailing unless it was blowing thirty. Backpacking was too mundane, so she scaled cliffs with some longhair named Harley who drove a pickup with a sticker that said LIVE TO CLIMB, CLIMB TO DIE. She's obviously drinking and drugging and has no interest in college or knowledge or anything. She's still sweet, don't get me wrong, but the people I see her with, they all look so extreme, and I find myself wondering what people like that do for sex."

"Probably kiss each other very, very gently," Sophie whispered, arranging the photos in neat rows.

Wayne started to say something, then caught himself and leaned forward. "What's all this?"

"What do you think of 'em?"

"I have no idea what to think. What are they?"

"Pictures of Brandon Vanderkool's work in chronological order."

"What do you mean, his work?"

"Just that."

"He did all—"

"It's his temporary art."

"*Wha?*"

She reached over to the side table for the weekly. "You heard about the nest he built on the flats, right?"

MADELINE FLOATED on three tequila shots through crowded Peace Arch Park with Toby, Fisher, Marcus and the King.

She took in the whistling skyrockets, the fizzling sparklers and the colorful fireballs arcing from cannons or buzzing on the ground. She sprinted ahead when an errant glow-in-the-dark Frisbee spun into view, trying to catch it, laughing when she couldn't.

In the month since the big party, she'd tended more grows than ever. The work kept getting easier, and the cash was pouring in faster than she could deposit it. Most days, her life felt exciting and daring. The catch was that Toby increasingly acted as if he owned her, especially now that he'd set her up just down the street from her father in the old Damant house. To which he had his own key.

Just now, for no apparent reason, he kissed her too hard on the mouth, then excused himself to a picnic table where three leathered bikers seemed to be waiting for him.

"The King's gonna make some sort of statement before the show," Fisher whispered to her as they approached the arch.

Madeline glanced around. "To who?"

"Hey, there's television cameras here. Don't kid yourself. And knowing him, he's just itching to get arrested."

Madeline scanned the crowd, then saw one large camera on a tripod and several others on bulky shoulders barreling toward them.

"We stand tonight in solidarity with other B.C. cannabis activists to protest America's corrupt administration," the King announced amid the crackling family fireworks. "Its brazen disregard for Canada's sovereignty is now so complete it stations drug agents on our soil, which amounts to an undeclared war."

To Madeline, this was comic theater, but nobody was laughing. Two more cameras arrived as the crowd swelled and the legalization rant droned on. She watched Marcus break up a bud and roll and light a joint as casually as if shelling pistachios. He handed it to the King, who took several quick inhales and held his breath behind a long smile before popping sloppy smoke rings at a camera.

"You see where *Time* wrote that the world's best pot comes from Vancouver?" he asked playfully. "So evidently some of you reporters must be tokers, since how else would you know?" He handed the joint back to Marcus, who snuffed it as another cameraman closed in as well as Mounties and BPs.

Madeline looked for a head looming above the others, both dreading and hoping to see Brandon, but then stepped back, not wanting her face to pop up on her father's television as Marcus handed the King an American flag the size of a large bandanna. He dutifully held it up and casually lit it, the boos and jeers followed by a collective gasp when the right arm of his brown angora sweater ignited too. The King was still smirking and unaware until Fisher ripped off his jacket and tackled him with it.

HE REAMED the barrel of the .22 bolt-action Remington he hadn't fired in decades, his hands surprisingly steady. Might as well do it now, he figured, before losing the gumption.

He'd watched his father clean it so many times. You couldn't talk to Henri Rousseau while he did it, either, as if the wrong comment might set the thing off. He was like that on most things, his father's goal being to get from A to Z with the fewest words possible. Wayne trudged upstairs to peel back the pain.

"Your daughter 'round?" The question had been posed so casually that he hadn't made much of it. Having talked to the same undercover Mountie a dozen times, he'd never liked his mildewed smell, but he wasn't bad company for a cop whose office was an old Dodge truck. "Madeline livin' here these days?" he'd asked again, as if small-talking, the implications snowballing a few hours after the fireworks ended.

Wayne changed into boots and pants he hadn't worn in years and found a moldy ankle-length raincoat he didn't mind throwing out, then shuffled outside, rifle in one hand, flashlight in the other, the George Bush mask Maddy'd given him years ago tucked flat against his stomach behind a belt on its tightest notch.

He crossed the ditch at its shallowest, narrowest point near the Vanderkool house. He'd bumped into Jeanette a week earlier and couldn't stop thinking about her. It had always defied some universal law that such a bright, pleasant woman chose to stick by Norm. Nowadays, the gaps in her thinking were as apparent as slats in a fence. She'd start talking about immigration reforms and end the sentence on the subject of glaciers hauling boulders north and south. "We're new. The land is new. Everything about this place is new," she'd said. "You can't shut the door even if you want to."

He cut diagonally across Boundary Road, tiptoeing past the Moffats' depressingly tidy property—who could devote his life to running a leaf blower?—and the Crawfords' grassy driveway to where Boundary bumped into Assink, the coordinates of the newly installed border cam he could see from his deck.

The camera, just like the thirty-one others he'd read about, was perched atop a metal tower twice the height and heft of a telephone pole and ten times as obnoxious.

He slid the mask on before entering the camera's range, which made it hotter and harder to see, then trained the flashlight on the camera until the lens swiveled toward him. When he flipped off the safety and raised the rifle, he heard his father telling him to hold his breath and squeeze the trigger as slowly as possible.

The discharge was quieter than he'd remembered. He reloaded and backed up to improve the angle. Aim. The second shot felt and sounded true. Still, he loaded and fired a third, missing badly. He scooped up the cartridges and scampered down the cool street, hearing the whine of a vehicle clearing the H Street hill just as Norm's porch light flashed on.

Milking time already? When the car sounded like it was already on Assink, Wayne abandoned plans to cross near the Vanderkools' in favor of the wider span in front of the Crawfords', where his stumble-hop turned painful and splayed him on the Canadian slope of the ditch, scraping the knuckles on his rifle hand, his head finding something soft to bounce off.

23

I T LOOKED like an indoor Christmas-tree farm at first until she inhaled the hot sticky air and realized she was standing inside a cannabis factory the size of a Wal-Mart.

Toby monitored her every reaction while explaining in a confidential mumble that he and his associates had rented the mothballed brewery eleven months ago through a make-believe coffee company. Seedlings were grown in old beer vats ideal for controlling moisture and heat. The ventilation system filtered odors, the tile floors provided drainage and a thousand lights were hooked to computers.

Half an hour into the tour, Madeline's hangover came to a clammy boil as she waited, out of earshot, for Toby to finish chatting with three deferential tattooed men. She still didn't know what he considered her—top grower, confidante, lover or simply convenient front woman until his crew finished digging an underground op beneath the Damant barn. But why did he bother with that when he had something like *this*? Her vibrating phone interrupted her speculation, so she turned and quietly answered.

"Madeline?"

"Who's—?"

"Brandon. Brandon Vanderkool."

She waited.

"Your dad shot out one of our border cams last night."

"What?" She checked on Toby's conversation, where two others had joined in.

"He looked like a ghost, but it was definitely him, raising a rifle and *pow,* out goes the light. Actually, two shots," he said breathlessly. "*Pow* . . . and then *pow* again. I didn't say anything, though. What would you say about lunch?"

"Huh?"

She looked up in time to find Toby striding purposefully toward her, thigh muscles popping, arms swinging, the other men watching him, then her, then him again as he slit his own throat with an imaginary blade.

"Next Wednesday at McGiver's?" Brandon said. "Noon or whenever you—"

"Okay." She cut off before Toby grabbed the phone, checked the last number—*Restricted*—and unclipped the battery. He spoke calmly, levelly, but his eyes were hot. "You know it's easy to turn these things on remotely, and then they can hear everything. You know that, right?"

She gently retrieved her phone and battery from his strong fingers and put them in separate pockets, her body encased in sweat.

He crowded her. "Who was it?"

"My father."

"He's got a restricted number?"

"He's like that."

"What'd he want?"

"He's ill, remember?"

"So, what'd he want?"

"Milk and Motrin."

"Sure hope you've got all the bad decisions out of your system." He'd lit into her just that morning about getting too drunk too often and being stupid enough to be caught on television with "those flag-burning idiots." He gestured impatiently toward the drying room and more tattooed men, his thick fingers welded to her lower vertebrae.

After a long silence, during which she scrambled to make sense of Brandon's call, she brushed his hand away. "I thought you said you'd never work with the Angels."

It wasn't clear he'd heard her until a dozen steps later. "There's bad Angels and good Angels. I had to jump your shit for their benefit, all right?"

He led her past labeled drying racks and four sallow workers busily vacuum-packing buds with some industrial-looking gadget Toby swore cost $3,000 and was worth twice that. "People want fresh pillows," he said, turning it into a marketing jingle. "The buds don't get crushed. Even the resin doesn't fall off."

Three middle-aged women appeared to be aggressively washing clothes by hand in the next room, engrossed in their labor, pouring liquid through cloth filters into a bucket, again and again, a mound of pot leaves on the table next to them. When Toby asked if there were any dry samples, they pointed blankly at a tray cluttered with crumbly wedges the color of wheat. He packed a glass pipe and offered it to Madeline, who shook her head. "Be a sport," he said. "Does the body good."

She took a couple puffs and tried to imagine having lunch with Brandon.

Toby thanked the ladies, who didn't look up, and then led Madeline through heavy double doors into the largest room yet, with a vast expanse of more flowering thick-leafed pot plants than Madeline had ever imagined. He pulled out two pairs of paper sunglasses, and they strolled beneath the fierce lights through the indoor forest, the air wet and thick with the reek and sting of chemical fertilizers. "You're looking at what might be the largest indoor grow in the world," he told her.

The hash was kicking in so hard that she couldn't stop smiling, although she fully expected dozens of policemen to burst into the room slinging rifles like the one in her father's basement.

"Now you can see," Toby said, offering his warm, meaty hand, "why we need to come up with new methods of getting much bigger loads across the border."

24

JUST BEING in public, especially in church, felt like a bold statement to Norm. Doin' just fine, thank you very much, was what it amounted to. A hard patch, no doubt about it, but we're makin' it.

It was easy to pinpoint the source of his newfound optimism. One of Pearl's most productive offspring had delivered a perfect calf, and bottle-feeding a stunning new Jersey—maybe the next Pearl—cast a hopeful light on everything, even if the mastitis hadn't completely stabilized yet and the feds were monitoring his property from aircraft and his wife was having a run of bad days. A healthy new calf was a healthy new calf.

The pews were unusually packed, as if church were needed more now than ever. Even Sophie Winslow was singing hymns she'd clearly memorized despite the fact that she drove a Subaru with a Darwin insignia. Still, Norm's mood soured, as usual, when people lined up for the stale wafer and cheap wine, hands clasped over their genitals like soccer defenders. Doc Stremler, of course, stood right at the front, another showy display of his superiority. Dirk Hoffman was close behind in cowboy boots, tight Wranglers and his signature red, white and blue shirt. Chas Landers was there too, looking as benevolent as a monk. But Cleve Erickson? Out on bail, apparently. Patera told Norm that he hadn't put up any argument at all and even offered the agents coffee. While everybody knew his sons were punks, Cleve was one of the last true dairymen and Norm had never questioned his word. Now he was just a name and a mug shot next to "Conspiracy to Aid in

Smuggling Contraband." Norm had nodded earnestly when Roony insisted Cleve was innocent. How could he know what his hooligan boys were doing with those smugglers cutting through his farm? Well, Norm knew, and others, no doubt, did too. Nobody seemed astonished when Gil Honcoop got busted on the same charge, not after he'd made such a stink about the Minutemen. And June and Cleo Schifferli, caught three days prior with twenty-eight pounds beneath fertilizer sacks, weren't missing communion either. Posting bail apparently wasn't that big a deal. Then Norm noticed Dr. Dawson, dressed even more vainly than usual, a silk handkerchief flashing from his breast pocket, as if he were hoping to dress his way out of his son's disgrace for smuggling Chinese women into the country beneath a fish truck. Well, good for him, Norm thought, right up until the dentist threw him a look that suggested he should be embarrassed about his *own* son.

Going to church had been Jeanette's idea. "You're done moping," she'd told him. "Get dressed." Once again, it looked like they were the only two not lining up in the parade of hypocrites, but on a more sweeping glance Norm noticed that plenty of others were staying put. Didn't the Sterks and Moffats always take communion? His mind raced with implications. Looking behind him to see who else wasn't partaking, his eyes settled on a familiar young man who nodded so confidently that Norm returned the courtesy before realizing it was that hustler who'd visited his milking parlor. Michael lifted his eyebrows and nodded again, more dramatically, then looked away.

Wait! Had Norm just agreed to something? The audacity! The kid was even working the church? His outrage gave way to arithmetic—eleven days until the next potential jackpot in his mailbox.

As the flock bunched near the exit, he forced himself to get it over with and go ask Ray Lankhaar how he was faring. He excused himself from Jeanette, then set out across the worn carpet toward where he'd last seen the gored dairyman, but he didn't get far.

"Norman!"

Dale "Shit-to-Power" Mesick called everyone by his formal name and loved to chat, but Norm was in no mood for small talk and couldn't bring himself to congratulate him on getting free money from rich fools. Plus, the thought of paying Dale to haul his manure away and turn it into electricity and cash was too much to contemplate, even if it would help with the goddamn stream monitoring.

"You shoot out that camera, Norman?"

He flinched, as if slapped.

"Easy, now." Dale shifted into a French accent. "Everyone knows *Monsieur* Rousseau did it."

He nodded vacantly and was straining to overhear a scrum of Lynden ladies behind him discussing Brandon when Tom Dunbar waddled up from the other side and bumped him off balance.

This hulking bastard, who routinely proved he could knock you onto one foot with just a nudge, watched Norm wince. "Didn't know you were so gimpy there. My older brother just got his knee replaced—better than new. But maybe you're a little squeamish about surgery, huh, Norm?"

He shook his head and missed the follow-up question, his entire being focused on the raging tissues inside his knee. Once that subsided, he found Jeanette in the corner of his vision, looking perplexed, listening to Alexandra Cole and Katrina Montfort like she'd just met them. Behind her, Sophie was chatting, eavesdropping, pollinating.

He excused himself from Big Tom and had started back to rescue Jeanette when one of the raspberry millionaires cut him off.

"How's that boat coming along, captain?"

Norm scrambled to recall the man's name—Arnold, Ronald, Roland? "Slowly," he said.

"Yeah? Well, slow can be good. How 'bout the dairy biz?"

"Lucrative as ever."

"You must love cows, Norm. That's all I can say."

He grunted and scowled but had no escape route. Behind him, he heard more banter about Brandon, and beyond that a crescendo of whispers that could have been about anybody.

"Seriously, Norm. None of you like to admit it, but why else would you spend so much time with 'em? I mean *every day*! It's not for the money, so what other motive is there? Seriously, Norm. There's nothin' wrong with it. You just *love* cows."

"Not the way you would if you ever got alone with one," he growled, the rich farmer leaning in with his good ear, then horse-laughing as Norm hobbled off toward Jeanette, distracted again, this time by Ray Lankhaar's profile. He scrambled for the appropriate words before clumsily grabbing his shoulder. Ray reared back and gave him the once-over.

"Been meaning to see how you're farin'," Norm began, realizing anything he said now was too late so he left it at that. Even after getting skewered by his own bull, Ray still looked a good ten years younger than he did. His face wore time well, with plenty of lines but all working in his favor. He'd once heard him attribute his youthfulness to the quart of raw milk he drank every morning to wash down a thick slice of his homemade cheddar, which he humbly speculated could cure stomach cancer.

Norm was spared from his stand-off with Ray when an Everson farmer he vaguely recognized leaned in to ask whether they were interested in cheap feed.

"Possibly," Ray said. "Whatcha got?"

The farmer told them what all he'd grown, then rambled on about how everyone was sick and tired of paying to haul alfalfa over the mountains. Norm nodded along, his feed bill having jumped to $7,000 a month even with a lame herd.

"Count me in," Ray said, after the farmer laid out his mixtures and prices, and they both looked at Norm.

"I'm good for at least one load," he muttered.

"Hear your boy's quite the *arteest*," Ray said once the Everson fellow pushed on. "A regular Michelangelo."

"He was on his dinner break," Norm said mildly, though he could feel himself heating up. "You can do whatever you want on your breaks." Then he navigated the crowd again, trying to ignore the smug glances. Was he limping? How had all these people suspended aging, and what did *that* cost? Jeanette, he saw, was chattering away at

Sophie. He couldn't get there fast enough, a compulsion rising to bust up the conversation.

His eyes suddenly locked with Michael's. Halfway across the room, the kid nodded slowly like he was confirming something. Norm bit down and looked away, enjoying the ambiguity of it. What was the risk? Nobody got hanged for a yawn or a nod. He beelined it toward Jeanette, but Alexandra Cole blocked his path and leaned close. "Have you tried Aricept?" she whispered.

"Come again," he said, irritated, trying not to lose sight of Jeanette.

"Slows the deterioration, especially in the early stages. My aunt's got it too."

Norm pursed his lips, blinked slowly and excused himself, arriving breathless and sweaty next to the two women in his life. Either the church was getting hotter or he had a fever. Sophie smiled, bowed and stepped away from Jeanette, who looked lost and off balance until he casually braced his palm against the shoulder she was listing toward.

25

BRANDON RODE around the valley with Dionne at the wheel explaining that her daughter got sent home sick again because either her immune system had gone on strike or she was just allergic to this place. Brandon made listening murmurs while tracking wing strokes in the peacock-colored twilight and picturing what he'd wear to lunch with Madeline, imagining something considerably brighter than anything he owned.

When the call about the suspicious van on Markworth came in, they were already eastbound on H Street. So Dionne flipped the lights and pushed the Crown Vic up to eighty after they cleared a knoll and could safely straddle the yellow ribbon. "We're coming home tonight," she muttered as they hurtled past a 35 mph sign at 100.

The van could be nothing or anything. Brandon had caught sixteen distraught aliens since the angry Chinese women had crawled out from beneath Greg Dawson's van. His latest roundup involved an old Lincoln on Jones Road. The driver, who lived nearby in Deming, handled the conversation gracefully enough and everything checked out until Brandon noticed there was no backseat. When he lifted the blanket he found six Indonesians lying sideways, head to toe, to the back of the trunk. Half of them started crying, the other half began praying.

Now he braced himself against the dashboard and hoped for a pot bust or, better yet, a false alarm.

Dionne slowed the Vic enough to make the Markworth turn and guessed right again by skidding onto Badger and sustaining her speed until they almost rear-ended a long avocado-green van with tinted square windows. It abruptly cornered onto Sunrise, squealing and rocking but making the turn. Dionne skidded to a halt, popped it in reverse, sped backwards, then shifted into drive and carefully tailed the van through a new neighborhood, nearly a block behind, not wanting to cause a crash.

"This is the difference between us and cops," she shouted. "Cops wait for backup!" The van rocked on its shocks through the next two turns, and the neighborhood turned into farms. When Dionne closed the gap, the van bucked off-road into tall grass and stopped. "I got the driver!" she barked, the Vic grinding to a halt and Brandon's head bouncing off the roof. "You take the van!"

Then she was out, sprinting faster than Brandon imagined she could while he felt his own body charging into the night toward that van door—before it opened. His hand wrapped around the sliding-door handle and he swung it back in a fluid, full-body yank as Dionne shouted at the fleeing driver. The door careened to the end of its track and didn't stop there, ripping loose in a screech of crashing steel, all of which he heard but didn't see because he was counting twelve faces warped with fear, their skin pulling back from their eyes and teeth.

He held up his big hands to try to slow their hearts. "All right," he said, then more softly, "s'all right. Just stay. Just . . ."

Dionne jogged back, pushing the gasping driver in front of her, head down and handcuffed.

"What ya got?"

Brandon pointed inside.

"Jesus. You haven't"—she rocked at her hips, waiting for oxygen—"searched 'em yet?"

"No."

"Then why don't you have their hands where . . . What've you said so far?"

"Asked them to stay put."

She glanced at his empty hands. "Get it free of the leather at least, for Godsakes." Then she shouted at them to put their hands on their heads, first in English, then in Spanish. *"¡Manos arriba!"*

Brandon pulled his gun, pointed it at the ground, double-checked that the safety was on and looked into the childish faces. Dionne continued shouting in Spanish until he said, "They're not Mexicans. East Indians, maybe, or Pakistanis?" Several nodded vigorously, as if not being Mexican might help. "And they're couples, husbands and wives, I think."

"Watch 'em!" Dionne snapped, then searched them one by one as another BP roared up, lights strobing and twirling.

Brandon finally got a clean look at the wheezing, downcast driver, a man of about fifty who'd once told him that the beauty of mathematics rivaled any sunset. "Mr. Pearson," he said respectfully. "What're you doing here?"

He was still thinking about him hours later while sipping his fourth pint and half-listening to Dionne tell the agents how petrified the aliens looked after Brandon ripped their door off like a fucking sardine lid and stuck his big head in the van. "One guy's got a knife, another's got a thirty-two, but they didn't budge. Isn't that beautiful?"

She'd been talking loud and fast ever since they got to the saloon, telling and retelling their story to as many audiences as she could find. "I come back waving my Beretta, and they couldn't have cared less. Brandon doesn't even unsnap, just asks if they're okay, and they shit themselves. Then he turns to this driver who's so out of shape that even I could run him down and says, 'Mr. Pearson?' Turns out the dirtbag was his fifth-grade math teacher."

Brandon wanted to explain that Mr. Pearson was actually his sixth-grade teacher, and one of his favorites, but by the time he'd marshaled the right words and waited out the laughter, McAfferty had taken the floor.

"All math teachers should be considered prime suspects," he said. "Who better to understand just how lucrative and easy this game really is?"

Brandon could sense everyone else in the bar listening to McAfferty and sizing up the seven BPs, including three new transfers from Arizona. He sorted the faces in the back and saw Eddie Erickson jerk his head back, then twirl the shot glass in his fingers.

"The honorable Mr. Pearson was probably pocketing a grand or two per alien to get them to Seattle," McAfferty speculated. "So he was looking at twelve to twenty-four thou for two hours of sweaty driving. And maybe this wasn't his first load. Maybe it was his twenty-first, or sixty-first, know what I'm saying? If he's been in it a while he won't have any problem posting bail. And if it's a big operation, they have *can money* for just this sort of thing and he won't even have to post it himself."

Dionne asked McAfferty for a smoke and stuck it behind her ear, then listed all the habits she'd been trying to swear off: the two daily scones, the three triple Americanos, the four—now six, sometimes eight—ciggies a day.

"The resolutions we make at first light are always different than the ones we make at midnight," McAfferty said, the other agents tuning in to his mock sermon. "I mean, we all have high hopes for ourselves at sunrise. Take last Saturday: I start the day, as I often do, by weeding the cemetery and paintin' the church. I avoid every vice I've ever indulged until lunch, when I cheat on my no-dessert pledge. By dinner I'm itching for just one drink. Then, of course, I head out for another, just to be out with the little people, you know? Another three gimlets into the evening, I spring for a pack of Pall Malls. At this point, fuck the filters. Know what I'm saying? And even this dreary joint suddenly seems packed with possibilities, though we're clearly the new pariahs around here." He raised his voice. "Because obviously it's our fault that everybody's smugglin' something."

He dropped back into an intimate tone that had everyone leaning closer except for Brandon, who wanted to leave before something bad happened. "But see," he continued, "you gotta understand I'm in this crazy mind-set where I think being a pariah makes me sexier. And by closing time, it's just me and two ladies I wouldn't notice sober if they had strobe lights in their cleavage. Know what I'm saying? So of course I close in on the one who smokes because I figure she's living for *now*. And nobody, even at last call, looks at me and thinks long-term, right?" The agents jackknifed with laughter, and Brandon did his best to snort along. "But at the last minute I go for the gusto and try to pick 'em *both* up because I'm suddenly willing to gamble they're a package deal."

Talley poured another round. "So?"

"Turns out—and this will probably astonish most of you—they aren't interested in me. I mean not even slightly. So I swerve home and call my ex again, naturally—two thirty a.m. my time, five thirty Sunday morning there."

"How'd that go over?" Talley asked.

"Wasn't all that well received."

"There's some phone service," Dionne offered, "where you can block yourself from dialing certain numbers after a certain hour."

McAfferty grunted. "As if that would stop me."

The bartender moseyed up as the story ended. "Can I get you the check?"

McAfferty looked up, stroking his chin whiskers. "Trying to run us out already?"

"Not at all." The bartender blanched, his eyes flicking to the dozen patrons standing in the back corner.

"Would you please explain to those Rhodes Scholars," McAfferty began, as the waiter retied his stained apron, "that the Border Patrol doesn't police drunk driving and doesn't give a shit how impaired they get. And after you do that, another pitcher would be much appreciated."

All the agents except Brandon turned to swap glares with the gang in the back. The bar turned oddly quiet until Eddie Erickson shouted into the lull, "Hey, Repeat! Aren't you even gonna say hi?"

Brandon blushed instantly, desperately hoping nobody understood that the nickname was aimed at him. Certain facts or phrases used to pop out of his mouth again and again. It took years for Danny Crawford to convince him to ignore the taunts, but the end result felt the same. He caught himself rocking at the hips and went rigid. By the time he risked looking up, McAfferty and Dionne were staring at him. Then Talley said, in a low rumble, "Just say the word, big fella, and I'll gladly shoot the douche."

McAfferty waved silent any further commentary, and Brandon remembered to breathe. Mercifully, Dionne asked him to keep her company while she had a cigarette outside. She hooked his arm with hers while she smoked and talked about her daughter. Brandon was too rattled to follow the story, but her voice was soothing. "You're still juiced," she said finally, stepping toward her car and tugging on his elbow. "Let me show you my place, then I'll run you back out here for your truck."

She was so concerned about being quiet that Brandon felt like they were breaking into the single-story, vinyl-sided house on a corner lot in one of those new cul-de-sacs that looked so alike that he wondered how anybody could remember which one was theirs.

Dionne gave him a quick, whispering tour of a small, bland house that smelled of new carpet, then pulled him into a tidy room with stuffed animals and a framed eight-by-ten of a cross-eyed girl in a Girl Scout uniform. He was relieved to not be alone but felt dazed, then cornered.

"What if Dallas wakes up?" he whispered.

"She won't."

"What if the chief or somebody—"

"I'm not your trainer anymore, remember? And we're way off duty, okay? So this isn't sexual harassment, if that's what you're jabbering about. Believe me, I know what that is."

"What if—"

"Brandon, I haven't had sex in twenty-seven months. We are gonna have sex, understand?"

He studied the carpet art on the wall, a landscape like you'd see at Denny's. It had always puzzled him how people seemed to fill their homes with random art. In Dionne's case, it was apparently all about matching colors with her bedspread.

When she started unbuttoning, he wanted to say he was having lunch on Wednesday with Madeline Rousseau. "I'm sort of a virgin," he whispered instead.

"Shhh." Two more buttons to go. "We all are."

"What I mean is I'm not very good for this."

She snickered. "You're a piece of work, is what you are."

"Really, in bed, I'm not coordinated."

"You're getting me going with all this hot talk, Brandon." She unclipped her bra and groaned as her breasts swung free like pale sacks of bird feed. He'd never even seen her in civilian clothes before. He couldn't have been more startled if an owl had flown out of her shirt.

As she reached for him, he scanned the room for hidden ledges, reading lights, ceiling fans, bedposts and other threats. He'd never heard about anyone else hurting themselves during sex. Who else bit through their lip or pulled their groin or cracked their cheekbone on a bedside table? Of the three women he'd had sex with, two of them were animal-rescue types, including the caramel-skinned veterinarian's assistant who seduced him in the single-wide she shared with eleven cats, two cockatiels and a beagle named Gandhi. That romance lasted only slightly longer than the other two, but he missed her the most, in part because her face was so expressive that he had a better chance of knowing what she was thinking.

Dionne's lips felt rubbery against his, her ringlets of hair fascinating his fingertips. She tasted like cigarettes and smelled like teriyaki and cotton candy. She simultaneously kissed him and finished undressing— not as quickly as she wanted, apparently, because she was groaning with exertion. He tried to focus on her face because the rest of her was science fiction. In fact, even her head didn't look the same this close, either, so he shut his eyes and told himself to go real slow.

She stepped away, ripped back the sheets and exposed her marshmallow-white body diagonally across a double bed no more than six feet long and unfortunately outfitted with head- and footboards. He stepped out of his pants and leaned across the bed to kiss her, his feet still on the floor. She scooted to the far side of the bed and patted the open space beside her. He did his best, climbing in on his side and bending at the knees so his feet hung off the bed behind him.

She kissed him again. Her tongue bullied past his teeth to explore his mouth. Though trying not to panic, he felt the familiar loss of pacing and control. And his legs were tightening. He wanted to explain that he needed to be on the bottom, with his knees up, but she was pulling his right arm to coax him to roll on top of her. So he swung his right knee across, careful to keep his weight off her as he rose up and straddled her hips with his knees. He bowed his back and neck enough to kiss her, slowly, feeling his body respond, enjoying the softness of her skin, the resistance of her lips.

Keep it slow, he told himself. Make her happy. Slow and happy. But her hips were too wide to straddle for much longer and his thighs started to ache. He tried to lower himself gently, but it all happened at once.

"Brandon, I can't breathe."

Her weight shifted beneath him and the footboard dug into his shin. Once he realized where she wanted to roll him, he whipped his head in that direction to help and whacked his mouth and chin on the crescent moon cut into the top of the wooden headboard.

"Oh shit!" she whispered, her breasts shuddering with stifled laughter. "I'm sorry. I'm so . . . Y'all right?"

Brandon slid his tongue along his lip, unsure if he was bleeding.

"Mama?" The doorknob clicked.

"Just a minute, hon."

Dionne pushed him toward the side of the bed, where he was lowering himself when a tiny snot-muffled voice said she loved Georgie but that he kept her awake when he ran on the wheel. (It was hard for Brandon not to interject that hamsters run up to seven miles a night.) So couldn't they put Georgie in the living room, if she kept the cage so clean that Grams wouldn't complain about the smell? Before there was a chance to respond, the little girl started listing everything that had gone wrong that day until Dionne interrupted to tell her to save that talk for the morning. "Back to bed, now, sweetie. You need even more sleep when you're sick, remember, so—"

"What's wrong?" a much older voice asked. "What's all the noise?"

Dionne groaned. "Jus' me and Dallas, Mom."

A pole lamp by the door flashed on.

"Jesus, Mom, what're ya doing?"

Brandon recoiled his feet and wedged as much of himself beneath the bed as would fit.

"What am I doing?" the lady asked. "You're the one waking every-body up."

Brandon heard heavy shuffling toward the bed. He pushed up on a crossbeam to squeeze more of him beneath it, then eased it back down, compressing his ribs.

"Let's go back to bed," the lady said. Then, under her breath, "Smells like a bar in here."

"Good night, Mom."

When she whispered for Brandon to come out, he replied in a low muffle that he couldn't move until she got off the bed, although the truth was he was more comfortable beneath it. But then he emerged, holding his mouth so he wouldn't bleed on her sheets and started climb-ing back inside his clothes.

"I'm so sorry," Dionne said, her cheeks purple with smothered laughter.

26

THE FARMER was facedown, as instructed, his bald spot shimmering in the lamplight, gray hairs twisting across his shoulder blades, arms locked at his sides, a sheet covering his lower half.

She lit six candles and rubbed oil into her palms, which while pungent was no match for the deodorant and cologne diluting the dairy stench wafting off the pink-skinned sixty-two-year-old bracing for the first massage of his life. "Remember to relax," she said gently. "That's why you're here."

"What?" He grunted, his voice nasal.

"Breathe, Norm."

"Can't hear with my head in this thing."

She lowered her lips to the face cradle. "Breathe nor-mal-ly."

She hadn't told him what to wear or not wear, just to "undress in there." So it was impossible to *not* look ridiculous. Leave his underpants on and he was a prude; take them off and he was a pervert.

To his disappointment, she started with his feet, her warm palms flat against his meaty arches, holding them. He was paying $45 an hour for this foot voodoo? Just thinking about it made his feet sweat, which made him self-conscious, and that made them perspire even more.

"Relax, Norm. Focus on nothing."

Nothing?

He began talking when Sophie started rubbing his feet and ankles, because otherwise nothing could distract him from the sensation of her hands moving on his skin; he knew where that would lead and wasn't certain yet whether it was supposed to go there. He raved about his healthy new calf, though the optimism sounded hollow. What he felt was desperation and foolishness. He wished like hell he'd kept his boxers on.

She set his feet down beneath the sheet as if they were fragile. He heard her lubricate her hands again, the squishy sounds alone arousing him. Then she started kneading his shoulders and upper back like a cat clawing a couch, her lower stomach tapping rhythmically against his head brace with the effort.

"What'd you do before massage?" he asked, desperate for a distraction.

"All sorts of things."

"Stewardess?"

"Pretty much everything, Norm."

"Like?"

"Relax."

"Just name one."

"Ran an art gallery."

"Paintings?"

"And sculpture."

"What else?"

"Just relax."

After an uncomfortable silence, he said, "Do you think it's possible that Washington and Jefferson grew marijuana?"

"Yes."

"But not to get high, right?"

"Wrong. Jefferson got high on Sundays before he wrote letters. George and Martha made pot brownies every Easter."

"Very funny."

"Relax, Norm. *Please.*"

He waited a couple beats. "So you suddenly decided to settle down on the border and rub people?"

"*Heal* people."

"Like faith healing?"

"No."

"I heard you were an astrologist too."

"Quiet, Norm. What does it matter to a Taurus like you, anyway? I'm your neighbor. Let me do my work here."

She rubbed him harder, grunting lightly with the effort, focusing on points around his shoulders, then below and even beneath his shoulder blades, pressing to the brink of pain and holding it like some precise torture. Norm held his breath to avoid audible groaning. She found a particularly tender lump and wiggled it beneath her thumbs before flattening and spreading it elsewhere like rolling bubbles out of fiberglass. The strange smells, fake waterfall and primal flute music no longer seemed so hokey with what felt like more than two hands on his back, one pressing slow and flat like a trowel, another two or three coming up behind it with agile, probing fingers. It didn't seem possible that Patera or the professor or anyone else could pay at the door and get this same treatment.

"Breathe," she whispered. "When I press down you need to breathe."

When the next whisper said it was time to roll over, he realized he'd slipped in-between dreams. How much time had blown by? Was it over already? He rolled clumsily, his knee barking. She held up the sheet to give him privacy, his self-consciousness returning like a fever. How long had he been out? Months of anticipation, then he falls asleep for most of it? He didn't pay for a nap! She worked his neck from the underside, pawing at it, then held his chin and the back of his skull and tugged, as if trying to pop his head off. Again, the hands felt too powerful to belong to Sophie Winslow, so he finally peeked. Her lips were less than a foot above his. Thank God she started talking.

He tried to remember exactly what she'd just said, but before he could she asked what he thought about his son's art.

Norm groaned. "Embarrasses me. Always has."

"How'd you know he'd be so good on the Border Patrol?"

"I didn't. I don't."

She lifted his left arm and stretched it slowly toward his ear, then held it there and massaged his left side in a way that made him want to kick his feet.

"You worry about him?" she asked, readjusting his ribs in slow motion.

"Since before he was born. Jeanette spoiled him, practically took his breaths for him. I don't care what she says, there's always been more than dyslexia going on there. And of course it didn't help that he was immature and so much bigger than kids his age. It's more than that, though. He's always related better to animals. Humans are a mystery to him. He sees everything but doesn't know what most of it means."

"We're animals too."

"But most of us aren't straightforward."

"What else?"

"Well, he sees shooting stars nobody else sees and feels earthquakes nobody else feels. 'Feel that?' he used to say all the time, especially one summer when he was twelve or thirteen. Jeanette called the earthquake people, and they said that in fact there had been an odd flurry of quakes in the area they'd assumed were too small for humans to detect. They were curious enough to send this timid little intern out to talk to him. So what's a father supposed to make of all that? By middle school he could read well enough to pass and could act fairly normal if he wasn't too excited or overwhelmed. But yeah, he still caught hell, especially after Danny Crawford left and there was nobody to look out for him. That's when Jeanette homeschooled him, which spared him the razzings but increased the isolation."

"So what's it like living with him now?"

"Like having a child who never grows out of the awkward stage. It's also kind of like having a priest in the house. I've never caught him in a lie. Don't know that he's capable of one. And . . ."

"What?"

"I keep dreaming he gets shot, but I don't do anything about it."

She moved to his legs, gracefully folding and tucking the sheet high on his left thigh. Her slick hands rubbed his left calf so vigorously that his entire body trembled, leaving Norm half-praying, half-dreading that her hands would climb above his knee.

"Cleve Erickson's situation surprise you?"

"Yes," Norm hissed.

"What about the Schifferlis?"

"No."

"The math teacher, Pearson?"

"No. Heard he got fired because he partied with former students."

"Has a young man who calls himself Michael visited you?"

"Yes," he said, before digesting the delicate nature of the question.

"Did he offer you money?"

"Yes."

"Are you taking it?"

"No."

"Will you?"

"Doubt anybody wants to go through my farm now they've got the cameras up."

Her hands rose to his left knee, her fingers studying its construction, then less gently maneuvering muscles and tendons on all sides of it. "You mentioned your healthy calves. Are things really looking better?"

He heard himself moaning. "One calf," he managed to say. "I just need a break." He caught a sob before it popped out. "I really, really need a break."

Her fingers continued probing his wounded joint. "If you knew you wouldn't get caught, would you take it?"

"The money?"

"For looking the other way."

"At what point is it too late to try to be honorable?"

"Wayne Rousseau thinks he can find honor by *experiencing* other people's greatness."

"By what?"

"How tempting is the money, Norm?"

"I think about it every day."

"Do you know how to sail?"

"Did it as a kid."

"A lot?"

"Enough."

"Enough to know how to sail across—"

"Wayne," Norm interrupted, "is an ass."

"There. That's better."

"Twice."

"Twice what?"

"My grandfather took me out twice. That's my sailing background. Only twice, but I don't have any clearer memories than those two afternoons."

"When I spoke with Jeanette at church, her spirits were as high as ever."

"Some days," Norm said softly, not wanting to mix the rubbing sensation with thoughts of his wife. "And other days making dinner's an adventure. She kept saying, 'Something's wrong with my mind.' And I kept saying, 'We all get old and forget.' "

"Ever cheated on her, Norm?"

"Once. And I've waited too long to tell her about it to be adequately punished."

"Or is it that you want to cheat on her again?"

His breath caught. "A man can't help but wonder," he ventured, "if a pretty lady other than his wife might have sex with him."

A recorder wound to a clicking stop.

"What was that?"

"The music."

"But . . . it's still playing."

"That's good. *Shhhhh.*"

Five minutes of silent frenzied thigh rubbing later: "Norm?" Her voice barely made it through. "Let that energy exit through your feet."

"Energy?"

"Just picture it leaving through your feet."

"What the—"

"Or think about your mortgage, how much you still owe, that sort of thing."

HE GOOSE-STEPPED back through the poplars toward his farm, cupping his hands to see if his breath stunk, his mind a jumble of virility and humiliation. How embarrassing! Well, at least she knows he's fully operable, right? Then came the shame of what he'd shared, things he'd never said aloud. But the truth was his body felt oddly youthful, a strange and blissful lightness overtaking him.

"Full Bonnie?" somebody yelled.

The professor. "What?" Norm shouted, neither slowing nor veering from his path to the boat barn. Manners be damned.

"Full body?"

"What're you saying?" Norm yapped, reluctantly straying closer to the ditch, daring him to repeat it one more time.

"Was it a full body massaaaage?" Wayne sang. "C'mon, I can smell the oils from here. Let me guess: It was perfect, except she missed one little spot, eh?"

Norm scowled at the scrawny elf, a marijuana cigarette burning between tiny fingers.

"You get naked in there? Or'd you leave your gutchies on? Don't feel inadequate, Norm. From what I gather, you probably wouldn't survive sex with that woman anyway."

"Hah!" was all Norm could get out before Wayne said, "Last two guys? One went temporarily blind in the left eye, the other broke his penis."

"Bull—"

"Oh, it can happen, my friend. If the ligament walls collapse and the chamber snaps, the whole thing fills up with blood."

Without thinking it through, Norm tried to parrot what Patera had told him. "Your miracle medicine there induces mental illness and panic disorders, as well as bipolar and delusional disorders and schizophrenia paranoid."

Wayne laughed at the sky. "That was truly wonderful. Would you repeat that please?"

"You shoot the camera out?" Norm demanded, jabbing his thumb down the road.

"Was gonna ask you the same thing."

"People say it was you."

"People will say anything, won't they? They'll say half the Americans along the border are on the take, that you've got the EPA crawling up your ass and that your son's in the new gestapo. Who cares what they say. You miss the camera, Norm?"

"Not a bit," he admitted. "They already replaced it, anyway."

"That's right, and I hear they're gonna be flying drones and blimps along here in no time. Personally, I hope somebody shoots them down too." Wayne scrunched his nose and sniffed melodramatically. "That yours?"

It took Norm a beat to catch up. Taking credit for the odor was admitting he'd been spraying much more manure than usual, which hinted at the trouble he was in—and Wayne, clearly, already knew all about it. One thing led to another.

"What's the latest on that evildoer your boy caught?" Wayne asked.

"How're those reinventions coming?" Norm countered. "Been thinking I might branch out too, maybe take up the cello and join some symphony that performs in Vienna."

Wayne took his ball cap off and shook his shaved head—the latest disguise. "You should get more massages."

Norm spun to turn and go, his knee almost entirely painless, awaiting the final retort. The professor never let him win; there always had to be another shot.

"What you don't understand, Norm," he began softly, "is that I envy you. You don't have to learn the cello or read the classics or indulge in any other last-minute self-improvement crusade. You're perfectly content being *you*."

Norm examined the compliment from several angles, then

stomped back to him. "That comment, more than anything else you've ever said"—all this under his breath, tit for tat, forcing the professor to lean closer—"proves that despite living across that ditch for thirty-one years, you still don't know the first thing about me."

"Touché!" Wayne shouted.

Norm's fading triumph was interrupted by the sound of a plane flying slow and low over his dairy, forcing him to kink his neck and stub his left foot just enough to tweak his knee.

When he stepped inside, Jeanette was waiting on the couch, a stress rash rising on her neck, her face so creased with worries she didn't look like his wife. In a flash Norm realized he'd forgotten that he was taking her to the memory clinic.

"Where've you been?" she asked.

JEANETTE FELT small and hollow in the large, brightly lit room across the long table from a young woman in a white lab coat who was lobbing questions at her as if she were a child. What was the date, the season, the month? What state, county and city was she in? The answers were easy, but she could feel the pressure and judgment behind them. This alarmingly loud girl asked her to repeat words back to her: *bird, drum, lake.* Next she was instructed to count backwards from a hundred by eight, which didn't seem fair considering that she'd never been able to do math in her head.

The lab girl interrupted her—had she already messed up?—to wonder if she could spell the word *earth.* Then again, but backwards.

"A moment ago"—now she sounded like a recording—"I asked you to remember three words. Can you tell me those three words again?"

Jeanette froze, the words hidden behind a wall of fear.

But the questions and instructions kept coming: "Please read the words on this page and do what they say."

What a horrible place! She was too nervous to be examined. This test wouldn't prove anything! Then she was asked to connect numbered dots on a page.

The woman checked her watch and looked up critically.

Feeling like a mouse on drugs, Jeanette heard herself breathing. She snuck another look at the upside-down title on the examination sheet: DEMENTIA BATTERY SUMMARY REPORT.

27

SINCE BRANDON was twenty minutes early, he drove around the block twice, then parked and strolled past McGiver's Café to scout the territory, debating whether to sit inside or out. Inside would be quieter, but outside he'd be able to see more. He picked a gap in the traffic and hoofed it across the street for another perspective, absently browsing an antiques shop, a used-clothing store and a locked nameless storefront with tinted windows and a long manifesto on its door about the *Nazification of Canada*. He got lost in the opening sentence: *Drug prohibitions make gangsters and addicts and homeless people out of our children.*

He walked in and out of the café three times before choosing a tiny wrought-iron sidewalk table where he sang softly to himself and gazed above the traffic at the rock pigeons strutting along the roof across the street. He was into his third iced tea refill by the time she showed up, twenty-five minutes late.

"You're easy to find."

He glanced around, confused, as if he should've sat inside, elated she was there and still *her*, but suddenly wordless and lost.

"Your shirt," she explained. "Don't see a whole lot of Hawaiian shirts around here, and I had no idea they made 'em that red or that big."

She'd almost kept walking, the awkwardness of the lunch settling in, but he'd clearly spotted her before she saw him. Amazingly, he seemed to still be growing, demanding more space, his chest and shoulders expanding, his face rounding, his Adam's apple settling into a fleshier neck. He had the same lopsided smile and unintentional pompadour, but didn't come off as an overgrown child anymore. More like an overgrown young man—until he spoke.

Just seeing her relieved him, even though she didn't look like the humorous tomboy on file in his mind. The thin hips, narrow shoulders, flat chest and monkey arms hadn't changed, but there was a momentousness about her like he'd seen in brides before weddings. He also noticed the new geometrics of her smile lines, eye radials and half circles framing her lips. Her irises were a brighter gray-blue, her voice huskier. Still, her mannerisms, her origami-like flexibility—shifting effortlessly from cross-legged to one foot beneath her butt—and her fidgeting hands, all but three nails bitten back, were all comfortingly familiar. He looked around, surprised all the other men weren't ogling her. And once he started talking, he couldn't stop.

He told her about his father's sick cows, then the Princess from Nowhere in limbo hell and the angry Chinese women hiding under a fish truck and another van full of scared aliens huddled like chickadees trying to keep warm in a birdhouse. And how trying to stop the buds and illegals was like trying to stop the tide or the sun or the wind. The words and stories just flowed. Talking to her was so easy!

Madeline realized she couldn't fake this one. Too much was going on to smile her way through lunch. For starters she had a nervous belly and a fogged head from the night before, which had somehow included topless chess with some manipulative creep who'd convinced her to call him later and talk dirty while he—from the sound of it—popped balloons in a bathtub. Now she lacked the clarity or patience to converse with anyone, much less Brandon.

His gushing monologue swung from intriguingly detailed to remarkably irrelevant to occasionally incomprehensible, but always loud enough for the other nine outdoor diners to hear every word. Though he was more coherent than he used to be, the quirks remained, and it came roaring back to her how Danny used to provide the subtitles. He hadn't even brought up that craziness about her father, yet why should she be surprised? He was incapable of hidden agendas. This was just Brandon Vanderkool unloading on the streets of Abbotsford, his eyes wandering above and behind and to the sides of her, his upper body rocking, his shoes drumming the concrete. Still, she felt something coming.

It was hard to talk over the traffic. Brandon could barely follow his own words and knew he'd jumbled some, what with all the distractions, including the congregating flocks—blackbirds on sagging telephone lines, crows displacing pigeons on the rooftops and a gaggle of purple finches in the collared sidewalk trees. He desperately wanted to point them all out, but if there was one thing he didn't want to be today it was the bird freak. Suddenly she looked away and then back at him, as if preparing to leave.

"How's your dad and sister?" he asked.

"Nicole is pretty much the same, just richer. And it'll take more than MS to slow Dad down. But when you called, you said something weird about him shooting a camera. What made you say that?"

"It was easy to tell it was him."

When she'd asked her father about it, his laugh was convincing, as was his aside that he wasn't so anti-American that he was taking up arms. "But you said whoever shot it looked like a ghost, so how could you—"

"By build and posture, by how his left shoulder hangs lower, by the cock of his elbows, by the way he walks on the balls of his feet and the—"

"Okay, Brandon."

"You wearing tinted contacts?" he asked.

"Nope."

"Really? I didn't know eyes got brighter with age."

"Thanks for noticing."

"Are you ovulating?" he asked louder, with the same head-tilting curiosity.

She looked at him incredulously. "So," she drawled, realizing that she was probably ovulating at that very moment, "why'd you want to have lunch?"

"I have to go to the bathroom," he said, jolting upward and knocking his chair over. "Please stay there." He picked up his seat and looked past her. "Please," he said again, then stomped off into the café.

It wasn't until he was gone that she heard and saw the birds behind her. Was he still obsessed? He'd once coaxed her and Danny into bicycling to a small Blaine cemetery after dark. When they got there, all sweaty from the ride, he started into his goofy calls, sounding like a cross between a kazoo and a geezer faking enthusiasm. *Who-ho-hooo-who-who.* She and Danny snickered until something called back. The dialogue continued for several volleys until a stout owl broke free from the canopy, gliding toward them over tombstones of Icelanders with names like Benedictson, Friedleifsdottir and Gudmunsson before realizing it had been duped and banking back into the trees. As Danny liked to say, "You don't forget time spent with Brandon."

She flagged the waitress, ordered sandwiches for them both and lit a Camel to ease the pinging in her head. There was no grand scheme behind this lunch. Her unease dissipated with the smoke and turned to amusement when she thought of the super-serious questions Toby had told her to put to Brandon, but she knew she'd ask them. She had to stay on Toby's good side so that when it was time to get out, he'd let her. She ground the last half of her cigarette beneath her heel as she watched Brandon stride back, glancing at the trees, roof and phone lines before laying two photos faceup in front of her.

"You on assignment, Agent Vanderkool?" she asked without looking up.

"In this shirt? Just wanted to warn you that your friend there's supposedly in the dope business. But you probably know that."

"Met him at a weird party," she began breathlessly, pointing with her pinky. So Toby was right. There is a mole. "Sees himself as a lady's man, I guess. Led us around like show dogs. Didn't catch his name."

"Tobias C. Foster." Brandon was delighted. She barely knew him!

"They recorded him talking to Hells Angels in Peace Arch on the Fourth. You're not in the dope business, are ya, Maddy?"

She closed her eyes and bobbed, as if listening to jazz, then forced a smile. "I come from a long line of wine drinkers." Once she got past the alarm that people were secretly snapping photos of her, she realized this was a heads-up, a favor. Brandon was looking out for *her*.

He could barely contain himself. She's clean—and smiling at him! "Well, I guess the Mounties assume you're in it because they know this guy's in it, right?"

"Whatever you say." She slid the photos back, having memorized when and where and at what angles they were shot. "What bird is that singing?" she asked, eager for a new topic.

"A starling. You hear a bird, it's probably a starling. People hate 'em, but they can sing anything. Mozart had a pet starling that helped him improve a melody by changing it to G-sharp. He had a funeral for it when it died. People got dressed up and everything."

Unbelievable. She asked about his work, the hours, the shifts, the upsides and downsides, then clicked through Toby's queries about the tools and habits of the patrol—how many agents, rigs, helicopters and boats, their staffing at nights, how often they patrolled the Cascades and the bays. She felt guiltier with each question.

She was interested in what he was doing! The last few times he'd seen her, it had been hard to sustain her attention. Now she found everything so interesting! He explained his strategy of rotating stake-outs on smuggling routes, then told her about all the ratting-out of locals and the drug busts of people she might know.

"Pot never was my thing," she finally said.

"Me neither," he said. "Only time I tried it was with Danny."

Just the thought of this amused her.

"It was the third Christmas he came back from college. Said he had something I had to try called Paul McCartney pot. Kept saying it was the stuff Paul McCartney smoked whenever he went to New York. 'Makes you happy,' he kept saying. 'Happy happy happy! All you do is laugh!' " Madeline started giggling, so he repeated it, louder, "Happy

happy happy." He wouldn't stop snorting until she urged him on. "So we smoked some the day he left, just a little, because we didn't want to get too happy seeing as how he had to get on a plane. But we didn't get happy at all. We didn't say anything for a couple hours. Danny barely moved. I drove him to the airport, then got lost coming home."

Madeline's laugh had everyone staring at their table. He scrambled to say whatever he could to keep her laughing, but couldn't think of anything to add. "You probably know this," he said, "but you laugh when you're beautiful."

She rearranged the words. The most she could recall being called was cute or appealing or, her least favorite, not unattractive. But *beautiful*? That was her sister's adjective. She tilted her head back so her eyes wouldn't overflow.

He tried again. "When you are laughing . . . What I—"

"Thanks, Brandon. Got it." She watched him demolish his Reuben and plow into the helpless fries, as focused on the food as if he were eating alone. "Still doing your art?" she asked.

"I wouldn't know how to stop," he said, not looking up.

"Still painting birds?"

"And people."

"Getting better?"

He shrugged.

Awkward with the silence, she said, "How's your mom doing?"

"She just took some big memory test to see what's wrong. Could just be menopause, you know? But she couldn't remember her favorite song the other night, and that really bothered her. She knew the notes, but none of the words or even the title."

"What was it?"

"A Beatles song."

"Back to Paul."

"Who?"

"Which song?"

" 'Blackbird,' " he said, unable to resist singing the rest of the opening line. Again, conversations stopped at the other tables.

"All right, Brandon," she said, reddening.

He couldn't see her expression because his mouth was skyward and bursting into " 'Take these broken wings and learn to *flyyyy* . . .' "

She simultaneously tried to shush him and memorize the moment, so busy thinking about how to describe it, how to do it justice, that she missed the disbelief and pity on people's faces. He missed every high note, French fry smithereens gathering in the corners of his lips. " 'All your life' "—she signaled the waitress for the check—" 'you were only waiting for this moment to *ariiise.*' "

To Brandon, the song sounded so perfectly executed that it was hard to resist starting at the top again, but he felt Madeline's hand squeezing his and when he looked down she was leaning toward him, sunburned, an eyebrow twitching, clearly moved. She was close enough to kiss. But how to get from here to there? He dared any of the jealous diners to think about wooing her. If necessary, he'd pound his head against a drainpipe five hundred times a day for Madeline Rousseau. When he opened his mouth to start singing again, she squeezed his hand harder. He felt hers trembling and covered it with the fingers of his other hand until it stilled.

28

SHE COULD feel the escalating stress and outrage in the trapezius knots, neck gristle and rigid joints of her moaning clients, especially once Dirk Hoffman's story started bouncing around.

He was returning home from the saloon at half past midnight when Agent Rick Talley's personal radiation detector went off. Nobody disputed that part. Exactly what happened next hinged on who was talking.

Agent Talley wrote it up as *a required vehicle stop* after Mr. Hoffman's truck made his PRD flash and beep. The driver appeared to be intoxicated. After he turned verbally abusive, Agent Talley gently subdued Mr. Hoffman in order to properly search him and his vehicle.

The dairyman's version: He was nearly home when Agent Hothead screeched into a U-turn and hit the lights as if he were Al Capone, then ordered him to step outside and "shut his fucking mouth." When Dirk asked what the hell was going on, Agent Hothead ordered him facedown on the street, where he was searched, held at gunpoint and berated in Spanish.

While no nuclear weapon was found on Dirk or in his truck, the incident made it common knowledge that the pricey new toys on the BP's hips were so sensitive they could detect such drive-by cancer patients as the sixty-nine-year-old Dirk Hoffman, who until then had managed to keep his radiation treatments secret.

This dustup unleashed other tales of harassment. Wildlife biologist Matthew Paust told Sophie he was interrogated for twenty minutes about exactly why he was strolling alone at night along the edge of *his* property. Alexandra Cole confided at the next bunko party that a new BP ransacked her brother's Audi after he visited a friend on Peace Drive. East Indians who'd grown raspberries along the U.S. side for decades stopped visiting Abbotsford relatives to avoid the humiliating questions and searches on the drive home.

And complaints about the border cams rose to a boil. They track us whenever we step outside! residents told local councils with no say over the patrol or its cameras. "How would you feel if you had a camera on you twenty-four/seven?" Melanie Mesick demanded. "Who's to say some perverted imbecile won't start using them to peer into our bedrooms?"

Still, the security and surveillance continued to escalate as Patera almost doubled patrols yet again to keep his ever-growing force busy. Most vehicles cruising the northern line after dusk were now green-and-whites. Few people took notice of the little flying drone when it first began traversing the 49th like some oversized, high-altitude bird, though they were alarmed to learn that the unmanned military aircraft's cameras could read a cereal box from fifteen thousand feet.

Patera wanted even more gadgets, urging the Blaine council to seek grants for a radiation alarm system at its busiest four-way intersection. He also insisted that local fire and police should be equipped with PDAs that could tap into FBI databases at the scene of an incident.

Nobody was surprised to hear that Dirk Hoffman had hired a hot-shot Seattle attorney to look into suing the goddamn Border Patrol. What everyone was waiting for was his next reader-board salvo: WELCOME TO THE POLICE STATE.

29

HE FELT his scalp burning as he shuffled into the Blaine liquor store, as if some cruel giant were focusing a magnifying glass on the top of his head. Walking back out, he heard childish squeals coming from the park and remembered this happened to be the one day of the year they turned Peace Arch over to thousands of shrill Girl Scouts from both countries. Just their luck, this heat wave. He rolled east toward the valley through the queue of semis crawling toward the only open Customs station, exasperated drivers hanging out their windows, too hot to smoke.

Norm took weather personally. Windstorms spooked him, cold snaps tortured his knee and when it climbed over eighty, the sun was an open flame on his skin. Roll him out naked in this heat and he'd be a charred husk within three hours. The weather girl swore this two-week scorcher would snap that afternoon with rain, wind and, possibly, thunder and lightning. Yet for now, the valley remained a cloud-forsaken oven. And to think he had to drive to the east end of it, without air-conditioning, just to give Ray Lankhaar a belated get-well-soon bottle on the hottest day of the year.

He passed five BPs rolling out H Street. While he didn't side with Dirk Hoffman and the other anti-fed nut jobs, it did make him queasy that his son was part of what had started to look like an occupying army. He'd asked Roony to pinch-hit for the afternoon milking after remembering his promise to swing by Ray's around three. He now hoped Roony still had enough on the ball to give them extra water.

South Pass Road suddenly featured three new toy ranches, their massive timbered gates announcing Hawk Heaven, Peace Meadows and Rainbow Ridge. The more useless the ranch, Norm observed, the grander its entrance. He saw that the county's largest blueberry patch had five new windmills on it, powering God knows what—as if further proof was needed that he was the least imaginative guy in the whole valley. Even with a thermos of coffee in his belly, he still had to fend off the swoons before the mirage of Ray Lankhaar's farm filled his windshield.

A row of firs and two massive NO CASINO! signs flanked the private drive curling up the knoll to a tidy house with a sensible metal roof. Beyond it were three freshly painted green barns and two rust-free silos flanked by freshly trimmed willows so the feed trucks had clearance.

Neither Ray nor his magazine-pretty wife, who'd never so much as blinked at Norm, answered the door, which forced him to trudge to the barns and have superior cow care shoved in his face once again. He hosed his boots, even though they were clean, to avoid that lecture. Ray prided himself on being the valley's only dairyman who insisted visitors wash up before entering his barns, which was typical of how he did everything. He bought the most expensive semen and bulls. He shoveled the manure three times a day, not just once. But it was his beddings—including, for the love of God, fresh sand every month—that flabbergasted Norm. Tropical resorts were less particular about their sand. He even sloped each stall to keep the lounging cows' heads slightly elevated. Why, so they could read in bed? The most galling aspect of this pampering was that it worked. He owned at least a dozen cows as old and valuable as Pearl, and his herd routinely produced the most milk per cow in the valley.

"Ray!" Norm shouted, hoping to just leave the bottle on the porch and bank the chit for a gift that would probably get written off as *table wine.* On his next glance around, he saw the baby-shit beige Mercedes parked on the shady backside of the second willow. Why would Ray invite him out when the doc was scheduled? He stepped quietly into the closest barn, grateful for shade, dangling the overpriced Merlot by its neck.

"Raymond?" he called, softer now, still angling for an undetected visit. He lurched back at the homicidal snort and shuffle of the penned bull that must have gored Lankhaar. Why hadn't Ray already auctioned the brute off? He was backpedaling gingerly when he heard rising voices and the sound—unthinkable on this dairy—of agitated cows. He pushed through a door hanging ajar, and once he'd stepped completely into the painful light he saw Ray shouting something through a surgical mask at the vet, who also wore one and was squatting next to a downed and bloated Jersey. Heat stroke? Maybe milk fever? But what's with the masks? Drawing closer, he noticed three other bloated cows moaning on their sides. Then a few more.

"Norm!" Ray screamed, standing over a cow that was spouting gas and foam. "Get over here!"

Bangs matted against his know-it-all forehead, Stremler looked up and glared, as if everything happening was all Norm's fault. "Put a mask on!" he yelled, folding a phone in a gloved hand and pointing at a box.

"Milk fever?" Norm asked.

"Put that bottle down and get over here!" Ray demanded, looking as wild-eyed as his ailing cows.

Norm wince-galloped over, his face instantly sweaty behind the mask. Hypocalcemia? Hypomagnesmia? Rumen acidosis? Despite the glare, he could see the gray roots of Ray's hair and, beyond him, another collapsing cow. Norm grabbed the upper lip of one already down and opened its mouth wide enough to slide a two-foot pipe down its throat and pour baking soda inside. It was reassuring to know that even sanctimonious Raymond Lankhaar got served a shit sandwich from time to time, but what the hell was going on here? As he ripped off his shirt and tied it off over his broiling scalp, his thoughts finally caught up with the action—the masks, Stremler's urgency, Patera's dire warnings. "Why so many down at once?" he yelled.

"Think I haven't wondered about that?" Stremler barked. Then, to Ray, "We've gotta open one up."

"What?"

"Now! Fifty-six is gone. We've gotta do it now."

"Oh, Christ," Ray whined. "Should I get a—?"

"I got everything here."

Norm ran the chief's warnings back through his head. That the government values its dairy product. That mad-cow could be spread with a spray bottle. That a toxin dropped in a bulk tank could kill half a million Americans.

Transfixed, he watched Stremler abbreviate the autopsy protocol. He didn't cut off a front leg or peel the cow open from the shoulder. He punctured and sawed straight into the belly until the entrails sloshed out onto the ground. The doc picked through this pungent ooze like a man shopping for melons, then slit a bloated blue-gray sack and ran his hands through its contents several times. He ignored Ray's questions before ripping off his mask and looking up to demand, "Where did you get this feed?"

"What's wrong with—"

"Where'd you get it?"

"An Everson farmer named Pal—"

"Dried corn," Stremler shouted. "Too much dried corn."

"You mean—"

"Yes! I mean killer levels of dried corn and who knows what else. How many have fed already?" The doc glanced around, his lips moving while he counted. Then another cow dropped.

Ray whipped off his mask and scurried toward his parlor as Norm recalled that Palmer had said he'd deliver his bargain feed that afternoon. "No," he pleaded, stumbling toward the shade. "Noooo!"

"What?" Stremler jolted upright, poised to quarrel over his diagnosis as Norm desperately punched numbers into his cell phone, messing up and redialing. "Do *not* tell me that . . ."

He left in a mad hobble, his mind so fixed on getting back to the dairy there was no room for other thoughts, passing cars on blind hills with his old truck screaming at over ninety on the straightaways. He was shouting "Roony!" before he got out and stormed into the parlor to find him propped against the back wall, listening to sports talk radio at such high volume that he didn't hear or see Norm until he was upon him. "Did Palmer deliver the—?"

"Yeah, don't worry. He came." Roony waved a hand toward the six full stalls.

"Stop the feeding!" Norm shouted, then yanked the hoses from 57's udder and pushed her massive head out of the trough.

"What?"

"Get 'em outta here!"

"Talk to me, Norm!"

"The feed's bad! How many milked already?"

"Two rounds and what you—"

"Get 'em out!" He yanked the hoses off 91 while Roony did the same with 17, all the cows now grunting and whining. One of them squealed and bucked her hind legs, grazing Roony's left thigh and sending him yelping toward the back wall.

Norm continued slapping the cows out, furious, yelling, then storming out back to where everything looked normal until he saw three tipped over on their sides, including—oh, *God*—Pearl. She looked up, and her gaze went through him. Of course. The first to feed would be the first to die. He dropped to his best knee and heard another cow fall, realizing he had no idea what to do other than to fill them with baking soda and apologize. He left Pearl to check on the others and found her twins splayed, blinking skyward. He stooped to soothe 59 as Roony hobbled from the parlor like some animated gargoyle.

Norm sensed that all his wrongs, his shortcuts and weaknesses and infidelities had finally returned to roost. He looked up, not so much for forgiveness as for explanation, and saw a blimp and a surveillance drone in the otherwise indifferent sky.

BRANDON WADED through hundreds of girls who came up to his hips. Dozens followed behind him, mouths upturned like they wanted to be fed, tugging on his uniform and demanding photos with him. He hadn't seen or heard any birds in days except for lazy gulls, crows and blackbirds, as if the heat had shoved the songbirds from the valley and left nothing but screaming Brownies, Juniors and Cadets whose voices sounded like wind chimes in his floaty, birdless blur.

For the first time in his life, he wasn't sleeping. Part of it was the grind of the night shift. Most of it was Madeline. After their lunch, it took great restraint not to call her every day. And the messages he left were never returned. He'd replayed the lunch in his head a few dozen times, looking for body language he'd missed or misunderstood. Her laughter was genuine, he was sure of that. Madeline used to be a Girl Scout too—a Girl Guide as the Canadians called them—and it was easy to imagine her at twelve, looking like a war hero with all her badges. Though he'd always known about this event, this was the first time he'd witnessed the craft-swapping horde of laughing, squealing girls spilling across the park and the closed freeway.

He tried to smile for the pictures, but he'd never been able to do that to anyone's satisfaction, the shots inevitably coming out lopsided, capturing little more than his uncertainty. Yet the requests kept coming, for photos of just him, of him towering over one or two little girls or entire troops. One kid shouted, "I want a picture with the dinosaur!"

Brandon finally escaped, to the irritation of bossy troop leaders, and was patting his empty pockets—he'd forgotten both his wallet and phone—when McAfferty and Dionne strolled up, apparently in mid-argument. "What the hell you doin' here?" Mac asked him.

"I'm scheduled."

"Of course. All hands on deck! Even if they worked until four this morning and they're too tired to line up their buttons and zip their barn door." He winked at Brandon, who pulled up his zipper and looked down at his shirt buttons. "Something huge might happen, like some little scout gets thirsty. Go find yourself some shade, bud. I'll wake you if we spot any pedophiles."

Dionne gave McAfferty a shove. "Would you *please* shut up?"

"Come on, you gotta admit this is a pervert's dream. Why else—"

"Do you *ever* consider your audience when you—"

"Never have, never will."

Agent Canfield wandered up. "How many days you got left, Mac?" he asked, sniffling hard.

"A hundred and fifty-six. Thanks for asking."

"Got some plans?" He sniffled hard again.

"Sure, little of this, little of that, mostly entrepreneurial stuff."

"Yeah, like what?"

McAfferty twisted the loose ends of his mustache. "Like creating memorable moments for paying customers."

"And how exactly do you intend to do that?" Dionne said.

"First rule of good ideas is to keep them to yourself."

"Come on, just a glimpse."

McAfferty scanned their faces. "You've all snow skied, right?"

Canfield and Dionne began talking simultaneously as Brandon pictured himself skiing with Madeline and Danny Crawford in a blizzard, following her voice all the way down the mountain. But what could he say about that?

"All right," McAfferty said, waiting for Canfield to clear his nasal passages. "Y'all know what it's like, or can imagine what it's like, to get stuck on a slow lift when you gotta piss like a donkey. Not only are you not gonna be able to for a long, long while, it'll also be mission impossible getting off the mountain and clomping up and down in the lodge to find a can while you're wearing boots that make you walk like Frankenstein, know what I'm saying?"

Brandon studied how he built suspense by interrupting his own stories.

"And complicating your desperate need to take a leak is the fact that your toes are turning into painful blocks of ice, right? So my idea," he said, slowing to a crawl, "is to sell a rubberized kit that runs down your legs and pools around your toes so you not only don't have to trek to the lodge pissoir, you can thaw your feet with your own urine. Whaddaya think?"

Brandon snorted along with the laughter, though his attention was fixed on a darker patch of sky than he'd seen in weeks.

"What if you've got more piss than storage space?" Canfield asked.

"Then it backs up your leg," McAfferty snapped.

"But what if you wipe out?" Canfield asked. "Then it'll be all over you like somebody nailed ya with a piss balloon."

"Now that," Dionne said, "sounds like a truly memorable moment."

"Everybody's a critic," McAfferty groused.

Brandon watched girls lining up, hand in hand, to march through the arch from the American to the Canadian side.

"Don't like that one? How 'bout strip bars in airports?" McAfferty asked. "For men *and* women. Who isn't bored and horny in airports?"

"When female pigs get horny," Brandon said, thrilled with his timing and relevance, "their ears pop straight up. Farmers call it 'popping.' "

There was a slight delay before the laughter hit, with McAfferty beaming like a pleased father, when all their radios started squawking at once. "Agents switch on secure mode." After only a few seconds, a supervisor's voice crackled through the Motorolas. "Dispatch just received a call regarding an alleged dirty bomb in Peace Arch." He then told McAfferty to divide the park into grids and assign an agent to search each section. "Anyone getting a positive PRD signal should respond to me immediately."

Dionne darted off, running pell-mell through the crowd toward her daughter's troop. Brandon felt fully awake for the first time in days, the noise and the multitudes coming into overwhelming focus, but he had no idea how to start looking for a bomb.

He began scanning his area for anything that didn't belong, though all he saw were hundreds of sunburned children with hundreds of sacks and backpacks. Was he supposed to look inside each one? More girls wanted their pictures taken with him. He kept moving, looking for people who seemed out of place, but it was all girls! Was he supposed to start asking them questions? He was ten minutes into his confused search, his head aching with panic, when he heard Dionne shouting for him.

He ran toward where she was pacing with her radio and staring at a picnic table beneath which sat a plastic red, white and blue cooler. "Yes, of course, it went off!" she snapped. "That's what I said. . . . Yes, I tried it twice. . . . Yeah, wires and a battery. That's what I told you. . . . Well, it's too late, I already opened it. . . . No, I won't. . . . I already told you nobody's claiming it. No. Look, it just started to pour. Hey, Brandon's here. I'll have him test it too."

Brandon pulled out his radiation detector and had taken only a couple steps toward the cooler when it started beeping and flashing.

"He just confirmed it, okay?" Dionne shouted into her radio. "I want my daughter out of this park! Right fucking now!"

Soon every BP, Mountie and park ranger was telling scouts and guides and troop leaders to evacuate the park, now. Most of the girls blamed this on the rain, yet their high chattering voices suddenly sounded different to Brandon. It was probably the exact same racket, but for him the squeals had shifted from glee to horror. There was another sound, too, that of the distant rumbling sky, and then, so much closer, a concussive thump somewhere on the wooded hill east of the park, where flames abruptly shot up above the tree line.

WAYNE STOOD alone in the overgrown soccer field, watching the northerly bend grass and trees, villainous clouds hurtling overhead as if late for some appointment in the States.

Franklin's instructions had been so easy to follow: *Make a small Cross of two light Strips of Cedar, the Arms so long as to reach to the four Corners of a large thin Silk Handkerchief when extended. Tie the Corners of the Handkerchief to the extremities of the Cross so you have the body of a Kite, which being properly accommodated with a Tail, Loop and String will rise in the Air. . . .* Ben's 250-year-old cheat sheet then went on to explain how to attach a wire to the top of the kite and a key and silk ribbon to the end of the string.

Despite the excited sky there'd been few signs of the forecasted thunderstorm, though it was blowing hard enough that he didn't have to attempt to run. He simply let the kite go. It swerved back and forth nervously, its silk body filling like a spinnaker, the sticks bending and its shape warping until it spiraled down into the field. Relieved to find the sticks intact, he waited for the wind to lighten and tried again. The kite climbed less erratically this time, just not sharply enough to get anywhere near the clouds, though he noticed—or perhaps imagined—a flash to the north.

Abruptly, the wind slackened and the rain began. It felt ridiculous, standing there with his kite in the grass at his feet, but he didn't feel like leaving. So he sat down, let the rain soak him and hoped for a storm.

What electrical activity there was looked hopelessly far away, but it was gradually getting gusty again. Fifteen minutes later he popped the kite up at the steepest angle yet, and it alternately dipped and rose as the sky growled. Wayne assumed the strands he saw protruding from the taut string were wind-related. The next time it happened, though, he raised his knuckle to the key.

The zap reminded him of the shock he got replacing the washer outlet in the basement. But wait a minute. Why, exactly, was he on his back in the wet grass? He moved his toes, knees and hips, his fingers, wrist, shoulders, neck and lips, feeling his entire body loosen as he stared, clear headed and exalted, into the infinite vault of rain.

Part Three

30

SOPHIE STITCHED together most of what happened by interviewing McAfferty, Dionne and Patera. But no matter how much she heard it still didn't add up, exactly, as if somewhere in this chain of events the reaction had been cubed.

The park evacuation actually went astonishingly well, considering that thousands of children had to be rushed from the grounds. Fortunately, the festivities were in their final hour and most troops were ready to leave anyway, especially once the curtain of rain started falling, which also helped the Blaine firemen extinguish the blazing house on Harvey Street.

Patera was in the park, speed-talking on two cell phones long before the ATF finally showed up in matching jackets, looking like some aging softball team. "This is *our* release," McAfferty heard the chief shout at one point. "*Our* agent found it."

Mac's take was that Patera's judgment had been warped by adrenaline. What amazing luck to have a bomb found by his very own crackerjack female agent—at a Girl Scout festival! You mean your agents aren't all men? That's right, folks. And not just any woman agent, but the mother of an innocent little scout at the exact same park that very afternoon!

Unfortunately, the story wasn't that simple. A lot was going on at once, and the potential connections were alarming if unclear. Everything was further complicated by early television deadlines and the time it took for the bomb squad to get there from Seattle.

And while Patera did eventually admit to one small and two large mistakes, he swore he never intentionally misled anyone. He simply tried to keep everyone as informed as possible. The problem was the urgency of local TV reporters. One such rushed conversation, according to the chief, went like this:

Has there been an evacuation?

Yes.

Why?

A bomb threat was called in to the Blaine sector.

What kind of bomb?

A dirty bomb.

A dirty bomb?

Yes, which would typically mean explosives tied to radioactive materials.

Has there been any confirmation of an actual bomb?

This, Patera told Sophie, is where he committed one of his two large mistakes. He should have just said, no—or "Hell no!" as McAfferty later suggested. But what he said was, border agents have confirmed some radioactivity in an ice chest of interest in the park.

What does the squad say?

Nothing yet.

And was there a firebombing of a nearby home?

The local station did respond to a house fire, yes. It's not clear whether it was arson.

And that's when Patera made his second big mistake, mentioning to a Seattle reporter that there was a simultaneous investigation—based on a panicky voice message from veterinarian Eugene Stremler—into the possible poisoning of several American dairies along the border. Patera's third, considerably smaller, blunder was speculating aloud on the possibility of a curfew.

A dirty-bomb scare that caused the evacuation of eight thousand Girl Scouts at Peace Arch Park was enough to lead a slow news day, especially with the kickers of dairy terrorism, a firebombing and an impending curfew. A war of sorts—what else could you call it?—had seemingly rolled over the Canadian border into the Pacific Northwest.

Meanwhile, the bomb squad treated the picnic cooler as if it were about to explode. Nobody else peeked inside, as Dionne had, or even approached it at all. They taped off a quarter-mile perimeter, then rolled out a wheeled robot outfitted with a video camera and remote-controlled hands. It had a hell of a time with the cooler latch, which gobbled another ten minutes, while Patera fielded more frantic questions right before the coverage went live. It was almost an hour before the deliberative bomb-squad commander blandly declared that the "dirty bomb" amounted to two six-volt batteries, some unconnected wires and a sack of kitty litter, which was emitting enough trace amounts of uranium and thorium to trigger sensors. There were no explosives in the cooler.

By then Patera had retrieved Stremler's sheepish follow-up message that the cattle fatalities appeared to have been caused by excessive fermentation in bad feed. The torched house, the chief was belatedly informed, had been abandoned and condemned for years. Not a single town council along the border was discussing curfews.

Bad news, though, spreads faster than good, so it took deep into the night before the truth began to cool the fear and confusion in the valley. There was a run on canned goods and ammo, and Tom Dunbar later admitted that he spent the night in a bomb shelter he'd built in the seventies. Others fired up ham radios and hid in basements, contacting one another and awaiting instructions. Many more went to bed numbed by the sensation that their country, their county, even their *neighborhood,* was under attack. And even those who got the full story before going to bed still found it hard to turn off the trepidation.

Daybreak arrived with a blinding fog that lowered the sky to the tops of the silos and steeples, which might have gone unnoticed if not for a raucous, low-flying flock.

Madeline jolted upright to what she assumed were Fisher's guard ducks alerting her to an ambush. Norm awoke furious that the goddamn EPA was buzzing his farm again. Dirk fumbled for his bedside .357 with one thought: air raid. Wayne dreamt through the bedlam, sharing a joint with Franklin and van Gogh. Sophie reached for her camcorder and shuffled to the window. And Brandon lay in bed marveling at the loudest skein of Caspian terns he'd ever heard, picturing its loose formation plunging through the whiteout, the agile, black-masked, white-winged birds held together by sound and faith.

31

THE BAD Moon Saloon was overflowing before dinnertime. Even nondrinkers showed up, drunk on relief. The more people came, the faster word spread, and the drinking, smoking and laughter soon spilled out into the lot and beyond to where cars coagulated along the overgrown shoulders of H Street.

Norm rolled up on the throng sleepless and unchanged. He'd had all he could handle of monitoring the health of his shrunken herd. He'd lost eight, including Pearl, and felt lucky that more hadn't died, though the future productivity of some survivors remained unclear. The fact that Ray Lankhaar had lost twice as many meant that Norm and three other dairymen could piggyback on whatever redemption he and his Bellingham attorney bullied out of Palmer's insurance company, which, knowing Ray, would dwarf the value of the cows—not that you could put a price tag on an animal like Pearl.

He'd wheeled a backhoe to the corner of the property with the best view of Mount Baker and dug her a roomy hole. He dragged her over, dropped her in, covered her up and left her with a one-word eulogy: "Thanks." Then he'd talked Roony into dealing with the rendering truck so he could skip that grim routine and grab himself a drink.

He considered driving on when he saw the size of the mob, but he'd already lit his fuse with the vision of a whiskey twinkling on the bar top. And he'd always found it hard to roll past the Moon even when it was empty. It was the only bar that served the whole valley—smack between Lynden and Blaine, Holland and Iceland, or heaven and hell, if you listened to Lynden drinkers. He limped past youngsters who so closely resembled older acquaintances that he nodded hello, getting nothing in return. Strangers, he remembered, can tell you how old you are without trying. The looks you get or don't get let you know exactly where you're at, where you're headed and where you can never go again.

Inside, it looked more like New Year's Eve or V-Day than some Sunday in late August. He was relieved and pained to spot Dirk, Shit-to-Power and a few other geezers his age. Hell, they were all older than plastic, older than television. But everyone was there. The Erickson punks, of course, but even Alexandra Cole, for Godsakes, laughing so fast and hard that people were backpedaling. There were dozens more he didn't recognize or else hadn't seen since they were kids. Almost everyone was half his age or younger, radiant and impervious to time. He covered a stool without drawing attention to his first public drink in over a year, ordering a shot of Crown and a bottle of Pabst to grease the first round of greetings. And another shot as Dirk and the others sidled up. "Great to see ya, Norm! Luck's gotta turn here somewhere, huh?" Even the great Morris Crawford sauntered over to give Norm his due, as if he'd done something heroic by poisoning his cows with cheap feed from some Everson yahoo. Part of it, he knew, was the Lankhaar factor. Hell, if Ray fell for the scam, anyone could. Chas Landers—his fifteen minutes already in the rearview—sidled up with whitened teeth and a heavy gold necklace to pay his respects. "Good for you, Norm," he echoed, as if hobbling in for a couple Crowns showed remarkable courage, everyone nodding like they'd been waiting months, maybe years, to drink with their old pal.

"What can ya do?" Norm said again and again with a gunslinger's wince, not really knowing what he was implying, yet every head bobbed as if bad luck had made him profound. A Deming dairyman he barely knew asked about his boat, then whistled at its dimensions and grinned like he was one clever son of a bitch to build an ocean yacht in his back barn.

Norm spotted Clint Honcoop and Cleve Erickson in the swarm,

their bald, sun-fried heads shaking with laughter, as if they'd been pardoned and their arrests were all part of the great mix-up.

People took turns impersonating grave newscasters from the night before while others spoofed Patera, giggling themselves blind after Dirk cautioned them not to underestimate the difficulty of what the chief had accomplished. "You have any idea how hard it is—how goddamn flexible you have to be—to get both feet in your mouth at the same time?"

"Seriously, Norm," Shit-to-Power bellowed from three stools away, "at your lowest, darkest moment yesterday you still couldn't have thought terrorists had targeted your farm."

He leaned back into a do-I-look-nuts grimace and everyone busted up, the laughter out of all proportion to the humor.

"Well, how 'bout ole Lankhaar?" Chas asked. "What was *he* thinkin'?"

All Norm had to do was lift his left eyebrow and they lost it again, mirth radiating in a half circle around him. *What was that? What'd Norm say?*

He felt his aches and worries dissipating. Even now, his straits clearly weren't nearly as dire as he kept telling himself they were. He made a silent vow to go out more often and toss back a couple if for no other reason than to get out from under his self-pity.

Chas bought him and a dozen others another round and waved off the gratitude, but Norm gripped his shoulder and pulled him close. "Why don't you just admit you kept at least ten grand instead of pimping around like this? We all know what cranberries are selling for." He cuffed Chas's stiffening neck as if to complete some inside joke.

"So what do you think's gonna happen to your buddy Patera," Dirk prodded, "now that he screwed the pooch?"

Laughter bounced around again until the riot of bar noise rose so high that Norm almost had to shout. "We've all screwed the pooch a time or two, haven't we, Dirk?" He threw back the free Crown and basked in moist smiles from women in their thirties and forties. Just three shots and he'd already drunk his way back two decades. "The chief was just trying his damnedest to do the right thing," he drawled, dragging out the attention. "Only thing he did wrong, in my opinion, was to expect the media wouldn't hang him out to dry. That and putting too much stock in the hasty conclusions of a certain high-strung vet we all know."

He felt his mouth running loose on him. Sober, he'd never take a shot at Stremler. That was one of the main reasons he didn't drink in public anymore—the self-loathing that followed. His father was a different drinker altogether. He had two whiskey sours every night in the privacy of his den. The first for arthritis, the second to examine his finances and the rest of his world in a more measured light. Norm drank to get drunk.

"You must be excited about the casino going up down the street," Shit-to-Power said.

"I don't like anything about it, but I don't blame 'em for a minute. If I was them, I'd stick it to us as hard as I could, then twist it a few times," he said, suddenly borrowing Wayne Rousseau's rant verbatim. "And this whole self-righteous, anti-casino crusade has a racist aftertaste to it, if you ask me."

There were grumbles but plenty of nods as well. "Right on," crooned a slender brunette with a reflective sheen of sweat in the hollow of her neck. "Somebody finally had the guts to say it out loud."

Norm felt like an oracle. Through his tangled audience, he spotted Sophie making the rounds, lathering men with the intense close-talking attention he'd hoped she reserved for him. He looked back at the brunette, who was still nodding in his direction, and experienced a fleeting notion that Sophie Winslow was too old for him. His fourth Crown went down like apple juice.

The next thing he knew, another young woman he didn't recognize strutted through the bar, amid booming laughter, wearing what looked like a bomb. "Make way for the suicide bomber!" she shouted. As she got closer, Norm could see it was just a computer circuit board strapped to her chest and something like Play-Doh in her hands. She tried to offer a drunken speech but kept saying "tourists" when she meant to say "terrorists," which doubled everybody over, including herself.

"So what's the story with that Space Needle bomber your boy caught?" Chas ventured once the moment passed, a payback bite to his voice. "Sure don't hear anything about him anymore."

Norm started to answer but didn't know what to say now that the conversation had swerved toward Brandon. And before he could coax words to the surface, he was distracted by the ever-present flash of Sophie's camera, snapping photos of the Jack Daniel's mirror behind him that reflected the side of his sun-spotted head and all the anxious pink faces hanging on his pause, leaning in for another hit of Norm Vanderkool, the room starting to list slightly, pleasantly, like a seaworthy ship in gentle seas.

32

BRANDON HAND-RAKED a mound of alder leaves, then tossed compact armfuls off a ridgetop overlooking the valley. The same southerly that swept the fog out that morning provided the lift, with the driest, largest leaves taking the longest flights. He did the same thing with sticks, then again with leaves, again and again, his mind freezing images at intervals from multiple angles.

He'd called Madeline again to tell her about the park fiasco. And when she'd called back, he was so excited that her words didn't sting until after she'd hung up. "Quit calling me," she'd said in a groggy whine. "I'm not your girlfriend, okay? We're not even really friends." Her voice turned husky and distant, the phone slipping from her mouth. "You need to stay away from me."

What had he missed? Wasn't her laughter real? And hadn't she reached across and put her hand on his? But the more he thought about their lunch, the stupider his singing seemed. What was he thinking? *We're not even really friends.* Her words moped inside him like a tumor. If he couldn't read Madeline Rousseau, who could he ever hope to know?

He found a calm stretch high on the Nooksack and waded to his boot tops with a heavy stick that he swung over and over against the flat surface, creating one misty rainbow after another until his feet were numb, his shoulders aching, and he was no longer thinking about Madeline or dead cows.

He sorted riverside maple leaves by color, licking their undersides and sticking them to similarly colored leaves to form an eight-by-three-foot quilt fading from red to yellow. He found piles of orange birch leaves and threaded a hundred together lengthwise by their stems, then attached one end to a steep bank and unfurled the rest into an eddy below, creating what looked like a skinny orange waterfall until it broke apart and looked like nothing. He dug through more maple leaves for the largest yellow ones, unfaded by sunlight, and fixed them next to one another in the riverbed with small stones, fashioning an underwater stripe—the yellow all the brighter through the exaggerated and distorted lens of the clear water.

Seasonal shifts had always unnerved him. Even after he learned how predictable they were, he couldn't shake the sensation that he'd blink and miss some critical phase. He often heard that barn swallows assembled in massive departure flocks, but he'd never witnessed any grand exodus and feared he'd already missed out again.

He gathered the flattest stones he could find and tried to construct a cone in the shallows, but it kept collapsing midway up. Then he studied the shed-sized boulders upstream and imagined thawing glaciers dropping them from their mile-thick floes, as his mother had described it, huge rocks settling randomly on the land like carrots and charcoal briquettes from melting snowmen. He covered several rocks, head-sized or larger, with wet leaves, and they looked like giant Easter eggs wrapped in tissue paper. He pulled his shirt off and plastered cottonwood leaves over his damp torso and face until he was nothing but leaves from the hips up.

"Why are you doing this?"

Brandon looked up, startled. He'd forgotten Sophie had followed him out and was still sitting on the bank, silently filming.

"What?"

"Why do you do all this?"

He started coating another rock with red maples. "It relaxes me. And the better I get to know the land, the more it feels like something's gonna happen. Is this it? No. Is it this? No. Is this—"

"You see things other people don't see, don't you?"

"How would I know?"

"I think you do."

"Reality's always more complicated than anybody says it is."

"Who said that?"

Brandon frowned and looked around. "Who's here but you and me?" He turned back to the river before she asked another question and he'd lost his feel for the rocks. He still couldn't find enough flat ones for the cone no matter how carefully he assembled them. He tried again, drawn to the moment before collapse, then walked down the river to look for even flatter stones. He was on his eighth failed cone when a Townsend's warbler broke his concentration with a high buzzy solo and he noticed his hands ached and he was shivering and hungry and it was almost dark. When had Sophie left?

He trolled through downtown Lynden with the heater fan on high, looking for food and a bathroom before remembering it was Sunday and everything was closed. He continued past the windmills; the old barbershop; the post office; the red, white and blue banners; and the stately elms flanking Front Street, noticing how their leaves had begun yellowing on the colder side of the street.

When he got home his mother was staring at photos on the dinner table. She was in all of them. On her father's shoulders at the beach. Graduating from high school. Getting married. Smiling in her garden. Slow-dancing with Norm at their thirtieth. "I just want to be who I've always been," she said. "Nothing fancy. Just me."

"You're still you," Brandon said, draping a damp arm over her, which was enough to snap her back and tell him to shower while she cooked.

He chewed his pork chops to the bones and downed a bowl of red potatoes and a quart of raw milk before telling her what the leaves looked like underwater and that there were more signs of autumn the farther upriver he went. It was hard to tell if she was still listening. He heard her breathing and glanced at her crossed legs, her top slipper bobbing slightly, keeping time with her heart.

"I know I blew that test," she said.

"No, you didn't."

"Yes, Brandon, I did."

"Then it's because you were nervous."

After a long pause, she said, "A cat has twenty muscles in each ear."

"That's right," he replied. "And sharks have been around longer than trees."

SOPHIE CAME HOME to two urgent messages from Wayne saying he absolutely had to see her. So she set up the camera and called him over for a drink.

He was twice as manic and bloodshot as usual, overgesticulating and making incomprehensible statements until he told her about getting zapped by the kite. "The world flashed into focus. And I felt no pain. None."

"You're a lunatic."

"No, I'm just getting closer."

"To death?"

"To what matters! You know what genius is, Soph? It's the thrill of originality so profound it can surprise you, move you, even lift you. How can anyone hear Glenn Gould, *really* hear him, and not be moved? He read music before he could read *words*. Or Coltrane, who spent eleven hours a day doing nothing but scales. Nothing but scales, Sophie. Or Einstein! That weirdo changed our notion of time! Don't just say it. *Feel* it! Changed our notion of time. Or Franklin! Ben might have been brighter than the next ten great men combined. These people were all too excited to *sleep*. Listen to this." He pulled out a typed sheet of paper, glanced at it for several seconds, then set it aside. "Max Perutz," he said.

Sophie shrugged behind the camera.

"Max Perutz was an Austrian who accepted the Nobel Prize in 1962 for discovering the structure of hemoglobin. P-e-r-u-t-z. And get this, just found this last night, this ridiculous genius apologized, in his acceptance speech, for not having made a more conclusive report."

He closed his eyes and delivered the words from memory in a bad Austrian accent. " 'Please forgive me for presenting, on such a great occasion, results which are still in the making. But the glaring sunlight of certain knowledge is dull, and one feels most exhilarated by the twilight and expectancy of the dawn.' " He glanced up, his eyes bulging. "That's all I want, Soph, the exhilaration of twilight. Even if it's vicarious! The expectancy of the dawn!" He rose, his hands reaching for the ceiling.

"Sit down."

"What?"

"Sit."

"Where?"

"Right there."

After he sat down, she flicked on the television and started the video.

"What the hell are—"

"Just watch."

"Oh, please tell me it's not Brandon. Please. Oh, sweet Jesus."

"Shush. Just keep your eyes on this while you give me the latest on Madeline."

33

SHE WATCHED Toby grunt out slow-motion push-ups in the grass next to the Impala while they waited for the chopper.

They were up to two flights a day, he'd explained as they bounced up logging roads into a quiet clearing ringed by blow-down and littered with shotgun shells. He had everyone working overtime to harvest and hump as many loads as possible while a suddenly tentative Border Patrol floundered in bad publicity. Curing times were cut in half. Growers and clippers doubled as smugglers. Five boats were in play now, and the ground crew tripled its daily volumes. But nothing moved product quite like a helicopter, the heaping backlog of B.C. bud flooding Seattle's market and overflowing into Portland and San Francisco and Los Angeles.

She was still unsure whether Toby was educating, courting or trapping her. She wasn't aware of any other girl in his life, but she'd lost the ability to talk to him and had gone from liking to tolerating to dreading his volatile affections and peculiar control over her. He'd told her, for example, exactly which skirt to wear today.

She wished like hell she'd never shared all Brandon had said over lunch. Toby's mole hunt had turned maniacal and he immediately fired three people—a clipper, a smuggler and a grower—without explanation. It didn't stop there. He interrogated everyone, even Fisher. She'd hoped the photos might help her escape now that her cover was blown. But the way he saw it, she was the only one he knew for certain wasn't

235

taking the pictures. That, however, didn't stop him from grilling her about Brandon over and over again.

After their lunch, Brandon had left multiple messages. He wanted to go out to dinner, tell her more about his work and show her his new dog. His last call spluttered around before ending with, "Not to get mushy on you, my friend, but you're well above average." She vaguely recalled leaving him a drunken retort. He hadn't called since, but it continued to unnerve her that he was such a fixture in Toby's thoughts.

He was still pumping on trembling arms, his sweat-glistened torso reminding her of the skinned and headless hogs she'd seen in meat coolers. It took the *woka-woka* of the incoming helicopter to get him, purple-faced, to his feet. "Turn around!" he advised, too late to spare her eyes and nostrils from the sandstorm.

He popped the Impala trunk and speed-walked two black hockey bags to the chopper, its registration number, she noticed, covered with duct tape. After three more trips to the trunk, they were loaded and rising before Madeline had buckled into the backseat. "Ninety-three seconds!" Toby called out as the Impala shrank below them.

She couldn't look down at the lunging greenery without reeling. "Aren't we too low?" Her eyes still burned from the sand, but when she shut them her stomach lurched. Though she tried staring up into the calm blue, that only made her dizzy. Mount Baker wasn't a relaxing sight either, naked from the hips down, melting back into the earth.

"Welcome to America!" the pilot shouted, leering back at her legs long enough for her to see a bloodshot eyeball behind his mirrored shades and an eraser-sized mole nestled between his cheek and nostril.

Toby was barking information at her. They were traveling at 118 miles an hour, heading 43 miles southeast into Washington to a drop spot they and the catcher both knew by GPS coordinates. She'd never seen him so amped. "Our only no-fly days now are sunny weekends," he yelled, "because of all the hikers and rangers."

The helicopter dropped in and out of green canyons. "Aren't we too low?" she asked again, louder.

Toby turned and grinned. "Gotta stay below the radar. At this elevation, we're not here, see? We don't exist."

We don't? She turned away from his little teeth.

Fifteen minutes later, he was jabbing a finger at a green clearing that looked no larger than a marina slip. They circled the spot twice, to see if the catcher had been followed, before falling into a stomach-lurching descent. Her mother had died instantly—and she'd never understood why that was supposed to comfort her. Who wanted to die without even a chance of saying good-bye?

The chopper leveled off into the tightest turn yet, then slowed and stabilized and settled on a surprisingly spacious and level pad forty feet from a green Toyota with a black canopy.

Toby told her to sit tight while he shuttled the bags. The truck driver looked as calm and respectable as a realtor showing property. The nameless pilot kept smacking his lips, trying to scare up saliva, and glancing at her legs.

Why had she been dragged along on this?

Toby climbed back inside, giddy and flushed, his minty B.O. filling the interior as he plopped down next to her and they lifted and twirled back into the canyon. Madeline shut her eyes until everything leveled again, and Toby was leaning his brawny torso against her, grinding her seatbelt into her pelvis and catching her mouth in mid-alarm with his own. She didn't kiss him back, though that didn't discourage his hand from sliding up her thigh.

She couldn't find her voice, but then it came louder than she'd intended. "Stop!" She felt the helicopter dip and heard the pilot shouting. Just as fast, Toby leaned away and was talking rapidly. Apologizing? Complaining? She couldn't make out anything beyond the revulsion pulsing through her. "I'm out!" she announced once she'd regained her breath.

He nodded. "We'll talk next month." While his voice was gentle, he wouldn't look at her. "You can't do this to me now."

34

THE RADIO calls kept coming, a new one right on top of the last. The border-cam dispatcher spotted a drive-thru station wagon in fields near Hammer Road and three people running with duffel bags near Jones Road. Locals phoned in suspicious vehicles on Froberg and Peace Drive as well. The freshest tip was that a sedan carrying two people up Foxhurst exited with just one. Brandon was the closest agent to this north-south road, so he sped toward it.

He'd volunteered for the graveyard shift, thinking he'd stand a better chance of making it through eight hours without facing smirks, glares or sarcastic questions about the bomb-scare fiasco in the park. He was sick of trying to read people and didn't want to talk to anyone except Madeline or his mom. The memory clinic had called his mother to say she'd scored poorly on their test, but that the results might have been skewed by nerves. They wanted her to take another exam. Though she was excited to get a second chance, Brandon felt his world slipping underfoot.

He followed Foxhurst toward the border, then veered off into dirt toward the big swamp. Setting out on foot, with night goggles now, he scanned the trees and sky for pulses of life. He reported to the supervisor that he saw plenty of tracks leading into the woods but couldn't gauge their age, which triggered second-guessing grumbles about chasing swamp ghosts when so much shit was going down in the valley.

The swamp wasn't even considered a smuggling route, as there was no easy route through or around it. Despite being larger than most lakes in the county, it was of so little interest that nobody had ever bothered to name it, though Brandon had always considered it the best place to find marsh wrens or Virginia rails.

He headed into the soggy woodlands toward the border, looking for tracks, trails or any warm-blooded life-form that flashed white in his goggles. It was hard to hear anything over the sucking sound of his boots, so he kept stopping and listening before pushing on again. On one break he heard the distant foghorn of a great horned owl, but forced himself not to reply.

He picked a fast route through scraggly trees and shrubs where roots offered enough traction to almost jog. Then he froze at the squawk of a blue heron that flushed a brood of mallards. Brandon scanned the air for rising ducks, but saw nothing. They were farther away than they sounded. A nighthawk or an owl might have rousted their bunkhouse, or perhaps they'd heard him running. Regardless, he strode toward the commotion until the swamp opened up. Here he stopped again and crouched, scanning the water and the sky and the water once more for motion, his gaze sweeping slowly across its surface. A raccoon or even an aggressive bass could have startled the birds, though he'd never seen a fish in this muck. He was about to resume wading when he saw something move. Through his goggles he could see its warm core. It was too large for a beaver or—then more ducks suddenly went berserk, and he lifted his goggles and shined a powerful beam on the muddy backside of a large man crouched hip-deep in sludge.

He appeared to be wearing army fatigues over a wetsuit that went up over his head, frogman-style, a large neoprene tube strapped to his back.

"Border Patrol!" Brandon shouted.

The man lunged deeper into the swamp. A car slowed on Zero, killed its headlights and glided past, its hopeful passenger within thirty yards of the line and charging for it. If he got there before Brandon got to him, he'd not only be free but could also stand on the other side and taunt him. This had happened to Dionne, who still fumed over it.

Brandon slogged diagonally away toward the shallower side, then galloped along its edge and, within fifteen yards of the border, holstered the flashlight and cut straight toward the man, charging through water up to his calves before finding a log to spring off. His foot slipped, so he got only half the launch he'd hoped for and splashed well short, chest-first. When he got up and sloshed ahead, the gasping man reached back into the top of his pack. That's exactly when Brandon bear-hugged him as a truck howled past just twenty feet away on Zero. They both went underwater for a long moment, but this guy was so winded that Brandon soon felt like he was rescuing him. He practically dragged him to firmer ground, then slapped on handcuffs and propped him against a stump.

It was hard to see what this one looked like even with a flashlight. His face was painted green and black, his eyes wild, his mustache long, his mouth a noisy funnel. Listening to him wheeze, Brandon examined the backpack. Whatever had been in the top compartment was no longer there, but in the main sack he found plastic-wrapped bricks of money on top of two double-wrapped bags of what he slowly realized were handguns.

35

SHE FELT stapled to the recliner across from three young diggers on her tattered sofa, beneath which she'd hid almost $14,000. The floor between them was mined with Subway wrappers, Burger King sacks and Pizza Hut boxes, the coffee table an avalanche of grease-stained magazines and unopened mail. Why was her bedroom door wide open, or as wide as it could get without plowing into jeans, bras and towels? Her bed looked ransacked. Had she dozed off? She recalled snatches of conversation, but who with?

There were four of them now, sharing a joint and talking high on the inhale like kids sucking helium. The couch boys looked like they'd survived a dust storm together. Looking closer, she recognized one—Maniac—she couldn't stand. The clean, older guy on the footstool was familiar, too: Duval. When he pitched forward to load a bong, a pistol grip rose from his coat pocket like an Afro comb.

What time was it, anyway?

When she'd moved in almost two months ago, she never saw the diggers. That was how it was supposed to be. They entered from the rear, had their own toilet and weren't even supposed to come in for water. Toby told her they were digging a subterranean grow twice the size of the one with all the ducks. He'd move her again, he promised, before a single seed was planted. Meanwhile, he said, just stay clear of the barn; the less you know, the more convincing your innocence. You're renting the place to be near your sick father and have no idea what, if anything, the owner does in his barn.

But the less Toby was around, the more his rules were ignored, and he hadn't spent the night since the helicopter fiasco. He'd apologized repeatedly for hitting on her so clumsily and had barely touched her since. But he gave her more work than ever, and she knew it wouldn't be completely over until he let her quit.

Diggers shuffled in and out now as if she ran a halfway house for construction stoners. It was almost fun at first, having people to play with at any hour, though the crew kept changing. When one of them rotated his shoulders, she noticed the heft and snout of another gun.

"Everyone knows a CIA lab in Laos refined heroin in the seventies," Duval began, as if answering a question. "Then they used Noriega, of course, to trade guns for coke with the Contras in the eighties. Remember that? And in the nineties, it's undisputed that the agency supplied the camels to haul opium to labs along the Afghan-Paki border. So why would the U.S. allow the legalization of cannabis when it knows it would forfeit its ability to manipulate the world?"

"But like what does pot have to do with all that?" one of the dustballs asked. "I mean, ya know, what does—"

"Everything starts with cannabis," Duval explained. "Everything."

"Amen," Maniac said. "She gets too fucked up."

Her eyelids fluttered. Who else could he be talking about?

"He needs to either get her out of here or . . ."

She couldn't hear what he said next, but then Duval added, "Well, she didn't get here by keeping her legs crossed."

By the time her eyes snapped open Toby had sprung through the front door, shadowed by Fisher.

"Let's go," Fisher told the diggers, and Toby rummaged around in the kitchen for a clean water glass. "Drive slow." He wheeled a hand to get them moving. "And stay off Zero."

The dustballs exited swiftly, as if trying to slip out before Toby finished hand-washing a glass to his satisfaction. He then opened two windows and stood before her, sipping water as if it were gin. "Told you not to party in here, and didn't I say there should never be any bud on the premises? Could've sworn I said that." He turned to Fisher, then swung back to her. "Or am I losing my mind?"

"You'd know better than I would."

He stared at her, then strolled to her bedroom, nursing the water, pushing the door and looking down at the laundry. "You better start taking better care of yourself."

"Or?" she asked, still startled by what the stoners had said. She cleared her throat, realizing she might cry, and held out callused and lacerated fingers. "Who else is gonna grow your goddamn plants?"

He raised a hand of his own, as if to slap her, then just said, "Please."

Her payouts were half of what they used to be. He blamed a slumping U.S. dollar but, according to Fisher, it had more to do with Vancouver ops getting ripped off, which had only intensified Toby's mole hunt.

"A little birdy just informed me about something." He rocked his skull from side to side like a prizefighter. "Your clumsy childhood pal, as you've described him, intercepted another load tonight. Imagine that. A big one, too. An *important* one."

"Three hundred and twenty thou," Fisher added, "and thirteen—"

Toby cut him off with an eyebrow, then examined her. "Talk to him recently? No? Well, you might ask what tipped him off because there were no sensors, no cameras, no nothing. We've never lost a load through that swamp before. So he obviously got a tip, eh? Or are you gonna suggest it's just dumb luck again?" He stepped closer, head swiveling, eyes wiggling. "I didn't realize you'd dated Monty. Some coincidence, isn't it? Your clumsy pal stumbles upon a smuggler you went out with?"

She glanced at Fisher, who wouldn't make eye contact, and cleared her throat again.

"Having trouble speaking?" Toby asked. "Get you some water?"

"I haven't talked to Brandon since that lunch I told you all about." It was hard not to slur.

Toby shaped his left hand like a pistol and pointed it at her chest. "If your friend's as unassuming as you say, why not just ask him where he's getting all his tips? I should think you'd be motivated to help me find that answer."

"I've got a couple questions of my own," she rasped.

"By all means."

"What happened to your no-pesticides policy?"

Bruised skin twitched beneath his left eye. In the background, Fisher was patting the air and shaking his head, mouthing, *not tonight*.

"And what about your no-weapons policy?" she asked. "What happened to that?"

"Let me know what Brandon says," Toby said after a long stare, then led Fisher out the door.

A half hour later, she braced herself against the kitchen sink and listened to her messages. One from Nicole reminding her of their father's birthday party. The nerve. Another from Helen at the nursery, wondering if she was still *sick*. Her father had called as well, "just checking in," trying not to sound worried. She looked through the window and across the border to where the Crawfords' and the Moffats' lights were burning. Beyond them, the Vanderkools' porch bulb. And was the basement light on too? She splashed her face and chugged water from the faucet, rinsing her mouth and soaking her hair, then walked outside.

36

BRANDON PAINTED from memory. He started out realistically, then veered toward the abstract until only what had to be there remained, a green-black face with domineering eyebrows and a long mustache. He painted fast, a productive frenzy coming on.

His mind shuffled images from the night: the mallards' hysterics, the smuggler's heaving wheeze, the chief's giddiness afterward, bursting disheveled into the bullpen, wearing jeans and his wife's reading glasses, brainstorming on a catchy nickname for the smuggler and settling on Swamp Man.

The gentle knock was enough to trip the three-dog alarm, Leo's yip followed by Maggie's yap and Clyde's startled half-bark. Brandon thought it was a false alarm until he saw Madeline standing on the other side of the glass door, her arms and ankles crossed, as if she'd been watching for some time. She looked wrung out, but it was her!

He quieted the dogs with a toothy whistle, then slid the door open. "You okay?"

"Me?" She looked at him, barefoot and shirtless in paint-smothered jeans, green and black smudges winding up his muscled torso, his eyes blurry. She smelled paint, sour laundry, damp dogs and basement mildew. A monotone behind him said, "Blue grouse," and after a few seconds there was a hollow sound, like someone blowing into a beer bottle.

"Half of your hair's wet," he said. "You look . . ."

Her smile tightened as she squatted to pet the wagging mutts. "Drunk? Hope I didn't set off any sensors."

"Where'd you cross?" Brandon sent the dogs to their pads with a finger snap.

She told him. He bunched his lips and shook his head.

The monotone spoke again—"red-breasted nuthatch"—followed by evenly spaced beeps, like a truck backing up.

"What're we listening to?"

"*Bird Songs of the Puget* . . ." He stepped toward the stereo. "I'll turn it off."

"Leave it," she said.

He started to speak but just stared at her with a half smile, as if he'd lost an amusing thought on the way to his lips.

She followed his eyes to one of his Rorschachs—complete or in progress, she had no idea. Two cold eyes above a familiar mustache. "Wow! Whatcha got there?"

"The guy I found tonight in the swamp."

She cut her laugh off. "You paint the people you—"

"All of them." He made a circular motion with his finger. "Every last one."

She took in the entire room for the first time. An extra-long, king-sized bed with neither foot- nor headboards. Bedside books stacked vertically. A desk and easels that came up to her shoulders. Gallon jugs of water. Three dogs curled on individual flying-saucer pads of ascending size. Canvases stacked a half dozen deep against every wall. A lamp in the middle with a moose silhouette on its shade.

"Double-crested cormorant," said the robotic voice before a screech like nails being wrenched from wood.

Brandon showed her more canvases stacked near the bathroom, talking in gusts about whom he caught where and what they did or said.

"These're amazing," Madeline said, squatting on her haunches to get closer.

"Yeah?"

"Not just for you, for anybody. But if you can make people look so real, why make them seem so weird most of the time?"

He hesitated. "I'm not trying to be a camera."

"How'd you catch that guy tonight, Brandon?" His cockeyed expression made her worry he was onto her. "I mean, did a sensor go off, or did you catch him on camera or something?"

"No."

"Somebody tip you? Some homeowner? Or a Canadian?"

Again he studied her, as if straining to translate a language he almost understood. "No."

"Well," she pressed, her mouth drying out, "so why are you always in the right spot at the right time?"

"I was looking for owls."

"Owls?" She smiled. "That's the reason you were there?"

"Yep." How drunk *was* she? Some of her words dragged, and she had a boneless quality to her. He was determined not to miss any body language this time.

"There wasn't any tip or anything?"

"Just the heron and the ducks," he said. "The mallards were going crazy. *Wack-wack-wack-wack-wack!*"

She lingered on a painting that looked like kids with psychedelic skin holding hands and rising off an invisible trampoline. She moved to the next one, then returned to the bouncing children: a huge boy and a slender, dark-haired girl. "You believe in heaven, Brandon?" She suddenly felt like she might start bawling.

"I believe in reincarnation."

She grinned up at him. "So what did someone do to come back as you?"

He paused. "Doubt it was a person," he said, then started listing the animals he felt closest to—Jersey cows, snowy owls, Australian shepherds, blue herons and so on—until he noticed her flexing forehead and wandering eyes. When he heard the western meadowlark's insecure melody, he wished like hell he'd turned off that CD.

"Why do you keep calling me?" she asked, her eyes fixed on

another startling painting, a flock of birds with Asian faces. "Haven't I scared you off by now?"

"I like you, Maddy."

"In what way?"

"Every way."

She focused again on the paintings, specifically a canvas of tiny but remarkably vivid faces, mostly gaping mouths, crammed inside what appeared to be the interior of a van. She caught his crooked smile on her. "Even after I tell you to get lost?"

"I shouldn't have sung 'Blackbird' at the restaurant," he said. "That was really stupid."

She felt ready to cry again. "No, that was fine. A little weird, but sweet. I need to lay down, Brandon."

She reclined on the bed and then, after a long moment during which he just watched her, she sat up, crossed her arms at her hips and started to pull her shirt off.

"I'm not good with—"

"Should I stop?" She froze midway, just above the pink birthmark next to her belly button.

"I'm good not—"

"You'll be fine."

"I don't think—"

"No?"

"I'm not in bed good, Maddy. I mean, I—"

"You prefer the floor?"

"No, it's just—"

She pulled off her shirt and dropped it on the floor.

"Fox sparrow," said the stereo, followed by a lewd whistle.

Brandon lay as still as he could as she pulled his pants and underpants over his long legs and enormous flat feet. She giggled when she saw he was too shy or scared to look below her chin. She climbed up beside his head and whispered, "Simon says kiss me."

He mimicked her every move. When her lips pressed harder, he returned the pressure, careful to keep his teeth covered. He tried to remember everything: the smell of her smoky hair and peppermint mouth; the rash on her arched neck that reminded him of a red-throated loon; the bulb of her chin; her oval nostrils; the white slits of her almost closed eyes; the yamlike shape of her right breast, slightly larger than its partner and leaning outward, as if pointing to something across the room.

He slowly raised a hand to align that breast with the other, astonished by its luxurious smoothness. There weren't any surprise ledges, headboards or bedside tables to worry about. Everything felt suspended in this safe slow motion.

Ten minutes later—or maybe twenty or thirty, while he concentrated on not moving, on not hurting her or himself, on not missing any sensation—she was suddenly, amazingly on him. Weightlessly, half-suspended, almost nonchalantly, as if it weren't some tricky, anatomical safecracking or awkward skirmish of elbows, knees and teeth. He marveled at the simplicity of it if he just let her do all the moving, her slender left arm with the mole near the elbow flung out to the side for balance. He watched her concentration escalate as it had when as a child she'd tried to convince him and Danny that she could do things with her mind like turn up the stereo. And the sounds! *Her* sounds! Madeline Rousseau's sounds! Her light growl got the dogs yipping, first Leo and then Maggie before Brandon snapped his fingers. She leaned forward and whispered that in a moment she would let him move *just* a little bit. No Simon says now, just a slight pleading for him to move—but not yet. When she finally, breathlessly, told him precisely how to move and he obeyed, her shudder reminded him of those old rockets that shook like they wouldn't make it out of the atmosphere without ripping into a billion pieces before they popped through effortlessly to float freely above the blue earth.

"Maddy?" he said, once he couldn't bear the quiet any longer. "Are you floating?"

"Uh-huh."

"Do you remember in school when they'd show videos of those old *Apollos,* back when they—"

"Brandon?" Her thoughts flopped between thinking it was the sanest, gentlest sex she'd ever had and sensing she'd hit a shameful new low.

"Yes?" he replied.

"Please just be real, real quiet."

He didn't notice the catch in her voice or the tears rolling into her ears. "Astronauts," he whispered.

"Please."

"It's just a sentence. You'll like it."

"Okay."

"Astronauts' footprints stay on the moon forever," he whispered, "because there's no wind to blow them away."

37

SOPHIE LISTENED to Tony Patera whine about the media under-playing Swamp Man and his ominous load of thirteen handguns and $320,000. But there was little time to contemplate that bust before it was steamrolled by an unrelated *Seattle Times* story that became international fodder by noon.

The "Space Needle Bomber" who triggered a multimillion-dollar increase in northern border security and strained U.S.-Canadian relations this summer is not the Algerian terrorist federal agents originally suspected, but rather the troubled son of a wealthy couple from a posh Seattle suburb.

While U.S. authorities initially thought they had Shareef Hasan Omar in custody, they actually had Michael T. Rosellini, twenty-six, who grew up in Broadmoor, one of Seattle's most affluent neighborhoods. His father is a vice president at CellularOne, his mother a programmer for Microsoft.

The mistaken identity was complicated by the twenty-three-day coma Rosellini endured after crashing his chased vehicle near Lynden on April 8. A subsequent search found a trunk full of explosives and three pounds of marijuana in the door panels.

Rosellini's former friends and coworkers described a troubled rebel who loved pot and couldn't hold a job. "He reinvented himself five times by the age of twenty-two," said one old friend. He was a punk rocker, a Nietzsche reader who liked to detonate homemade bombs in abandoned quarries. More recently, he frequented a Seattle mosque to show his support for oppressed Muslims and to agitate his Presbyterian parents. Three photos showed his progression from a clear-eyed senior to a shaggy Alaska deckhand to a bearded Costco worker who, with his mother's East Indian coloring, arguably resembled Shareef Hasan Omar, also pictured.

With the help of federal sources, the newspaper pieced together Rosellini's recent exploits. A letter from a Seattle imam introduced him to leaders of a radical London mosque, but he was not embraced. He showed up next at Toronto mosques, exaggerating his ties to a London imam. Again he wasn't trusted, though somehow he acquired fake identities—one of them was Hassan Mahjoub, a reputed alias for Omar—as well as explosives.

It was unclear what, if anything, he had targeted. The Space Needle map found in his vehicle turned out to be a tourist pamphlet. Rosellini's unconscious fingerprint didn't help much, because neither he nor Omar had ever been arrested and printed. The mystery, however, was over once he awakened. The FBI's only public comment was that he was being held on drug, explosives and other potential charges, including conspiracy to levy war against the United States.

Friends were split on whether Rosellini was a con man, a believer or a wannabe, though none of them believed he was capable of harming anybody but himself.

Sophie watched the news sink in, nobody knowing quite how to react. A collective attention-deficit disorder took hold. People half-listened to one another, and even the prime minister couldn't contain his smirk when asked if he found it ironic that Canada had caught so much hell from Washington, D.C., over someone who turned out to be a U.S. citizen.

Sophie received multiple copies of a *Maclean's* cover story called

"America's Clumsy Wars on Drugs and Terror" in which former UBC professor Wayne Rousseau was quoted as saying, "The U.S. is the paranoid bully of the world. From where I'm sitting, it looks like Americans are being terrorized by themselves. It's a new wrinkle on FDR's famous apothegm: All we have to fear is . . . *ourselves*."

38

THE FATHERLY thrill that came with seeing both his daughters in his house at the same time quickly faded. The same tension that used to take hours to surface arose immediately with Nicole's forearms-only embrace in exchange for Maddy's bear hug. Meanwhile, her mannequin husband arrived with the wincing smile of someone serving soup at the Salvation Army for the very first time. Wayne's friends, Lenny and Rocco, acted subdued from the beginning, nibbling around the kitchen, peeking at him to see if he was missing the undercurrents.

Nicole dominated the dinner conversation, as if afraid where it might lead without her guidance, rattling on about neighborhoods getting renovated in Vancouver. Wayne resisted pointing out that gentrification is hardly a synonym for progress. He winked, smiled and passed the curried vegetables Maddy had cooked, which Rocco and Lenny praised, and Nicole and Mitchell picked through.

It irritated Wayne that Nicole hadn't said a word about his cameo in *Maclean's*. He hadn't received so much praise since his retirement party, which allowed him to indulge the daydream that he might ultimately be remembered for his ability to elucidate American hubris and hypocrisy. Who knows? Maybe relations would hit such a flashpoint there'd be a CBC retrospective on him, with producers scrambling for footage of incisive lectures or tracking down bootleg videos like Sophie Winslow's doozy of his impromptu jousting with Congress. He'd stayed up the night before making notes on future essays, just the fearless ideas themselves, each more provocative than the last. People would want to hear his thoughts. It didn't matter when or even if he published them. They wanted to *hear!* So he wrote and wrote, but the pot wore thin and he went from feeling like a modern Mencken to a washed-up simpleton. His comments in *Maclean's,* he noticed for the first time, in fact, weren't exactly what he'd said and suddenly sounded like arrogant cheap shots.

That, no doubt, was what Nicole thought. He told himself to let it go, but how could they not even mention it? He waited patiently for the mannequin to quit chewing. "So, Mitchell, what do you make of that scary Canadian terrorist turning out to be a wayward American?"

"Well, Wayne," he began in his affected baritone, "it doesn't change the fact that we've got problems of our own, that our asylum policies are the most generous and foolish in the world."

"That's your reaction?" Wayne tried to control his voice. "Blame Canada anyway?"

"I think we just look at this sort of thing differently, Wayne. We don't have to agree on everything, do we?"

Wayne caught Nicole's glare and took another bite.

Lenny shifted the conversation to real estate and the crazy prices for Zero Ave. properties. "Even trailer lots are double what they were three years ago."

"Location, location, location," Nicole said. "If your business is drug smuggling what better place to be?" She glanced at her sister, then began lecturing everyone about the benefits of foreign index funds, hinting that Wayne desperately needed to finally get smart with what little money he had.

So there will be more for you? he wanted to ask.

"I think she may be right on this one, Wayne," Mitchell added dulcetly. "You seriously might want to get some guidance on some of this stuff, given that it's not your primary area of interest or expertise."

Money had never mattered to Wayne, even before he was dying. "Perhaps I'll find someone," he said through his teeth.

"Well, I *am* a broker," Nicole blurted, rolling her eyes. "Earth to Dad! Your daughter's a broker with Kunkel and Bradford."

Madeline smiled at Lenny. "Welcome to our family dynamics. If you stick around long enough, you might get the impression that my sister isn't bashful with her advice."

Nicole dropped her fork. "Yeah, Larry, stick around and you'll figure out that my sister's a drug dealer."

"*Lenny,*" Madeline corrected.

"What?" Nicole snapped.

"And FYI, I don't deal drugs, but I'd rather sell them than whatever it is you're pushing."

"And what, exactly, do you know—"

"Stop," Wayne scolded. "Both of you."

"It *is* a birthday party," Rocco added with a smile.

Nicole cut a chicken breast into pieces so small there was nothing left to slice. "You're not the least bit curious how she could afford to rent the Damant house?" she asked Wayne. "Didn't that strike you as a bit odd? Hmmm, why would she want to live there?"

"To be near her father?" His eyes flickered between the two of them, his wife alive in both of their faces. "To get more space?"

"Smoke some more *medicine*, Dad. What about her Nissan? Pretty nice car for someone who quit her job at the nursery, eh? Oh, I'm sorry. You didn't know she quit, did you?"

"Refresh my memory," Wayne said, "exactly how many kids have you raised?"

"*That's* your reaction?" She tugged at the neck of her blouse. "So happens that a doctor and a broker don't have a whole lot of time left over to overpopulate the planet. But of course sixty-hour workweeks aren't something you'd know a whole lot about."

Wayne looked at Lenny. "Who would've thought a daughter of mine would end up living the American dream?"

"That wasn't funny the first ten times you said it, Dad."

"A broker and an anesthesiologist," he said, without looking up from his food.

"What?"

"You always call him a doctor." He took another gulp of wine.

"Dad, that is so ignorant."

Wayne couldn't stop himself. "Guess he'll come in handy if you need to put a dog down. But wait, that's right, you two don't have any time for dogs either."

Nicole's chair fell backwards as she shot upright. "Enjoy your gift, Dad." Then, to Madeline, "Don't expect me to visit you in jail or rehab."

Madeline exhaled melodramatically. "Thank God."

Nicole picked up her chair. "You're changing, Dad, and she's an addict."

"And you've already said twice as much as you needed to say."

"But you haven't?"

Wayne muscled a smile. "Please, let's just try to start over here. Please."

Mitchell rose, white-faced, his jaw tendons popping. "Think it's a bit late for that."

They collected their bags and coats as if the house were on fire, dumping the angel cake onto a plate so Nicole could take her pan, and left with a *whomp* of the screen door.

Wayne realized the next time they came to the house he'd be dead. He went to the kitchen window to watch them pull out, but instead saw Norm Vanderkool hobbling to his mailbox with a look of dread. He apologized to his wife in his head, then aloud to Rocco and Lenny. He sighed and reluctantly turned to Maddy, chewing the corner of his lip. "Please tell me," he said softly, "you didn't quit the nursery."

39

GOOD NEWS usually comes in person, bad news in the mail. That's why it stunned Norm to get a letter from the EPA lady telling him that after a month of testing and two photo flyovers they'd determined that his lagoon wasn't contaminating the creek. He had to read it twice to make sure that's what it said, then again, slowly, to revel in its conclusion. Everything was couched in stingy language about ongoing monitoring and future potential penalties, but strip all that aside and the score was Norm, 1; U.S. government, 0.

And this came when he was already on a roll. Three healthy new calves and he was down to an almost routine dozen cases of mastitis, only three of which appeared to be staph. And with the settlement Lankhaar's attorney had already scared out of the Everson farmer's insurers, Norm was due to ultimately receive twice what he could have gotten at auction for those eight cows—even if one was Pearl. Now he was just waiting for the first of three $12,000 checks to clear: enough to buy some two-year-olds and maybe—yes, maybe!—the mast and rigging from that guy in Anacortes and—who knows?—possibly start shopping for a twenty-five-horse Yanmar. Everything was lining up in the good column. Jeanette seemed to be tracking better. And despite the ongoing waves of embarrassment at the Border Patrol, Brandon was not only still alive but also still employed and helping with the bills. Even milk prices had shot up twenty-three percent.

So when this BP with obnoxious sideburns and an oversized mustache swung by that afternoon to ask in a somber voice to please accompany him to HQ, Norm's mind couldn't catch up. When it finally did, his first thought was that Brandon's luck had run out. As Jeanette had shouted the night after he caught that guy with all the guns, "How many lives do you think he has?" And now this dour agent. "Brandon?" Norm said hesitantly.

Agent McAfferty seemed to understand. "He's fine. This has to do with you, Mr. Vanderkool. The chief would like to talk to you."

"Have him call me," Norm said, relieved and slightly confused. "I've got—"

"You need to come to the station, sir."

Sir? He studied the portly agent, reading the name tag again, his anger rising.

"Please," McAfferty continued, gesturing such that Norm thought he was about to grab his hand.

He flinched, his nerves suddenly afire, then reluctantly stepped outside. "I'll meet you there," he grumbled, feeling for his keys in the wrong pocket.

"Think you'd better come with me, sir."

He sighed, looked back at the house, then limped out to the idling green-and-white, his knee grinding on cue. Without thinking, he glanced down Boundary to see Sophie pretending to trim a hedge and then, reluctantly, across the ditch to where Professor Smokestack stood on his deck in checkered shorts, his legs as thin and pale as bones.

The station seemed practically abandoned compared to the last time he'd shown up, just two agents in the bullpen and a skinny supervisor plunking away at a computer with his back to the door. Norm followed McAfferty into the hall, then noticed that the man sitting in the holding pen looked familiar, even from behind.

"Luther?"

McAfferty stopped when he realized Norm was dawdling, and started wheeling his arm like an impatient traffic cop.

The man wouldn't turn to face Norm and in fact leaned farther away. Luther Stevens, the former high-school principal? The man Norm once feared Jeanette had fallen for?

"This way, sir," McAfferty said, then walked him brusquely down the hall.

Patera looked like he'd aged a decade since Norm last saw him. He didn't stick his hand out like some gift as he usually did, and instead grabbed Norm's shoulder as if to steady him.

"The hell's going on?" Norm asked. "What's Luther doing in—"

"Come on back."

Patera led him into another room, where that SOB McAfferty and some wooden-faced poser named Rawlins pulled up chairs. Their boss talked in sweeping phrases about how, as Norm no doubt knew, the patrol had been dealing with quite a few delicate situations lately, and that the last thing they wanted to do was jump the gun. He glanced at Rawlins, checking to make sure his wording was right. "But we've still got a job to do here, see. And, well, Agent Canfield caught three illegals cutting through your property last night."

Norm felt short of breath.

"And under questioning, well, you see, one of them said, well, he said the landowner—in this case, you, Norm—were—"

"Getting paid for their safe passage," McAfferty interjected impatiently. "Said he understood that you—he knew your name, Mr. Vanderkool—were getting compensated to the tune of ten grand a month."

"No. That's . . ." Norm felt another swoon coming on, and the sound went out of the room. He wiggled his jaw, futilely trying to pop his ears, then shut his eyes and waited, realizing that he was just nineteen months younger than his father was when he stroked out.

"Norm?"

"I never agreed to any—"

"That's what we assumed," Patera said, glaring at McAfferty, "but this situation is particularly delicate, because one of the illegals in custody is someone we deported years ago by mistake, someone we later learned was the right-hand man to Ahmad Saeed Jaballah."

"I didn't. . . . The who?"

"Jaballah recruits out of Montreal for the Egyptian al jihad. They call him al Kanadi, or 'the Canadian' in Arabic. So, as a courtesy to you, Norm, before this likely becomes an FBI matter . . . See, there's also the unsettling matter of a sudden spike in your checking account."

"You're looking at my—"

"Pretty standard these days, Norm, in a case like this where—"

He started giggling, feeling so dizzy that it took him a few beats to collect himself.

IN THE DAYS after his inquisition, Norm thought he noticed stares and double takes, but he hadn't been out enough to know what people thought or knew or heard. He'd avoided venturing into public, except in passing, until now.

Even after his explanation about the settlement payments on the bad feed, the SOB wouldn't let it be. He'd straddled a chair backwards and asked him point-blank if he'd *ever* been approached by *anyone* offering to buy access through his property.

Norm hesitated. He couldn't coax himself to actually say no, but he somehow managed to shake his head. He wasn't under oath, right? And if he hadn't been paid, what the hell was the issue?

"Mr. Vanderkool, are you telling us that you've never once been solicited by anyone trying to run drugs or illegals through your farm?"

Norm blinked faster. If he said, "Well, yeah," he'd be admitting he'd lied. But if he mumbled, "No, absolutely not," he'd have lied twice. Patera seemed to encourage the evasion, nodding along with his quarter-truths and even telling McAfferty, "Enough already," as if his own judgment were on trial too.

"Nothing about receiving payments on the twenty-third of the month?" the SOB persisted, his mustache twitching like a lie detector. "Is that what you're saying? Nothing along those lines at all from some friendly young buck calling himself Andrew or Michael or William?"

Norm's heart galloped. Stalling, staring at the agent, daring him to continue, he finally muttered, "Imagine every living soul along Boundary Road has heard that bullshit." He took a series of shallow breaths.

"But this hustler, this kid, never said for what, and I, of course, never agreed to anything. Quite the opposite."

Suddenly Patera wasn't reeling the SOB back anymore, and all the oxygen left the room as Norm recounted the entire affair with the kid on his porch and how he saw him again in church and all the confusing nodding that had ensued. By the end of it, his clothes were soaked and the BPs stepped out for a discussion.

Being driven home by the insufferable agent in surly silence, he lowered his window to breathe and to dilute his stink, wishing like hell they were driving faster, at least the speed limit.

"You surprise me, sir," McAfferty finally said, turning off Northwood onto Boundary, exchanging an intimate little index-finger wave with Sophie Winslow and creeping slower and slower toward Norm's house. "I would have expected the father of Brandon Vanderkool to be considerably more candid."

Norm's attempted laugh came off as a grunt. "Don't be so hard on yourself," he said without glancing at him. "My expectations usually miss the mark too."

The new publicity-shy BP didn't put out a release about catching a suspected terrorist. What got out traveled by word of mouth alone. And Norm saw the rumor twinkling in Sophie's eyes—"Please come talk"—and in Wayne Rousseau's urgent wave over and in the glances he got at the Chevron the one time he'd risked fueling in Lynden. He'd skipped church too.

Duke's Steakhouse was the first real test, so he struggled to look better than he felt. It was Jeanette's idea to go out, and Brandon had jumped on it. What could he do, demand that she cook?

She wore a festive floral scarf and a smile to match as she excitedly told Brandon about some fossils found just east of Mount Baker. She'd taken the second memory test that afternoon and come home invigorated, confident she'd redeemed herself. Even her teeth glimmered, as if all the health food and exercise was not only healing her but peeling back the years.

Meanwhile, Norm felt about 109, just cut him open and count the rings. He did his best impression of amiable attentiveness, despite sweat crawling high enough to sting his freshly shaved neck. Neither Brandon nor Jeanette grasped what he'd endured at the station, dismissing it as yet another amusing mix-up in a long parade of them. But Brandon was harder to read than usual. A powerful melancholy had seemingly settled inside him over the past several days that, for once, he couldn't shake off by morning. He looked older, too, like a man sucking it up, wrestling with problems he was trying to conceal. This Norm saw as progress.

Morris Crawford strolled over before the meal arrived, looking like Sam Shepard in a plaid shirt rolled to mid-forearms and long jeans so perfectly cut and faded that they looked formal.

Norm rose to greet the popular raspberry man, his head swimming slightly. Something about him had always created an intense desire not to be one-upped.

"So how's the yacht comin', Captain?"

Norm had heard Crawford spin the same question dozens of times, yet he'd never been able to ascertain exactly where it fell between admiration and amusement.

"Beautifully," Jeanette said before he could respond. "We're thinking about entering one of those around-the-world races next year."

His rush of gratitude was so complete that he didn't know what to add as Crawford casually clasped Jeanette's left hand, then shook his and addressed Brandon through a smile. "Danny was just asking about you. Said to say hey if I saw you, so 'Hey.' "

"When's he coming back?" Brandon asked, as he did every time he saw the man.

"Maybe Christmas?" Crawford replied hopefully. "We'll see. Meanwhile, could you do us all a favor and tell that patrol of yours that they've got more important things to do than harass your old man?"

There it was, laid out just like a grinning congressman would've, acknowledging that he *knew* yet placing it in the most flattering light. Norm's mind was so jammed he didn't hear Brandon's response, but by the quiver in Crawford's forehead he could tell it hadn't made any sense. Then the raspberry mogul was off, flattering a waitress with a parade wave and sauntering down the steps as if he owned them.

Norm had skipped lunch and still couldn't muster enough appetite to dent his sirloin before he saw—oh, please, no—Dale Mesick pointing him out to his suspiciously well-preserved wife and plodding over. The true test: almost everyone else offered one face to yours and another to your back, but Shit-to-Power had only one face.

"Hey, Norman," he said, his peroxide doll a step and a half behind, her tongue fussing with spinach caught in her bright teeth. "Good to see you and the family, my friend. Y'all remember Melanie?"

Norm tried to fold his napkin next to his plate, but either the cloth was too starched or his fingers couldn't finesse it, so he rose to greet head-on whatever he was up against.

"What's this B.S. anyway?" the stubby bastard demanded, far louder than was necessary. "First we hear Doc Stremler's running dope, then it's some big-shot terrorist paying a fortune to cross your farm?"

Norm hadn't got a third of the way up before his bad knee locked. His other foot, pawing the carpet for leverage and traction, for some reason found neither. When he tried to make fun of himself nothing came out, as if he were suffering an odd power outage that would pass if he just let it. Before the full swoon hit and the chandelier spun, before he toppled backwards and lost consciousness, he experienced a passing fantasy—simple enough to realize, if he'd had time to whisper his request—that Brandon would cradle him like a child, one arm behind his neck, the other beneath his knees, and quietly carry him from the sweltering restaurant into the cooling night.

40

UNTIL NORM'S stroke, the growing roster of busted locals had been as titillating as it was unsettling. News of Eugene Stremler's arrest flabbergasted just about everyone, especially those whose animals he'd cared for and those he'd enlisted in his anti-casino brigade. But the rich-vet-gone-bad zinger—Customs found forty pounds in his Mercedes trunk during a rare random search of NEXUS lane vehicles— was soon upstaged by news of Luther Stevens. The beloved principal, caught with 160 pounds in his wood shop? Still, from what Sophie could tell, people seemed more shocked by Norm's alleged involvement.

When rumors first slipped about illegals buying access across his land, Sophie heard outrage. Things had gotten so absurd that even stalwarts like Norm were getting slandered. There was, however, another reaction. If Norm, Luther and the doc really were involved, then all the rules had changed, right? If they think it's okay to cut themselves a piece of the pie, what's to stop the rest of us?

And something about those busts and rumors brought on a mass confessional in which people almost lined up to tell Sophie about their indiscretions. Even the mousiest locals suddenly had stories. They started mild, with tales of sneaking undeclared cases of whiskey over the line, but often swerved into the bizarre. Beekeeper Tawni Metz admitted smuggling eight thousand queen bees to Victoria, where she sold them for $100,000. Another's crime was profiting off the Beanie Babies craze in the nineties. Several farmers fessed up to hauling in hundreds of gallons of Canuck Gold, the Canadian version of Roundup. Elderly couples told Sophie about repeated trips to Canadian pharmacies for discounted Lipitor, Celebrex and Zoloft. Others shared old family secrets about rum-running uncles and grandfathers who bushwhacked the same routes bud runners used today. A few came forward saying they'd recently sold overpriced border parcels to shady out-of-towners.

To Sophie it felt as if the citizenry were undergoing some sort of group therapy. Even quiet Vern Moffat took a break from his leaf blowing to tell her how his younger brother had smuggled eighty pounds in the false floor of a horse trailer. "Nobody wants to get in there and shovel the manure out." Smaller indiscretions—an ounce here, a gram there—were more prevalent, of course, back when the border wasn't watched so closely, and there were also the oddball things people or their "friends" snuck over the line—whether grizzly hides, black-bear teeth, whale bones, wolf skulls, moose meat, crane jerky or Cuban cigars. Katrina Montfort veered off-topic to relate a twenty-five-year-old story about her teenage affair with a hazelnut farmer who kept hopping the ditch to sneak into her parents' house on Peace Drive.

Sophie chronicled all of it, and people increasingly asked to go on camera. After three vodka tonics, even Alexandra Cole ventured into the light to describe exactly how the bank could tell which locals were laundering money, without naming individuals or businesses but making it tantalizingly clear who was about to get busted.

Still, the tiny blood clot that lodged in a narrow vessel in Norm Vanderkool's brain while he rose to shake Dale Mesick's hand at Duke's on a two-for-one Tuesday took the fun out of this mass confessional, especially since Norm increasingly appeared innocent and wrongly maligned. They'd even ransacked his bank account!

The clot lasted just long enough to give Norm what the doctor called an ischemic stroke, though it did enough damage to launch a new prevailing notion: The increased security is *killing* us. Sophie heard rumblings about an anti-government posse forming to "take the county back," a mood summed up by Dirk Hoffman's new reader board: BP GO HOME.

As it played out, many agents were already on their way. Within a week, headquarters transferred fourteen of them to the southern line and flew a cost analyst out from D.C. to examine the sector's books and particularly its handling of the border cams, which reportedly malfunctioned whenever temperatures rose above seventy-one degrees. Patrols were trimmed, and the green-and-whites soon blended in with the tractors and trucks lumbering along Boundary, H Street and beyond.

When Brandon Vanderkool quietly resigned to take care of the family dairy while his father recuperated, it felt, to most, like the end of a very peculiar era.

41

HE STROLLED through the dairy, picking up after Roony again—a bucket knocked over here, an empty juice bottle there, a bright jug of bleach and a pair of torn yellow rubber gloves dangling near the parlor exit, which helped explain why some cows had hesitated when he shooed them out that morning. He took a bright silver ladder out back and spray-painted it gray, then rearranged the pallets near the parlor's entrance so the northeasterlies wouldn't make them want to turn around and put their butts into the wind, which complicated everything.

He hopped on the Super Slicer and cut bales, then pulled a trailerful past the feed trough. He noticed 73's swollen left eye and absently started checking the others, finding limps he hadn't spotted in 17 and 69. It was getting harder to keep weight on some older ones, particularly 11 and 28. He strode around back to bottle-feed the youngest calf.

Dionne, McAfferty and the rest had tried to talk him out of it, yammering about all his wasted training and talent, his knack for the work, his *gift*. And Patera had initially refused to accept his resignation, insisting he take a week's paid vacation to think it through. But the chief had eventually relented, in part because he was told to relieve or transfer another fifteen agents by December. Besides, it was obvious that Brandon's father needed more recovery time.

He talked well enough and seemed the same physically, yet he looked strangely becalmed. He took his time eating, dressing and listening. When he did step outside, he shuffled through the dairy like an old man reminiscing. There was no argument from Norm when Brandon took over and left him with just the books. He routinely overslept and retreated after breakfast to his boat barn, where he hadn't spent so much time since the gleaming hull had arrived on a flatbed and a small mob of doubters watched to see if it would fit inside.

When Brandon had called to tell Madeline about his father's stroke, she apparently hadn't checked caller ID because she groaned at the sound of his voice. He was so surprised she'd picked up that he hadn't known what to say, then she started lecturing him—again—about what a mistake it had been. But now it wasn't just a mistake, it was a "huge mistake." Perhaps his all-time favorite hour had been reduced to a gigantic error. "We're totally different people!" Then gentler, but still raspy and foreign: "I was so messed up. Please just forget about it."

As if memories were optional. All he'd managed to blurt before she hung up? "I can't not forget."

He spent hours auditioning combinations of words that could change her mind before finally coming up with the perfect response to her comment about how different they were. He'd tell her his mother's story about the moose that fell in love with a cow named Jessica in Vermont and courted her for seventy-six days. A moose and a cow! Seventy-six days! Complications arose once he pictured Madeline asking what happened next. He tried writing everything down, hoping his words would look more persuasive on paper. Maybe he could read them to her over the phone. But the longer he rewrote and rehearsed, the more garbled the words seemed. He forced himself to give it a break when he realized he was rocking so fast that his neck was swinging.

Luckily, he could lose himself in the rhythm of the dairy. He'd switched out all the bedding, regraded the barn alleys and changed the metal tracks on two sliding doors to a quieter plastic. He'd cleaned the vacuum controller and convinced his father to buy better semen. And today he intended to take advantage of a dry, windless lull to spray the fields without stinking up the valley. He could see his breath that morning, and the leaves were turning so fast they fit into his notion that everything was rushing by.

When he wasn't working on the dairy, he poured himself into his paintings and forms. His rock cones, knotweed structures, leaf mosaics and oil paintings kept surprising him. Sophie often tagged along, snapping and filming with such an odd intensity that it sometimes felt incomplete when she wasn't there, setting up her tripod or adjusting her video camera.

After a grumpy new feed truck driver rattled up and filled the silo, Brandon shed his rubber boots and bib and stepped out of the barn beneath a quiet, birdless sky. He piled the dogs into the front seat and headed to town to get more tetracycline and ampicillin, studying the loopy telephone lines along the ditch where his mother swore barn swallows had assembled by the thousands one September. If they'd already left, why hadn't the seabirds arrived yet? What if all the brants, wigeons, scoters, buffleheads, mergansers and trumpeters decided to forgo the exhausting flight and winter up north? Then what?

He was surprised to see the feed truck again, parked just a few blocks down Boundary in the primitive dirt and grass driveway leading to Dirk Hoffman's roadside outbuilding on the northern fringe of his L-shaped property. The massive rig was parked so hastily that its last three feet were cantilevered sloppily into the oncoming lane. Puttering past, Brandon noticed that the rear of the truck was listing more to the left than the slope warranted.

"He have a flat?" he asked the dogs, their ears lifting. He pulled over and climbed out, the dogs clawing after him and flopping out his side. He shut the door, then crossed Boundary to have a look at the left-rear duo of deflated Goodyears. The driver was shouting inside his cab, probably yelling into a phone at somebody, Brandon figured, about those tires. He strode up to the cab, picturing the size of the jack this job would take, the dogs behind him in a single file from smallest to largest.

The man's window was open, and Brandon's head filled it without him having to step on the foot rail. "Got a flat?"

The driver was so alarmed he dropped his phone, then frantically groped around near his feet as a small voice whined through it. "Hold on a sec!" he growled, smothering the phone against his chest. "Having a row with the wife. Ya mind?"

His tone was hostile enough to start Leo yapping, which got Maggie going and Clyde too, halfheartedly. Brandon backed up, silenced all three with a wave, then strode back to the rear wheels again with Leo still acting like they'd treed a raccoon. On closer inspection, the tires didn't appear deflated so much as sunken to their rims, though the soil looked dry and solid. He circled the truck as the driver's griping rose into a wail. "Well, that's what credit-card companies do!" The other twenty tires sat plump and firm atop the sun-baked earth.

Brandon glanced across Boundary and Zero. Was she there? With the curtains drawn and no cars in sight, the Damant house seemed abandoned, as it had since the cheerful couple left for a retirement home a year ago. The forgettable barn, slightly back and to the left, looked as unused as ever.

It wasn't until the feed man hopped down on his foot rail to ask, with his arms flailing, what the hell he was doing that Brandon's eyes followed the narrow dirt road leading from the rear of Dirk's outbuilding through the maze of leased raspberry fields toward Pangborn Road. When he glanced back across the ditch at the Damant barn and then down at the sunken wheels, he pictured it all at once.

The question was, who should he call first?

42

MADELINE'S HEAD felt severed from her body. She had no aware-
ness of time or place or even self. Her first fingerhold was recognizing
Brandon's voice spluttering through the phone, asking if she still lived
in "the old Damant place."

By the look of the dust-swirled air and the smoke-smeared ceiling,
the answer was yes. Then she noticed her sweat and realized she'd
overslept. The next thing he said came through remarkably clear, yank-
ing her upright and making immediate, head-throbbing sense.

After hanging up, she tried desperately to connect Brandon's words
to reality and stumbled over clothes through the debris of another forgettable smoke-out. An enormous black fly slammed itself suicidally
into a small windowpane. She peeled back the kitchen curtain and saw
a Volvo hurtle past on Zero and then the feed truck across the ditch on
the far side of Boundary. Beside it was the unmistakable silhouette of
Brandon Vanderkool, slouching like a sunflower over some apple-
faced man breaking his neck to talk up to him. And behind him, fanned
out in formation and also staring up at him, were his three devout
strays, the wiener dog, the little shepherd and the old Lab.

Shit! She could move only so fast without the vertigo kicking in.
She pulled on some pants and stuffed clothes, books and pans into
garbage bags, taking anything that was clearly hers. Everything else
stayed. She guzzled from the tap and glanced at the wall clock. Five
minutes had already whirled past. Two trucks roared along Zero, their
backdraft shaking the house.

She reached into the cabinet beneath the bathroom sink for her large toiletries bag and panicked at its lack of heft, frantically unzipping it and staring inside at nothing. Then she clawed through shampoos, soaps and deodorants, but it wasn't there. Had she moved it again? She checked every stash she'd ever used or even thought about—under the couch, in the duct behind the heating vent, in the cabinets above the fridge, behind the panel in the office closet. *Fuck!* She'd lost another six minutes. She had to get out now, *now!* She grabbed the three garbage bags and scurried barefoot from the house.

She stared at the smashed front-left panel of her Maxima, the cause of which she couldn't pinpoint, and after looking east and west for Mounties—Brandon's back to her—she sped down Zero and crunched into her father's gravel as an angry face from last night floated through her head, shouting that she'd run a red right before he'd slid into her. She parked behind the fence and speed-dialed Fisher to give him one loud sentence: "A truck just fell into the goddamn tunnel you never told me about!" Then she ran to the sliding door on her father's deck with a throat so dry it hurt.

A frenetic piano melody rang out from the basement while she drank from the faucet until she felt human again. She finally descended into the paint-fumed cellar, which was cluttered with canvases splashed with blacks, blues, yellows, golds, greens and browns all in similar swirling dashes, one horrific imitation after another of van Gogh's famous last painting of a flock of blackbirds flying over farmlands into a menacing sky.

Her father choked, blushed and clutched his bony chest, his pinched face and spindly arms all so remarkably paint-splotched that he looked like a living rendition of the painting he was struggling to replicate. But from his stricken expression, Madeline realized she looked even worse.

He dropped his brush and swung his childlike arms around her, wet paint and all, her relief rising like anesthesia until she cried loud enough to compete with Glenn Gould's desperate piano.

43

THE DECISION-MAKING process was second- and third-guessed, then mocked. Why hadn't they waited and made certain they'd actually catch someone before raiding the first tunnel ever discovered along the Canadian border? Why had they forced the Mounties' hand and left border cops with nobody to apprehend but chemo-ravaged Dirk Hoffman?

Patera argued that the sunken truck tires blew any chance of surprise. Still, the prospect of apprehending smugglers in the act at eleven in the morning seemed bleak. As Agent McAfferty asked Sophie, "What self-respecting douche bag gets to work before noon?"

Dirk professed complete ignorance of the nearly finished, ninety-yard tunnel that stretched from the Damants' outbuilding just north of Zero to his large shed just south of Boundary. He'd sublet that entire thirty-acre rectangle, he explained repeatedly, to a Ferndale raspberry farmer named Daniel Stickney. "Talk to him!"

No drugs were found inside the tunnel or on either side of it. What the Mounties did discover on the Damant side, however, was a barn full of lumber and dirt. The adjoining "party house," as they called it, was owned by Roland P. Nichols, who apparently didn't exist. Madeline Rousseau had been spotted there twice, yet under questioning she claimed she'd visited it only to see an acquaintance named Marilyn, who was sharing the house with others. No, she didn't know her last name or whereabouts, nor was she aware of any tunnel. Her father backed her up, swearing that she'd been living in his guest cottage for the past two months, caring and cooking for him on a daily basis.

This investigation was eclipsed three days later by a raid on a former Molson brewery east of Vancouver, in which seventy-three officers participated in the seizure of an indoor pot farm so huge the Mounties didn't know how to describe it. "Thousands and thousands of plants" was all they said publicly, "worth tens of millions of dollars." Nineteen people were arrested, including reputed kingpins Emmanuel "Manny" Pagaduan and Tobias C. Foster. This bust was the culmination of a yearlong undercover investigation, according to the Mounties, who suggested the brewery farm and the border tunnel were part of the same operation.

On the American side, locals marveled at the audacity of such a long four-by-four-foot underground passage, built to last with half-inch plywood, two-by-sixes and rebar. Its architects even thought to wire and vent it, though apparently hadn't factored in the possibility of a twenty-ton feed truck parking on top of it. If this million-dollar tunnel, as everyone soon called it, had been uncovered a month earlier, Patera might have brokered further investments in northern security; but with nothing to show other than vague conspiracy charges against a Ferndale berry farmer, in effect it weakened his case. No congressional delegation flew out to gawk at this outrage, no budget adjustments were advocated, no editorials called to fortify the border, no Minutemen held vigils. The U.S. media spun it as comic relief, another aside from the border buffoons, especially once one reporter realized the pissed-off but still uncharged Dirk Hoffman was the cancer patient who'd previously set off false radiation alarms.

His guilt or innocence was hard for most locals to ascertain, but his take on things was as clear as ever: WELCOME TO AUSCHWITZ. This greeting looked more out of place the longer it stayed up. The BP accelerated its exodus, and the entire valley quieted as raspberry fields were put to bed, illegal farm workers returned to their homelands and fair-weather residents abandoned their toy ranches. Customs interrogations softened, too, and the few remaining agents grew increasingly reluctant to confront anybody, especially after the immigration-detention centers maxed out. The Princess of Nowhere herself was sent back to Brazil the prior week, once it was finally sorted out that she spoke an oddly accented mix of Portuguese and her native Tupian. Captured illegals were now simply put on the street with the promise they'd leave the country voluntarily. Consequently, arrests amounted to little more than annoying paper shuffles and flimsy agreements. "Catch 'n' release," as McAfferty called it.

The border cams—first feared, then ridiculed—were now forgotten. Nineteen-year-old Americans resumed crossing the ditch for the ritual thrill of legal drinking. More Canadians ventured south to buy groceries and gas and awaited the September 10 grand opening of the Lucky Dog Casino just over the line. Bud smuggling slowed down, as if there'd been a cease-fire or the outlaws themselves had lost interest, although a better explanation surfaced in *The Economist,* which concluded that the rising Canadian dollar had accomplished what the drug czar and Border Patrol and police forces couldn't.

What lingered was the gossip about Brandon. People obsessed over his Superman-like ability to detect a tunnel where everyone else saw dirt, pavement and a ditch. They shared testimonials of watching him build strange things—could you call them sculptures?—throughout the county.

Sophie finally persuaded even Jeanette Vanderkool to discuss Brandon on camera, but it didn't go as planned. As soon as she asked about his childhood, Jeanette insisted they change places. Sophie sat in front of the camera, grinning apprehensively.

"Everybody shares themselves with you," Jeanette said. "Who do you share yourself with?"

"The dead, mostly." She smiled at her camera. "My first partner kept demanding more distance, then got it. *Boom.* An aneurysm. We talk a lot. My second one left for a blonde who didn't ask questions. Died in a convertible two years later. We talk too. And, of course, my father. We did an oral history of World War II together at the V.A.s in every air force town we moved to. I'd do the recording, he'd ask the questions."

"Who'd you do it for?"

"See, I didn't realize it, but all those letters from the publishers and TV stations were rejections. It didn't seem to matter, though. Most people didn't ask or seem to care who or what it was for. My father was the sort of person people told everything to."

"Did he die in battle?"

"No. Riding a lawn mower in Houston, when a truck tire bounced down an off-ramp over his fence and killed him instantly."

"Do you make this stuff up as you go?"

"Who'd make up something like—"

"Well, it's just such a freak—"

"Freak accidents, in my life, have been the norm. I was hanging up my ice skates when I was fourteen . . . I was really into skating as a kid. Dreamt of the Olympics and everything. So I was hanging up my skates in this locker when someone asked me a question. I pivoted like this and a skate fell down and the blade slit my wrist." She raised the scar to the camera. "Took two surgeries to sew the ligaments back together. Everyone thought I'd tried to kill myself. That was the year before I was sleeping in a tent with a friend—an acquaintance, actually—who died instantly when a gum-tree limb fell on her and didn't even touch me. You want more?"

"Where have you lived?"

"Nineteen different states. You want the cities?"

"What jobs have you had?"

"Stewardess, research librarian, nursing assistant, substitute history teacher, sex instructor, masseuse. Lots of things."

"You taught sex-ed in the schools?"

"No, I taught groups of women how to get comfortable with their sexuality."

"You're serious? You've got all these men primping for you, but you're not sleeping with any of them, are you?"

"Marilyn Monroe once said sex is the opposite of love. I'm afraid there's some truth to that when it comes to men."

"Poor thing. You've never had a good man, have you?"

"Is Norm a good man?"

"A great man. A wonderful man who worries too much." A desperate expression washed over her face, as if she'd just lost something. "Did you," she said, "did you answer my question?"

Sophie ran a pinkie finger around her tight smile. "I'm a lesbian."

Jeanette paused and tilted her head. "Oh, that is so delightful."

"Why's that?"

"I'm asking the questions today, Sophie Winslow. So what are you really doing with all this?"

"Dad always said he wanted to do an oral history of *now*. To do as many interviews as it took in one place and time until the truths rose up. That stuck with me. I'd wonder what it would be like to know what everyone on a plane was thinking at the same time. If you lined all those thoughts up, would it add up to anything? So when this place came to me, it seemed as good an opportunity as any to try, for once, to get my arms around a people and a place and a time. You know, a community time capsule of sorts. I lucked out on the timing, of course, but it took me a while to figure out what my real subject was."

"And that would be?"

"Your son."

Jeanette cocked her head as if to shake water from her left ear. "Come again?"

"He's your son, but he's our story. He's not only unique and honorable, but he's also the only one who's incapable of . . ."

"Of what?"

"Of posing. Do you have another half hour, Jeanette?"

44

NORM STALLED in the boat barn, pacing along the full length of the fifty-six-foot-six-inch mast he and Brandon had roped—in sections—to the truck and hauled from Anacortes in the slow lane with his hazard lights flashing. Why hadn't he waited until he'd found a good price on a short rig? The taller stick would come in handy in light air, sure, but fifty-six-six? Christ. He'd read enough to know that the bigger the mast, the bigger the sails and the bigger the trouble.

He'd pulled the trigger on the rest of the rigging, too, from some salvage guy in Sacramento, of all places, who swore it was all brand-new and should arrive by the following weekend. Flipping through the Yanmar catalogue for another look at the two-cylinder twenty-five horse, he pictured his shiny sloop swaying in the boat-lift slings at the marina, rocking his head slightly to enhance the fantasy.

He didn't know what exactly explained it, whether the stroke had cleared his head or if it was the removal of his daily burdens or what Jeanette would probably call karma. He just knew things looked as different as they did after the first snowfall. Brandon, especially. He was far better at running the dairy than Norm had expected and seemed to communicate more easily than ever. But Norm still couldn't make sense of the notoriety he continued to generate. The tunnel discovery was a freak show unto itself, with people always stopping by to fawn over him. And he flatly couldn't believe what Sophie had told him about the pothead professor taking a serious interest in Brandon's art. Plus she now was throwing an art show cocktail party strategically scheduled just hours before the grand opening of the casino. Jeanette said it would feature some of their son's work that nobody had ever seen. He'd even received an invite in the mail. When would it ever stop?

The idea of everyone standing around staring at Brandon's paintings went down like castor oil. He'd never understood art for art's sake, which left him bored and snickering at the suckers who bought into it. Brandon's took it a step further and confused and embarrassed him, as if it exposed something unflattering about the Vanderkool gene pool.

When daylight flashed inside the barn, Norm could hear crescendos of laughter coming from next door. The party sounded large even by Sophie's standards, so apparently even the anti-casino doomsayers were turning out en masse to see just how cheesy this "Vegas-style" monstrosity was inside, after first checking out the artwork and grabbing a few free drinks.

"Brandon?"

The youthful voice puzzled him, since he'd assumed it was Jeanette coming to scold him about being late for the party. He stepped out from his semi-enclosed workstation, looked down and saw nobody. "Hello?" he hesitantly replied.

A moment later, a slender, short-haired woman with bright eyes ducked out from beneath the broad camber of the hull. It took Norm a couple breaths to recognize Madeline Rousseau.

"I'm sorry," she said. "Didn't mean to interrupt—"

"No bother."

"Saw the light and couldn't resist peeking," she explained. "I had no idea how big it is. You could go anywhere in this, couldn't you?"

"If I can get her out of the barn."

"Can I have a look inside?"

"By all means."

She climbed the stairs, stepped confidently aboard and spun a Lumar winch. "Look at the size of these suckers." She disappeared below, clucking and whistling. "Had *no clue* it would be this . . . awesome."

Norm didn't notice the knee twinges as he descended into the galley.

"Bronze portals, laminated beams, teak trim. You're a real crafts-man, Mr. Vanderkool."

Norm blushed. "Don't look too close." He'd heard the pro-fessor had put her in rehab for a couple weeks. He'd also heard she went away to college in Ontario, or had gone to see an aunt in Manitoba. He unlatched the electrical box and waved her over to see the color-coordinated wiring, feeling like a sweaty kid showing off his science-fair project. "Got it all labeled, see? Bow light. Anchor light. VHF."

She at least feigned interest. "I'm stalling," she confided after he shut the box. "I don't feel up to going to Sophie's quite yet."

"Me neither."

She laughed, and Norm wondered why he'd just now realized how pretty she was. He'd always thought her sister was the beauty. "You were looking for Brandon?"

She smiled. "Been thinking about him a *lot* lately."

Norm scrambled to catch up with the significance of the words and the smile.

"I got my job back at the nursery. And if I can stay sober"—she tapped a knuckle on the cabin trim—"I'll apply for winter quarter."

He nodded, admiring her candor.

"So part of my plan," she continued, "is to get back into sailing—not racing, just sailing—which got me curious about your project here. What do you still need?"

"Plenty." Norm inhaled as Sophie's party clamor crested again. "For starters, an engine, so I'm—"

"What else?"

"Little things, sails being the biggest, but I'm a long ways from being able to afford even a Yanmar, so—"

"Why not just buy some used sails online and drop her in the bay?"

He laughed awkwardly. "Think I'll have a hard enough time

maneuvering her with an engine, Madeline. You see, I don't have all that much experience under sail."

"I'd love to help you figure it out," she said. "We could learn how to sail her together, Norm—in and out of the marina, if we had to, until we can get an engine for her."

He turned away, pretending to sneeze. The biggest difference the stroke made was emotional. He couldn't remember ever breaking down quite like he had earlier in the week when the tall doctor in her white lab coat gave them the verdict on Jeanette's condition: "It looks like early Alzheimer's."

"*Looks like,*" Norm had repeated petulantly, zeroing in on the chink in the diagnosis. "So you don't actually *know* what it is."

The doctor looked at each of them confidently, patiently. "My experience tells me that's what it is, but there isn't a blood test or—"

"So you *don't* know," he snapped.

"That's true, but—"

"Well, why do you—"

"Norm," Jeanette said calmly. "It's okay. I've got it. It's almost a relief. Really, it's okay. I've known it for some time."

It wasn't her graceful acceptance so much as her attempt to comfort him that got him blubbering. But even little things uprooted him now. Jeanette's reminder notes that she posted for herself all around the house. Brandon bottle-feeding a calf. So something as incidental as Madeline Rousseau calling him Norm for the first time could move him, much less her offering, in the gentlest way imaginable, to teach him how to sail his boat.

45

BRANDON WAS PINNED in a corner behind two Lynden ladies he vaguely recognized, both chattering simultaneously about the "quite unusual" photos and paintings on the walls and desperately trying to drag him into their conversation.

He'd never known how to react to this sort of attention. Ever since kindergarten, he'd heard his work called unusual and bizarre or, worse, weird. No response beyond a shrug or a blank stare had ever come to him. It never seemed like the sort of thing you talked about. Besides, Danny Crawford always said that the less artists said the better.

"What makes you create these things?" asked the one with the pastry flakes clinging to her lipstick.

"Yes, what *compels* you?" pressed the one with the goiter.

They might as well have asked him why he breathed. After hesitating, that was the question he answered. "Because I need to," he mumbled. "And because I want to." He stared down at the ladies until their heavy eyelashes fluttered like hummingbird wings trying to lift them off the floor.

Brandon hadn't foreseen any of this when Sophie casually asked if she could show some of his work at a "little gathering." It sounded as if a few of his canvases would be mixed with other art and a few people would eat cheese and crackers and glance at it. Instead it was only his stuff. On every wall. Even in the bathroom. Twenty-three recent paintings and more than fifty photographs of his outdoor work. Several sequences showed him building cones in the river and on the flats, or his thorn-stitched structures getting ripped apart by the currents, or the rainbows he created by swinging a club off the water. There were shots of many columns on riverbanks, in trees and ravines. Then still more action photos of him, from up close and afar, throwing sticks into the sky or hanging see-through tapestries of leaves that he'd completely forgotten about. The paintings included clusters of foreign faces—more expressions, really, than faces—and others of bird flocks, the largest canvas being a silver ball of flashing dunlins, as well as his most recent—a three-panel portrait of Madeline, the first nearly photographic in its precision, the second more abstract, her face flushed with anxiety, and the third, almost surreal, of her pink-tongued laughter.

Luckily, almost nobody—except these puzzled elderly women—was paying much attention to the art, beyond the most easily understood paintings in the entrance, including one of his mother sprawled in dandelions and another of a lineup of cattle wearing the faces of his father, Dirk Hoffman, Cleve Erickson, Raymond Lankhaar, Roony Meurs and other local dairymen with features too small to make out.

For the most part people were talking and laughing, not seeing. And as the house filled and the volume climbed, most of the giddy chatter was about blackjack, craps and slots, about how much money people were going to win or lose, what Katrina Montfort had heard about the decor and the buffet, everyone gorging all the while on Sophie's free liquor.

Brandon's mother passed through the door in a sequined top and so much makeup that he almost didn't recognize her. She looked hesitant, though her smile bloomed once she recognized people. She hugged Sophie, then Alexandra Cole, then anyone within reach, embracing some of them twice. He started toward her in case she needed him, but felt blocked by the sea of expectant faces. The room was filling fast, and he reminded himself to try not to watch and listen to everything at once.

He'd agreed to come only after Sophie told him Madeline might show. Having talked to her so persuasively so many times in his mind, it kept jolting him to remember that he hadn't actually spoken to her since he'd called about the tunnel. When he finally asked her father about her, he said she'd be back pretty soon and left the rest dangling.

Now he wished Sophie hadn't mentioned her at all, so he wouldn't have spent so much time searching for a strand of words so simple that he wouldn't trip over them—such as, *Something that amazing can't be considered a mistake.* Yet by itself, that seemed even worse than saying nothing. So he worked on combinations of ideas that incorporated an apology, though he couldn't pinpoint what he'd done wrong. He wished he'd heard Danny Crawford apologize more often so he'd know what a great one sounded like.

He found McAfferty in the kitchen, mid-story with Dionne and Canfield. "This was a two-day wedding. Two days! And it was one of those weddings that's so small it's too intimate, know what I'm saying? Especially when you don't know anybody, which I didn't. And this congregation didn't split along traditional bride-and-groom lines, okay? The two camps here were crossworders and gays." He topped off everyone's champagne glass and glanced at Brandon. "What's up, Picasso? So I wake up and stumble into this way-too-intimate lodge on this way-too-special wedding day, and there I am, a hungover, hetero noncrossworder with no place to hang. Know what I'm saying? The gays are all chatty lovebirds on the couches. And the thoughtful brainiacs are at the breakfast table obsessing about *thirty-seven down.*"

"So what'd you do?"

"That's the point, Candy. What do you think I did?"

"I would've hung out with the crossworders," Dionne said.

"We know that, but what'd I do?"

"You lucked out and guessed thirty-seven down," Canfield said, "and the crossworders adopted you."

McAfferty scowled and turned to Brandon.

"You talked the gays into Bloody Marys," Brandon said, "and had a good time."

McAfferty beamed at Dionne. "Didn't I just tell you the kid's a misunderstood genius?"

Brandon was studying how McAfferty's hand nonchalantly cupped Dionne's waist when a bearded man who stood no taller than his sternum burst into their circle, apologized extravagantly for interrupting and introduced himself as the dean of something. He told Brandon that he absolutely had to speak with him at his earliest convenience, then excused himself just as profusely and waddled off.

"From what I can tell," McAfferty offered, "you're a big hit with old ladies and midgets."

"You're all midgets," Brandon said, scanning the barrel-bodied throng again for an agile tomboy with chestnut hair, his ears straining all the laughter for one laugh in particular. "How many days you got left?" he asked.

"A hundred and twenty-two," McAfferty said. "Thanks for asking. Who'd have thought I'd outlast the chief?"

"Don't count on it," Dionne said.

As part of the Blaine reorganization, Patera was supposedly getting transferred to the Baton Rouge sector, which bordered, as McAfferty noted, on absolutely nothing. But Congress had put all personnel changes on hold after a new GAO report concluded that for many miles, no delineation whatsoever remained of the U.S.-Canadian border. Much of the overgrown seam would need to be resurveyed again, not only to police the line, but also just to know where it was. This sounded all the more ominous after a House committee released a portion of a jihad training manual that advised terrorists to enter the belly of the beast through Canada. With this news arriving near the end of an election season, incumbents and particularly desperate challengers from northern states were demanding an immediate and renewed commitment to border security.

Sophie grabbed Brandon and introduced him to her "bunko gang," six effusive, middle-aged women who stood there drinking, tittering and gawking at him, their eyes shining with liquor.

"Go ahead," she said. "Ask him."

A woman with a laugh like a power tool wondered if there was "any chance in hell" he could build a form on her property. When he looked puzzled, she added, "I'd pay you, of course." Then she pointed at a photograph of a slate cone he'd built.

"You have slate on your property?" he asked.

"Pardon?" she said.

"What kind of rock have you got?"

"I don't know"—she looked to the others for help—"that we have any. But of course, we could bring in whatever you need."

"Kinda needs to already be there."

"What?"

He shrugged.

They waited.

Talking was a letdown after the day he'd had. That morning he'd counted thirty-two species, including skinny oystercatchers, black-bellied plovers, western sandpipers and Pacific loons fresh from the north. The valley felt alive again. The night before he'd driven out to the old Sumas Customs House before sunset and waited thirty-five minutes before a lone Vaux's swift swooped into view. After that slender bird disappeared into one of the two bulky chimneys, there was a pause before another dozen dove into the hole, followed by hundreds more, foraging the twilight for insects on their downward spiral, several hundred swifts forming a tall funnel that swirled into the same chimney like a genie returning to its bottle.

ONCE NORM and Madeline arrived, the house was already crammed with people excusing themselves back and forth to the makeshift bar where Morris Crawford was pouring doubles and flattering everyone. It took Norm five minutes to find Jeanette, who pulled him over to a wall to show him photos of what looked like a bare-chested man covered in leaves from his hips up. Norm turned tropical red as he slowly recognized the subject, then turned and instantly spotted his son above the crowd, surrounded by a clot of ladies in the far corner. The throng of excessively cheerful people between them was spiked with people to be avoided: Professor Rousseau, Shit-to-Power, Raymond Lankhaar and—good God!—Agent McAfferty.

"It's all Brandon!" Jeanette gushed, as if some phenomenon was taking place that he hadn't processed yet.

He glimpsed Madeline caught in a scrum of laughter in the doorway. Then he was practically mobbed himself, as if they'd confused him with someone else, their squealing voices ringing in his ears. Even Wayne grabbed him to smirklessly congratulate him on his son's show, gesturing grandly with the hand that wasn't attached to a cane. Norm overheated in the attention, his vision blurring, a palpable desire rising to escape back to the barn, where he could look at his boat alone and anew through the lens of Madeline's confidence.

BRANDON'S EYES floated past her twice before he recognized her. Her hair was shinier and curled around her face, her skin darker, her posture straighter in a long-sleeved blouse and new jeans. He watched her tap his mother on the shoulder and suddenly the two of them were hugging, rocking side to side like they'd just won something. Then he saw Sophie pull Madeline to the trio of paintings he'd made of her. He blocked out the questions from the ladies below as she covered her eyes with both hands as if the images were too awful to bear straight on. He glanced down and asked the Canadian lady to please repeat her question, then looked back and lost Madeline altogether as more voices lobbied for his attention.

"Please, Brandon, would you explain this."

He turned to the painting in question. It was like staring at his blood under a microscope and being asked, *Well?*

Another lady with thinning hair impatiently muttered that art is definitely in the eye of the beholder, but that frankly she didn't get it. "I'm sorry, but most of this looks like child's play to me."

He watched his mom lead his blushing father to a painting of her catching written words with her hands, and to another of him patting Pearl's distinctively patterned brown-and-white head. Even across the room, Brandon could see his face clench toward a sob. Then he looked everywhere for Madeline again, feeling claustrophobic, new words churning in his head. He saw a shadow flicker across the room, and another, and a series of fluttering images, ducking low enough to see the forked tails out the window. The ladies, with their backs to him, were discussing blackjack strategy now, so he crept to the sliding door and quietly slipped into a twilight that looked digitally enhanced.

A dozen barn swallows had gathered on the telephone and power lines looping from Sophie's house to Northwood. Another dozen were approaching from far north of the ditch, then an incoming cloud— multiple clouds, actually—that broke up as they neared the three lines, the birds spinning like ice skaters or stunt pilots before lining up side by side and carrying on in high, grating voices that sounded like glass marbles rubbing against one another. He tacked toward their temporary roost at a forty-five degree angle, the din of Sophie's party fading beneath the excited banter of the assembling acrobats. As the sagging lines filled up, they created the illusion that the weight of all these little birds was pulling the telephone poles toward each other and that the swallows were about to be launched from this flexed slingshot.

SOPHIE ASKED Alexandra Cole to give her two-finger whistle to get everyone's attention. "I'd like to make a quick announcement and introduce a special guest," she said, which created so much simultaneous chatter that Alexandra had to whistle again.

"Brandon," Sophie shouted. "Where are you?"

A voice rose above the murmur. "Think he stepped outside."

"Well, good," Sophie said over the laughter, "because I'm breaking a promise here. I told him I wouldn't draw undue attention to his work, but I simply can't resist. I wanted you all to get a chance to see some of it, and I hope that some of you find it as stunning as I do." The chatter and laughter rose up and people crowded the walls with cocktails, most of them squinting at the art for the first time. "Listen!" she pleaded. "I took the liberty of inviting a far better judge of such matters, Dr. Matthew Egan, the respected dean of Fine Arts at Western Washington University. Dr. Egan?"

For most people the little man was just a voice. "Young Mr. Vanderkool's art, I believe, reflects perhaps as well as any art I've seen, the

American psyche in the twenty-first century," he said, to rising snickers. "I'm very serious," he added while several conversations resumed. "His fixation with nests, for example, obviously expresses a grave concern with security."

More giggles skittered across the room, but every painting and photo was getting examined now. "And the nests are crumbling," someone blurted with mock gravity.

"His work with leaves," the dean continued, "shows he's obviously been influenced by the great Andy Goldsworthy, but Mr. Vanderkool's quilts look more like flags, susceptible to the slightest breeze." His voice rose confidently above the crowd noise. "And what to make of these paintings of startled smugglers and illegal immigrants?" He pointed at a portrait of the Princess of Nowhere. "Again, his focus appears to be the instant before collapse—or surrender. I haven't had the pleasure of conversing with the artist, but it's obvious to me, given the variety of people and birds he paints, that he celebrates all living things. Or consider his self-portrait," he demanded. "Clearly, the leaves are feathers and . . ."

The laughter and raspberries rose, drowning him out with conversations about the casino and football and weather and an Oktoberfest celebration in Bellingham. Wayne Rousseau, however, was just warming up, holding court in his corner as people leaned in to hear him disagree with the dean and suggest that in fact Brandon's art was all about turning order into disorder and chaos into a plausible pattern, the subtext being how *temporary* everything is. A shrinking bevy of ladies tried to follow his subsequent pronouncements about how dyslexic geniuses were often viewed as oddballs in their own time, about the latest movements in landscape art, about da Vinci's obsession with flight, about how van Gogh's very last painting was—

"Oh, my God!" Alexandra Cole shrieked, gawking out the window. "What is he doing with those *birds*?"

HE ESTIMATED there were fourteen hundred shoulder to shoulder on the lines, with dozens more in the air entertaining the others and still more congregating. He was standing perfectly still, slightly west of the raucous flock yet close enough to make out their long, midnight-blue wings and cinnamon breasts. Several incoming birds whirled near his head before swooping up to the black lines. It became a game, with swallow after swallow seeing how close it could come to his head, his hips, his bowed and extended arms, circling and dipping, finally swirling back to the lines. Their voices rose to a crescendo and were instantly lost in a mad, simultaneous flutter of wings, as if gunfire had launched them airborne in a swarm that extended, then collapsed as it veered southeast across the valley toward the treed hillsides below Mount Baker's stone flanks.

He watched them fade over the golden fields into a hazy mob before disappearing into the blue-black sky itself. He felt so much a part of them that it half-startled him to look down and find himself still there, left behind, alone and buzzing like a tuning fork. He took a breath, shuffled his feet and heard the party behind him, sounding too close. He decided to go find Madeline before he lost the nerve or the words. But when he turned he saw that everyone had already spilled into Sophie's yard and the street, all of them seemingly staring at him. He glanced around behind him, to see if there was anything else they could be looking at, but there wasn't. Turning back, he spotted his sequined mother leaning against his father. He saw Sophie filming, then heard and saw McAfferty and Dionne clapping, with others joining in. But it took him a few beats to realize that the lone figure striding toward him was Madeline Rousseau, her arms extended from her sides the way they did when she was telling you something that amazed her, or the way they did when she was about to give someone a hug so big that it required an elaborate windup.

He apparently wouldn't need to summon the perfect magical sequence of words after all. He wouldn't have to say anything. If he just stood still and waited, she'd walk right into him.

ACKNOWLEDGMENTS

Thanks to the inspiring Gary Fisketjon for helping me improve this novel. And thanks to Kim Witherspoon for being a patient and daring advocate for my work.

Anne Collins offered valuable input, as did other early readers, including Jess Walter, Valerie Ryan, Denise Lynch, Robin Franzen, Andy Parker, Craig Welch, Jennifer Langston, Jennie Nelson, and my parents, Levin and Janet.

Joe Meche and Larry Wilson generously shared their wisdom on birds and cows. Tom Schooley, John Flory, Dan Ewer, Gwen Schnurman, Gary Hirsch and three agents with the U.S. Border Patrol also helped with the research.

Other inspirations included Andy Goldsworthy's art, Temple Grandin's books, Jane Laclergue's exuberance and Steve White's manic phone calls.

And thanks beyond words to Denise and Grace Lynch for just about everything else.

A NOTE ABOUT THE AUTHOR

Jim Lynch lives with his wife and their daughter in Olympia, Washington. As a journalist, he has received the H. L. Mencken Award and a Livingston Award for Young Journalists, among other national honors. His first novel, *The Highest Tide,* won the Pacific Northwest Booksellers Award, was adapted for the stage and has been published in eleven foreign markets.

A NOTE ON THE TYPE

The text of this book was set in Sabon, a typeface designed by Jan Tschichold (1902–1974), the well-known German typographer. Based loosely on the original designs by Claude Garamond (c. 1480–1561), Sabon is unique in that it was explicitly designed for hot metal composition on both the Monotype and Linotype machines as well as for filmsetting. Designed in 1966 in Frankfurt, Sabon was named for the famous Lyons punch cutter Jacques Sabon, who is thought to have brought some of Garamond's matrices to Frankfurt.

Composed by Creative Graphics, Allentown, Pennsylvania

Printed and bound by Berryville Graphics, Berryville, Virginia

Designed by Robert C. Olsson